Win a holiday for 2 to Portugal!

Joe Walsh Tours

To celebrate the release of *Three of a Kind*, **Poolbeg** and **Joe Walsh Tours** are offering one lucky reader the chance to win a week for two in the fabulous four star Estoril Eden Aparthotel on the Lisbon Coast in Portugal.

The Estoril Eden, a beautiful, modern hotel overlooks the Atlantic Ocean and is a few minutes walk from the beach. The hotel and the nearby towns of Cascais and Estoril offer excellent facilities to guarantee a truly relaxing and memorable holiday.

This **excellent** prize includes flights, transfers, 7 nights accommodation on a bed & breakfast basis, and the services of a Joe Walsh Tours representative.

Let Joe Walsh Tours take you there . . . www.joewalshtours.ie

To enter, all you have to do is answer the following question:
Q. What is the name of the Portuguese Coffee Fiona likes to drink in *Three of a Kind?*

Answer: _____

Send to: *THREE OF A KIND* Competition, Poolbeg Press, 123 Grange Hill, Baldoyle, Dublin 13.

Name: _____

Address: _____

D0968288

_____

Also by Alison Norrington

Class Act
Look Before You Leap

Three of a Kind

ALISON NORRINGTON

POOLBEG

Published 2005
by Poolbeg Press Ltd
123 Grange Hill, Baldoyle
Dublin 13, Ireland
E-mail: poolbeg@poolbeg.com

© Alison Norrington 2005

Typesetting, layout, design © Poolbeg Press

1 3 5 7 9 10 8 6 4 2

A catalogue record for this book is available from the British Library.

ISBN 1-84223-186-3

Typeset by Magpie Designs in Goudy 10.5/14 pt
Printed by Nørhaven Paperback, Denmark

www.poolbeg.com

ACKNOWLEDGEMENTS

Three Of A Kind actually began as *Taxi Shoes*. Thanks to Trish for such a fab title – it was a big inspiration to write the story.

Thanks to Bridin for making me aware of the Hague Convention.

Thanks once again to the people of Wexford for your kind words, overwhelming support and encouragement.

I enjoy talking with and emailing other Irish writers, but a special thanks to Tara Heavey and Melissa Hill.

Thanks to Catherine Daly and Marisa Mackle for a great welcome onto the ace website *www.writeon-irishgirls.com*. An inspired idea, Catherine.

I'm now (finally!) on-line at *www. alisonnorrington.com*. It's always so nice to hear from my readers and I'll answer any of your questions (or moral dilemmas – believe me, I've had plenty!!).

Once again I would like to thank my family – Mum – for everything! Your ability to see the big picture and then to focus in on the details. Ian – for your open-mindedness and balance. *Up the Ramp* was born in Lisbon in February 2004 – keep up the good work!!

Ryan – for your brilliant sense of humour and overwhelming interest. Conor – for your artistic eye and blatantly honest opinions.

To all my friends for listening and reading – sometimes at the same time!

Thanks to Maura for the most reliable support and help, especially at school collection times!! I owe you a lunch (or three!) and to Mary, Jane and Catherine – we need another night out!

Thanks to Ger, once again, for lots of advice and support.

To Poolbeg and their great team – Paula, Lynda, Emma and Claire. And to Gaye, once again, thank you so much for your advice and help.

Thank you to everyone who bought *Class Act* and *Look Before You Leap* and I am looking forward to hearing from you all at *www.alisonnorrington.com*

Alison
xx

Be not longing
For more than you have.
Stop.
Reminisce.
The good times that you've *had*.

For that split-second moment
The carousel stops spinning
Is yours to enjoy.
So take stock of living.

Ian Norrington

PROLOGUE

August

Fiona perched in the back of a caramel Lisbon taxi, fidgeting on the slippery leather seat, desperately trying to avoid rear-view-mirror eye contact with the swarthy Portuguese driver. He stank of cigarette smoke, despite overdosing on pine air fresheners. Breathing in warm, recycled air, she bent forward, hugging her knees and looking down at her tanned elegant feet, her toenails neat and free from varnish, as a large teardrop fell and splashed on her cheap leather sandals. She watched as the single drop trickled down and lost itself between her toes.

Charley fell into a Dublin taxi, her battered Reeboks feeling heavy on her disorientated, drunken feet. As she stumbled, laughing, at the back door, the cabbie hollered at her to mind herself. She slurred the address to him, not

1

noticing how he shook his head at the pathetic sight of her. She was asleep before he could warn her not to get sick on the upholstery.

Helly felt nauseous as she hopped into a black London cab. She'd had a great night at the gig and hadn't touched anything but water. A niggling notion taunted her perplexed mind. She'd felt this way before. She stretched out her legs on the back seat, her Jane Brown sandals glistening in the flashing orange glow of streetlights as they nipped towards Belsize Park. As another wave of warm sickness churned in her stomach, she knew. She wasn't ready to face up to it.

But she knew.

Six months ago it had all been so different . . .

It had all started at Mother Redcap's market. I'd swear my sister Charley was half-pissed, but I'd kinda got used to that! Although she seemed to have got worse. Well, first we'd had to push her car to the brow of the hill and then roll it down just to get it started, and then, when we'd finally arrived in Dublin, I'd got out of the car and trod straight into a dried knobble of dog shit.

A great start to the day!

But still, we'd had such fun, bartering and bargaining with Madame Lydia outside her cloaked and veiled tepee of a market stall, challenging her that as she'd advertised 'One hand €25, two hands €40' she could read one hand each for the pair of us for forty. I mean, two hands is two hands, isn't it?

But Madame Lydia's scary feed-the-world cleavage had

wobbled and the hairy mole below her smudged mouth and lip-sticked teeth had shook as she'd argued her point. She was wily and wizened and had coped with worse than us on a Saturday morning, so we eventually conceded to pay the €25 each for a reading of our left palms. She'd said the left was the best, as we were both right-handed and that meant something. Damned if I can remember what!

Charley had been her usual noisy self and had jibed at me, as Madame Lydia retreated back into her 'room', questioning why I thought I needed the predictions of a back-street nutter anyway. "You've got it all, honey! What more could you want?"

She had also been annoyed at me for giving in to Madame Lydia so easily, slapping me on the arm and hissing, "Helly! You're way too soft. I'd easily have got us both in for the €40!"

So, we'd pulled aside the threadbare, red-velvet curtain and entered her small beaded room, pungent with the smell of cheap joss-sticks. We balanced on rickety pub-reject stools as she squinted and frowned at our sweaty left palms. We were sceptical as she squeaked some old flannel about European connections and travel, blah blah blah, pregnancy in the family, blah blah, and when she came out with the news about sex with a dark handsome stranger we actually shrugged our shoulders.

Yeah, we'd heard it all before.

And it took me only seconds to decipher it all. Our younger sister Fiona was in Portugal, so there was the vague reference to travel, Charley was no stranger to sex with strangers (the dark and handsome bit I couldn't verify). As for the *pregnancy, it'd hardly be me, with two children already and on the pill! Therefore, one of my two sisters was about to give me the chance to blow the cobwebs off my flat-packed, save-for-a-rainy-day cot! Dan would complain like mad when I asked him to go up in the loft once again.*

Actually, if I recall it correctly, Charley was so disgusted at Madame Lydia's efforts that she'd thrown down her money and, as Madame grabbed at it, quicker than George Best in a bottle shop, Charley spat, "OK, so where's the video cameras? This is a wind-up, right? An absolute farce! You're shite! I'll tell you your bloody fortune all right!"

And that was about the size of it. I don't really put much trust in tarot or palmistry – it was just for the fun of it really. It's a rare occasion that I get back to Dublin without the entire family so I was up for anything.

Little did we know how things would turn around in such a short space of time . . .

Chapter One

4 months earlier . . .

April

Helly crossed the cool room, ducking to avoid the low, exposed beams and turned the volume-knob clockwise, her slender fingers skimming the button lightly. She loved this song. It brought her early days with Dan to mind and made her feel guilty about her recent intolerance of him, reminding her how she'd once loved his scraggy clothes and passion for music. It had been in the heady days of love when they had both enjoyed his busking days on the London Underground.

They marvelled together at the fabulous acoustics and the ever-changing audience. He hadn't really needed to busk for the money, but Helly loved the way his charm oozed out of his scruffy jeans and slightly too-tight T-shirt and was sure that the women always threw in a coin as they passed him by just for the flash of muscle. She loved the really deep underground stations like King's Cross or St Pancras, where she could hear his throaty saxophone vibes from the top of the first set of old rickety escalators. And how they used to wait for a quiet spell to kiss and how he'd grab and tickle her as she tried to clutch at the coins in his cap. It saddened Helly how things had changed over the years. Their 'new' house was an imposing red-brick, Victorian semi in 'rich London' – a term coined by her mum. Helly was convinced that Dan thought they'd got one of those executive removal firms in. You know, the ones who come armed with bubble-wrap and boxes and take control of everything as they take down and pack up your possessions, organising the removal and then setting it all out in perfect order in your new house.

Only we didn't have the executive crowd in. Just the usual removal men with hosepipe veins and forearms like hams. But we'd done the rest.

Me and Toby and Jack. My seven and five-year-old sons.

They're brilliant and I wouldn't be without them. Energetic, cheeky, loving – and that's just the first two minutes. Despite their youth, they're more fun than Dan these days. And sometimes more mature. He's nowhere near as affectionate lately. I used to love his hugs, spontaneous displays of love that would make me melt. He'd envelop me in his strong arms and I'd lose myself for a few seconds in the soft cotton of his XL rugby shirt, breathing in his smell – his deodorant and aftershave, tinged with the Lenor from his clothes. But they're rather rare these days – hugs from Dan. He's far too engrossed in his work and his band, and the respect I once had for him is eroding faster than a sandcastle in an incoming tide.

By contrast to those heady busking days, the only six-pack in our house these days is in the fridge. I'd started hula-hooping after Jack was born, to regain my once-toned tummy, but I never got it back as flat as it used to be. And neither has Dan with his! My pregnancies had been boringly run-of-the-mill. I had often felt invisible in the shadow of the preggo horror-stories that some of my friends had had. Though I shouldn't complain.

But I'm ambitious. I wouldn't mind going through it all again.

Just one more time.

Just try telling Dan that!

The exposed red bricks of Helly's basement studio gave it an earthy, natural feel which, coupled with the terracotta floor tiles, emanated a warm, rustic glow.

Scrutinising the antique Afghan coat, her most recent 'find' at a flea market in Paris, she hung it carefully on the old pine door. Diego, their much maligned and misunderstood golden spaniel, crept in, sat behind Helen's legs and barked.

Just once.

But loud.

"Jesus!" she jumped, her hands jerking involuntarily. As she clutched onto the gnarled door, she leant against the antique wardrobe that housed her new and spare stock of eclectic, vintage clothes. "You're a bloody nuisance, Diego!" she snapped at the expressionless hound.

"Why can't you be a friend instead of a handicap?"

OK, so he pulls the 'puppy eyes' and I feel mean, but let's remember, he's man's best buddy!

Diego got to his feet, turning his backside to Helen as she placed a pair of early 1970's beaded slippers into her large holdall. Without a backward glance he sashayed out, wagging his tail lazily for extra impact as he farted.

"Ugh, Diego!" she called after him.

The colour photos she had hung on the brick wall had sat on top of the stereo cabinet and on the windowsill in their old house. They had become so familiar to her that she had stopped seeing them. Rather, she had seen them, but hadn't actually *looked* at them. Not for a long time. She moved across to the wall, lifting her hand and lightly running her finger over Fiona's face as it smiled back out at her from behind the glass. The photo had been taken a good six years ago, probably around the time that Fiona had first gone to Portugal. Her dark hair had been cut fashionably short. And it shone in chestnut streaks beneath the sunlight. Beside it, Helly had hung an 'action shot' of herself and Charley as they played with Toby and Jack when they were toddlers. Charley was crouched on all fours in their parents' back garden and Toby was on her back. Soaking up the memory of that sunny afternoon, Helly smiled at their matching cow's-licks which sprouted on the left-hand side of their fringes. Jack had only just started to walk so she had given him a piggy-back as they chased Auntie Charley and Toby. She looked down then at the photo of herself and Dan, cheesy and tanned as they had posed on the slopes in

Aspen – way before Toby and Jack's time. He had his arm around her shoulders and her smiling, pea-green eyes were shining – in direct competition with her glistening white toothy grin. And yet she realised that she had no photographs of them all together. As a family. She knew that it would be an amazing shot, what with the family trait of sparkling green eyes. But she also knew it would be virtually impossible to gather them all together for such a picture.

She had always read how the middle sibling was supposed to be the rebellious one. It was one of those 'goes without saying' things that she'd often seen on morning telly. Like, if 'he' mirrors your body language, he's interested – and if 'she' fiddles with her ear when she's talking, then she's lying. If the morning programmes and the glossy magazines were anything to go by, it just had to be true about middle-sibling rebellion. You only had to ask Raj Persaud or Dr Ruth or Twink. Anyone worth their salt knew it. It was supposed to be something to do with the eldest child taking on the responsible and mature roles, forced into paving the way for their siblings, and the youngest being allowed to always be the baby, the cosseted, protected one. Which only leaves the middle sibling as the one who has to rebel for any attention.

Obvious really. When you thought about it. She didn't really need Raj Persaud or Twink or even Trevor McDonald to explain it.

Only, Helly's family was different to that.

She'd always been confused by her mismatched sibling situation. Coupled with a do-gooder mother with strange

9

misplaced loyalties, and an alcohol-dependent father, Helly had felt shoe-horned into the position of the Sensible Grounded Sister from an early age. And nothing had changed over the years. Her eldest sister, Charley, still lived in Dublin and was still a party-gal. Helly worried about her intensely. In the last year and a half she seemed to be getting worse, increasingly diluted and deluded. Charley had always been a flirt but had never been one to fall in and out of bed with different guys. And now she did. Frequently. And if the hapless Kevin knew anything about her antics, then he said nothing. Their younger sister, Fiona, was stuck in Portugal in a wrangle with her ex, Luís, the father of her child. Helly pitied Fiona for being too afraid of him and wished she could help her to find a confident voice, loud enough to fight back.

Yes, nothing had changed – even now, when she had two great sons, a husband and her own 'shabby chic' boutique just off the Portobello Road. She accepted that twenty-four hours a day simply weren't long enough, that seven days a week was ludicrous and that fifty-two weeks in the year was absolutely farcical. Much like every other mother on the planet. She knew that Dan loved her and their two boys, but he had gradually grown more selfish over the years. Owning his own graphics company had its obvious pressures – she realised that from running her own business – but she had begun to resent his commitment to his blues band, feeling the strain of his frequent absences from home.

Helly had first met Dan under the table at a student

party that neither of them had wanted to be at. They'd been looking for their shoes under the rickety table in a dark corner, where piles of empty bottles had fallen drunkenly onto their sides. Much like most of the students there. It was after two in the morning after all. She had loved her shoes, which were similar to Dorothy's legendary ruby slippers, and she'd been dismayed when he found his Elvis-like blue suede boots and realised that someone had poured beer into one of them. Well, they'd hoped it was beer. Even as teenagers they joked that they'd be 'sole-mates'. It was only a matter of time then, before they realised they wanted to be together forever and decided to move from Dublin to London, and so began Dan's busking 'career'. Her sisters had been envious at the announcement that they were moving, desperate for some excitement in their lives and frantic that Helly was leaving them with a cranky mum and sloshed dad. Helly recalled kissing them and making them promise to visit at least twice a year.

As much as I love them to pieces, my sisters have always been a headache and a worry, and they take no responsibility for themselves. And my parents? Mum has recently discovered email and mobile phones and it's really not funny! She talks into a mobile as if it's a walkie-talkie. Dan teases her, saying she'd be better off with two empty tins and a long piece of string!

Helly and Dan had been so in love back then, when they'd first moved to London. Her mum had detested the idea and Helly recalled the morning that she first told her. Her mum had been drying her hair in front of the old

11

mirror whose silver coating was peeling at the edges, and she had laid down her white hand-gun hairdryer slowly. Helly had listened to it ticking as it cooled, counting down the seconds until her mother exploded. Her mum simply couldn't understand her wanting to start a new, exciting life with Dan.

But she had – more than anything in her entire life, she wanted a new, exciting life. With Dan.

Those were the days when it was impossible to keep their hands off each other and, almost instantly on arriving in London, Helly took on a sassy, new confidence that meant that sex was *always* on the menu. Liberated by her freedom, away from the frowns of her mother, Helly became the woman that she had always dreamt of being. She often lay in bed at night and thought back to those early days when she had playfully dragged Dan into the woods for a daring 'quickie' and how he had loved her even more for skinny-dipping at midnight in the Serpentine. But it was all just a memory now, tucked away, along with her brow-raising bikini waxes and days when 'no' meant 'yes', and 'yes' meant 'what-are-you-waiting-for?'. But now, two children and a career down the line, Dan didn't bother flirting with her any more. And Helly missed it. She still found him highly attractive and was certain that he had his share of female admirers – especially on the gig circuit. He still had the same style of cropped, slightly wavy, dark hair – although possibly slightly less of it, and she was beginning to really notice the light creases of crow's feet kissing the corners of his eyes. He was a great-looking guy, and she loved him. On paper they had an impressive CV *en famille*. Two bright children, a fantastic house in North London, her funky new Mini, his impressive Audi TT. They had the look, the lifestyle, the careers and the joint credit cards but Helly wasn't entirely happy. She knew that she should be. She was aware that her sisters were envious that she 'had it all'.

But I haven't.

And it's not nice, knowing that they're still envious. I just want them to sort themselves out. You've heard the Oasis song about the family full of eccentrics?

Just ask me about it!

Mum's probably to blame. I'd say she's the one with the banjaxed genes. A woman who, encouraged by wildcard Charley, perpetrated a fake insurance claim for burglary by breaking her own kitchen window. From the inside! Thank God Dad copped on to it and managed to tidy up the mess just before the police arrived. She'd thought it was a great idea, until she realised she'd have to stash all the 'stolen' items at Uncle Jack's farm for two months! Life without her microwave had been hell. She'd been banging the drum then about fat-cat insurance companies charging too much anyway.

So I'm told by Dad.

I don't visit too often. The last time was when I saw Madame Lydia with Charley.

But there's more to my life than my dysfunctional family. I can see how my life seems like the clichéd, roses-round-the-door image of contentment to my sisters, but the truth is I'm the ultimate example of money-not-buying-happiness.

I'd expected, on getting the house of my dreams, that I'd reached my destination. Only I hadn't. I had the trimmings, the mint sauce without the lamb. And, despite Dan's pre-occupation with his 'other' life, I had become convinced that another baby would truly make me Little Bo Peep. I suppose it was Madame Lydia in Dublin who had put the idea into my head . . .

Dan had needed help to sit up on the sofa when Helly had first mentioned the appeal of a daughter. OK, so his condition hadn't been helped by the bottle of wine that he'd virtually finished alone after he'd been rehearsing with the guys, but still, the reaction wouldn't have been much different sober. Hysterical laughter would have still prevailed. Eventually he had realised she was serious. She really wanted to try for a daughter.

"But, Helly babe, you're so busy, and you're doing so well now at Pink Turtle. How would she fit into our lives? How *could* she?"

"Dan!" She'd sat beside him and put her slender forearm around his broad shoulders, pulling herself close to his side. She'd nuzzled into his warm neck, resting her head on his shoulder, breathing in his familiar scent, enjoying the moment. His voice had sounded more gravelly and deep as it reverberated through his body and into her ear at such close range.

"We don't have the time, Helly. Why now? We're both busy with our lives, and we're a great family as we are." He'd rubbed his tanned hand across her tummy and smiled, "You're lovely just as you are. We are. We all are."

Helly had felt sick.

Sicker than when I'd been pregnant before.
Sicker than the-hangover-from-hell sick.

Right down to the very core of her body, Helly wanted another child. More than anything else. Even with the prospect of sagging breasts and even more stretchmarks.

Chapter Two

Charley woke, feeling immediately sick, to the sounds of next door's *Breakfast Ireland*, and lay still, waiting for the 'spinny rooms' to start. She knew Mr Kelly wore a hearing aid but cursed the fact that the bedroom walls simply weren't thick enough. That, or he needed a stronger earpiece! And it wasn't only her bedroom. When she was in her living-room she could hear Mrs Kelly whipping up scrambled eggs in their kitchen, and when she was in the bath she could hear – well, it was adjoining Mr and Mrs Kellys' toilet ... The muffled sound of the telly presenter chirping the week's new breakfast recipe did her no favours either. She could make out the words 'mushrooms', 'spinach' and 'tabasco'. Breakfast was the last thing on her mind, thanks to the state of her stomach. She was buckled and knock-kneed and yet she should have been used to it all by now. But despite her 'full' social life, she still hadn't quite mastered the art of the hangover. Except for hair of the dog – that always worked for her.

But not on a work day.

Not a good idea.

Not again.

As usual, it had all started so innocently. She'd finally coined the jingle for the nappy advert and had switched off the light in her plush office in Fitzwilliam Square, turning her back on the static nylon carpet and beech-effect filing cabinets. She simply couldn't resist when the girls who, by day, were so far up their own arses she was surprised they didn't carry torches, suggested they go for a quick drink or two. So they'd shared a couple of bottles of red wine, and then a couple of large gin and tonics were slipped in before they'd decided to hot-foot it across to Dawson Street for a meal. And there they'd had four vodkas and then four large wines. Or was it five? Which were swiftly followed by two sambucas as a special 'treat' to round it all off.

As Charley rubbed at her gritty eyes, attempting to peel her velcro'd tongue from the roof of her mouth, she vaguely recalled an argument between herself and the MD's secretary. Her sister Helen was always giving out to her about drink-fuelled arguments, but what did she know? She was like the Olympic flame – she *never* went out!

As she lay, warm and cosy beneath the duvet, curled on her side, she opened her eyes and scanned the room through slitted, stinging green eyes, relieved to see that it was her own. Yesterday's mascara sat in lumpy chunks on her eyelashes and traces of dry ruby lipstick were streaked across her pillow. She breathed in the stale drink-and-garlic pong that seemed to lightly dust her white cotton duvet. Dropping her hand down beside her bed she snatched at the air as she grappled for something to rehydrate her parched mouth.

No water.

Nothing.

She must have been in a bad way to forget the water.

Then she stiffened and froze as she heard a sleepy groan from somewhere behind her. She fought through the cat's-cradle net of the inside of her head to recall who might be in bed beside her. Turning over slowly, she faced a pungent tunnel which, on blinking, she realised was the beddy-breathed open mouth of the 'Spanish' waiter from last night. The name 'Miguel' came to her mind as she gawped at him. Oblivious to her staring, he frowned hard and tensed in his sleep as he snorted, sucking in a chunky snore, making her jump. Disgusted, she flung back her covers and jumped out of bed, her head banging in protest. Dragging herself to the bathroom she stepped onto cool tiles and punched the 'on' button of the fish-shaped radio. As she stepped under the steaming cascade of water, squirting a blob of zinging lemon gel into her hand, she felt her long hair suddenly cling to her neck and shoulders, warm and wet under the jets.

Only to be reminded by the giggling, chirpy presenter that today was her birthday.

Her fortieth.

Smiling, she relaxed under the warm water as she

remembered that she wasn't going in to work today. Again.

There was little to beat an invigorating shower to bring Charley back to life after a heavy night out. She loved the feeling of the stretchy lace against her bum as she sashayed across from the bathroom, back into her bedroom, in her burgundy lace knickers. She felt, despite her squeezing headache, rather sexy. And feckit, it was her birthday and she had absolutely no intention of feeling forty today. Today of all days. The exotic 'Miguel' was now sitting up in her bed, his neat tree-of-life chest hair looking most tantalising. She couldn't help but notice the lusty twinkle in his eye – if he could hear the muffled sounds of Mrs Kelly hollering at Mr Kelly, then he wasn't letting on.

"You're one dead sexy woman, you know," he said without a trace of a Spanish accent, his voice thick with lust as he admired her toned and St Tropez-tanned body.

She took great delight in the fact that her firm breasts hadn't caught up with the rest of her – they were clearly unaware that she was forty and were stuck somewhere around twenty-nine. She was delighted that she wasn't yet able to tuck them into her knickers, and supposed it made up for the fact that the signs of the drink and cigarettes were beginning to show around her eyes and lips.

"Course I know I'm sexy," she replied. "You don't think you can get to my age – I mean, you don't think I don't know that!"

"Come here . . ."

She smiled as she knelt down on her antique pine bed,

watching her legs sink into the sumptuous duvet before she 'whooped' as he grabbed her, flipping her and pinning her down.

"You're the original Italian Stallion," she cooed, wondering whether there was a trace of Latin blood in him at all.

"Mmmmm," he groaned as he nuzzled her neck, her boobs squashed against his chest hair. As he playfully bit her earlobe he wondered whether she'd figured out yet that he was just plain Michael, olive-skinned, from Stillorgan.

She wriggled from beneath him, her lacy knickers riding their way up between her bum cheeks as she slid off the bed. She stood before him, topless and confident of her body in a way he knew was hard to find in women in their twenties. She slid open her wardrobe door, pretending to look for something to put on.

He knew the routine. It was many a morning he'd woken up in a strange bed, to find the lady of the house was playing hard to get. He crawled across the bed on all fours.

Charley clocked him in the mirror and braced herself for his grip. His hands were firm and yet gentle on her slender hips as he stood behind her, nuzzling into her dark hair and snaking his hands up her torso, across her belly button, over the slight raise of her ribs, until they were cupping her breasts. She threw her head back. She knew the effect her long silky hair had on the guys. They loved burying their faces in it. Thankfully, thought Charley, they never noticed the cow's-lick that she

21

detested – since childhood she had hated the way that it forced her fringe upwards slightly. Holding her shoulders lightly, he spun her to face him, her hair splaying out and falling in strands across her face, her eyes. In her mouth. He kissed her full and hard, surprising her and forcing strands of her dark hair into her gums. She held her hands against his chest and pushed him away, for a split second. Just time enough to run her fingers through her hair once again, and remove it from her mouth.

Before the clock had moved on three minutes she was feverishly polishing her mirrored wardrobe with her backside.

At a speed of 'nots'.

I'm *not* going to work.

I'm *not* forty.

I'm *not* looking for love.

I'm *not* cut out for a relationship.

She panted while he grunted and groaned as she tried desperately to convince herself that she really *was* better off without a permanent man in her life. Then her mobile bleeped, a muffled sound from her bag. Momentarily she was distracted, but 'Miguel' wasn't near to giving up. Once again it bleeped and she lost her concentration.

"Ignore it," he panted, his eyes fixed on his own close-range reflection as he conga'd his way into Charley. Damn, he knew he looked good.

She tried, but couldn't as the mobile bleeped again.

"Stop! It's either three messages or one really long one. I have to look." Michael cursed as she pushed him away lightly.

He pulled on his jeans swiftly as she pulled out her phone and pressed the buttons to read her texts.

"Oh Helly! What are you thinking of?"

Michael looked up, only very slightly curious. "Bad news?"

"Listen to this. *'You know how lavender is really relaxing? Well, do you think that lavender farmers are completely chilled out and serene the whole time?'*"

"What?" he gurned at her.

"I know. It's my mad, housebound sister. She's always sending me these really profound and unanswerable texts. Sorry."

"Is she disabled?"

"No. Well, not really. She's just a busy mum with two kids, a perfect husband and a fabulous house. Jealous? Me? Never!"

"Oh. Well," he frowned, puzzled as he pulled on his T-shirt, "maybe some other time?"

"Yeah," Charley lit a cigarette, throwing her phone down onto the bed, and checking her watch, "maybe. Any chance of a lift to the airport? I've got to catch a flight to London."

"Sorry, no can do."

"No problem," she said cheerily. "I need to check my emails first anyway."

By now it had all caught up with her. Charley groaned as she lowered her gaze, reaching out for her third oversized latte, her hand shaking involuntarily as she clutched it.

"Arrggh, I think I must have Parkinson's! Fuck!" she

23

cursed under her breath, irritated with herself and her condition as she decorated the chrome table with splodges of hot coffee. She was blaming it on the unbalanced rickety table-legs on the uneven pavement. It suited her to. She'd deliberately wiped from her memory the champagne breakfast she'd treated herself to at the airport. Oh, and then again on the plane. She'd then hopped onto a train at Stansted and had whizzed through into central London surprisingly quickly. They'd agreed to meet at Starbucks in Belsize Park and now the watery sunlight was reflecting starkly against the silver table and slicing through her pounding head. But she couldn't bear the claustrophobia of sitting inside. Her puffy eyes and poor complexion were evidence of yet another night on the sauce and too many cigs and she was a poor advert for the coffee giants on this bright, yet crisp April morning as she huddled into her parka, her track-suited legs crossed loosely. She'd wanted to look brat-packy, but at 40, and after yet another evening of over-indulgence she looked brutal. It was obvious that she'd annoyed her boss with her colourful excuse for another day off. But hell, hadn't she warned them that her fortieth was looming? What more did they want? A letter from her mammy?

The thought of her mother reminded her of the birthday email that she'd received from her parents only that morning. It had been sent at 02:45 so she supposed that Dad was keeping Mum awake with his snoring, despite her buying him numerous nose-clips and contraptions. And Dad, the poor devil, was forever trying to lose them. Charley knew it was her mother who had sent this email as she'd inadvertently attached loads of email spam in the shape of porn junk screaming *'Do You Want a Bigger Penis?'*. The truth was, Charley did, her short-term and sooo-on-his-way-out 'boyfriend' Kevin being the cocktail sausage of sexual partners and as such, not daily fare. She got a little every fortnight but it wasn't nearly enough to live on. And she worried at her willingness to accept this, knowing she was really scared of being alone.

She had read her mother's jumbled email, sent 2:45 am.

From: Mum & Dad

To: Charley

Time: 02:45, 10th April

Subject: Happy 40th, darling

"Happy 40th, darling. Have a fantastic day with Helly and give her our love.

I've just ordered some new conservatory furniture, so you must come over and see it. It's peach with a bambaloo frame. You know, we're only the other side of Dublin, why don't you call over at the weekend? I hope you've not thrown off your coat yet, pet, it's still too cold for that. Dad keeps trying to take the new bambaloo furniture into the garden but I keep telling him it's too cold even to snow! Anyway, I'll ring you later, love. Have a great birthday, pet, and give Kevin a big kiss from us. He might be a little boring, pet, but he's a good man. You don't want to be on your own."

At least it was an improvement on the phone calls during which her mother always took great delight in asking if she was even *looking* for someone to get married to. In an absurd turnaround, she'd begun to encourage Charley to *stop* taking her contraception. She knew it was an ominous sign that her mother was aware of her loudly ticking body-clock. Nothing changed in her mum's life – except that she got worse. She was still over-ordering from the catalogue and hiding her wacky buys from Charley's dad, and still over-reacting at the mere mention of any male friend of Charley's. And then there was her strange fixation on peach, not to mention that she was the Queen of Crap Expressions. Her daughters took great delight in every new coinage. The latest had been that Mrs O'Dwyer had 'got better to die' – that was the latest 'number one', beating all previous mispronunciations and mistakes.

Feeling a pang of sadness, she stared into the huge mug at the brown sludge at the bottom and yearned for a quick shot of vodka while she waited for her sister. Kevin was playing on her mind. Like a loyal puppy, only not so playful or cute. As she swirled the cold mug in her hands she thought back to her twenties, a time when she had been so sure of herself. She could literally *hear* her own voice as she had lain on the beach in Greece, lined up beside her friends, colourful and pert in Dayglo bikinis. They'd laughed at the rickety sunbeds but had listened to her when she spoke, her voice confident and warm, "No, I'm never going to *need* a man. I hate women who are afraid to be on their own. What kind of life would *that* be?"

But her self-esteem had plummeted in direct proportion to her alcohol consumption rising. She cheered up as she reminded herself of her promise, that every birthday with a zero at the end was a milestone. She'd decided that it would mark a change. She'd decided to face up to moving on and splitting with Kevin for a start.

She was confused about the distinction between social drinking and alcohol dependency, and with that more blurred than ever, had decided to take the opinion that drinking was merely a national pastime, a bit of a laugh. She'd grown up with pub culture – it had been an intrinsic thread which ran through her adolescent life and she couldn't imagine a life without it. She often argued that even the 'soaps' revolve around pubs. What would *Fair City* be without McCoys? *EastEnders* without The Vic? And *Corrie* without the bloody Rovers? The truth was, she felt, these programmes had deceived an entire generation. She grew up thinking this was life 'on the outside' post teenage angst. The cruel words of her ex-boyfriend Donal often reverberated through the cotton-wool cloud of her mind. The suggestion that her liking for drink had rung the 'last bell' of their relationship. Ridiculous! She had been heartbroken after the split but Donal had convinced her mother that Charley had a drink problem and, at thirty-eight, she wasn't prepared to listen to his incessant preaching.

And then she'd visited her sister Fiona and her partner, Luís, in Cascais.

It had been horrible. She just couldn't get back to Dublin quick enough. She had always been wary of her sister's boyfriend, but what had happened in Cascais had changed her perception of life and tarnished her outlook ever since.

So she'd gone straight back to work after the visit, to her job as an ad copywriter, taking minimal delight in making up ditties and jingles for a living. The bonus for Charley was that she could work from home sometimes if she wanted to.

Or rather, if she needed to.

Chapter Three

Helly suspected that Dan thought she didn't notice how these days he sprang out of bed every morning, a good half hour earlier than usual. Helly would lie, eyes closed, remembering how she wanted another baby to rekindle what they'd once had – not to drive a deeper gap between them. And this morning had been no exception. She had sat on the edge of the bed and looked back to his 'side'. He had thrown the covers back in a lump and his pillow had fallen onto the floor.

Obviously in a hurry!

She heard the radio burst into life downstairs as Dan boiled the kettle and then heard Toby and Jack stampede out of their rooms and down the stairs. She sighed deeply and rubbed her hands over her face in an attempt to revive herself and face the day with a smile.

As she came out of the shower Dan called up the stairs

to her, his voice rich and calm, "I've just put their lunchboxes in the car for you!"

Helly cursed under her breath before she shouted back, "Thanks, love!"

She strode across the landing, back towards her bedroom, hearing the bubbly sounds of her sons giggling and laughing as Dan sang in the kitchen. "Boys!" she yelled. "Get your coats on for me. There's rain forecast for later!"

As she padded barefoot across the waxed wooden floor of her bedroom, the large sash window letting in chunks of light, she bit at a strand of loose skin beside her thumbnail.

It's Charley's 40th and she's flying in for the day. I invited her for dinner tonight as I haven't seen her for a while, but she says she can't make it. Well, she probably could make it but she has another agenda.

Two, in fact.

The first being that she can't stand kids. Not just mine – everyone's. It's her level of intolerance, you see. It's extremely high. But she wasn't always like that. It's probably made worse by her second agenda – her love affair with alcohol. She reckons she can only cope in the company of children when she's jarred. She claims it knocks the rough edges off them!

So she's on a morning flight and we're meeting later for coffee – probably to cure her hangover from last night.

Pumping serum into her palm she rubbed it between her hands and smoothed it over her blonde hair. Helly was blessed with strong features which allowed her to go for a tightly cropped, boyish hairstyle which really suited her, although she'd always thought her eyes were too big.

It had marked a serious turnaround when Charley had said to her, a few years back,

"You know, Helly, your hair would look fabulous really short. You know, like 'Lisa Stansfield' short."

"Don't be ridiculous. You mean 'Judi Dench' short?"

"Exactly."

And so she'd toyed with the idea for a while until a particularly foggy morning had transformed her already naturally frizzy hair into a brillo pad. So she had taken the plunge and never looked back.

She had always been able to get dressed in nanoseconds. Ever since she was a teenager. She hummed as she slid into her calf-length suede skirt and tugged on her Emma Hope spike-heeled boots. Grabbing yesterday's pink Chloe vest she pulled it over her head, scanning her bulging wardrobe for a suitable jacket. The April air still had a chill to it and she wasn't prepared to brave it in a vest alone. Since her arrival in London, it was second nature to her to blend individual designer items with flea market or Camden Market buys and she had an exceptional eye for it, often pulling old clothes from the back of her wardrobe and mixing them with designer items. It was Dan who had first suggested that she try opening a boutique of her own, and she now frequented the Paris flea markets along with the London and Brighton ones looking for bargains to bring back and sell in Pink Turtle. Stamping down the stairs she herded the boys out of the front door, pausing only at the hallway mirror to smear two stripes of colour onto her lips.

Crucial if your eyes are big!

She dashed out of the door, bundling into her new black Mini Cooper amid a flurry of schoolbags and lunchboxes, treading awkwardly on the empty crisp bags and sweet wrappers that were already littering the interior. She turned the key in the ignition and checked over her right shoulder for a space to nip out into.

As they drove toward the school they passed the Victorian Salvage Company that she was dying to visit. She had fully intended to fill their new house with the original features that had probably been ripped out in the eighties and was just waiting for Dan to spare her some time so that they could discuss it. She felt lonely and cold, realising he couldn't schedule her in for any spare time.

Helly dropped the children off at school, dodging the huge 4x4's and sleek bobs which sat perched at the wheels, and then decided to take a gamble with her time, cutting through the traffic to call in at the shop for a while. Claire was helping her out there today, but she hadn't anticipated so many telephone calls and customers when she walked through the door and she'd spent much longer there than expected. So now, as she walked towards the café, she knew she was already late for Charley. Not that Charley would mind – or even notice – depending on how hungover she was.

The minute she turned the corner she noticed Charley's pained morning-after-the-night-before expression from fifty paces.

"Jesus, the state of you!" she called as she drew near.

"Hey," Charley oozed sarcasm as Helly scraped a chair

from the table, "what happened to 'Happy Birthday to you'?"

Helly leant across the table, kissing her sister on the cheek. She sat down and shivered slightly. "God, it's a bit cold out here. Can't we go inside?"

"Can't."

"What do you mean, can't? Why can't you?"

"Cos I feel too sick, that's why!"

The vehemence of her reply bypassed Helly – she was used to it. Especially in the light of the hangover.

She kept her denim-jacketed elbows off the table to avoid the numerous splats of coffee swimming and wobbling on the chrome surface.

"So will I get you another one?" she asked Charley, indicating the three mugs on the table and wiping up the mess with an abandoned serviette.

"Yeah, what you having?"

"A mocha frappuccino."

"Go on then." Charley brightened up slightly. "Forget the lattes, I'm ready for something stronger. Are there any with brandy in?"

"Charley! It's only lunchtime! Were you drinking on the plane?"

"Oh, give me some credit! Anyway, it's past twelve. And it's my fecking birthday! C'mon, Hel, you're a right dry shite these days."

"Charley," Helly hissed, "pull yourself together! Look at the state of you!"

Charley ignored her, sticking her fingers in her ears as she began to hum loudly while she perused the extensive coffee menu. Helly went inside to order, leaving the humming, oblivious Charley.

She came back, putting down the two large mugs onto the rickety table as Charley grimaced, "What the hell's that?"

"Caramel macchiato. I changed our minds."

"Jesus. As if I didn't feel sick already!" Charley shifted in her seat, looking around her. "Feckit, Helly, can't we go to a nice wine bar or something? Even a pub would be better than this! Thought this was supposed to be a *birthday* celebration."

"Did you get my text?"

"Christ yeah. What was that all about? Lavender farmers!"

"Don't you ever think about things like that? I mean lavender is so relaxing, isn't it? Imagine working on a lavender farm? You'd be floating all day and night."

"Helen, you really need to get out more." And she stuck out her tongue.

As they sat at the table in the bright sunshine Helly ignored her embarrassing sister, held her steaming mug aloft and wished Charley a Happy Birthday.

"Happy Birthday!" Charley smiled, speaking a little too loudly. "Jesus, I was happier yesterday when I was a *year* younger!"

Helly was already tired of smiling, placating the frowning suits that had left their personalities at their desks with their laptops and photos of their wife and kids, and were sitting at adjoining tables, looking at them strangely.

It's going to be one of those days again. I hate it when she's like this, so bloody contrary and awkward.

And hungover.

Helly watched Charley's eyes light up and turned to see what she was looking at. Not surprisingly it was the guy behind the counter, making the coffees.

"Yuck. Charley please! You really should be more choosey."

"Why?" she grinned. "You know I'm a woman who has '*NEXT*' written in my knickers."

Helly groaned and took a gulp of coffee as Charley continued, "As Colin Farrell once said, whoever I bang is bangin' me back!" Charley brightened at the reminder of male company and relaxed as she began to fill Helly in on the latest in her life. "You know, I had an email from someone from school yesterday."

"Go 'way. Who?"

"Through Friends Reunited. Wanting to meet up for a drink."

"Who!"

"Do you remember Johnny Quinn?"

"Urrgh, the one who used to flash his willie in PE?"

"Yeah."

"Yuck, Charley, he was rotten *then*. God only knows what he's like now at forty!"

Charley pushed Helly's arm, causing her to spill some of her drink,

"No need to bloody shout it out! Anyway, I replied to him before I came out this morning." She nearly mentioned that it was after she'd asked Michael for the lift to the airport, but chose not to.

"No! What did you say?"

"Thought I'd check him out. I sent him a real saucy email."

Helly drew her chair in closer. "Go on."

Charley sat back further. "Can't tell you. Too rude. Actually I took an excerpt from an erotic novel that's been sitting around for a while. He'll either piss his pants or come in them."

"You're some bitch."

"Yeah," she giggled. "Fun though, isn't it?"

"So what if he replies with a real hot answer? Does that mean you'll be meeting up with him? Who knows, I may be wrong about him – he might have turned into a prince by now."

"Come on! Don't believe the Ugly Duckling story, girl – you'll only be disappointed."

"I don't know, for a gawky teenager you didn't turn out too bad."

"Thanks a bloody lot!"

"Anyway," said Helly, "isn't it supposed to be *Friends Reunited*?"

An hour later the sun had broken right through the patchy light cloud and the caffeine was lifting Charley's mood. Helly was on the verge of removing her jacket but thought better of it, remembering that she'd rushed the ironing of her pink vest the day before and she had deodorant stripes down the sides. As they sat and people-watched in the fresh air, they grinned at the builders who bundled in and out with their takeaway coffees and sandwiches, leaving dusty footprints on the welcome mat. Helly watched as Charley came to life, all signs of hangover forgotten as she switched into 'babe mode'.

"Hey, darlin', you can join me in a drink later," said a guy with Brad Pitt looks and toned abs straining through his T-shirt, winking at her, his dusty leather pork-pie hat making him strangely extra-sexy.

"I'd love to," she grinned. "But with the size of your ego? I don't think we'd both fit."

His mates had laughed and slapped him on the back causing him to spill his coffee as they beefed their way back to the site, waddling as if their balls had swollen to the size of their heads.

"You're cruel," Helly laughed.

"The Princess of Piss-take, actually." Charley smirked as she finished the last dregs of her drink, suddenly feeling a little better about herself.

"OK then, ready?" asked Helly.

"Yeah, fancy some shopping?"

Helly checked her watch, "Well, I've got a while yet before the school-run, but I would like to call back in to the shop and check on Claire." She stood and tucked her chair in under the table, despising herself for the mumsy act, but it was hard to shake off in an instant. "I forgot to ask you, what did you think of the Paddy's Day Parade?"

"I didn't go!" Charley shook her head as she stood, checking her lipstick in her hand-mirror. "I know I said I would, but I didn't bother this year. Just couldn't be arsed really. All those eejits dressed up as leprechauns. And they've got the nerve to wear the hats that say, 'Kiss me, I'm Irish'! I mean, fake ginger hair and green clothes – it's not a great look, is it? No wonder they have to beg!"

Helly laughed at her reasoning as Charley linked arms with her. "Well, you must at least have had a few Irish coffees?" She was testing the water, curious as to her sister's reaction.

"No, I didn't."

Helly felt relieved, having been certain that Charley would have spent the entire Paddy's weekend pissed.

Until Charley continued, "I spent the weekend at Winston's actually. He's got some fantastic Jamaican Rum. A hundred-and-fifty-one per cent proof!"

"Winston?" Helly screeched.

Charley wondered whether half the dogs in London were heading their way at that very second.

"That guy from the gospel choir. He's got a stall on Moore Street Market.

'*Ahh wiiiishh aah knew hoow it would feeeel to be freeee! Aah wiiish aah could teeell!'*" Charley began to demonstrate her version of gospel.

Helly sighed and tried not to feel embarrassed.

My sister really is as eccentric as hell, but an absolute gem. The trouble with Charley is, she only got drunk once, but it seems to have lasted about eighteen months!

OK, so she's more Courtney Love than Nina Simone, but since she's joined the Killiney Gospel Choir there's no stopping her. She's even texting me recipes made from papaya and coconut milk!

As they dodged through the bustle that had burst from a Tube station, Charley smiled at Helly and asked, "So how is Dan? You don't really talk about him much."

A cloud crept into Helly's smile. "That's because he doesn't really talk to me much any more. He's too busy."

"Yeah, but so are you, what with the brats. I mean boys. And Pink Turtle and the flea markets. You can't blame it all on him. You have a great life, Hel. All that freedom and independence."

This is what annoys me. Charley's always had a soft spot for Dan, right from Day One. And I thought marriage was supposed to be a 'partnership'!

"I know. But he knows my routine – there're no surprises! I'm at Pink Turtle from nine thirty to three. I took on Claire to run it from three till six and some weekends. I go on a day-trip to Paris once a month for the markets. That's hardly nine-to-five, is it? He's either continually at the computer doing his graphics work or he's gigging with the bloody band. I just don't seem to fit into his life any more. It's as if we're growing apart. And I'm only thirty-three. I thought that kind of thing starts to happen in your fifties."

"Ha, don't believe it! If some of the guys I go out with are anything to go by, it's happening all the time. I'm just glad they're not promising to leave their boring wives for me. That'd be a complete fright. You know what they say – a wife only lasts for the duration of the marriage, but an ex-wife is for the rest of your life!"

"But I'm so happy in every aspect of my life, except for my relationship with Dan. Well, I must admit, at home I feel like a housekeeper, mum, chef, accountant, nurse and skivvy."

"Don't be ridiculous! You're busy with your shop and he's busy with his music. What do you expect? You're married! Why do you think I haven't got married?"

"Em, perhaps because nobody has ever asked you?" Helly reminded her.

She took umbrage at the suggestion, "No. Actually. Because my motto is why buy the book when you can get it out of the library? Anyway, I've got friends who consider marriage to be the new extreme sport. It requires nerves of steel *and* insurance!"

"You're just sooo unromantic, Charley."

"Not at all. I am a true romantic at heart. I just also understand the need for good sex. Are you and Dan having any?"

"Huh! Not with each other. The trouble is, I desperately want another child." Helly's voice softened. "I want to try for a daughter. But the prospects of it has put him right off sex."

She saw Charley's horrified expression as she asked, "So are you still on the pill?"

"No, I stopped it last month. It was my last pack anyway and I thought I'd be able to talk him round."

"What!"

"It'll be OK. He's not coming anywhere near me anyway, unless we have at least two layers of clothing on. Each. It'll do my hormones good to have a break off the pill for a while. It's not exactly as if he's mad for me at the moment."

"Jesus!" Charley knew when to lay off.

Helly continued, "The problem is, Charley, it's become routine and monotonous and I can't help but think about being pregnant again. Though I suppose I should count my blessings and thank God for the kids I have and my antique clothes."

"Yeah, and your fantastic wooden-floored Victorian house!"

The taste of envy filled the air-space as Charley's words sat before them, truth laid bare in an ugly fashion.

It only took a split second for Helly to decide to keep quiet about her exciting meeting tomorrow. A stylist for the new chart-topping girl-band Quattro had called into Pink Turtle and had been so impressed by Helly's eye for co-ordinating eclectic pieces, she'd arranged a meeting for her with the record-label PR guy – to talk about the possibility of her supplying the costumes for their latest UK and Ireland tour! Helly was bowled over by the thought, but extremely nervous too.

But now she simply smiled at Charley, not wanting to fan the flames of jealousy even more.

But the smile didn't quite reach her eyes.

Chapter Four

Fiona looked at her reflection in the mirror, the stark fluorescent lighting of the café toilets enhancing her light tan. The click of her heels echoed and sparked off the tiled floor as she fidgeted. Leaning in toward the mirror she placed her fingers along her hairline and gently tugged upwards. She'd seen the programmes on the telly where the plastic surgeons did this to show the promises of face-lifts, the success of the scalpel. She had hoped that her appearance would have improved, what with the perma-tan and Portuguese year-round sunshine – she hadn't counted on the cruel effects of stress though. Or the lure of the countless pastries. She worried about her flagging appearance and felt a wave of disappointment as she turned sideways and viewed her protruding tummy and bum – she was nearly 'deeper' than she was wide! She'd tried repeatedly to console herself with the popularity of the J-Lo bum, but she knew hers was double the size. She grabbed at the tops of her thighs, dreaming of the day that she could save enough money to afford liposuction. She had begun to despise her appearance and, as an avid and talented violinist, since the birth of *Riverdance* had dreamed of being a leather-trousered, sleek-haired violinist who'd swing her glossy hair and pout shiny lips to the camera. She'd watched every appearance of Sharon Corr and Vanessa-Mae and had yearned to mix the classical violin with a more funky, sexy image for herself. Instead, she remained a couple of stone overweight and the turmoils of the last year hung heavy on her.

Literally.

She pulled her auburn hair back into a low ponytail, feeling the dew of perspiration on the back of her neck. Hoisting her leather bag up onto her bare, tanned shoulder she moved across to the sink area and washed her hands, her long elegant fingers brown amongst the white sudsy foam. As the door opened beside her, the garlic smell wafted in and she heard the sizzling of cooking and the brash voice of the swarthy, sweaty proprietor, whom she'd nicknamed 'Betty Swollocks', barking from behind the counter as he cuffed his forehead with his sleeve and demanded to know what his customers wanted for breakfast this morning.

It had taken her a while to get used to Portuguese coffee, but five years on she was a hardened Lisboeta, starting her day with a turbo-charged *bica* with a bag or three of sugar stirred in. She took her usual small table by the front window, which allowed her to watch city life rush past as she ordered her *bica escaldada numa chávena fria*. She wanted the piping hot *bica*, the bitterness offset with heaps of sugar, but insisted on having it in a cold cup from the shelf. Like many of the regular customers she'd learned from experience and so refused to take her *bica* in a cup from the top of the coffee machine which would usually be so hot she'd burn her lips before she'd even tasted the bitter-sweet drink.

As tired as she was of Portugal, Fiona still loved getting lost in the vibrancy, the anonymity of the city. It reminded her of Dublin or London and in any case she was always grateful for any excuse to get away from Cascais, the village where she lived.

Now she enjoyed feeling invisible as she sat in the window sipping her coffee, wondering what her daughter Adriana would be doing with Luís today. She hated these times alone and yet knew she should be enjoying them, taking the opportunity for time out. If only she had some money on her to spend in H&M or Mango she might get the chance to relax and make the most of her day in Lisbon. Ah, well, window-shopping was a torment with no money to gratify her desires, but it was better than nothing.

Her phone bleeped, vibrating in her pocket. She only had incoming calls and texts these days, her serious lack of funds meaning that phone credits were way at the bottom of the list of financial priorities. Her eyes filled with tears as she read a lavender-farm quandary from Helly. It was only her family's texts and calls that made her feel loved. She couldn't really afford to ring them, but was so desperate lately she'd been scrimping on decent food so that she could make a couple of calls to her sisters in Dublin and London, needing the blanket of their sympathy. But she still couldn't bring herself to admit to her parents what a pig Luís had turned out to be.

Years ago a giggling Charley had nicknamed Luís 'The Onion' due to his ruthlessness in business and his ability to make grown men cry, but it hadn't bothered Fiona much. Being a copywriter seemed to mean that Charley always had obnoxious foodie names for everyone – she'd once labelled Helly as 'The Doughnut' because she was "sickly, sugary and sweet on the outside and oozing with yumminess on the inside". But Fiona hated that Charley had entitled her 'The Banana Skin' because she was always slipping up. Not so much physically, more on a day-to-day, coping-with-life basis. Fiona was embarrassed about it. But, thankfully, Luís was ignorant of the title. Fiona often wondered at which point his sense of humour had melted away, in the transition from love-of-her-life to ex.

She felt the vinegar tears sting. Discreetly she pressed at the corners of her eyes, to dispel the emotions that still seemed to be queuing to pour out. This wasn't the time or the place. But nowhere was – at home, in bed, during the day, she continually elbowed back her emotions when it came to Luís, still holding out a minute fragment of hope.

She pinched at the miniscule handle of the coffee cup, and swigged down the bitter remains.

She left the café to be faced with a rickety, yellow tram, clanking its way around the narrow cobbled streets.

She stood back, making brief eye contact with the uniformed driver as he pulled on the old levers, exchanging gruff pleasantries with the pensioners and tourists on board.

Lisbon always used to lift Fiona, never failing to overwhelm her senses, but not any more. She sat in her usual spot on the rocks, by the river, watching the orange and white ferries glide across the sun-streaked River Tagus from Cais do Sodre. She felt her thighs spread a little on the warm pavement as she sat, her legs dangling down over the rocks as she stared at the seagulls rooting and pecking at the moss-covered stones. As she looked up at the imposing Cristo Rei statue that towered high across the river, Christ's arms outstretched, welcoming, she recalled how much she had been in love with Lisbon when she'd first arrived.

She'd sent her sisters insane with her perspective of the European San Francisco, boasting its 'Golden Gate' bridge and its trams. She used to adore the forty-five-minute train ride from Cascais to Lisbon, with its views of the river, Belém, and the Disciples statue – or, if she sat on the other side of the carriage, the sight of the cars as they zipped and nipped through the traffic beside the train-tracks. Isabella, the mango-seller, was always outside Cais do Sodre station to greet her with a smile, her boxes of fruit stacked against the station wall as her regulars fiddled with coins to buy them. Fiona used to make sure to buy a couple, just to try and help, but she was in no position to now. She used to delight in the bright graffiti'd walls at Cais do Sodre and the sweet, heady waft of the Camel cigarettes the students smoked as they gathered outside the station, debating where to go instead of school.

But that was in the past.

She slipped slightly on the mossy ground as she got to her feet, beginning her walk up into the city centre. She paused for breath, sweating in the blanket of heat, her eyes shaded with her sunglasses, and she was aware of the intense perfume of jasmine and orange blossom. The green tint of her shades did little to hide the familiar rich colours of the jacarandas, bougainvillaeas and geraniums which seduced her. She had often thought it ironic that in Ireland she'd taken little interest in the countryside, the names of flowers for example, and yet in a bustling city such as Lisbon she couldn't help but notice the fantastic gardens and floral tapestries that surrounded her.

Feeling slightly puffed out and uncomfortable around the waist, she tugged at the band of her jeans in an attempt to stretch them a little. She hated feeling stuffed and knew she was putting on more weight. As she prepared for a bout of self-deprecation she was approached by two American tourists looking for directions, their oversized shorts and brightly sloganed T-shirts confirming their status. She was often taken for a local Lisboeta, due to her long auburn hair and sunkissed complexion. She directed them to the nearest tram stop, glancing at their inappropriate footwear – one wearing calf-length yellow socks with trainers and the other flimsy flip-flops – they had obviously never heard the local saying, "*Abril, águas mil*", the voice of experience which linked April with "a thousand waters".

Having stopped to catch her breath, she was now ready for the rest of the steep hill. She dropped her shades down from her hair, over her eyes, and caught her reflection in a deli window. She grimaced at the sight of pink and brown raw meats displayed on skewers, on a bed of green and black olives and straight-from-the-tin button mushrooms. It was true: Lisbon was no friend to vegetarians.

But it wasn't the meats that caused her to look again: it was the small card in the window next door advertising for staff.

Twenty minutes later she had taken one of the rickety trams which climbed and dropped as they rode over the reputed seven hills of Lisbon (although she now knew there were many more than seven), and had made her way to the centre of the city. As she began her walk up another steep hill she paused to look in the shop windows and cringed every time she saw her puffed reflection looking back at her. Her excess-weight issue was always thrown to the front of her mind in Lisbon where nobody was fat. The city's numerous hills saw to that and Fiona hated her chubbiness as she wheezed and panted to get to the top of the streets.

Perhaps she should have stayed at home and cleaned her tiny apartment which she'd tried desperately to make homely with cheap pictures and the slightly broken shell-mobiles that were sold on the seafront. She hated the cold floor-tiles and the rusty balcony, always deploring the fact that the apartment never got quite enough sun to wipe out the chill-factor inside. But she loved her pastel-pink front door. It was the first thing that had attracted her to rent it. There was plenty of tidying to do there, and then there was her intermittent violin practice, but given the opportunity for a day of escapism in Lisbon there was little contest.

But her buying days had disappeared with Luís. His weekly treats, meals out and surprises for which she pined were now distant memories. That and the comfort of snuggling up to his broad hairy chest every night, the way he used to caress her forehead as she woke, the way she'd nestle in the crook of his tanned arm as sleep took them, soulful traditional *fado* music soothing them.

As usual, the thought of Luís brought with it a feeling of misery and an overwhelming homesickness and Fiona realised once again how much she missed Dublin and London. Dublin: the DART, grey skies, pollution and puke on the street corners on a Sunday morning. London: red buses, the Underground, grey skies, pollution and road rage. It made no sense but she missed them intensely. But nowhere near as much as she missed her sisters, Helly and Charley.

"Yeah," she said softly to herself, suddenly remembering Charley's birthday, "I must ring them both tonight."

Fiona had lived in her small apartment in Cascais for the last year – ever since Luís had walked out on her.

On *them*.

On her and Adriana.

Or, more precisely, since he's thrown them out.

The fantastic views over the sea didn't make up for the

fact that her modest apartment was still a far cry from the huge, red-roofed home that she'd shared with him for the previous four years. She missed Luís desperately and resentment burned in her whenever he mentioned Bella, his new Swedish girlfriend. And, with her limited maintenance from him, coupled with his strict instructions forbidding her to work, she felt trapped in a country that she had once held so dear.

She constantly wrestled the 'brave face' on, to fight away the sadness of the last year, often taking walks around the trio of small sandy coves that Cascais was arranged around and stopping for ice cream at one of the trendy little restaurants with Adriana.

Today, in pensive mood, she felt saddened that the initial appeal of Portugal – the clichés of sardines and port – were touristy memories.

She looked down at her faded, worn jeans and felt the tears sting at her eyes once again as she got on the train heading back for Cascais.

Chapter Five

Helly had enjoyed her day with Charley and she'd tried to cajole her into getting a later flight and joining them for dinner, but Charley's irritation with everyone under the age of eighteen was too strong.

"I'm sorry, Helen, it's just kids. I can't help it. It's nothing personal against Toby and Jack but, well – you know me."

"It'd probably do you good to spend some time around children, Charley. You're so obsessed with your own life, it'd be good for you to give some time to others for a change."

Charley harrumphed and forced a wobbly attempt at a smile, "Noooo way. I can't stand it. And the noise! I don't know how you and Dan do it. It cuts straight through me!"

"Why have you changed, Charley?"

She shrugged, avoiding eye-contact with Helly.

"Charley! I've got a photo of you with Toby and Jack at home and the three of you are so alike! They adore you. You were such fun with them."

"Oh Helly," she sighed, irritated, "please!"

"They do notice it, you know. How you avoid them. They do miss you. We all do."

She saw Helly's disappointed expression and felt bad. "Oh, you know I love them to pieces. But just not tonight. I had a really late night and, erm, an early morning."

"But they love you so much, Charley, and hardly ever see any of my family. It all revolves round Dan and his Auntie Pat and bloody Uncle Brian."

"I know, babe. Maybe next time, eh?"

Helly knew there'd be more chance of seeing a Rolf Harris revival than making Charley child-friendly.

"It'd be different if you could just take their batteries out for a few minutes!" Charley teased.

Charley rang Kevin from the airport and then also on her way home, but not before her usual stop at the off-licence. She tried to use different ones on different days as she'd started to tire of shop assistants commenting on the frequency and quantity of her purchases. All that scaremongering about drinking was ridiculous. Her dad had drunk for his entire life and he was still around! She filled a carrier bag with bottles of red and white wine, grabbing at some crisps to balance out the alcohol-to-food ratio. The shop assistant shot her a cursory glance, fully aware that the random handfuls of crisps and peanuts were a cover-up. She'd seen it too many times before.

When she got home she was planning to slump onto the sofa and watch the re-runs of *Friends* as she finished off two of the bottles of red, but she'd no sooner uncorked the first bottle when Kevin arrived. In her more homely moments Kevin was the comfy but tatty cushion that you didn't want anyone to see, but you loved snuggling up to in the evenings. His appeal shrank in proportionate dimensions to the approach of the weekend. On a Monday he was a great fella, but by Friday he held as much appeal as last week's TV guide.

She sat cross-legged in her leather armchair, glancing sideways at him transfixed by the television, slumped on the settee, his legs stretched out before him. Bored with the monotony of him, she felt Rebellious Divilment appear and begin to tug. She decided to spice up their evening and slid out of the door and up the stairs. Straightening the crumpled duvet that she'd left in a hurry after Michael's departure earlier in the day, she smiled at her reflection in the huge wardrobe mirror. She pulled on stockings and suspenders, her new lacy knickers and basque. She looked damned good. Even if she was forty! Especially because she was forty! Strutting out of the bedroom, she paused to tuck in a couple of stray pubic hairs, and then grabbed her black pashmina, securing it at her neck like a cape. She spun around at the door, plucking up a dirty T-shirt from the laundry bin and rubbing away the streaky marks on the mirror that she'd made during the sex episode that morning. Tiptoeing down the stairs, her skyscraper stilettos wobbled beneath her. She stood at the lounge door, seeing the back of Kevin's turnip-like head before the telly. Leaning provocatively against the door, she rolled the dimmer-switch down. Kevin looked up toward the lighting and then back at the telly as she cleared her throat, priming herself to talk in her huskiest voice.

"Hey babe, Super Pussy!"

Without looking around Kevin simply replied, with a sniff, "Oh, great, babe. Soup please, love."

By early evening Helly had the dinner on the go. Charley had gone to catch her plane straight from Pink Turtle and Helly was disappointed that her 40th had only warranted a day-trip.

The kitchen was permeated with a warm blanket of chilli as the spicy smell was wafted around, and the spotlights shone down on the tomato'd spatula and the scattered kidney beans that lay belly-up on the worktop. Dan hummed as he ripped open a scatter of white window-envelopes with slick corporate logos. Toby was struggling with his tens-and-units homework and Jack was trying to read his library book at the kitchen table. The atmosphere was unusually calm, the beech units with their chrome fittings a relaxing backdrop to the kids' studious moments despite Diego skittering and shuffling excitedly at Helly's feet.

He's always nice when there's food on the go.

Helly sat on a high stool by the island unit central to her large, square kitchen, beside the rainbow colours of the loaded fruit bowl placed tantalisingly beside her. She crunched into a red apple, sketching her ideas eagerly as she prepared her paperwork for tomorrow's meeting with the record company PR guy and Kaz the stylist. She didn't even notice how Dan had stopped humming and was now throwing the letters away with the crumpled envelopes.

Earlier she had been annoyed with him. It had all been fine until he'd said only an hour ago, "If the doorbell goes it'll be for me."

"Oh," she had grimaced as she struggled with the tin opener and a particularly stubborn tin of tomatoes.

"Yeah, we're auditioning for a new guitarist."

"Here?"

"Yeah."

"Dan!" She had tried not to screech, noticing how Toby and Jack had looked up from their work suddenly. "And you only thought to tell me now?"

"Sorry. I forgot to."

"Great. And what time? And how many of them? I'll never get the boys to sleep."

"You will. It won't take long. There's only one guy calling in tonight. We're seeing the other one at Gav's tomorrow."

"OK, that's not so bad then."

And just as she grabbed the tin opener again he had added, "Oh, and we've got another gig this weekend. On Saturday."

"Dan! Since when?"

"It's a cancellation. It only came up today."

"Dan! You're never here lately."

"Mum," Toby interrupted, "Dad is here *sometimes*."

"I know honey. But I would like to see more of him, wouldn't you?"

"Yeahhhh!" Toby had sung, pulling back his chair and running to hug his father. Jack was in hot pursuit, copying every move that his elder brother made.

Helly had sighed and turned back to her wok, resenting the fact that, once again, the weekend was virtually taken up with Dan's drumming.

Jono, Gav and Kyle are great guys, almost like brothers sometimes, but I need some female company! I live surrounded by men. Not ideal, especially when faced with gorgonzola boots, computer games and a congenital inability to do more than one thing at a time. I suspect Charley would love it. So between the band and the business Dan's never got time for me — for us.

And when his arse hits the sheets it somehow activates a sleep hormone!

I just can't stop thinking about the idea of getting pregnant again. I don't know how Dan can't see where the space is in our lives for nappies and bottles and coagulated baby sick down my back!

I'm not too old to start again.

Neither is Dan.

But maybe too selfish?

Nick strode up the three steps that led to the large Victorian house in one huge step, his guitar under his arm. Impressed by the gleaming brass knocker, he rattled it against the glossy black door twice. He loved the challenges that being boss of his software company brought, but was also aware of the need to balance his frenetic business life with something more recreational, and his guitar had always been his source of relaxation. He was quietly confident. He was always quietly confident.

He knocked again.

"Dan! Door!" Helly bellowed inside the house, irritated at how her husband was able to ignore the front door and yet hopped on any ringing telephone as if it were his only lifeline with the outside world. He knew she was struggling to cook dinner, keep an eye on the washing machine and the children, *and* prepare for her meeting tomorrow. Annoyed, she put down her calculator and turned down the bubbling chilli before she trotted down the hall, cursing under her breath with every step, Diego in hot pursuit. She grabbed the latch and yanked the door open.

It took milliseconds for the blush to sting her cheeks.

Nick felt fifteen again.

It was unusual for him – a man of experience who knew it took more than a bunch of garage forecourt flowers and a box of Milk Tray to impress. He was an expert in the present-giving arena and knew the demands were a stout heart, a steady hand and an encyclopaedic knowledge of the branding of exceptional lingerie.

And yet.

Yet, this attractive woman standing before him rewound his emotions back to a time long ago and pulled at something buried right in the heart of him.

Yes, for once, it wasn't entirely below the waist.

Helly did her best to keep calm.

Not easy when your guts are doing backflips and you can feel the blotchiness rising up from your neckline like mercury in a thermometer. But I put in a good performance.

It must have been at least a count of six before we spoke.

"Christ! Helen!"

"Sssh," she hissed. "What the hell are you doing, Nicky?"

"Em, I've come to see Dan. For the audition."

She snapped a huge smile onto her face as she mentally screamed for composure. "You're not serious! Here? But does he know?"

Nick grinned, his bleached white teeth glistening in the evening light,

"I hope so. He asked me to be here at six thirty."

"Oh," realisation hit Helly slowly. "Right, OK. No, sorry, Nicky, I mean, does he know about *us?*"

"Us?" he teased, his voice way too loud. "What 'us'?"

She ran her hand through her hair, "The old 'us' – does he know?"

"I don't know. You mean you never told him?"

"Course not!" she hissed. "Did you?"

"Helen, I never knew Dan was 'Daniel', *the* Daniel. Until two seconds ago I never realised I'd be knocking on the door of The Woman Who Broke My Heart. How could I tell him?"

Helly exhaled in a big puff and looked down at his boots.

Timberland. Still trendy!

"Sorry, Nicky. I wasn't thinking."

I was in shock, in fact.

"But, Helen," his voice lilted slightly as his eyes danced, "you look great. Better than ever. Fate, huh?"

Yeah, fate. And now he's auditioning for my husband's band?

He always did put the 'mmmm' into music.

She heard Dan calling from upstairs and panicked. "OK, please, em, sorry, come in."

At this point I would have usually hollered for Dan, but when faced with a mishap from my past I rarely do what is 'usual'. Thankfully Diego provided a welcome distraction as he wagged his tail furiously and licked Nick's hand enthusiastically. It was just as he began jumping up, snuffling his wet nose into Nicky's crotch, that my usual dislike for Diego re-emerged. Dan came skittering down the stairs right on cue.

"Nick. Hi."

She was saved from the intros by the sound of Jack yelling for her from the kitchen.

I was glad of the excuse.

Chapter Six

Butterflies danced, uninvited, in Fiona's tummy at the prospect of seeing Luís. He dropped Adriana off at six, as arranged, following behind as she ran into the apartment clutching her bag full of goodies. Fiona hated herself for the self-inflicted abuse, but couldn't resist looking out of the window at Bella, who she supposed knew the price of everything and the value of nothing, relaxing in his gleaming new car outside. She watched as she stretched open the large newspaper, the words *Diário Económico* emblazoned across the front cover, its vivid colours toned down by the heavily tinted windows of the car. She winced in pain. As if Bella could read Portuguese anyway! A pang of jealousy washed over her yet again, at the thought of this stranger being near to her Adriana and possibly even having some influence over her.

As Luís made a fuss of Adriana, his voice husky and soft as peanut butter as he begged for kisses and hugs,

Fiona wanted to cry. Despite the time that had passed, it still hurt so badly to see the ease with which he dropped the smiles and the pleasantries the second he turned away from Adriana to face her. She had to say something to him but was afraid of his response. His bullying, gruff voice. His angry eyes and the way he threw his arms about when he was cross. Which was often. She wondered how he'd ever been so tender with her, and continually puzzled about his decision, almost overnight, to leave her – or, rather, for her to get out of his house and leave him. She'd wished Charley had stayed on an extra few days last year. Just when she needed her. It hadn't struck Fiona that Charley leaving Cascais had coincided with Luís deciding that he no longer wanted to be part of her life.

As she watched him hug Adriana she had goaded herself, drumming up bravery and motivation like an American public speaker at a conference.

'Say it. Don't be scared of him, just come out with it. No time like the present.'

The job advertised in the window at Mango had tormented her for the whole train journey from Lisbon to Cascais and she knew she'd have to mention it to Luís.

"OK then –" she attempted.

He was brusque as ever as he strode toward the door. "I will see Adriana again in two weeks. I do not have a date yet, but I will contact you."

"Em, Luís, I've found a job. In Lisbon."

"No!" His voice was booming, his eyebrows set in an angry 'V'. "I told you before – no work! I give you money every week. I want Adriana to have her mother at home."

"Yeah?" she challenged, opening her eyes wide and throwing her arms up. "And what about her father? I'm sure she wants to have him at home too!"

The look of disgust quivered from his stubbly neck right up to his patchy hairline. Fiona panicked as his eyes flashed. The fact that he resembled a Mafia boss didn't help.

"But Luís," her voice turned to pleading and she was annoyed at herself for letting it, so soon anyway, "we can't survive on what you give us."

"Why? You want for nothing."

"No," she spat, angry now at his chauvinistic attitude, "except for a life!"

He glared at her and she wondered how there had ever been such intense love between them. She spoke out and surprised herself: "I'm going back. With Adriana."

His tanned face reddened and it frightened her. It wasn't the progressive reddening that happened to everyone else – the red wine being poured into the glass and the fill line getting higher and higher – it was a sudden, instant burgundy and she winced at the anger flashing in his dark eyes.

"Back where?"

"To Dublin," she gushed, "or London. I don't know yet. Anywhere! Back to my family. To the people that love me. I'm not staying here. I can't do it any more."

His voice was deep and slow. "I told you before, Fiona. You will not take Adriana from Portugal. She was born in Portugal and I am Portuguese. I want her to grow up Portuguese."

"But what about *my* life?"

"Like I said to you before, your life is here as her mother."

"This isn't fair, Luís. A double-dose of mother doesn't make up for an absent father! You're behaving like an old-fashioned fool. It's ridiculous – you only see her a couple of times a month! And you say I can't work because you'll take away the maintenance money you pay me! I may have been a doormat this last year, Luís, but I'm getting better and I'm getting stronger and you cannot treat me like this. It's only a matter of time before I do something that *I* want. Only a matter of time."

His eyes darkened further as he stepped towards her, his voice a whispered hiss, "I know all about this, Fiona, and what you are planning is child abduction. The Hague Convention promotes the protection of a child if born to a national in the national's country. I have a *right* to insist that she stays here."

She glowered with anger. "How dare you suggest that I'm trying to abduct her! I am her mother and I have rights too. It's ridiculous! Us holed up in this apartment while you swan in and out of her life whenever it suits you. We're virtually prisoners here in Portugal and I will take her to London!"

"If you do that, Fiona," he was suddenly strangely calm, "then abduction is precisely what you'll be doing. I will never give my permission. You will be hearing from my solicitor."

He turned once again to the listening and frightened-looking Adriana, swapping his Incredible Hulk expression for Santa Claus's, kissing her gently on the cheek.

Fiona didn't see him go. In her attempt to hold back the tears she had left the room, locking herself in the small bathroom where she broke down in huge suffocating sobs. She didn't understand why Luís had gone off her so suddenly, although she suspected that Bella was an issue long before they separated. She berated herself for succumbing to motherhood so fully. She knew he felt he'd gone down in the pecking order, but wasn't the welfare of a baby, a child, more important than that of a fully grown man? She felt dowdy and old. And she hated herself for it. Her stifled sobs echoed in the bathroom and were interrupted by the thud of the front door as he left.

Within seconds Adriana was knocking on the toilet door. "Mummy, I need wee. Mummy?"

The muffled sounds of quite excellent guitar had provided a distracting and yet exciting percussion to my attempts at helping the boys with their homework. I found it worryingly hard to concentrate, primarily due to my heart pounding in my neck, my ears, my legs! How could Nicky be here? In my house? Jesus, it's years since I last saw him! I feel dizzy and vile. I can just imagine Mum's face, her cat-arse mouth, if she knew that Nicky was back to cause mayhem in Helen Murphy's life once more. Only I'm not Helen Murphy any more, am I? I'm Helen Donovan now. And it'd do me well to remember that.

Once I'd finished helping Jack to calculate 2p+2p+7p in about twenty different ways, I bolted from the kitchen chair whilst the boys sorted their schoolbags.

"Come on, boys, it's time to go up and get washed and undressed. And you can tidy that room, Toby, please." She spoke distractedly as she rooted in her bag for her lipstick.

"But, Muuum!" Jack's voice was shrill and loud as he protested, tearing right through her head.

"But nothing!" She applied the colour to her lips and smoothed her hair, smiling at her refreshed reflection as she continued, pressing her lips together to release the promised colour-spheres that the TV ad promised. "Go on, Toby, love. You're old enough to know better."

I clap my hands double-quick and feel stupid – I'd never normally do that – but it works and the boys scoot out of the room in a flurry of arms and legs and attack the stairs.

Kicking off her diamanté beaded mules, she climbed the first flight of stairs, treading softly on the Roger Oates runner which clung on for dear life to the wooden stairway with brass fixings. She paused in the dim light of the landing and looked into the spare room that Dan had claimed as his own and that he'd filled with his hobby material. As boss of his own graphic-design studio he had two computers, loaded to the hilt with the latest graphics software. She was proud of him and had stood by him in the early years of their marriage.

She'd been studying design at the Grafton Academy when she'd met him at that party. Little did she know she'd meet Daniel there – the accountant's son from Blackrock. Neither of them had really wanted to be at the party. Helly had been keen to start work on her latest project and Dan hadn't been in the mood to listen to someone else's music. He'd just put his first band, Steel Pillars, together and would have preferred to be making music himself. They'd laughed at his saturated suede boot and he'd got into her taxi home as they'd left the party together. Of course the Cinderella jokes had been rife, what with him travelling home with only one boot on, but magic pixie-dust had been sprinkled over them and the laughter and fondness for each other had intensified, until their first kiss had blown each of them away.

Over the next few years they'd continued with their overwhelming infatuation with each other. Helly had excelled in her flair for clothes and frequented the second-hand shops, dragging Charley or Fiona with her to help buy carefully selected items which she usually had sold on within a few days. Dan had gone on to college to learn his graphic design skills. Those had been fun times, the two of them living with her parents while she worked from home. When Dan had finished college, Helly was well on her way to gathering loyal customers who would have killed for her 'eye' when it came to spotting a trend.

They had been each other's first loves and they both felt that the other was the better deal by far. Helly had never thought she'd bag a gorgeous, talented and charming guy such as Dan, and he had never dreamt that such a stunning, artistic and truly beautiful girl would ever look twice at him. When she was twenty Dan had surprised her by suggesting a move to London. It coincided with a fantastic job offer for him there and, as much as Helen hadn't wanted to leave her parents and sisters, she knew that this was the break that they'd been waiting for and she had been madly excited at the prospect of the trendy London markets and clothes shops.

Now, she stood on the landing looking into his full room, in which only minutes before, Nick had been showing off his musical skills. She strained to hear their conversation as they chatted in the kitchen, finding it hard to compete with the roar of the kettle boiling.

And we'd been here a few months, were just settling into London life when I met Nicky. I'd absolutely no intention of starting an affair. I mean, Dan was my life. My love. We'd been out for the night in Wardour Street and I was sitting at the bar in Romeo's nightclub. Dan had gone to the toilet and Nicky had appeared within seconds, hopping onto the empty barstool in front of me. I'd told him that my boyfriend was sitting there, but he'd grinned cockily, and said that he didn't care. He wasn't going to let the evening pass without talking to me. I remember seeing Dan walk back across the dance-floor as he approached us, and I was both excited and nervous at what was going to happen. Of course, Nicky was all charm and manners and apologised to Dan, offering to buy us both a drink. Dan had declined his offer and Nicky walked away. I can still remember how the bubbles had popped in my stomach as he'd looked back at me and winked.

I was confused but yet so, so excited.

As she turned quietly she caught the golden shine of the cymbal that balanced delicately above Dan's drum-kit – one of his drum-kits – and the dull gleam of his saxophone which was gathering a velvety film of dust in the corner.

It's great to have a husband with a full life, but it's too full to think of me, or what I want.

And I'm only thirty-three.

I don't really know if I want another pregnancy. Maybe I'm clutching at straws. I am a little worried that it would mean my commitment to Toby and Jack would be affected, that my commitment to my work would be damaged and that our small amount of freedom would be taken from us.

And then there's the ruination of my figure and seriously disturbing notions of ante-natal classes with nubile twenty-three-year-olds!

Not to mention the horrendous thought of being perpetually held hostage by a crying baby.

Helen silently turned to face the second flight of stairs which led to the children's bedrooms; she could hear Toby in hysterics as Jack began to cry. Clicking back to reality she ran up the stairs two at a time, her long legs quick on the steps. She glanced in at Toby's bedroom, horrified at the mess inside.

Messy. Just like Charley's room always used to be.

Is there an untidiness gene you can inherit?

She pushed open the door of Jack's bedroom to see him striking out at his jeering brother as he leapt across his bed. Helly wanted to laugh at the sight of Toby as he leant against the wall, buckled up with laughter. It was nice to see him so happy.

She sat on the bed next to Jack, scooped him up in her arms and sat him on her lap.

"What's going on, Jack?" she asked lightly as she kissed his forehead and wiped his tears.

"He's laughing at me."

"Oh Mummy," Toby spluttered, "I can't help it." He struggled to speak between his fits of hysteria. "He was saying his prayers and —"

Jack interrupted, "Miss Grey was teaching us prayers today, Mummy."

"Yeah but Mum," Toby offered, "'Blessed art thou a monk swimmin'?'"

Helly started to laugh and was pleased when Jack joined in.

"But Mummy," he whimpered, trying to stretch his face into a sad one despite his giggles, "I didn't know what Miss Grey was saying and one of the other boys told me it was that."

"He was kidding!" yelled Toby. "That's just a joke!"

The three of them laughed, their giggles infectious.

The trilling sounds of the phone ringing brought a sudden halt to their laughter and they all hopped up from the beds in an attempt to race for it. Helly playfully pushed them back down onto the duvet, catching a glimpse of them rolling onto each other on the bed as she darted for the door. She flew down the stairs, grabbed the cordless from the hall table and ran into the lounge, flopping down onto the large leather sofa.

"Hello?" she panted.

"Helly?" The voice at the other end sounded unsure.

"Yeah, who's this?"

"Fiona."

"Are you OK? You sound weird, what's wrong?"

Helly recognised the gasping sounds of her sister crying

as she tried to disguise her tears.

"Hey, what's wrong? Fiona, whatever has happened?"

Click – she had hung up.

Helly rang her back immediately. She seemed to have stopped crying, but her voice was muffled and thick, as if she were talking into a pillow or eating a doughnut.

"Sorry," Fiona sniffed through her stuffy nose.

"Don't be daft. Are you going to tell me what's wrong?"

"Oh, it's something and nothing. Luís has just upset me again, as usual. The truth of it is, Helly, I want to come and stay with you."

"You want to come to London?" She hadn't meant to screech it.

"So much it's driving me mad. I hate it here now, Helly."

Helly listened to the deep sniffing and coughing as Fiona began to cry again. "I hate to admit it, but life without Luís is shite. I can't take any more."

"You're insane! Do you remember when you first told me you were going to Lisbon – and I thought you said you were moving to Lisburn?"

"Yeah," Fiona managed a giggle but it was more of a snort.

"Honestly, what are we like? When I told Mum we were moving to Belsize Park she thought we were heading for Belize!"

Fiona snorted out a laugh. "And I suppose Dan's uncle is still 'Brain' as opposed to Brian?"

"Ha, bloody ha. But you know, it's so hard not to say it to his face – as I once did! I'll never live that one down, will I?"

"Never, ever, ever!"

They both went silent. Helly picked up the conversation.

"But I thought you liked being a Lisbian?"

"Helly, stop it. I'm being serious!"

"Oh but Fiona, please. You can't expect me to believe that you'd rather be in London than Lisbon! You were *made* to be a Lisbian."

"For the thousandth time, it's a Lisboeta, not a Lisbian."

"Well, it *should* be Lisbian. Stands to reason."

"Well, I might as well be a bloody lesbian, for all the male attention I get here. Helly." Fiona's voice softened, "You don't want me there, do you?"

"No! Yes! I mean, oh God!"

"I'm so unhappy here," her voice was once again full and thick, "and Luís is being such a shit. He doesn't even *see* Adriana – only about once a fortnight."

"So nothing's changed then. What's he so busy at? Or is that the one and only 'Stupid Question of the Year'?"

"You got it in one. I think I preferred the days when he used to try and hide his bit of extra-curricular from me, but the veneer's even slid from that now. Not that it matters any more. He's not coming back to me and that's that. I hate *her* though. Not him. Smug Swedish bitch that she is."

"And how's Adriana taking it all?"

Fiona looked down at her four-year-old daughter, her amazingly long silken black eyelashes resting on her rounded cheeks as she slept. She lightly traced her finger over her small pert nose and her freckles, like finely chopped wet grass. "She's fine. She hardly misses her father. He never spent much time with her when he *was* here. He'd been gone for nearly two weeks before she even asked for him! I suppose it's me that's hurting."

"But Fiona, London? Why do you want to come to London? There's no comparison between Lisbon and London."

"It's not Lisbon; it's Cascais. I'm a good bit away."

"I know, I know, but still. I know how lonely you must feel but, believe me, the loneliness will come with you. It's in your head. You can't leave it behind like a pair of old shoes."

"Don't be ridiculous, Helly. It'd be a dream to be in London. I'd see you all the time for a start. And it'd be so easy to get a cheap flight over to see Charley, Mum and Dad. Flights to Ireland from here are a ludicrous price."

"Well, I'm living and breathing it here and I'm lonely. I'm desperate for some female company. Dan's either designing flash company logos or booklets, or he's venting his frustrations on his drum-kit. He's even auditioning for the new lead guitarist here. Right this minute!"

Not that I'm complaining.

"Well then, it'd be even better if I came back to you. I'd be doing you a favour too." Fiona knew she was pushing it, but couldn't resist it. In for a penny, in for the full two pound.

"Now, don't push it," Helen laughed at her cheek.

"You've got a lot to consider."

"But Adriana and I need a new start. Me and Luís are well and truly over now. He'll never come back to me, and I have to accept it . . ." her voice trailed along, "I need a new life." She paused. "So what about the other band members? Any nice ones?"

"They're great guys, Fi, but you just wouldn't want to go there. You're really better off in Cascais. Just think of the comparison. Cascais – sunshine, fresh air, relaxed pace of life. London – exhaust fumes, lousy weather and the crowds always walking in the opposite direction to you."

"You're exaggerating it."

"You'd have to contend with the traffic here, the drugs, the crime. It's a dog-eat-dog city, babe. And then there's the celebrity obsession. It's ridiculous! More than half of the mums at the boys' school are trying to be either Victoria Beckham or Sienna Miller."

"You're deliberately making it sound terrible. There are thousands of people who live in London and love it. You're just trying to put me off."

"I'm not, Fiona. I'd love to have you back, but you're not thinking clearly. Portugal is a fantastic place, full of charm and great food and, erm, other stuff."

"Well, I suppose becoming a resident of any city means that its streets lose their charm. These seem well soured now."

Helly remained quiet.

I've really missed Fiona in the years she's been gone. She followed me from home to London and my parents went doubly grey overnight with worry. But I took her under my wing and we had great fun in those early years. And then she got the job as a nanny for the Portuguese family and the rest is history. I was even jealous when she'd met Luís those six or seven years ago! He was sex on legs.

"Helly," Fiona sounded weary, "you have to understand. I'm homesick. I miss London. I yearn for a small place on the outskirts where I'm surrounded by families whose children make excellent playmates for Adriana."

"Ha, we all want that! Fiona, I can't tell you what to do and I'm not about to stand on the moral high ground, but London is a different place now. It's noisier, ruder and brasher than ever before."

"OK, so times change. Things move on." She began clutching at statistical straws. "The education system isn't working properly here. There's an illiteracy rate of 10% at the age of 15. That's twice that of Greece and three times that of Spain!"

"Yeah, but you can't feed me that one. You'd told me before that Adriana won't start school properly until she's six."

"And the clothing is so expensive!"

Helly resigned herself to stop trying to talk Fiona out of her turmoil and listened for the full thirty-three minutes. Finally she suggested that she ring Charley and wish her a Happy Birthday.

Why is it always me who has to try and sort out all their problems?

She was exhausted when she finally pressed the large button on the cordless to disconnect the call. She was surprised that the boys had gone back to their rooms – they usually put an abrupt end to any call she was on, with their shouting or arguing.

Now I'll just get my boots on and take Diego out for a quick trot before I bump into Nicky again.

With any luck, Dan will turn him down and wait to see the other guy at Gav's house tomorrow.

I can't imagine how I'd cope with life in Nicky's presence again.

She jumped up from her stretched-out position on the sofa as he came into the room.

She threw down the phone as if it was on fire. It thudded onto the leather sofa, drawing attention to itself as it bounced.

"Sorry," Nick smiled, "I didn't mean to interrupt."

"No! No. Em, I was just finished."

He loved the way she ran her hands through her short hair.

I always run my hands through my hair when I'm nervous!

He remembered how she always did that when she was nervous. He didn't want to make her uncomfortable. He extended his right hand.

Clean short nails.

Still!

And he squeezed her hand, pulling her slightly closer.

Electricity jumping from his palms to mine.

What's that all about?

"You're looking great."

"Thanks. You too."

I can't bloody concentrate. What's wrong with me? The

way he stares into my eyes with that steady gaze and dead sexy grin.

And how kind of him not to mention the extra wrinkles tickling the corners of my eyes!

"So how are you, Helen?"

"Helly."

"Oh," he smiled, his eyes warm and dancing, "Helly now, is it?"

She nodded.

He whispered, "The last I heard you were getting married and I presumed you were going back to Ireland."

"Well, we didn't."

Nick smiled a cheeky, wide grin as he flirted, "What, you didn't get married?"

"No," she smiled, still attracted by his charm, "we didn't move back to Ireland."

"Shit!" he teased. "So, 'Helly'? It's cute. Suits you better than Helen actually. Better than the old Helen clichés, Helen Back, Hell Raiser and all those. It's different. Helly," he tried it for size, "yeah, it really suits you. I like it."

Yeah, and I still like you!

At least the bubbles popping in my stomach and the unexplained buzzing in my ears tell me I still like you.

But why now?

Now, when I'm getting zilch attention from my husband?

Nick followed her down the hallway and into the kitchen. She lightly turned the volume button on the stereo, soaking the silence with David Gray. Acutely aware of Nick's close presence, she lined up the mugs to make large cappuccinos for them.

Nick silently admired her slender fingers and her light touch. He felt a stirring in his boxers as his mind switched back to the adolescent he'd been all those years ago, as he imagined her touching him with the same light touch and passion. He turned and flicked through her sketches and ideas for the girl-band tour, pretending to be interested in the colourful and impressive drawings. Then moved to stand beside her as she measured out the scoopfuls of coffee.

"So, Helly –"

His voice was low and throaty and she felt the hairs on the back of her neck rise at his warm breath. Her heart banged so dangerously loud in her chest she feared it might break her ribs, or worse, that Nick would be able to hear it. She froze, the goose pimples standing out across her chest and arms.

He breathed his warm softness into her ear, slightly nuzzling it as he spoke, "I didn't think I'd ever see you again."

Helly closed her eyes and breathed deeply, struggling to compose herself. Nick grasped her gently by the shoulders and turned her to face him. Despite her attempts to avoid his gaze full-on, he tipped her chin lightly and she automatically raised her head. She could literally feel the sparks jumping between their mouths.

"You're more beautiful than ever. You broke my heart, Helen."

Against all sense and reason Helly closed her eyes and leaned in towards him, their lips virtually touching.

The silence was broken by the sounds of Nikes on the wooden hall-floor. It was Dan.

Shit – it's Dan.

"Hey, Nick. So you've met my wife then?" Dan's perfect smile and white teeth lit up the spot-lit kitchen. He hadn't noticed the pink flush on Helly's cheeks nor how they'd sprung apart as he'd entered the room. He playfully scuffed Helly's blonde crop as he walked past her.

It's lucky it's supposed to be scruffy!

I still feel like his pet dog though.

No, he has more fun with Diego.

"Yeah, I've met Helly." Nick felt uncomfortable at his lusty thoughts. He turned away slightly. "She's beautiful."

Dan was dismissive; it was old news and he was used to people being impressed with his wife's good looks.

You see, it's more interesting to Dan to discuss gigs and media talk. But I'm used to that and, hey, it suits me right now. I'm disturbed to find that my feelings for Nicky have surfaced. Completely uninvited. I wasn't expecting this and I don't know how to handle it.

I brace myself not to laugh as Diego again nuzzles his warm nose into Nick's crotch.

Lucky Diego.

Chapter Seven

Charley was afraid to open her eyes.

She was aware of the droning hum of early morning traffic outside, and knew instantly it was a foggy morning. She could hear the thick denseness of the rumbling, fumy blasts, knew the minute she opened her front door she'd be enveloped in a foggy blanket of chill. Her tongue resembled carpet, metres of it, all rolled up into the small confines of her mouth. She knew that the second she opened her eyes the headache would cut the eyes out of her. As she breathed deeply, unaware of the beddy, stale smell of her room, she forced herself to recall the events of the night before. She remembered that she'd kicked Kevin out. She was surprised it had taken her so long and had absolutely no regrets at getting rid of him. Relief ran a lap-of-honour around her head, to the sounds of 'Chariots of Fire'. She'd rung some of her mates who were out for the night. It slowly came back to her, the pieces of the jigsaw scattered in her mind. She remembered ringing Helly in the early hours.

"Oh, God. She'll be mad at me again now," she whispered to herself. Fragments of disjointed events taunted her, the recollection of calling the police creeping back into her mind. Slowly she put the pieces together, remembering how she'd left London in the evening, had failed miserably as 'Super Pussy' and then hit the city. And the bottle. She had shared numerous bottles of red in Eliza Blues and then had gone on for cocktails. She dimly recalled at least four Sea Breezes and Bucks Fizz, but the thought of alcohol now churned her stomach. Then there were the glasses of champagne at midnight. She rushed to her feet, slamming open the bathroom door as she dived for the toilet. She needed a cure – and quick!

As she yodelled into the loo she puzzled at the memories of the police. Wiping her mouth with a handtowel, she walked back into her bedroom, the sting of the acrid smell dulling her head all the more. As she opened her window, breathing in the thick morning air, she looked down to where her car was usually parked only to see a navy blue Saab in its place.

She then remembered. Her car had been stolen.

Hence, the police.

Huge blocks of intense morning sunlight made enormous orange rectangles on the tiled floor of Fiona's apartment. It was the only time the sun hit the apartment, and she'd flung open the shutters to make the most of it. The aroma of her culinary skills usually competed fiercely with those of the sardines and garlic wafting across the quayside from Cascais' restaurants. It had taken her quite a while to be immune to the smell of fish cooking every day and found that the heat seemed to intensify the smells but her current craving for smoothies meant that her small kitchen held a pleasing scent of colourful blends of fruits. Her French pal, Claudine, made angular shapes as she leant her lithe body up against the rails of the balcony, watching Fiona blend strawberries and kiwis with natural yogurt.

"I mean, Fiona, I cannot stand it there any longer. I have worked hard for him and that bloody bar, building it up from nothing. He's a bloody Seagull Manager."

Fiona turned, gurning as she threw in a few chunks of ice and placed the lid on the blender. "A what?"

"A Seagull Manager,"

A smile crept across Fiona's face. "Claudine. What have you been listening to now? I've never *heard* of a Seagull Manager."

"Oh," she sounded surprised and a little confused. Claudine often misquoted English phrases and relied on Fiona to translate and put her right on things. "Well, I heard an Englishman in the bar the other day. He was saying that he liked being a Seagull Manager." She gesticulated wildly, her blonde curls bouncing lightly as she became more animated. "He says a Seagull Manager flies in, makes lot of noise, shits on everything and then leaves! That *is* Xavier."

Fiona grinned, holding the lid and pressing a button to make the blender squeal with excitement as it chopped through the chunky fruits and slippery yogurt.

"So," she raised her voice as she spoke to Claudine, "what are you going to do?"

The blender groaned and moaned as it ground through the ice cubes. Fiona turned it off.

"Going to do?" Claudine's voice was slightly muffled. "Going to do nothing. I 'ave quit!"

Fiona turned to face her only to see her tugging at the cups of her bra, and fiddling with herself beneath her T-shirt.

"What the hell are you doing now?"

"Oh, these bloody 'Haribo'!"

Fiona watched in amazement as Claudine pulled out two small 'Haribo' sweets – miniature rubbery fried eggs – rubbed them between her fingers and then re-positioned them back inside her bra.

"Claudine! Please! Why've you got jelly sweets in your bra? Or do I really not want to know?"

Claudine smoothed down her tight fitting T-shirt proudly.

"Look," she ran her hands over her pert breasts, "new nipples!"

It struck Fiona, while she dribbled embarrassingly as she laughed, that it had been weeks since she'd found anything funny. The thought dampened the smile on her face and filled her eyes with tears. Claudine took two steps – from one side of Fiona's kitchen to the other – and put a slender arm around her.

"Hey, what is wrong? Why you cry?"

And that really set her off. The old reliable show of sympathy and tenderness that triggers the dam-buster. Fiona knew from years of experience that tears not only changed her voice into a deep, wailing vibrato but also seemed to disable her mouth from forming words properly. She'd meant to say something like 'I want to go home. I hate him. And I hate what he's doing to us,' but it came out something rather like "Ahhh waaaa go ohhhm ...." *Dribble, dribble, sniff,* "Ahhh aaat im . . ." *dribble, sniff, snots on sleeve,* "Ann ahhh aaat wo iiissss dune to aaasss ..." *sob, sniff, dribble.*

Claudine was relieved when Fiona had got the worst of it out of her system. She was relieved – partly because she could barely understand the wailing sounds and also because there was a limit to how much squeezing and hugging a girl could do. They sat on Fiona's small balcony, watching the schoolgirls stroll down Travessa da Misericordia, their calf-length claret socks slacking as their mouths gaped to eat the huge pastries they'd bought from Panisol. The balconies overhead were, as usual, heavy with wet washing and Fiona burst into a giggle as an elderly woman stuck her head out her top window to talk across the street to her neighbour.

"Blimey 'ell!" Claudine whispered. "A horse looking out from a horsebox!"

The mood somewhat lifted with humour, they sipped at their ice-cold drinks as Adriana sat quietly by their side colouring in pictures of Barbie.

"I just hate myself. I was never this low. Ever!" Fiona

was just able to talk without crying. "My self-esteem's as baggy as a pair of old knickers. I have to get out of here. Anywhere would be better."

Her lip wobbled with emotion as the tears reappeared. Sniffing loudly she wiped her eyes, fixing back her 'brave face'. She smiled at Claudine, a watery, weak smile as she joked, "You know, I could go to Helly's. I could get a job, get financially sorted. Maybe in a year or two I could even afford a few shots of Botox."

She placed her cold glass down, the sun shining on its pastel-pink contents, chunks of strawberries floating in the icy drink. She walked back into the shade of her apartment, leaving Claudine to soak up the sunshine. Pulling off a strip of kitchen towel she wiped her tear-streaked face.

"Luís is such a bloody hypocrite! It just makes me feel worse when I think of the lies. He always said how he hated 'fake' women. You know, I once asked him if he thought I needed an augmentation." She cupped her breasts as she spoke.

"Why? So you could hear him say you didn't?" Claudine frowned, never fully understanding Fiona's poor body image and obsession with surgery.

Fiona looked indignant. "No! I was desperate to be attractive to him. I suppose I was asking for his approval." She sneered. "And, as usual, he said he hated fake women. And here he is now, with a size 6 who has lipo-suction that she really doesn't need!"

"So you think going to London will solve all your problems? But you won't be able to afford surgery for a long time yet. Surely a house, job, car and daughter come first?"

"Of course they do! But I'll get work. Adriana can start school. I can start working." She paused, looked troubled. "But Claudine, what if this is simply grass-is-greener syndrome? What if it's a case that I *think* I'm not allowed it and so I want it?"

"Oh, I know what you mean. You mean, like the date you have with the ugly guy that you can't *wait* to get away from, until you find that he doesn't fancy you! Then he is suddenly attractive! George-bloody-Clooney!"

Fiona was irritated at the comparison but let Claudine off with it. "Yeah. Kind of, I suppose. I can't explain it, but London is so appealing right now and I'm not sure if it's enhanced because of Luís' demands that we stay in Portugal."

"Can you not go for a holiday? Go to visit your family? He cannot complain at a holiday?"

"I can't even afford to eat properly, never mind a holiday. No," she shook her head dejectedly, "there's no chance."

They were silent for a while.

"Fiona, you need to get out more, meet some new people. Listen – I will be going to my art class again this week. How about you come with me?" Claudine pulled that I'm-feeling-sorry-for-you face that made Fiona want to cry. Again.

"Art! I wouldn't be any good at that."

"You do not know until you try. Come on, it is fun. And before you put an excuse in the way, there is a

89

crèche there so Adriana can come too. It is only for an hour."

Fiona's eyes narrowed to slits. Claudine moved in for the kill.

"Please. You will enjoy, I promise."

Morning sunlight striped Helly's kitchen walls, reflecting a mini-starburst off the chrome splash-back and cupboard-door handles. Helly laid the white slices of bread out on the worn, wooden chopping-board. She'd bought it on a market years ago and had always wondered about its origin – too dark for cherry and yet too red for walnut. Years of impact had softened its surface in sliced grooves. A thin layer of split fibres set in stripes marked it at haphazard angles. As she buttered at high speed she slammed filing-cabinet doors in her mind.

Toby and Jack dressed. *Slam. Done.*

Diego fed and walked. *Slam. Done.*

Packed lunches nearly ready. *Slam. In progress.*

As usual her household routine was well organised. But today Helly had bigger fish to fry, and thanks to Charley's late-night telephone call, her head felt confused and mushy. Kind of like the tuna mayo she was cramming between the bread slices which she then sheared into four squares.

Crusts off for Jack. *Slam. Done.*

As she deftly arranged her children's lunches into plastic boxes she stared out at the moss-covered patio, its slippery surface glowing almost neon in the sunlight. She had to meet Kaz the stylist and the record label guy at ten thirty. She hadn't found the time last night to check over her work. Well, it was more that her brain was buzzing with excitement at the electrical currents that seemed to fly off Nicky.

"Helly! The toast is burning!"

Dan's booming voice broke her trance and she sprang to the toaster and hit the large lever on the side, causing two smoky charcoal squares to leap out onto the worktop.

"Oh Mum, it stinks in here now," Toby complained with a whine, wrinkling his button-nose in disgust.

"Open the patio doors then, love. Let some fresh air in."

No sooner had Toby pushed open the French doors than Diego bounded out, sliding on the green slabs as he sniffed them.

Helly's arms worked independently of each other, her left reaching to pluck two bananas from the rack and her right grasping two small cartons of orange juice. As she zipped up the lunch boxes on auto-pilot, she thought back to her own childhood. The truth was she'd been making lunches for schoolchildren for nearly twenty-five years. In the way that often happens in busy households, the routine of her schooldays was never questioned. Dad was always slightly half-cut and she knew better than to disturb him in the mornings. Helly took it upon herself to make the breakfasts, school lunches and dinners. Her mother was perpetually preoccupied with her own life. Or other people's. Helly had often resented how her mother could invite the troubled housewives of the village to their house, at any hour of the day or night, and sit with them to put the world to rights, and yet seldom had time to listen to her own children's dilemmas. Helly had always wondered where the line should be drawn between being supportive, and a walk-over. She yawned as she dumped the two schoolbags onto the table. Charley's middle-of-the-night call had disturbed an already fitful sleep as she'd tormented herself with memories of Nicky. She'd learned over the years that a phone call from Charley, in the early hours, is always confirmation that she's drunk.

Again.

I could barely understand her. She was slurring and moaning down the phone. It was all I could do not to shout at her, but I didn't want to wake the boys up. It was tempting though – the noise might have woken Dan and the interruption of sleep might have stirred some serious love-action with my husband.

But I knew better really.

I sometimes think I almost hate him for it.

There was a time when he loved early-morning sex.

Loved.

Past tense.

He doesn't seem to feel like that any more.

Early morning, late morning.

Afternoon, dinner time, night time.

Take your pick from the deck.

Pick a time of day – any time of day, but don't tell me.

The result's always the same anyway. It seems my not-so-well-hidden agenda has flattened his libido.

He moans that it's all about baby-making now and it's

turned him from sexy to sad.

After heated words with Dan, he finally agreed to take the boys to school. Of course he would be late for work and he hadn't given in easily, but finally Helly had made him feel guilty enough to agree. It meant she had an hour to get herself washed and dressed and mentally prepared for the all-important meeting. She finally decided to wear her good-luck underwear. Her lace balconette bra and matching thong always brought out her flirty, assertive side.

Yeah – just what I need to clinch this commission.

Flirty and assertive.

And confident.

Although I suppose another pregnancy would mean that my fantastic armour of underwear would be relegated to the bottom drawer and I'd be back into Mothercare belly-belchers.

But it would all be worth it.

The silkiness of her three-quarter-length skirt lightly brushed against her bare bum-cheeks as she strode confidently into the grand hotel reception area where they'd agreed to meet – but had her good-luck La Perla thong always felt so constricting? Had she put it on back to front? Or was it twisted or something?

She approached the receptionist, politely asking for the toilets. The receptionist smiled, her heavy foundation crinkling at her eyes, and directed Helly toward the left of the foyer. Her DKNY sandals clicked on the marble floor of the ladies', the blue spotlights and chrome giving it an almost space-age feel. She locked herself into a cubicle and struggled and wiggled to adjust the thong which she found was not actually back to front, but just a little too tight.

Kaz the stylist was waiting for her in the hotel bar. The smart, trendy PR guy with her she introduced as Dominic. He rose, pulling out her chair for her. She knew instantly that he liked her and she warmed to his kind face and open smile. She smoothed her skirt as she sat down and was immediately reminded why she hadn't worn the La Perla thong for ages.

Christ, I feel like a wedge of Edam. The damn thing's cutting into me like a cheese-wire and I'm sure the tears beginning to well in my eyes are obvious! Thank God I don't have piles! It's a known fact that girls with piles can't wear thongs.

Perhaps another reason not to try for another baby?

Helly managed a smile, although she suspected her eyes had a pleading kind of look to them as she hurriedly placed her portfolio on the large table and she excused herself, leaving her potential new client to look through the ideas that she'd sketched out. The reprieve was instant the moment she stood up and yet she couldn't wait to get back into the toilets. Once locked in the sumptuous cubicle she breathed out with relief as she tugged off the offending, expensive thong, stuffing it into her handbag.

Charley felt terrible. Even the smooth coolness of her desk irritated her. The hum of her computer rattled her.

The attention-seeking sounds of paper being sorted angered her.

Her usual hangover remedy had been ingested over an

hour ago and she felt no better; yet. It had irritated her that the MD's secretary had noticed a couple of bruises on her arm, and when she pointed them out, Charley had no idea where, when, or how they happened to be there. She was desperate to put on her sunglasses, the fluorescent lighting in the office bearing down on her like an inter-rogation spotlight. She rummaged in her jacket pocket for the sunglasses, wondering if anyone would notice. She inadvertently stuck her finger through a small hole in the pocket and looked down at it without thinking.

"Ohhh," she winced quietly, as she felt the contents of her head fall forward and bang onto the insides of her forehead. She couldn't figure why she was finding ciga-rette holes in her clothes lately and if it hadn't have been for the couple in her sofa too, she would have suspected that somebody was tampering with her laundry. Sucking in a deep breath, she yearned for the rush of wit that had been in such abundance the night before. The clear head and the confidence that her Best Buddy gave her. Glancing down at her bag she caught sight of the small glass bottle that would set her straight.

Only a quick swig.

It wouldn't do any harm.

Bending forward on her chair, trying not to look down, she grappled beneath her desk with her bag handles. Pulling out the vodka, her chin almost resting on the desk, she poured some into her plastic cup beneath desk-level, feeling splashes of vodka hit her ankles. Sitting upright, she brought the plastic cup onto her desk, adding a splash of the lemonade that she'd had in her drawer for the last two days. Sipping at the strong drink, she relaxed as she began to go over last night and her discussion with the police. She placed the innocent-looking drink onto her desk beside her plastic pen-holder and pink files. She started as her shrill telephone rang loudly and, rubbing her forehead, swiftly slid up and out of her seat and headed for the post room. She wasn't up to talking to anyone yet, least of all while she was still replaying last night's events in her mind. She remembered thinking how dead-sexy one of the policemen had been and cringed as she recalled how she had played up to him. His Starsky-like dark curls and strong features were slightly blurred in her memory, but she was sure that her re-collection of his gorgeous green eyes was spot-on. She'd reported her car as stolen. And, as the last twelve hours seemed to run in bursts of fifteen minutes in her mind, she couldn't piece it all together.

It was ridiculous. She always parked her car outside her flat and now it was gone.

Stolen from outside her front door.

Her thoughts were interrupted. Her mobile was vibrating wildly on her desk.

As if things couldn't get any worse

The policeman with Starsky-like curls and green eyes sat at his desk and rang a mobile number he had been given the night before. He remembered the attractive woman vividly – her dark hair and green eyes. He could have fancied her if she hadn't been quite so jarred. As he waited for her to answer he knew the story already. It was typical of her type. He had the conversation virtually pre-recorded – "Yes, ma'am, no visible signs of forced entry or break in. No, ma'am, nothing seems to have been taken. No, your CD player hasn't been touched ... the hand-brake was on. Yes, it was locked … no, ma'am, we can't explain it. ..." – knowing full well the car had been found exactly where she'd parked it *before* getting smashed out of her head.

Helly was enjoying a celebratory glass of wine with Kaz and Dom when her mobile rang in her bag. She was desperately trying to control her excitement at being offered exclusive supply for the entire tour and Kaz had even hinted at the possibility of future work with other groups later in the year. In her high spirits she reached down and groped in her loaded handbag whilst still try-ing to hold her champagne flute elegantly. She smiled as she pulled out her phone, pressing the 'OK' button and swiftly whisking the small phone up to her ear.

She saw their surprised expressions as she spoke into the phone but thought nothing of it until she saw him blush, and Kaz burst into laughter.

Yeah – he actually blushed.

It was only then I held the phone away from my hot ear and noticed that my lucky lacy thong was dangling from it!

Ten out of fucking ten for style, Helly!

Chapter Eight

Nick threw a sprinkling of lemongrass into the stir-fry, his tousled, dark-blond hair absorbing the spicy aromas that the hazy clouds of steam carried upwards. Jabbing lightly at the concoction with his wooden spatula he leant across to check the final stages of his recipe. His skill with a pestle and mortar was renowned amongst his mates – the mess he left in the kitchen afterwards even more so. He loved living alone, sure that too much female presence in his life would bring with it criticisms and moans about his technique with the dishwasher. Or rather, his lack of technique. But Nick was ace at keeping pasta moist and knew the best organic butchers in London. He toyed with thoughts of Helly as he flicked the wok high, causing the baby sweetcorn and mangetout to hiss excitedly. The guys were due around at seven, and he was dying to throw in casually his news of being the new guitarist in the blues band. He'd probably show off and mention the attractive wife of the drummer also — but he'd take his time. There was no point in steaming in like a hormonal acne'd teenager. It simply wasn't Nick's style.

He was tormented by the recollection of Helly. She had broken his heart when she had told him she was marrying Dan all those years ago. OK, so he knew how it had aggravated her, the way the other girls used to openly flirt with him, but he'd never actually gone off with anyone else. Helly was different to them anyway. He knew she was seeing Dan and him at the same time, but he'd felt sure that he would be the one to win her over. Nothing could have been worse than that evening when she'd cried as she'd hugged him and told him how sorry she was, but Dan had asked her to marry him. And that she'd accepted. He had kicked himself ever since for not asking her first. He had lost all his faith in justice for a long time after that. They were meant to be together. It had broken him, completely changing his life from that point onwards. He knew that women found him attractive and so, immediately, he'd begun to treat 'em mean, to keep 'em keen, using every woman that had come his way, making sure to break it off before it ever became too serious.

But now Helly had stirred something up inside of him that was unbalancing, something of the old Nicky. Resting the fragrant spatula by the side of the sizzling wok, he wondered whether she ever went to the band's gigs.

He made his way toward the bathroom, bending and

swiping at his trainers that were sitting on the wooden floor emanating a cheesy pong, knocking them into the understairs cupboard. As he tugged on the bathroom light-cord the extractor fan whirred into action and Nick looked at his reflection in the spot-lit mirror, liking what he saw. Self-assured and confident, he squirted a small gloop of gel into his palm and scuffed his hair a little more, pausing just to check that his Gallagher-style uni-brow was still a thing of the past. Nick had to admit though, only to himself, that he was getting bored with cartoon-women. His fixation on Pamela Anderson types and Jordan look-a-likes had had the bucket of cold water thrown over it. He was bored with chasing short skirts and silicone. He knew that most men lusted after a suc-cessful relationship with a beautiful woman, but had begun to worry himself with his latest thought: a beauti-ful relationship with a successful woman. It was as if a microchip of maturity had been implanted into his brain overnight, and he now Arnold-Schwarzeneggered as he struggled to decode the latest instalment. He wasn't sure if it was yet *de rigueur* to strive for brains over beauty, but he was finding it hard to fight the feelings. As he switched off the bathroom light, instantly silencing the fan, he decided to ask his mates some gentle probing questions.

At this thought, he moved to the window to check for any sign of the lads. The furrows on his forehead relaxed as he looked down at his precious vintage Mercedes 280SL, its red paintwork a strange brown beneath the orange street lights. He still felt the same adrenalin rush as the very first day he'd spotted the car. He leaned towards the window as he lustily ran his eyes across its smooth bonnet, proud as the glints of streetlights hit off the chrome hubcaps and front grille. He wasn't driving it much and the fact niggled at him. He knew that the sunroof was beginning to rust and the 1971 motor needed to be driven routinely and that to let it sit was the worst thing he could do. But he was also swimming in enjoyment of his recent discovery of how women swooned over men who cycled to work. All in the name of enviro-friendliness, of course. Nick couldn't stress the importance of that enough – the emphasis on the environmental issue. Otherwise you were simply a crash-helmet-wearing, trouser-clipped Mr Bean who *had* to cycle to work. Nick knew that his expensive mountain bike, complete with the latest accessories, was tantamount to the image of eco-aware Noughties Man. But yet whilst it was so 'him', it wasn't truly him at all. Ever since the love-of-his-life had turned her back on him he had disguised his lack of confidence behind a polished façade. He was still Nicky, the impetuous, romantic, down-to-earth guy that she'd fallen in love with, only he was buried beneath the flash clothes, the slick products and the lifestyle that impressed. He'd never really tried to find anyone to match up to Helly. He'd settled for second-best – the bimbo airheads who were impressed by his years at charm school. And yet his sister's words often rang through his head: "For a guy who claims to have had a lot of women, you sure don't know much about them."

The intercom buzzed loudly, indicating that the lads

had arrived to watch the footie on his 42-inch plasma screen. Sliding on the polished wooden floor he hit the entry button, pausing on his return at the coffee table to scruff the magazines up a little – excessive grooming or tidiness was still laughable amongst his peers.

He rubbed at his forehead, recollecting the problem he'd had with the Merc last time he'd driven it.

He really had to get that sunroof looked at.

Helly's mood matched her fraying socks. She stood at the cooker, her worn pink socks that she loved wearing around the house falling lazily to her ankles. She wasn't happy at the request for burgers tonight. She hated the way that burgers came in packs of 8 and buns in packs of 6. She knew she was being difficult. She was just in one of those moods. She knew why, but Dan couldn't figure it, although he'd been slightly surprised at her complete lack of enthusiasm when he'd told her that he'd said 'yes' to Nick. He was in the band.

And to top it all she'd had Charley on the phone again, spouting what she'd already told her, "Christ, Helly. I'm so embarrassed. They found it where I'd parked it yesterday!"

"Charley, you've got to get a hold of yourself. It's a clear sign of how out of control things are getting. And it's getting worse. Why don't you come over to us for a while? Or go to Mum's?"

"No can do, sorry. I'm so, so busy. Oh, and did I mention, I've a delicious boil-in-the-bag curry waiting for me?"

"You're not serious. Look, I'm sorry I couldn't talk to you properly this morning. It was *such* a bad time."

"S'OK. No probs. So, please, save the lecture. I'm feeling bad enough as it is. It was just after all the drink . . . I forgot."

"Charley," Helly's tone was abrupt, "I've gotta go. I'll talk to you later. I'm halfway through cooking dinner and I've got to go shopping yet. About two hours, OK?"

"Whatever."

"Oh don't be like that!"

"Well, I'm out at the gospel choir tonight."

"OK, so I'll ring about ten-ish?"

"Whatever."

She smiled to herself as she placed the dinner plates on the table. The promise of work for the girl-band tour had lifted her, but between being embarrassed as she'd waved her kinky knickers in the restaurant and then being landed with Charley's problems once again, it was all starting to be too much. And she was worrying about Fiona too. Distracted by her anxieties, she wrestled the rubbish into the bin and cleared the worktops with a squirt of the Dettox spray and a few wide swipes of the dishcloth. She washed some strawberries to eat with ice cream for dessert and then called the boys and Dan to the table in the dining-room. If they were going to eat burgers, then she wanted them sitting at the table at least. She knew she'd be up against opposition, but they were getting a little too fond of the idea of plates on their laps, with the telly blaring. As they sat to eat she heard her mobile ringing in the kitchen. Pulling out her chair to go and answer it, she caught Dan's look of disapproval and paused.

"C'mon, love. You wanted us all to sit and eat together in here. Let's do that, eh? Whoever it is can ring back."

"OK," she conceded, sitting down again.

"It'll stop in a minute. Stop worrying. Enjoy your food."

As if!

Dinner was disappointing and, while she suspected Dan's lack of conversation had a lot to do with it, she blamed the burgers. It was always the same whenever she served up fast food. They ate it too fast. The one opportunity they had as a family to sit together and eat was over before she knew it.

She took the plates back to the kitchen, only to find her mobile floating in the sink. She'd always hated the 'vibrate' option of the phone and if it hadn't been for Dan insisting that it was a great idea and constantly activating it, this wouldn't have happened. She must have left the phone on the worktop. Obviously, the vibration had caused the phone to dance along the worktop until it reached the sink – and she hadn't been there to save it as it free-fell to its demise. She felt like crying in anger as she plucked it from the water, wiping it on the tea-towel as she walked into the lounge.

As she paused and glanced in at the three men in her life she realised, with a pang of sorrow, that her sons were growing up too fast. They were slouched on the sofa, the stances of teenagers seeming strange on their soft young bodies, as they watched *The Simpsons* with Dan.

"Here," she said, putting the phone on the arm of the settee beside Dan. "See what you can do with that for me. It vibrated itself into the sink. I think it's finished."

He looked up at her, a confused look on his face. Then he took the damp phone and began to fiddle with it. Toby and Jack both sprang up, demanding to help him.

Helly decided to take her chance to catch up on the day's events. She was desperate to tell someone about her new job.

Dan seemed so preoccupied when he got in from work. And then it was a quick, rowdy dinner, followed by the swimming phone, the telly and the kids.

Perhaps I'll tell him later. Maybe in bed.

Maybe not.

It'd be another great excuse for him to avoid sex.

Sometimes the load was just too much. She felt rejected by her husband, surplus to requirements to her children and leaned on by her sisters. She escaped to her bedroom. She lay on her bed, looking up at the cream ceiling, her burgundy velvet bedspread luxurious beneath her, and she ran her hands across its luscious pile. The vanilla pods that she'd placed by the radiators were wafting a glorious scent around the room and for the first time in days she began to relax. The sensual feel of the room, the pleasing aroma and touchy-feely fabrics made her yearn for the human-touch of her husband. Without meaning to, he was making her doubt herself, her appearance; he was beginning to make her feel ugly. Her eyes filled with tears as silence roared between her ears. It started with a low indiscriminate buzz, which was slowly getting louder in her head. Before long the hum of nothingness was overwhelming and Helly stood up abruptly to slice it, jostling her paperwork on the bedside cabinet.

She paused and then picked up her papers. Flopping back down onto her bed, she lay on her tummy this time and flicked through her sketches. Apart from planning the look for the 'girls' she had been trying to sort out the timescale on her jumbled calendar, which had now given her a scrambled brain. She glanced across to the blue tartan miniskirt she'd picked up last week, as it lay on her chair, and wondered whether the early Madonna, string-vesty look might work on the four attractive girls.

I love my work. Apart from my family, it's my life!

Her thoughts drifted to Nick.

His hairy forearms pumping over the guitar strings.

His classy, manly watch and the bulge of his forearm muscle as it moves . . .

The way he used to kiss me, so soft and yet so strong.

The way he used to make me laugh spontaneously and unexpectedly.

The way he used to massage my back.

I'm so excited about this new commission for work, but I must also ask Dan when their next gig is.

Helly jumped as the phone rang. Bought back to reality with a bump of realisation, she grabbed the unit from her dressing-table.

"Hello?" She tipped her head to the side and wedged the phone into the side of her neck as she turned toward her laptop, which sat on her bed, and clicked to connect

107

to the internet – she didn't hold out much hope – the thing was always losing its connection halfway through paying for something with her credit card.

"Helly. It's Nick."

She felt suddenly warm. Almost sweaty.

"Nick," she didn't know why she was whispering, "why are you ringing here? What do you think you're doing?"

"Helly. I'm ringing to speak to Dan."

She kicked herself as she heard the humour in his voice.

"Oh, yeah. Right. Course you are. Well, em, hang on there and I'll shout for him."

"OK."

"OK."

"Thanks."

Helly snarled at her reflection as she passed the mirror and then leant over the banister to call down to Dan. She tried to avoid the usual throaty holler that she'd have used, opting instead for a light, feminine tone.

Dan called back up the stairs to her, "S'OK. I've got it."

She heard him connect the call with the handset from the downstairs hallway and before she could get back to disconnect the bedroom phone he called up, "You still going food shopping this evening?"

Great. Completely reinforce my role as chief cook and bottlewasher right while Nick's listening in!

She didn't reply, instead disconnecting the phone and flopping down onto her bed, shaking her head. Shopping was the last thing she wanted to do at that moment in time, but she had to. It was unnerving how the feelings of neglect Dan was causing were having a bigger impact on her than she'd have expected. She wondered whether it was possible to fill the gap that neglect was making on her confidence, with fantasies. Fantasies about Nicky…

It had already been a tiring day, what with sorting the new pieces she'd bought in Brighton last month for the shop, the dog-walking, the tidying, the talking to the mums outside the school, cooking the meals, but she was still faced with the huge weekly shop. When all she wanted to do was to get into the bath.

Their brand new, claw-footed bath …

Charley stood in the cold community centre, its bare, stark walls throwing voices back at them in an unfriendly manner.

Winston came in, sharp in his slick suit and short dreadlocks, took one look at Charley and frowned. "What's with the jeans, babe? Been for a paddle?"

She looked down at her legs, as did the three people standing nearby. She guessed she looked ridiculous in her rolled-up jeans, her Che Guevara T-shirt and rasta-coloured scarf, but she wasn't about to let Winston piss on her parade. She was performing to an audience.

"It's the fashion, Winston, haven't you noticed? Christ, cop on!"

"Fashion, me arse! Roll them down. You look stupid."

"Thanks for your opinion. And your problem is?"

"No problem, sugar." He turned to face the people beside Charley. "Have you met Marcia, Clive and Ray?"

The two guys shook her hand so ferociously her voice vibrated as she spoke. "Pleased to meet you."

"Pleased to meet you, Charley."

The hall was soon filled with rich voices as the twenty-six men and women rehearsed, singing softly.

If only Charley understood the concept of harmonising, thought Winston – 'Many Rivers To Cross' simply didn't sound the same with her squalling and slurring in the background.

As she walked in the early evening sunshine Fiona's skirt was pinching at her waistline, a constant reminder of her poor shape. She knew that Claudine and Adriana would be waiting for her down on the beach. The huge orange sun was still shining, a fat peach suspended low in the blue sky. The shops were mostly open, apart from the handbag and shoe shop that always closed bang on six.

She'd been trying to teach Adriana to play the violin. It was supposed to be a bonding, relaxing process and yet she was becoming irritated at Adriana's lack of interest. She'd watched the pushy parents and rebellious teenagers on *Jerry Springer/Ricki Lake* and had promised herself not to push her own interests onto her children, yet she still found herself disappointed when Adriana didn't embrace the things that she herself loved. She felt slightly guilty at her attempts to influence Adriana back – but she didn't want her becoming *too* Portuguese. Just in case she ever got back to London or Dublin.

Walking across the road to the beach area, she pondered on the job that she'd seen advertised.

"Perhaps I should stay here and immerse myself in Portuguese life," she whispered, tired of fighting with her feelings.

She perched on the sea wall watching Adriana burying Claudine's feet in the sand. A huge seagull sat a few feet away from her and she scrutinised its huge beak and starey eyes. She adored living by the sea and knew it would be one of the hugest wrenches in moving away from Cascais. Perhaps she should go to Dublin after all, where the sea was in easy reach.

She felt guilty at the prospect of taking Adriana from Luís, despite his behaviour and his hot-and-cold interest in his daughter. She yearned for Helly but didn't want to go back to London with her tail between her legs. She wasn't sure if it was worth firing Luís up about it if she wasn't sure what she wanted to do, stuck as she was in the twilight zone.

"Yes, maybe," she looked down and spoke to her hands, "we should just go back to Ireland. Perhaps it's time to go home." Her sunglasses hid her bloodshot, teary eyes.

She'd had an emotional day and to cap it all her waist was stubbornly swollen to that point between two notches on her belt – one being too tight and the other too loose – and she wasn't about to give in to it. She knew it would have been easier to discard the belt altogether but she was dogged in her attitude that the belt wouldn't win!

She was desperate to talk to Helly and was plagued with memories of her sisters. Helly was always so reliable and sensible while Charley had always been wild. Fiona sometimes envied Charley her complete disregard for what other people thought and her free spirit. She thought back to when they were teenagers and how Helly had found out that Charley had gone for a photoshoot at a 'model agency'. Helly had always been more like the eldest sister than Charley and Fiona remembered with a smile how Helly had dragged her into Dublin and barged into the photographer's studio in the back room of the agency, despite the roaring receptionist and the red neon '*No Entry*' sign which flashed above the door. Fiona had been so filled with excitement at Helly's dare-devil actions that she hadn't been prepared to see Charley, perched on a stool with a red-velvet backdrop, wearing a pair of gaudy, ridiculously high-cut, pink lace knickers.

Only a pair of pink lace knickers.

Charley had screamed and strangely, Fiona thought, grabbed a T-shirt to hold up against her ample bare chest. The photographer, Geoff Something-or-other, had grabbed Helly by the shoulders in an attempt to spin her around and out of the door. Helly was having none of it and pushed him away from her. Charley was screaming at Helly, Helly was screaming at Geoff and Geoff was falling backwards, a clumsy, gaping dancer as he collapsed onto his tripod and camera, bringing the whole thing crashing down. And when Helly had barked at Charley to "get some clothes on for Christ's sake" – she did. Without argument or fuss. But Charley had actually always done what Helly told her to. Though Helly had to get really, really angry first.

Her memories of growing up in Wicklow and thoughts of her family only made Fiona even more desperately unhappy.

She'd really believed that Luís would marry her. She'd wanted to marry him for so many reasons.

Like – she loved him.

Like – they'd made the beautiful Adriana together.

Like – she'd mentally planned the rest of their lives as family.

Like – she thought that he'd loved her. Loved *them*.

She pushed her sunglasses up into her hair, resting them on the top of her head, her chestnut hair with natural auburn highlights gleaming and glossy in the sunshine. Claudine always moaned enviously at Fiona's naturally straight hair, trying to improve her poor body image. But Fiona didn't realise her blessing, except maybe when she sat and watched Claudine spend ages with her GHD hair-straighteners.

The bright sunlight caused her to squint slightly as she gazed dreamily at the blue sea, the small white surf whooshing as it lapped. What once had been streets of cultural paradise were now simply reminders of her failed relationship as she mourned for the hopes that she'd had.

Fiona watched as Adriana played with Claudine, her long dark hair swinging as it cascaded down from the bright pink clip, her dark brown eyes sparkling as she jumped and giggled. She almost envied her daughter's innocent, uninhibited approach.

Luís had been so supportive and kind at first. He had held her hand through the Portuguese formalities, helping her to settle in and make it 'home'. She had sometimes wondered whether he was verging on being a control-freak, but then always felt guilty as she realised, as he often said sternly, he was 'only trying to help' her.

It was second nature to the Portuguese to be polite but reserved, kind and friendly, but Fiona realised that however long she stayed, she'd never be considered a 'local'; she would always be the Irishwoman that had "had Luís' child for him".

That's how they described her.

And it stuck.

Unlike himself.

Claudine had been the first to point out the cold look in his eyes, the look that now frightened her. As swift as the sleight of hand a conjurer uses to pluck a card from behind your ear, Luís' concern often mutated into anger. Anger that she'd done something 'wrong', or had somehow 'failed' him. He was always worse if he felt that she was not spending 110% of her time with Adriana.

Yet he clearly cared about Fiona.

Then she got it.

What he actually cared about was her continual commitment to mind *his* daughter.

Chapter Nine

Dan was glad that Helly had gone shopping. It gave him the chance to ring the automated banking number and check on the dire state of their account. He was really starting to worry about their financial situation and hated himself for being too cowardly to mention it to Helly.

He let out a relieved sigh when Nick rang him later with the contact name and phone number for the new venue. The chance to fill in for the cancellation was just what they needed on so many levels and he had jumped at the chance of the Saturday-night slot. More gigs, hence more money. And the extra exposure on the London circuit.

As he sat at the island unit in the kitchen, watching his two sons squealing and laughing as they battled over the rugby ball outside, he berated himself for the way he was acting with Helly lately. He wasn't proud of himself for rejecting her like he was doing, but the serious situation with their money had somehow knocked the libido clean out of him. He was trying not to show his worry, plastering on a smile and a shrug whenever she handed him the dreaded white envelopes with the plastic windows which always revealed his name. It wasn't helping how she was obsessing about another child and he knew she'd stopped taking the pill.

As the boys came bursting in through the French doors, squabbling and skidding their muddy trainers on the polished floor, he snapped back to reality.

"Hey, c'mon now, lads. Back now. Shoes off at the back door. You know the rules, boys."

He heard Helly grappling with her key at the front door and vowed to himself that he'd be nice to her this evening.

Helly sighed as she sank back into the warm bath, the slightly too-warm water washing over her, soothing and smoothing her irritability. Her secret bout of tears had stung her cheeks a blotchy pink and her eyes were blood-shot and felt like pickled onions.

It had been bad enough, struggling at the front door with four bags of shopping as she'd tried to open the door with her *car* keys. She had wearily walked into the kitchen and dumped the carrier bags, stretched to transparency, onto the kitchen worktop, then immediately turned to the fridge for a chilled glass of wine.

Dan's bare feet had shooshed against the ceramic floor as he entered the room, his wide shoulders back and his chest puffed proudly, filling his T-shirt, as he rubbed his hands together in a gloating fashion.

"Hey, babe," he had sung, slapping her bum lightly as he made for the water filter jug. "The boys are asleep. Already!" As he poured himself a large glass of water he had noticed her swollen wine glass resting beside the slumped bags.

"Oh, like that, is it?" he'd smiled.

Helly had prickled.

And then I'd been more than surprised when he'd said:

"Look, leave that shopping, I'll unpack it. Uncle Brian and Aunt Pat have said they might call around later, for a look at the bath. Why don't you go and have a nice relaxing soak before they arrive? I know you're dying to."

Helly had felt her shoulders relax and she had given Dan a light hug. She had felt calmed by the silence in the house and needed this. She had kicked off her shoes in the hallway, leaving them lying sideways on the rug as she'd climbed the first flight of stairs to the bathroom. Grabbing at the taps eagerly, she'd enjoyed the roar as hot water plummeted noisily into the new claw-footed tub, creating mushrooms of buffeting steam that hung heavily in the air.

Now more relaxed, she'd felt the need to use the loo and had sat on it, plucking a magazine from the under-sink cupboard. She flicked through the mag, enjoying her 'me' time, even though the pages had already begun to sag in the moist air. She was soon disturbed by a cool gust of clear air as the bathroom door had swung open, dispelling and wafting the veil of steam at exactly the same time as the churning knot in her stomach unravelled itself as a lengthy, rattling fart. Helly had looked up, slightly embarrassed, expecting to see an aggrieved Toby or Jack who'd been woken by the roar of the water or a bad dream – or even worse, Diego. Instead, as she'd squinted to see through the thinning steam she'd seen Dan and his uncle and aunt, Brian and Pat, looking in at her, horrified.

"Jesus, Dan!" she'd hollered, feeling herself redden.

"Oh God – sorry, Hel." Dan swiftly closed the bathroom door. "I thought you'd left the bath running – I just wanted to show Brian the new bath."

Great – I can't even piss now without an audience!

Talk about being caught with your pants down.

I'd planned the absolute mother-of-pampering-baths. I'd intended to buff with the loofah to get my skin glowing, I'd already picked out the varnish I was going to use for painting my toenails and now it's all ruined. I was planning to wrap up in fluffy bath towels for a while letting my skin dry in its own time. And what had I got instead? I could hear Brian and Pat making squeaky sounds as they fussed over Dan. The question was, would it be rude to get into the bath now that I know they're here? Or should I be polite and wait until they've gone?

Political correctness had washed over Helly like unwanted kisses from an ugly admirer as she'd struggled to shake off her irritation. Feeling like an aggrieved public schoolboy, shoe-horned into last year's uniform, she'd forced herself to turn off the bath taps, resigning herself to do the right thing and smile and be pleasant to her visitors. She pulled on her track pants and hoody top, running her fingers through her damp hair, and then put on her lipstick.

She came into the kitchen to find Dan and his aunt and uncle standing out on the patio. She was just about to switch on the kettle when she noticed Dan's neat writing on the notepad by the phone. Glancing up out of the kitchen window she checked that he was busy, rattling off his plans and intentions for the grotty patio. The words danced in flashing neon lights off the page at her – almost like a 'screamer' from the Harry Potter films. It was Nick's address and phone number. She grabbed her handbag and rooted for her mobile, then remembered that she'd handed it to Dan earlier after its swimming lesson in the sink. The French doors opened and Dan's voice became louder as he re-entered the kitchen, still talking 'decking' to his Uncle Brian.

"Dan," Helly smiled, "have you shown Brian and Pat the plans? The ones that your garden designer friend drew up for us?"

Dan beamed, obviously delighted that she remembered. "No. Pat, you're gonna love these. Come through to the lounge."

"I'll bring in some coffee." Helly squeezed a smile as they traipsed through her kitchen, wet shoes and all.

She clattered with the mugs and spoons for a minute before she tore off a sheet of paper and copied down Nicky's mobile number and address. She wasn't sure where Westburton Terrace was. But she'd make it her job to find out.

She had no sooner taken in the tray of coffee and biscuits when Dan announced that he was going out. He casually threw in the fact that "the band" had plans to rehearse for a new Saturday-night gig at a new venue. He was delighted that they'd called him to fill in for a cancellation. As he chucked his mug of coffee down his neck, at the same time continuing, "Need to rehearse . . . new guitarist . . . back later, babe . . .", Helly was shell-shocked. And so, with a hug and kiss for his aunt, a slap on the back for his uncle and a hair-ruffle for Helly, Dan was gone.

Out for the night.

As she'd felt her short hair rearranged in new spikes on top of her head she had noticed the strange look that Pat was giving her.

Probably due to my new 'do'!

It just bugs me so much how he lives for his work and his band and yet expects me to keep the kids going. And so now he's gone again for the night.

And he'll probably come home and not want any physical contact. It doesn't feel good, knowing that other women are beating their husbands off them with a stick, and mine feels repulsed at going anywhere near me.

It was in that split second that I made the decision. And it was out before I'd even given it any thought. I just said it,

"Pat, Brai – I mean, Brian. You wouldn't be free to baby-sit for us on Saturday night, would you?" She watched their blank faces. It wasn't often she asked for baby-sitting help, and was half expecting them to say how busy they were playing Scrabble or something equally exciting like clipping each other's nose-hair.

Their silence spurred her on, "It's just that I haven't

been to one of Dan's gigs for so long. He puts so much time and effort into the band. It'd be nice to support him now and again. Don't you think, Pat?"

And so they'd agreed!

And so I now lie in my bath, having cried with despair at the prospect of Dan coming home and making crap excuses for not wanting to make love to me, and cried at my confusion at the way my mind and stomach are in chaos at the reappearance of Nicky.

Oh, and did I mention the sheer nerves I feel about what I could possibly wear on Saturday night?

Really – is it worth all the tears?

Dan got in after midnight and Helly felt the bed dip as it took his weight. Her relaxed senses winced at the smell of cigarette smoke and stale beer that came from his hair and skin. Oblivious to the odours, in only the way that you can be after a night in a pub, Dan snuggled up behind her, his warm arms and bare torso lush against her back. Helly snuggled her bottom in toward him as they 'spooned' until she felt the beginnings of movement against the back of her thigh. She tried to wiggle in closer to him but found herself left on the cold patch of bed as he turned his back to her, sticking his backside out in her direction.

So now he's misconstruing every move!

He's becoming paranoid.

Why is it that he's reading everything as a ploy for sex? This baby thing is clouding his vision, taking over our lives and I really don't like it.

He's an expert at nookie-avoidance tactics now.

"Pat and Brian are baby-sitting on Saturday," she murmured.

"Really?" Dan turned back to her. "Who for?"

She climbed up onto him, straddling him.

"For us!"

That moved him all right.

"Yeah, I thought it'd be nice if I came with you on Saturday night."

He looked puzzled but smiled.

Must be the booze.

"Really? I thought you'd lost interest in the band. It's been ages since you've come to a gig."

I'm glad it's dark 'cos I'm blushing. Talk about guilty conscience.

"I know. I've missed it. You don't mind, do you?"

"No, no. Course I don't. The guys will be glad to see you. It's just been so long since you've shown an interest. Thanks."

He hugged her and kissed her on the forehead. Helly lost herself in the moment and closed her eyes. It wasn't until she let out a light moan that he remembered his anti-sex agenda.

"Oh Helly. Do you mind if we don't? I'm just so tired tonight."

"No," she climbed off him, and lay beside him, lonely, "course I don't."

He leant across and kissed her forehead again.

"Thanks, babe. Night."

Helly lay, staring up at the darkness, sick with rejection.

"Dan?" Her voice was light and clear in the silence.

"Yeah?" he groaned, his back to her once again.

"Did you have any luck with fixing my mobile?"

"Yeah. It's OK. I left it on the fireplace in the lounge."

"Right," she smiled to herself, "thanks."

Chapter Ten

She woke bright and early the next day, excited, with only two days to go till her big night out.

She sat in the car outside the school gates, watching Toby and Jack run in, their faces alight with enthusiasm, their eyes dancing. Then she fumbled with her phone and pulled the scrap of paper from her jeans pocket. She didn't really know why her fingers were shaking as she programmed in Nick's mobile number, but the minute she'd entered it, under the name 'Mmmm', she had an overwhelming urge to send him a text message. She was dying to let him know that she was going to the gig on Saturday night. Especially after him asking her!

The reality is this – I'm in panic mode and, as usual, I was talking when I should have been thinking. Dan mentioned this morning that they'll be dropping off their gear at the venue Saturday afternoon so they can take the Tube to the gig, all in the name of severe alcohol consumption.

Jesus! As if I weren't worried about it all enough without pickling my brain at the same time . . .

Helly had taken the car home and hopped onto the Tube to work. She loved the walk from Notting Hill Gate Tube Station to her shop on the Portobello Road. She wasn't sure why she'd ever named it 'Pink Turtle' but was glad she had – it had a ring to it that made people remember. The throb of the Tube Station was soon a distant memory as she strolled in the early morning sunshine along Pembridge Road, her knee-high boots as comfortable as slippers and her full three-quarter skirt swinging with a flirty kick as she walked. She stopped en route to look through the window of the Retro Store, admiring the Jasper Conran boots with suede heels that Isaac had stuck a price-tag of sixty pounds onto. Her eyes scanned the second-hand goods in the window and she also spotted Miu Miu sandals *and* Prada stilettos that she'd definitely pay the fifty quid on the price tag for. Isaac caught sight of her at the window and squinted as he read the slogan on her T-shirt through the glass, laughing and giving the thumbs up at her 'I CAME INTO THIS WORLD WITH NOTHING – AND I STILL HAVE MOST OF IT LEFT' message. She stopped to look at the antique silver that was displayed outside the fine art and antiques shop, fingering the twisted knives and forks, wondering whose mouths they'd fed over the years.

This time of the day was when Helly truly began to relax. She often waited for the bubble to burst – for someone to recognise her as a plain, nondescript fake in the trendy streets of Portobello. It hadn't happened yet.

Pink Turtle was just at the beginning of Portobello Market, which hosted a general market all week, selling value for money fruit and veg, pashmina shawls, bagels, sunflowers, lilies, tulips and cleaning products, but she really liked the weekends, when the clothes market was in full swing.

As she unlocked her cerise pink door she checked her window display and was pleased with the way she'd hung the chiffon floral tops from delicate threads, and the rose petals that she'd scattered on the floor of the bay window. She'd really wanted to go along to the Orange Café for breakfast, but remembered how she'd decided to cut down for the next couple of days, on the run up to her night out at the gig. She didn't want to be bloated on Saturday. She left the door wide open, letting in the morning sunshine, and turned to see Gonad, the white Westie pup that belonged to Penny from the shop next door, trotting in and lying in the doorway, slumped in the sun. She switched on the music, the sounds of Billie Holliday filling the shop as she checked her till and stock, and began pottering and planning her day. It wasn't long before Penny stuck her head around the door.

"Hey, Helly. Gonad all right there? He's not annoying you, is he?"

Helly laughed. "Only in the way that I'm jealous! He looks so relaxed and comfortable."

"Well, it's your shop. If you want to lie down in the doorway, no-one's stopping you!"

"Not so good for trade though, is it? You going down to the market?"

"Yeah, I was going to. What do you fancy?"

"I'd like some bananas and kiwis, and could you get me some of that soya milk from the Neals Yard shop?"

"Oh, exciting weekend coming up?" Penny grinned, recognising the usual female signs of careful eating.

"Nothing much really," Helly tried to play it down, "just going to one of Dan's gigs on Saturday night."

"Oh, right. OK, so you don't fancy your usual chicken pesto sandwich and skinny raspberry muffin today then?"

"Don't tempt me. No, thanks. Just the fruit. Cheers, Pen."

Their conversation was stopped by the arrival of four German women tourists cramming themselves through the narrow doorway as they loudly admired Helly's antique clothing display. It was a common joke around the area, post-*Notting Hill* – about the influx of cheesy tourists all virtually *expecting* to see Julia Roberts or Hugh Grant. A man whizzed by on his bike, his wicker basket on the front stuffed with sunflowers and lilies from the market. Helly watched her 'customers' touch each other on the arms and coo at the excitement of seeing something akin to the movie. Helly wondered whether they actually expected to see the London businessmen wearing bowler hats and carrying enormous black umbrellas too.

Penny soon returned with blue carrier bags jutting with the angular shapes of fruit. She sat behind her counter, peeling the banana and was just about to stuff it into her mouth when Kaz came in.

"Helly, I'm looking for something for tonight."

Helly hopped up from her high stool, placing the banana down beside the till.

"For the girls?"

"No," Kaz smiled, "for me. My husband's taking me out tonight, it's our fifth wedding anniversary and I fancy something new. Mind if I rummage?"

"Go ahead! Try this rack with the lace vintage dresses."

Helly pulled a handful of light dresses from the rack and rested them over her wicker chair as her mobile rang. Leaving Kaz to excitedly plough through the clothes, she stepped out of the shop door, standing with the sun beating down on her cropped blonde hair as she answered her mobile. It was Fiona.

Fiona was in a middle ground, a no-man's-land where the power of rage and the isolation of helplessness scrabbled for the front line. She was constantly haunted by herself, by who she *used* to be, how she *used* to look. Lately she could literally feel the elasticity leaving her skin, like air slowly invisibly leaving a balloon, an almost silent hiss that no-one but she was aware of, yet her face was a constant reminder. Exfoliators seemed no longer to slough and refresh, only to redden. She was left slightly buffed and still wrinkled – only pinker. The depression had started to sink in when she realised her eyebrows were slipping lower and a permanent frown line, an angry exclamation mark, sat between her eyebrows. In her twenties she had thought the merest hint of the indentation gave her a feisty look, now it only gave her an air of somebody troubled. Somebody unable to cope. Alone with her reflection in the echoey bathroom, the silver-edged mirror told no lies and she could see her life beginning to etch itself permanently onto her face. And sickeningly her mum could hit to the core of her insecurity in a sentence.

"You won't believe what she said!" Her words were tinny and hollow as they bounced off the tiled walls.

Helplessness had won over rage and Fiona was finding it hard to breathe with any regularity as she clutched the phone to the side of her head.

"Go on." Helly knew that, once again, her work would have to wait.

"She said 'Fiona, I hope you're not still wearing those stupid half-cut T-shirts. You're too old for all that now. You know, I saw a young woman in Wicklow Town last week in one of those tops and she did not have the stomach to wear it. And I certainly didn't have the stomach to look at it! What do they think they're doing trying to dress that way anyway? No, Fiona, it's no good trying to recapture your youth, dear. It's all gone!' I wouldn't mind, Hel, but I never wore clothes like that. She didn't ask for Adriana or me or anything. I'm worried about her, Helly."

Helly snorted, clamping her hand over her mouth just in time. She felt ready to explode with laughter.

"Helly? Did you hear that?"

"Yeah, mmm, yep. I heard it."

"You're laughing, aren't you?"

"No, I'm not!"

"You are. Helly," Fiona's voice fragmented as emotion

overtook her, "please, please, don't laugh at me."

Her heart-wrenching sobs tugged at Helly with a strength that overwhelmed her. She immediately felt guilty at finding humour in their Mum's wry and yet ridiculous remarks, but thought that Fiona should be used to it by now. Their mother had always been banging the drum for some worthy cause, usually on far-flung shores, but had always failed to see her family's problems and dilemmas. She had never been there for any of them. Ever. But she was a kind woman, although her loyalties were questionable as far as Helly could see. For Helly the most troubling sign was the complete lack of sense of humour in Fiona. She'd always been over-sensitive about her looks and yet, strangely, would always find a way to laugh at herself. It seemed that things were considerably worse in Cascais than Helly had originally thought.

"Don't you have any friends there?"

"No. Well, I mean there's Claudine, she's my only proper friend. The others are all afraid of Luís and his financial and commercial power. Swanning around the bloody place with his bulging wallet and his crombie. He thinks he's Donnie-Fucking-Brasco!"

"How about if I come over?" Helly gushed, regretting it the instant it came out of her mouth. She'd already committed to fly out to Paris with Kaz and wondered how she'd fit in the two trips.

"Oh my God! That'd be fantastic. Do you think you could, Helly?"

"Yeah," she forced the jovial tone. "That's it then. I'm coming over to you. Don't even listen to Mum. You know what she's like; she can't help it. Look, you've been through enough but you need to toughen up. Give me a few days, I'll be over. I can't wait to see Adriana either. You know Mum. She's a crap grandma. She never even asks for Toby or Jack."

"I know. It's just hard. I feel so cut off here. So low. Thanks for the chat, Helly."

"No problem."

"So will you really come over?"

"Consider it booked!"

The trouble was, having become so accustomed to being the responsible one, the one who always takes the lead, Helly found it hard now, all of a sudden, not to jump into action at the slightest whiff of discontent.

I don't know how Dan will react to my absence. He'll probably go bananas. It's not so much my absence, rather my lack of presence. The ruination of routine. The disturbance to Dan's daily recreational activities. And then I've got to check whether Claire can cover the shop for the few days. And what about Kaz and Quattro?

She was glad Kaz hadn't heard her phone conversation. She was determined to make a success of Quattro's tour wardrobe and she knew her ambitions would mean an extra surge of dedication to her work for a short space of time.

Helly was suddenly worried about asking Dan if he'd mind her going away for a few days. He surely wouldn't. After all, he'd been so busy with work and his gigs, it'd be nice if he took an easy week off. She wondered whether he'd enjoy taking the boys to school and being home for them and putting them to bed at night.

After all, it's no big deal.

I do it every week.

By Saturday night she hadn't mentioned the Portugal promise to Dan yet and was hoping to pick her moment tonight, when his easy-going nature was more pliable after a few bevvies. Helly had devoutly ransacked the kitchen cupboards to eradicate anything that would give Pat reason to cast judgement and so the tins of baked beans with tiny sausages in them and anything curried in tins had been thrown into the small cupboard in the bottom corner. She knew that when Brian and Pat arrived to baby-sit they'd be armed with sweets and chocolates and that the kids would have a *great* time. But she was under no illusion that Pat loved to rummage through her kitchen cupboards too. She heard their car pull up outside and liberally dusted bronzing powder between her breasts to create a more substantial cleavage and then cursed herself for overdoing it.

"Shit! It's too bloody shiny now!"

She tugged at her new bra as she rubbed vigorously at her glistening chest.

It's ludicrous really. But it's true – my self-awareness has escalated since the re-emergence of Nicky and I love it. I feel impetuous, excited and yet dangerous. He's reawakened something in me. Something raw, something real and something rather scary has been unleashed inside of me. I am ridiculously impetuous, and feel completely irresponsible. Just what I need, don't you think? After a lifetime of being responsible for my sisters and now for my family, I'm certain a short sharp blast of irresponsibility would do me good.

And since when did I pay attention to the adverts for teeth-bleaching? And now I'm painfully aware of my appearance – and I want to be hot for Nicky. I want him to want me again.

Perhaps to make up for Dan not wanting me.

She listened from her bedroom as Pat gushed and kissed her little nephews at the front door. Looking down onto the streetlamp-lit road she felt the confetti of butterflies punching to get out of her stomach as she watched Nick pull up behind Brian and Pat's car in his vintage Mercedes. She quickly crouched at her dressing-table, reaching for the haemorrhoid cream, and squeezed a tiny amount onto her little finger, dabbing it gently around her eyes, marvelling at how the skin almost instantly tightened, dispelling any signs of wrinkles or bags. She'd been cautious of trying it at first, when Penny had come into the shop and recommended it. It didn't seem right, putting the cream that was designed for that particular aperture on display around your eyes. But she had to give it to Penny: it worked. Albeit temporarily.

She stood upright, and brushed down her thighs which were clad in her worn 501's as she slipped her fake-tanned feet into a pair of pink strappy sandals. She quickly sat down again to put the finishing touches to her deep cerise nail polish and, in her haste, lightly wiped the wet varnish onto back of the other hand just as Toby skittered into her bedroom.

"Jesus!" she spat, splaying her long fingers like an elegant starfish as she wiped at the pink streak on her hand and groped for the varnish brush again.

Toby was watching her admiringly, his large eyes translucent with innocence and yet sparkling with devilment.

"Mummy?"

Her heart warmed as she turned to his sweet and light voice.

"Yes, love?"

"Why do you always say 'cheeses'?"

She hugged him loosely, taking care not to knock her nails again, and kissed him firmly on the forehead. "I love you, Tobes. Run down to Uncle Brian now."

Toby refused to and instead pulled at the curtains and sighed as he looked down at Nick's car. "Look at that car, Mum!"

Helly was continually amazed at how her young sons seemed so aware these days and she crossed to the window and lightly put her arm around Toby's shoulders. They looked down at Nick's to-die-for red 1971 Mercedes 280.

Helly was determined to be the one at the front door when he rang and challenged Toby to race her down. She booted it down the stairs and noticed the mixed reaction when she entered the kitchen. 'Brain' immediately focussed on her chest, which was encased in an elegant lace-strapped vest. Pat scanned her long slender arms which were glowing with a light shimmering of bronzer, and then stared at her face as if it were a bar code as she took in every detail of her make-up and the effort that had been made. Helly noticed her sneer at her jeans. Dan suddenly became strangely possessive of her, even making

135

a point of crossing the room to put his arm around her shoulder gently – but firmly.

Then the 'bing bong' of the doorbell broke the frozen moment.

"S'OK, love," she cooed surprisingly calmly to Dan. "You chat with Brian."

Slicking her hair, she took a deep breath as she reached to open the front door.

"Hey!" He smiled a wide smile as his eyes glistened beneath the streetlights.

She felt herself blush. She was certain Nick wasn't married. There were no rings and his dress sense was cool and urban, unlike John, the bass-guitarist, whose ironed shirt tucked tight into jeans screamed "night away from the wife". She was sure that he hadn't changed, that he was still warm, funny and considerate.

And it excited her.

The couple of glasses of wine at home had already started to get her blurry and by the time they got on the Tube at Chalk Farm she was ready for a party. Even despite the fact that it was packed with tourists, Helly, Dan and Nick squeezed in the carriage to join in with the shuffling and jostling of the Tube tunnels. It was crammed – standing room only. Helly stood face-to-face with a tall Asian guy whose dark brown eyes were topped with long silky lashes and she couldn't help herself admiring them. Lost in her half-pissed thoughts, she was brought back to life as Dan insisted on teasing her by lightly pinching her bum from behind. She couldn't believe he was putting on this show of affection to the public. She knew she looked good but she couldn't believe that he was groping her here – in the 'safe' environment of the bloody Tube train! Excited and encouraged by his cheekiness she lightly dropped her hand down to her thigh and stretched it back slightly, feeling his denimed thigh.

This is the first time he's been suggestive in months!

Just for good measure she discreetly ran her hand up along his thigh to his crotch and cupped him in her varnished hand, giving a tight squeeze. Slightly too tight – just to get the message across. She felt the swell almost instantly and it excited her. Discreetly, she rubbed the palm of her hand against the warm bulge and paused as his warm hand grasped her wrist and began to tickle her palm. Running her fingers across the back of his hairy hand she began to caress his fingers, pulling gently on each one.

He isn't wearing his wedding ring!

She grabbed onto his ring finger again to check.

Cheeses! This isn't Dan!

In a heightened state of alertness, she moved her head to the side of the Asian guy, scanning the carriage only to see Dan behind him holding onto a chrome pole with both his hands as they jiggled and wobbled into the next station. Catching her eye, he winked and smiled across at her.

The question is – whose balls have I just been squeezing?

Feeling sick, with a lump in her throat the size of Russia, only colder, Helly turned to see a grinning and slightly flushed Nick.

As the doors whirred open she felt instantly sober, trying to disguise her beetroot face from the grinning Nick.

The playfulness and confidence were shaken in her, and so by the time they reached the pub she was subdued. The blackboard outside advertised their gig for nine, with an extra mention for the live rugby the next afternoon. Nick laughed as he put his hand on the small of Helly's back, directing her lightly in through the doorway, as if aware of her dampened spirits.

"Live rugby? In a pub? How ridiculous! All the beer'll be spilled and everything!"

Chapter Eleven

Charley swore at the telly. Really loudly. With absolutely no regard for Mr & Mrs Kelly next door. Not one bit.

"Another bloody nappy ad! For Christ's sake! Is it really necessary?"

She stood up and punched at the remote-control button to switch channels and then threw it down onto the rug. As she walked to her kitchen, her marshmallow velour socks baggy around her ankles, she was aware that she was frowning but by the time she had taken huge gulps from an exceedingly large glass of wine, her face had begun to soften.

She did everything she possibly *could* to avoid children; she certainly didn't want to be watching them on the damn TV. *Especially* babies. As if it wasn't bad enough having to listen to her daft mother banging on about her body-clock, she then had to listen to her two sisters talking about their children. It always struck her how their voices warmed when they said their children's names. Charley felt the glow of love that Helly and Fiona had for their children. Even when they'd been naughty, Charley felt envious at their family 'unit' and hated being on the outside, although she knew she had put herself there. And then, to make things worse she'd had to write a jingle for a nappy advert only recently.

It was hard for her. She hadn't always been this angry. If she'd only realised that as time passed she'd find it increasingly difficult to look at a nine or ten-month baby without feeling a surge of sadness and wonderment. And she feared that it would only get worse as the years went by. How many times had she kicked herself for not being stronger? How many times had she regretted the 'day-trip to England'? And so she blamed herself, repeatedly. And yet, nobody knew.

Charley made a point of having absolutely *nothing* to do with children from that point onwards. Her family had noticed the strange shift but had stopped puzzling over it, simply accepting that it had almost coincided with the onset of her heavy drinking. She'd once adored spending time with Toby and Jack and even her friends' children. Charley, the nut-case, had always been the one to kick off her shoes and roll up her jeans and start to play 'it' in the park, or to sling off her jacket and lie on the floor with the children, agreeing to be 'banker' if they let her buy the most lucrative Monopoly streets.

By the time she had shuffled back to her armchair she noticed that the huge glass in her hand was virtually empty and so turned on her heel back to the kitchen. She snatched the bottle by the neck and swung it, nestling it in her dressing-gown pocket as she retreated back to the comfort of her lounge.

"Feck it," she shrugged, lifting the bottle to her mouth, "why bother with a glass anyway?"

But as she poured the 'pain relief' into her, the bad, sad feelings just weren't melting away like they usually did.

Helly shifted her bar stool so that she got the full belt of the air con. She was cooking but the adrenalin buzzed through her like a pinball. In the spot-lit bar the walls, sweating rivulets of moisture, were pounded by the blues band. It was hot, smoky and as full as the last bus. Her hands slid on the wet icy glass as she lifted it to her mouth and gulped huge mouthfuls of the Bacardi. The place already stank of smoke and stale beer, but she was loving it. The excitement somersaulted inside her as she waited for Dan, Nick and the guys' slot. They were on soon. And she was already dizzy! As she sat alone at the bar she looked around at the distressed oak beams and 1930's beer and Oxo ads that were framed on the wall. It was an unlikely venue, but she supposed the fact that it was the size of an aircraft hangar helped. She checked her watch. With only five minutes to go she necked the last of her drink and ordered another from the smiling, glass-flipping barman. Feeling the chill of the air conditioning blowing down across her bare shoulders, a wave of goose pimples puckered over her.

"Hey," a deep voice murmured in her ear, making her jump, "order one up for me while you're there. My shout."

She spun around on her stool, nearly poking out his eye with her nipple which she feared was jutting with the cold. He noticed. It would have been tough not to. She composed herself as she watched Dan approach them, looking dead cool in his Ramones T-shirt. She ordered two pints, which were placed on the bar within seconds. Dan lifted his and drank half of it in one go, wiping his frothy moustache as he '*aahhhh'd!*'.

"Rightso then, Nick. You ready?"

"Bring it on. I can't wait."

Dan kissed her on the forehead, placing down the empty glass, the white bubbles clinging to the sides and sliding down from the top, shocked that it was all over so quickly.

"OK, babe." Then he whispered in her ear, "Really great to have you here. Thanks."

She smiled at him as he walked away, watching as Nick turned and gave a sexy wink in her direction.

Just like the first time I met him.

He hasn't changed. He's still cooler than a frozen Martini.

My God, what the hell am I doing here?

What am I thinking of?

But she couldn't deny that she was attracted to him.

Just like before.

Fatal.

By midnight Helly had got in with a crowd of strangers who were seated at the largest round table there and who were attacking the cocktail list at a ferocious speed. She'd had to sit down – her ridiculously high sandals were crippling her. It was after the first four drinks that she realised she needed to sit down, and then after the next four the temptation to remove the shoes overwhelmed her. They were pinching at her toes, and her arches and calves ached like mad. The empty glasses gathered on the huge table as she joined in. She found out through their conversation that they were a blend of ex-school pals, ex-boyfriends and work-colleagues who had obviously known each other for years. It was great. She had little problem focusing short-distance. She could make out the shapes of the numerous empty glasses and bottles on the table, but when she tried to see something further she realised she was seeing two of everything. And the buzzing in her ears and the thudding of the bass in her abdomen continued.

Nick, Dan and the guys had pulled up chairs too and their shiny, sweaty faces laughed as they joined in the piss-take with their newly formed mates. For Helly the voices became a mass of sound as she found she was no longer able to distinguish one sound from another.

"Dan. Dan." Helly slurred slightly. "Want go home. Feel sick."

Dan frowned at the inconvenience. "Helen. We've got to pack everything up yet. That record label guy was dying to see us. I've got to stick around and see him. *And* get our money! We won't be leaving here till gone two."

She shook her head frantically, staring at the floor.

"No, no. Sorry, can't do that. Need to go bed. Need go home. Now. Feel sick. Anyway, I've got record company connections now, so don't need record label guys. Wanna taxi. Dan, please."

"Christ!" Dan whispered under his breath.

Nick noticed and whispered to Dan, "Problems?"

Dan rubbed his forehead as his shoulders dropped. "You could say that. I'd forgotten what a nightmare she is if she has too many drinks. She hasn't been to a gig for years."

"Do you think she'll puke?"

He grimaced and nodded. "Probably." He looked up at Nick with an odd expression on his face.

"What?" Nick stepped back, unsure of his expression.

"You wouldn't do me a favour, mate, would you? Just this once?"

"Sure, fire away."

"You wouldn't take her home for me, would you?"

"What?"

"Just this one time. It's no problem, is it? I'll ring a taxi and pay the fare. If you could just see her in safely and then get the cab back here."

Nicky hesitated and took one look at Helly who was now resting her head on the table, in a large puddle of spilled drinks. Flat beer was dribbling off the edge of the table and hitting the leg of her jeans, causing a dark wet patch.

Dan wasn't sure what to do. He was torn between wanting to look after his wife and get her home safely, and worrying that he'd miss his chance at promoting the band. And, of course, there was also the worry that Helly would get sick – right there in front of everyone. He knew instantly Nick was the right guy to help him out.

"OK, mate. I'll do it."

Dan slapped him on the back, causing him to jolt forward slightly. "Thanks, man. If you're sure you don't mind. Here, I'll give you the cab fare. Just make sure she gets home. My aunt's there minding the kids."

He thinks I can't hear him! The bastard. Does he think I'm actually looking forward to seeing bloody Pat and Brain? I know I'm a little wonky, but I can just imagine their faces.

But hey – Nicky is taking me home. . .

Yummy, yummy, scrummy.

Helly was glad to get out of there. The vacuum of silence inside the taxi helped her to relax and the cool air calmed her stomach a little. She sidled up beside Nick on the shiny leather seats of the black cab. Unaware of the taxi driver's eyes on her in the rear-view mirror, she looked at his thick neck bulging like a fat-lardy cake over his collar. She clutched her hand over her mouth to stop the laughter getting out.

"Look at the head on him," she whispered very loudly to Nick. "Like a dog dressed in a suit for a comic photo."

Nick held his laughter as he noticed the indignant expression of the cabbie and clutched his hand over her mouth as she giggled into it. Hot and wet. He looked at her. She hadn't changed either. Despite the wedding ring, the beautiful house and kids, the designer husband, she was still Helen. Her free spirit and reckless outlook may have been numbed slightly, but Nick knew it was still there. And it had only taken a night on the town to start bringing it out again.

"Sshh!" He got her in a light headlock, pulling her in closer to him, which she loved as it meant she was within breathing distance of his lips.

She pulled away slowly and sat back, her eyes sultry and her pupils extremely dilated.

"I bet you're still a real shag-fest, aren't ya?" Before he could reply she continued, "I bet you could peel an orange in your pocket."

He laughed out loud, "What the hell's that supposed to mean then?"

"Oh," she shook her head in a lazy, uncoordinated way, "I've seen your fingers on those guitar strings. Don't think I haven't noticed."

She didn't give him the chance to reply, speaking as if from a distance, possibly even thinking aloud, "You know, I do love Dan. But I love to be separate from him too. I work hard. He neglects me though. I keep the house nice, I cook, I raise the kids. All he has to do is sort out the bills. And you know?" Her voice rose many octaves as she forced herself to sound sober. "I try to keep myself nice. I gave birth twice in three years, you know. I've got the Pink Turtle antiques clothes shop on the Portobello Road *and* I've been asked to help the stylist for Quattro too. I'm a busy girl, you know."

His eyes were sparkling as he smiled widely at her. Before she knew it he was nuzzling into her neck, the magnetism of attraction overwhelming him. He had never hit on another man's wife, but the urge now was simply too strong. They had been so hot together. His feelings were taking over and it didn't happen often. It had been years since he had felt so intensely about someone.

"Remember when we had sex in a taxi?" she grinned.

"Hey, Helen, easy."

She giggled, hopping up to straddle him, and grinning playfully as she looked straight into his eyes.

"Do you still *love* music though? I mean really really love it?"

"It's been a part of my life since I can remember. You know that."

"Me too. So, do you still sing too?" Her eyes were doing a drunken dance as she struggled to look sober.

"Yeah," he humoured her, enjoying her flirting and thankful that Dan was nowhere to be seen. "I was lead guitarist *and* singer in my last band." His hands slid down onto her jeans-clad arse as she sat astride him. It still felt as good as ever – firm and high, although maybe not quite as slim as he'd remembered.

Her voice was husky as she spoke, punctuating her broken sentences with small pecks. Little, tiny, kisses. On his nose. His cheek. His forehead. "My karaoke song – is 'Say a Little Prayer' – by Aretha Franklin – you see – I've learned – through bad experiences – that ballads are – simply – inappropriate – for karaoke – Dan's sister – used to get up – just when – everyone was singing – jaunty numbers – and sing – 'We've Only – Just – Begun' – it – was – sick – the whole place – went quiet – every-one stopped – having fun – and started staring – into their beer – she – completely – killed – the – atmos-phere."

Nick was staring at her intently, his eyes glazed and lusty.

"I remember your singing." His voice was soft and low.

She stopped her butterfly kisses and tried to focus on him.

Lifting his hands up, he gently cupped her face. She could feel his breath as he gently pulled her toward him. Finding it difficult to breathe, her heart raced in her chest, threatening to pound its way out through her throat. She frowned and pulled back slightly.

"You are amazing." His voice was husky and deep, and yet soft. "Still."

"No, Nick. We can't. Not really. Not properly."

"I can't stop thinking about you."

"Well, you must. I'm a married woman."

"You're fantastic. Why did you leave me for him?"

She couldn't find the words.

He continued, "I want you, Helen. I never got over you. I still love you – have always loved you. I don't want your housekeeping skills, your parenting ideas or your contribution to a joint account. I want you, Helen. You are still so amazing."

Her eyes filled with tears. "Thanks, but you know why I left you."

"Cos you were getting married?"

She looked away. "Not only that."

She closed her eyes, the bumps of the London streets grinding their torsos together in jerks as she felt his warm breath on her cheek. Her stomach flipped a million times as she felt his soft, hot lips on hers. At first she was unable to move them, lost in the feel of his tongue as it probed lightly between her parted lips. Suddenly she grabbed his hair at the nape of his neck and pushed her mouth onto his. Hard and full. They kissed just as they had done all those years before, Helly's red lipstick smearing across her face as she lost herself in the past and the present.

Helly's head pounded and her bedroom was still wobbling. She had fought off Pat's disgruntled offer of helping her up the stairs, and now she was there she couldn't settle down. It was worse if she turned her head quickly. A strange nausea churned in her stomach, a cocktail of embarrassment, regret and shame mixed in with the overindulgence of alcohol. She'd managed miraculously not to be sick in front of Dan's aunt and uncle when she'd got in. She vaguely recalled Nick holding her up at the front door and handing her over to a confused-looking Pat. But she'd only been sick three times by this stage. The cabbie had managed to stop down side streets, but hadn't been pleased with the condition of his passenger.

How could I have done that?

They say the difference between stupidity and genius is that genius has its limits, and after a night of sod-the-consequences hedonism I can fully go along with that. I reckon that's the price you pay for nudging your way in on an evening, when you're severely under-practised in 'going out'. I must admit, I'm flattered by Nick's attention but also a little unnerved. It's easy for me to be annoyed with Dan, but now I'm worried how easy it could be for me to be distracted again. Especially if Nick persists with this particular line of questioning. And what have I done? I can remember the cringe-worthy ball-squeezing on the Tube, but what about the rest of the night? I just have these vague recollections of kissing in the taxi!

God, it just doesn't bear thinking about.

What have I done?

Chapter Twelve

Fiona was on fire. She'd spent the day trying to really boost up her tan, worrying about her appearance now that Helly had promised to visit. Claudine had taken Adriana to the park for the day and so Fiona had gathered up her towel and Factor Eight and made for the secluded beach that the tourists couldn't find. There was no way she was going to lie about in her bikini in full view of the public. She had slathered the oily lotion onto her bare skin, even letting down the straps of her bikini-top as she lay sunken on her towel, making a body-shaped indentation on the sand as she practised sucking in her tummy. It had been lovely. For the first five minutes. She was almost asleep even. And then the wasps appeared. She tried to ignore their nasally Spitfire hum as they circled over her, nose-diving occasionally and making her squeal as she leapt up, swiping at them. By the time they'd finished playing with her she realised she'd been tarred and feathered by the combination of sun lotion and sand, her legs two chunky wedges of heavy-duty sandpaper. Luckily the sea had been warm, the sand lifting off her bronzed body quickly as she squatted in the knee-high water, afraid to go any deeper for fear of the local squad of jelly-fish, but also unwilling to display her torso to the few locals that she shared the beach with. It was bad enough that Luís had finished with her, without advertising the mess he'd left behind! She had finally managed to force herself out of the water and lay in the sun to dry, managing even to sleep for a while. The sun eased the tension from her muscles as she lay on her warm towel, allowing the heat to penetrate through her dark skin. Her thoughts drifted to a better life, a happier life, and she dreamt of a new, fictitious fireman boyfriend who took her into the fire station for rampant sex, and then cosseted her as he made love to her in the four-poster that she had in her new, fictitious bedroom. She woke with a start at the sound of another whining buzz, leaping to her feet and knocking over her bottle of sun-tan lotion, watching it glug out, soaking quickly into the parched sand. Cursing to herself as she whipped up her towel, folding it roughly and shoving it back into her beach bag, she muttered, "As if! Four-poster in the bloody bedroom! Knowing my luck, if I went to London I'd end up on an estate where even the arms of the chairs have tattoos!"

She'd arrived back at her apartment before Claudine and Adriana and took the opportunity for a quick shower to degrease herself after the suntan lotion. She dried herself off, then looked in the mirror, pleased at her deeper bronzed reflection. The enlarged freckles over her nose and cheeks had virtually joined together and a deep bronze glow across her shoulders, chest and arms meant that she looked great. She tugged on her light trousers and black vest and waited for her daughter and best friend to come home. They were going to eat at Claudine's apartment.

For the first time in weeks she felt good. If only her clothes weren't pinching, she'd be on top form.

"So, my sister's coming over."

"Well, that is *fantastique*! Do you know when?"

"Fantastic? It's completely insane! I mean, where am I going to put her? My spare room is tiny *and* full of junk! It seemed like such a great idea on the phone yesterday when I was upset. And look at me!" She joggled her tummy in her hands.

Claudine smiled, stretching out a long suntanned leg as she stood elegantly on the warm deck of her apartment.

"But you look fine. Your tan is gorgeous. Don't worry, we'll work it out. Do you fancy something sweet?"

"Yeah, OK."

Fiona was always ready to eat. Like the new-born chick in the nest, she always had her mouth open. Claudine's voice became muffled as she sang softly in the kitchen and Adriana's light giggling danced in the warm air as she played dollies on the balcony. Fiona looked across at her daughter's tanned, dumpy feet, poking from beneath her as she knelt, her chubby tanned legs folded under her. An immense feeling of love overwhelmed her as she scrutinised her small, discarded sandy sandals and her salt-tangled hair.

Claudine broke the spell, handing her a plate. "Gateaux. Always good for the soul." She sat down. "So? You are all set for the art class?"

Fiona grimaced, and then shrugged as she stretched her mouth as wide as possible ready for the cake. "As set as I'll ever be."

"We should leave soon – in about thirty minutes."

Fiona balanced her plate, on which sat the bulging pastry. She lifted it to her mouth and stuffed it in, the light buttery pastry crumbling as it mixed with the cool cream and strawberries. She chastised herself for falling off the diet wagon so easily, but realised it simply went along with her lifelong trend of debit-and-credit eating. Simply, if cake was lunch, then salad was dinner.

"And what will Helly say when she sees me?" she managed to say between bites. "My haircut's horrendous and my sagging arse is *not* what she's expecting to see. Especially coming straight from image-conscious London!"

Claudine giggled, "Yes, Xavier said the other day it looked like two badly parked Volkswagen Beetles."

Fiona's eyes widened in disbelief, "What did? My backside?"

Claudine nodded, grinning.

"Oh he did, did he? Right, I'm glad he finds it funny! And how many other people has he shared that sentiment with?"

Claudine was desperately trying to stop grinning and so pushed the majority of her cake in at once.

"Fuck you lot! You're all laughing at my expense. Just because you've got the hots for him. There's no need to laugh at *all* of his jokes, you know!"

Claudine composed herself, "I do not have the hots! He is a nice man, funny, but that's it. Just a friend."

"Oh come on," Fiona calmed a little. "If he suggested that you jump off the bridge, you'd at least lean on the railings. He was a Seagull Manager not so long ago and now he's a love-bird?"

Claudine stuck out her flaky-pastried tongue and Fiona mirrored her.

"At the end of the day, Fiona, I am suffering from single girl's sunburn. At this rate I will need a Do-It-Yourself bodybaster to oil my back. Just because you are off men, my love, it does not mean we all have to be ..."

"No, I'm sorry."

Fiona wished she could be more like Claudine. Luís hadn't wasted any time in finding a replacement so why couldn't she? She worried so desperately what effects a new man in *her* life would have on Adriana. She didn't want to confuse her, and yet she needed to feel like a woman too. Every time she met a new guy she became awkward and embarrassed and her mum was there on her shoulder, her conscience and opinions like a stuck record in her memory. She'd had a few dates since Luís' departure, but they'd all ended miserably. She'd been on a couple of dates with Xavier soon after Luís leaving. She hadn't wanted to but he'd coerced her, all in the name of 'I'm Only Being A Good Friend To You'. They'd sat in the fish restaurant and Fiona had listened to him ranting on about the numerous 'MILF's' that came in and out of his café bar.

"MILF's?" she'd queried at the time, still enjoying the way the candlelight disguised his acne-scarred skin. He'd grinned, his teeth polka-dotted with stray knobs of broccoli, and had replied, "Mums I'd Like to Fuck."

She'd gone straight off him.

"So," Claudine wiped her mouth and dusted the flaky pastry remains from her lap, "what about the job in Mango? It sounds great for you. I will look after Adriana for you. You might even get part-time. It is worth asking, no?"

"I don't know. Luís was furious even at the suggestion!"

"He is an arrogant pig though."

"Obviously, I know that. The trouble is, the jobs I'm trained to do have either already been wiped out by technology or they're on their way out."

"So that is it! Why don't you retrain? Do a course, Fiona. Learn a new skill ready for your new life. Luís cannot complain at that. You are not actually *working*. Just training to work."

"OK, so what will be the hot jobs for 2015? Plastic surgeon?"

"Yes, great idea!"

"No, Claudine, I was being sarcastic."

"Oh, but you're probably right. How about travel agent or psychologist? Computer expert?"

"Matchmaker maybe? Hopefully I'll do a better job than I did on myself. I'm even annoying when I'm sleeping according to Luís."

"What? How?"

"My snoring! He hated my snoring. But don't you hate being told you snore? What more offence can you cause than telling someone they're irritating when they're sleeping? We never really had a chance, did we?" She laughed at herself.

"No, seriously, Fiona, how about training as a travel consultant? Not an agent. Not in a high-street shop window. But a specialist Portuguese travel consultant? You would be great! You speak the language, you know the place. It is a *fantastique* idea!"

Fiona's mouth was stretched like a hammock between her two ears.

She really couldn't argue.

For once.

So, she had her first art class this evening.

She wasn't really into painting and hadn't held a proper artist's paintbrush since she was in her last two years at school. Claudine seemed so confident with the whole idea and so Fiona simply tagged along. She had worn the floral dress that hid all her lumpy bits and, on walking into the packed school hall, was glad of the security blanket of its bias-cut and colourful print. She wasn't completely fluent in Portuguese so didn't understand everything but managed to copy the rest of the class as they gathered A2 sized paper and clipped it onto their easels, mumbling between themselves. She hated feeling like the new girl, but lost herself in the anonymity of it all, hoping that everyone had noticed her glowing topped-up tan.

She watched as Claudine approached the tutor, pointed across to Fiona and nodded, smiling. Fiona stepped forward to introduce herself. She'd have been much happier leaving it all to Claudine, but didn't want to appear ignorant.

"'Ello, Fiona."

"Em, hi." She felt ditzy as she stepped awkwardly from foot to foot, beaming, unsure of what to say.

Claudine smiled and walked away, leaving them to it.

"You 'ave done art class before?"

"No. Well, not since school," Fiona gushed, taking in a million and one points of the tutor in micro-seconds. The misshapen toes of her shoes, the small hole in the ankle of her tights, her tweed skirt with the hem which had only slightly begun to fall down – right up to the mole on her chin and her long dark hair which was twirled and held in place by a single pin.

The tutor's voice bought her back to reality, "Perhaps you would like to model tonight? It often breaks ice for new students?"

Fiona looked around for Claudine, who was busy preparing her paints and easel. Before she could reply the tutor had caught her firmly by the elbow and was steering her into a side room.

"Now, remove dress and put on kimono." She eyed Fiona up and down as she frowned, "Mmm, I think it will fit you. Maybe too tight. Try anyway."

Fiona blushed as the door closed behind her, panic ringing in her ears as she cursed Claudine and her ideas, and hating herself for not having the confidence to walk away *now*, while she still could. She undid her dress and hung it on a hook that jutted from the door, sliding her arms into the silky kimono and double-fastening the flat belt securely. She sheepishly opened the door and stepped gingerly onto the cold, tiled floor. A half-moon of wooden easels surrounded her, strangers' faces poking around the sides as the tutor spoke loudly in Portuguese. She indicated a sumptuous chair, draped with a fuzzy-haired blanket-type thingy, which had been placed high on a table in the centre of the class. She pointed and smiled, indicating to Fiona to step up onto the table and sit on the chair. She searched the faces for Claudine, who she finally located, but couldn't quite figure her fretful expression.

Fiona clambered up onto the table and tried to appear comfortable in the slippery kimono as it stuck, full of static, on the hairy blanket, while she slid around inside it.

"Fiona, please? If you don't mind, please. Now, please."

The tutor had turned to Fiona, her eyebrows arched high in question. Fiona didn't get it. She was already blushing.

"Please?" once again the tutor asked.

And then realisation hit. She watched the tweed-suited woman as she tugged at an imaginary belt at her waist. They wanted her to remove the kimono.

"Oh, no. I couldn't! I'm sorry, but no. I mean, I just –"
She stood, the backs of her thighs pinching at the silky
kimono, giving the impression that it was wedged
between her bum cheeks.

"Now, not to be shy." The tutor smiled, obviously
hardened to rookies who weren't keen on flashing the
flesh. "It is good if you are shy. It breaks ice."

Fiona's face was burning, so hot that she feared that
her eyeballs would catapult out of her head and splat on
the windows across the room. She could feel her
burgundy glow as she stood and untied the loose belt,
feeling faint as she slipped the kimono off her arms. She
heard a snigger from across the room, only to see two of
the younger guys tittering at her. Then she remembered
her underwear! She was wearing her huge strapped,
'industrial' bra and her skimpy lace knickers that her
fleshy hips bulged over. She only had to look at the tutor's
face to realise that she wanted a nude pose.

"Holy shit!" she whimpered to herself, sitting back
down on the chair, wrapping the kimono around her,
feeling the burn right down her chest and remembering
the Persil white triangles that were etched across her
boobs, an embarrassing indication of her intense tanning
session.

"It's OK, Fiona," the tutor's voice cut the ice, "we have
all had to model for the group." As she spoke she twirled
her hand high in the air, indicating the old men and
women who were smiling and nodding, annoying the
fuck out of her.

Fiona wasn't so worried about them. But she was

worried about the three younger, and yes – attractive, guys who were smiling, paintbrushes held aloft, as they waited to see what Fiona was trying to hide.

Claudine cringed behind her easel, mouthing the words 'sorry' and 'I didn't know it was nudes!" to Fiona, looking every bit as bad as Fiona felt. Her pulse banging in her neck, she was reminded of Charley's 'topless' photo-session all those years ago. She recalled how envious she had always been of Charley's wild behaviour. Then she closed her eyes and thought back to Luís, how badly he'd treated her, how she'd struggled for the last year emotionally and financially, and with a deep breath she threw caution to the wind and threw off the kimono, whipped off her bra, flinging it behind her, feeling quite liberated as she did so. She neither noticed nor cared that it had landed on the hand of the mannequin in the corner.

She relaxed back onto the fuzzy blanket, the welt marks of her bra indented in red streaks beneath her boobs and up over her shoulders. She didn't care at that moment.

She would go so far as to say she wouldn't even worry if Luís walked in.

Chapter Thirteen

Helly nudged her way around Camden Lock Market half-heartedly, nonchalantly checking the crafts as she berated herself. She was lucky to have got the boys to football training this morning and had nearly been sick again when she'd swerved and careered along the road. Dan would have gone ballistic if he'd known. She'd had to dive into a café for the toilet and hadn't known whether to yodel into it or sit on it. She'd ended up doing both, to her horror. There'd been a queue the length of the Great Wall of China waiting to go in after her and her feet couldn't carry her away quick enough. The morning air felt chilly on her today, which she blamed on her low blood sugar, after her excesses the night before. Her Mongolian yak-hair scarf was wrapped around her neck twice and still hung weightily as it scraped her legs. The fluff tickled her fifteen-denier'd knees as they sat like two rock cakes above her knee-length boots, and she cursed herself for not wearing trousers. One of the mums, Martine, from the school was always friendly at the school-gates and had arranged with Helly to meet for Sunday morning coffee at eleven. Helly was grateful for the hand of friendship and was looking forward to someone to talk to. She'd already rung Claire and she'd agreed to run the shop for the day. Helly was now purely killing time prior to eleven o'clock. As she turned the corner for the runway of the next aisle of stalls she bumped straight into Martine, the school-mum she was meeting.

"Hey," Martine smiled, "are you OK? You look terrible."

"No. Not really." Her mobile trilled. "Sorry, I'll just get this."

"I'll go and order the coffees. Latte or cappuccino?"

Helly's stomach churned. "Ugh, latte, I suppose. Thanks,"

She whined into her mobile, already seeing that it was Charley on the other end.

"Jesus, you sound manky!" said Charley.

Helly groaned, "Make me feel worse, why don't you? I've got a terrible headache."

"Don't tell me about it! It must be the drink!" she joked, dripping in sarcasm.

"Oh, sorry," Helly shook her head, sorry for bothering her hapless sister. "Perhaps we'll talk later when you've sobered up!"

"Helly! I meant you! I was only messing though. Don't

tell me you're bollixed! At this hour?"

"For a change," Helly managed a miniscule smile. "What're you doing?" She heard laughter from Charley's end.

"I'm actually at work."

"Go 'way. You've gone in? On a Sunday?"

"Funny. OK, you've made your point. I've actually got loads to catch up on. Give me a ring later, yeah?"

"OK. I need to talk to you. I'll ring you about six."

"Make it after seven if you can."

"Why? Where you going?"

"I'm taking the dog for a walk."

Helly frowned, "Dog? You haven't got a dog."

"No, but you do."

"What?"

"Well, not exactly the dog, more the dog-lead."

Helly couldn't cope, "Oh Charley, what are you talking about?"

"It's my latest man-trapping trick. I tried the drop-your-shopping one last week, but it didn't steam my pudding. Not my style. I know men love ditzy and vulnerable, but I just felt like Mum."

Helly closed her eyes as she tried to concentrate.

"Helly, I went out with a carrier bag with holes in the bottom. On purpose! Go shopping, fill the bag and watch your purchases spill out onto the pavement. And watch the men fuss. It's great!"

"You're cracked. Are you that desperate? What about Kevin?"

"Kevin! He's history! Gone! You've heard of IBS, well,

I had IGS. Irritable Girlfriend Syndrome!"

Helly couldn't take it all in. "I need to sit down. I need coffee."

"OK," Charley knew the feeling. "I'll catch up later."

Helly remained silent.

"You OK, Hel?"

"No."

Charley was surprised to hear Helly's voice quiver as the tears came.

"I'm going to Portugal to see Fiona," she choked, "and I'm going this week. The sooner the better." Charley felt her words hang in the air heavily as she whispered through her tears, "Nicky's back."

And she hung up.

Charley knew it was hard to find a decent man, but she was of the mind-set that believes that when Cinderella left the Glass Slipper, it was no accident. She'd recently come up with a series of scams to lure the cute guys. And today was the I've-Lost-My-Dog plot.

She felt stupid, but only fleetingly. She supposed it was actually putting it into words that made her realise the daft scenario she was getting into.

She was going to take an empty dog-lead into Phoenix Park and just *watch* the cute guys offer their help. She knew it'd be great fun.

She was desperate to talk about it, and so with Helly hungover she decided to ring Fiona.

"So, yes, I'm going when I've finished this ad. It's just, you get a completely different crowd at the weekend."

"Is that so?" Fiona's voice was thick was sarcasm. She couldn't quite believe what her sister was actually planning on doing.

"Listen, if you were spending your days trying to conjure up lifestyle rhymes to advertise tampons, you'd do anything too." Her voice was drowned out by a passing bus as it splashed through shallow puddles.

The sisters laughed down the phone, both of them realising how they hadn't really laughed together for so long. They all needed a burst of fun really.

Charley added in, just for divilment, "It was all wasted on Kevin, you see. And there was I dying to get the chance to show off my playboy bikini wax."

"Charley! You never did!"

"I did too. I'm always in the beauty salon."

"You're so lucky. That's one of the reasons I want to go to London. It'd be so much easier to look after my health there."

"But why do you really want to leave Portugal? It must be fantastic being a beach bum, sand in your pants every day. Don't tell me – I bet you're slathering on the factor 40, have fabulous blonde highlights that are completely natural and your bikini doubles as your bra. I *bet* wearing shoes feels weird to you."

"Don't believe all the hype. It was like that when I first came here, but not any more. I spend my days taking Adriana swimming, or walking along the coast road to the lighthouse, or punching numbers into my bloody calculator. I'm forever struggling to pay the bills. If it wasn't for Claudine I'd be in a serious depression. I just really want to get out of here. Anyway, how about you? Are you really drinking as much as Helly says?"

"Oh, don't mind her! She's getting more and more like Mum. Don't worry about me, it's her we should be talking about. I never got to the bottom of her tears today, but she said 'Nicky's back'."

"Who? Nicky who?"

Charley realised instantly that she'd blabbed. Obviously Fiona had never been told about Helly's affair with Nicky – she realised that younger sisters rarely had the perceptions of the older ones. She thought quickly. "Oh, I don't know what she meant!"

Fiona continued, "Well, don't try and change the subject. How about the drinking?"

"Oh, give over! The evenings are so long and my social life is hectic."

"But she says you keep missing work?"

"She's a grass! Look, I'm like a celebrity: Wednesday is my Monday."

"You do know that chronic drinking is known to cause early menopause. It can also shrink your ovaries, interfere with orgasm. Amongst many other things."

"Bloody hell, now you really sound like Helly! It's just a fun thing to do after work – a stress-buster."

"Oh right. And you wouldn't think of starting yoga?"

Charley stuck her tongue out at the phone and cut the conversation short with a flippant remark. But as she put down the phone she realised that she hadn't been *completely* sober, any evening, for weeks.

The dog-lead felt daft in her hand as it swung aimlessly beside her. She'd deliberately worn her light summer dress and denim jacket and her chunky silver chain glistened nicely as it sat on her collarbone. The sunshine danced lightly through the trees and Charley crossed her fingers hoping that the showers would stay away. Three teenage girls 'whooped' as they skated past her clumsily, clutching at the air as they grasped for balance from each other. The diluted sunshine had bought out the joggers again, their bare, hairy legs catching Charley's attention. She simply couldn't concentrate on looking as if she'd really lost her dog while those toned muscles bulged, prominent under the tanned skin before her eyes. She forced herself back to the task in hand. She'd already decided that she'd call the missing hound Diego, on the basis that it'd be simple to remember if she imagined it was Helly and Dan's dog that she'd lost.

But still, it didn't sit right.

And she felt ridiculous.

"Diego! Dieeeegoooo!" she sampled the idea with a squeaky call. Her voice cut through the warm air, intruding on the ambience. An elderly couple, sharing a limp sandwich and a park bench, looked up at her. Stretching her face into an awkward smile she nodded in their direction. She called again, *"Diegooo! Here boy, Diego? Diego!"*

A tap on her shoulder made her jump. She turned to see two teenage boys wearing beanie hats and earphones.

"Lost your mutt?"

"Em, yeah." She nodded, holding the lead up, unsure

whether to tell them to feck off. She wasn't sure whether enlisting their help might attract more attention to the cause, or whether that would be a good thing or not.

"Want some help?"

"Oh. OK, yeah. Thanks. He's called Diego."

The taller of the two held out his palm. "It'll cost ya, mind."

She sneered, and went for option one. "Feck off, you little shits!"

They threw down their skateboards and whizzed off, laughing and jeering as they went.

She frowned, looking down at her Sophia Klokosalaki shoes, eyeing the delicate ankle straps and coquettish low heels. Taking a deep breath she stepped onto the soft muddy grass and sank slightly as she squelched toward the flower beds, wishing for Helly's floral Boden wellies.

"Diego!" She really meant it now, determined that she'd stay only fifteen minutes more before calling it a day.

A husky voice spoke so close to her ear that she felt the warmth on her neck. "Hey, missus. Lost something. Again?"

She spun around to see the curly-haired copper from the other night, his hands pushed deep into his jacket pocket and a cheeky smile plastered on his face.

His extremely good-looking face, but still.

"Yeah," she felt really stupid now, "I've, em, lost my dog."

"Your dog?" He looked wide-eyed as if he was having trouble getting it.

"Yeah! My dog. Diego."

"What kind of dog is he?"

"Oh, he's a … em. Well, he's a –" she looked down at her hands, desperate to think of something, "a boxer! Yeah, he's a boxer dog. Four years old. Beautiful."

He looked down at the dangling lead, "And you use a flimsy lead like *that* for a four-year-old Boxer?"

She hadn't thought of that.

"Yeah!" She forced the confidence out of her. "Well," she shrugged, "me ma bought it for me when he was a pup and he won't go out on anything else now. God love him. He's *really* fussy."

"I see. He loves it so much, he's run off?" He was speaking strangely to her, dragging each word out, making her feel like a right eejit.

"Yes." Sheepish was creeping in now.

"C'mon. I'll help you look."

"Thanks."

"So we're calling 'Diego'?"

"Yep."

"And your name is? Again?"

She grinned, flashing her white teeth with a sparkle in her eye, "No, it's not 'Again', it's Charley."

He extended his hand. "Charley, I'm Steve. You probably don't remember."

She tried really hard not to blush, "Steve. Yeah. Thanks."

Nick pounded the treadmill while watching the pert bums of the women on the exercise bikes. He felt odd. Apart from the fact that his insides shuddered with every strike of his striding feet and the cool, piped air was dehydrating his mouth, he realised that feeling a strong connection with Helly was one thing, but since she'd jumped on him in the back of the cab, things were now entirely different. He wanted her even more. Married women weren't his style and yet she had certainly stirred up something. Plucking at his towel as it dangled over the side bar he wiped his saturated face, sweeping the salty sweat from his eyes. He recalled that she'd told him she was going to Portugal and was desperate to remember whether he'd mentioned his sister in Lisbon. The chemistry between them was clouding his memory. And his judgement. Punching at the buttons to take it down to the cool-down of a walk he conceded that he must have mentioned it. After all, it wasn't every day that Portugal came up in conversation, unless one of his middle-aged business cronies was bleating on about golf and the Algarve. Helly both confused and yet intrigued him. He knew it'd take more to impress *her* than being able to julienne a carrot. He knew that generally women were looking for men who could fix a car *and* grill a steak for dinner. He wasn't sure how to pitch himself at Helly twelve years down the line.

Or even if he would.

But he really wanted her.

Steve had helped Charley look for a while, deciding finally to simply take her number and offer to report her missing dog when he went on duty later.

She'd flirted outrageously with him as she'd fumbled

for a pen, and then asked him for one. It had been great when he'd finally stopped a gorgeous executive-looking man for a loan of his pen. What an ego boost! They'd said their goodbyes by the lake and gone in separate directions, casting a look back at each other.

She picked absent mindedly at a loose flap of plastic that jutted from the side of her bus seat. She rarely got on the bus sober, but the 134 had virtually pulled up beside her as she'd rolled up the dog-lead and stuffed it into her denim jacket pocket on her way back to the DART. Delighted with herself, she sat on the top floor of the double-decker and watched the masses of people as they navigated around each other, ants busy finding their way through the maze. The spring evening air felt great now, the freshness in the fading sunshine suiting her mood. She'd always gone for dark men, and yet Steve wasn't her type. And yet he was. She was muddled and excited and felt ridiculous that, at forty, she was getting excited over a guy. The embarrassment factor was quite high too, what with the unfortunate mistake she'd made about 'losing' her car, and now the lost-dog-syndrome. He probably thought she was a chronic amnesiac; she supposed that was why he took her number rather than gave her his. And it was a bad omen, being monikered 'again' so soon into the relationship. A man sitting behind her stood abruptly and pressed the bell for the next stop. As the bus lurched to a halt he stumbled and sat on her lap, his bulk squashing her legs. It bought her back to reality as she realised this too was her stop. Smoothing her dress once again and refastening the buttons that were loosened, she clipped down the narrow stairs, stepping out into the cool evening air.

Fiona read to Adriana. The soft glow of her bedside lamp, crafted into the shape of a castle, gave the cosy room a warmth which made bedtime extra special. Small rectangles of orange light shone from the 'open' windows of the castle, making it one of Adriana's favourite things. Fiona loved this time together. Despite the dilapidated condition of her apartment she had made sure that Adriana's bedroom was perfect. It was all she could do to try and bridge the gap of their far-from-perfect lives. As she read from the Disney storybook she watched Adriana's large brown eyes blink, as she soaked in the magic of *The Little Mermaid*. As always their story time ended with tickles and nose-rubs and lots of hugs. It was the only time of the day that a ringing phone annoyed the life out of Fiona. It was their special time together, and it was precious.

"*Mummy, o telefone.*"

She smiled widely at her daughter, "I know, baby." She kissed her on the forehead, "You go to sleep for Mummy. I'll come back in to see you when I've finished."

"Mummy?" Adriana's soft voice called. Fiona turned at the doorway. "*Eu te amo, Mummy.*"

"I love you too, baby."

"Well, she sounded terrible." Fiona was telling Claudine about her phone call with Helly, whispering so as not to wake Adriana. "She was in an awful state." Claudine plaited her own hair lazily as Fiona spoke, "I couldn't get any sense out of her. She was just crying."

"Do you think it is her husband?"

"She didn't say. Although, the other day we spoke and she was giving out about him. But I suppose I'm really anti-men at the moment. As far as I can see, marriage turns people into tyrants or bores."

"You are still tainted after your Luís experience – and you have had a string of disastrous dates since then. But you could be right. I mean, why do people bother?" She paused as realisation dawned. "Why *did* you bother, Fiona?"

"I never married Luís! I wanted to. I would have done if he'd asked me. At least if I'd married him I'd be *entitled* to half of the house and our stuff! But it wasn't so much why I bothered, more why did I stay bothering. I think you stay in a shit, abusive relationship because you lose faith in yourself. At the end of the day, Adriana might not need a dad but she does need a father figure."

"That's why I am glad I am not a mummy."

"Well, I'm glad I am. I'd be lost without Adriana. It's just this place. I've got to get away from Luís, from here."

Charley had got in from her short walk from the bus stop via the off-licence. She'd thrown the dog-lead onto the kitchen worktop, wondering whether she should have 'weathered' it a little. It looked so gleaming and new and un-doggy. She was glad she'd kept the receipt; she might even get her €15 refunded. She'd been thinking on the bus, hoping that Steve wouldn't be too aware of her address. If he realised she was living in a flat it'd completely kibosh the concept of her having a dog. Grabbing a bottle of red, a corkscrew and an enormous glass she carried the ensemble into her bedroom and poured a huge glass of wine as she logged onto the internet. Glued to the screen she gulped mouthfuls of the fruity, rich drink as she lazily checked out 'Google' for the correct procedure for reporting lost dogs to the police. She wasn't entirely sure that Steve was being 'professional' by taking her phone number, but then, she didn't really mind too much. It was only then she noticed the twenty-five emails waiting to be read, and she felt excited. Scanning through the names of 'sent by' she realised that they were all from her family and friends. Worst still they were mostly titled 'DOG MAY BE MAN'S BEST FRIEND, BUT WOMAN'S IS DEFINITELY 'THE RABBIT'', which was the subject of the dildo-inspired email she'd teasingly sent to Johnny Quinn. She stared, the realisation sinking in quicker than the wine. Holding the glass to her mouth she hid behind it as she filled her mouth and clicked on the message from her mum and dad. As she swallowed she closed her eyes in dread.

She prised them open and read it.

CHARLEY. CAN'T IMAGINE WHY WE'VE GOT THIS FROM YOU. IT'S BAD ENOUGH GETTING THAT DISGUSTING PORNY JUNK MAIL, BUT THIS BEATS ALL. HOPE IT'S NOT FROM YOU. YOUR FATHER WOULD GO BALLISTIC, SO I'LL DELETE IT AND DENY ALL KNOWLEDGE.

MUM

BY THE WAY, WHAT'S THIS ABOUT RABBITS BEING WOMAN'S NEW BEST FRIEND? ARE DOGS SUDDENLY OUT OF

FASHION? AND WHAT ARE 'LOVE BALLS'?

She quickly clicked out of it and onto the next one, from Kevin.

CHARLEY

THERE'S NO NEED TO RUB IT IN. YOU'RE CRUEL AND CHILDISH TO SEND ME THIS. I HOPE YOUR AGE CATCHES UP WITH YOU SOON. YOU'RE HEADING FOR TROUBLE KEEPING ON THIS WAY.

SORT YOUR LIFE OUT AND DON'T BOTHER CONTACTING ME AGAIN.

YOU'RE A SAD ACT.

KEVIN

As she continued reading she cringed at the realisation that she'd replied to Johnny Quinn's email as REPLY TO ALL rather than simply REPLY. And now everyone had read her saucy, rude and extremely sexually teasing e-mail.

"Dammit!" she spat as she grasped her wineglass quickly, causing the burgundy liquid to splosh over the edge and all over her dress. "Everyone I know got that sex-filled email!"

"Mum, it's only an idea." Fiona was exasperated, regretting ever mentioning the travel consultancy idea to her mother, but forcing herself to talk about anything rather than mention how excited she'd felt after her topless stint at the art classes. Thankfully the tutor hadn't protested when she'd kept on the knickers – there was no way *they* were coming off.

"But Fi, I'd help you out. I've been to Future-ventura!"

"Mum, with respect. It takes more than a two-week

package tour to make you an expert."

"Nonsense. Once you've seen the run of the place! So, if you set up this travel yoke you'll be staying in Porcheegal then, love? So do you think you and Luís would make it up then?"

"No, Mum. He's a complete pig." She walked into the bathroom as she spoke, squirting an over-generous blob of apricot exfoliator into her palm, and hooked the phone in the crook of her neck as she made circular shapes on her face, neck and chest.

"Honestly, Mum, forget about that travel idea. I really want to get out of this country."

"So you'll be bringing Adriana back to Ireland then? Oh, how exciting! It'll be lovely having one of my grand-children around. What with Helly's two being rooted in London, though God only knows why she wants to be there."

Fiona panicked. "No, Mum. If I'm going anywhere I'll probably head over to Helly's for a while."

She heard the silence roar until she couldn't bear it, and continued,

"*If* I go anywhere, Mum. Luís is still being difficult about things."

"Oh, pet. Think carefully before you do anything dras-tic. Is there really no chance you'll get back together?"

"No, Mum. Bye, Mum. Love ya."

Fiona shook her head as she disconnected the call, resting the phone on the tiled windowsill as she rinsed the grainy particles off her face with cold water.

It was hopeless trying to talk to her mother about

things. She always got the wrong end of the stick. She was aware of the impact that age was having on her parents, probably more aware than Helly and Charley. It was no secret that the seventies was an age where genders began to converge. She knew that it wouldn't be long before her mother would begin to sprout facial hair and Dad had already started to become easily upset if his routine was forced to change. OK, so it was irritating how they both liked to be *days* early for appointments but at least she was glad that they weren't yet at the stage where they could have eloquent discussions about recent operations. Thankfully, her parents both had good health.

She pulled the cord, turning off the bathroom light, her scrubbed face feeling a little tight, and checked in to see that Adriana was still asleep. She was a dream; her eyes like a doll's, closed when she lay down and springing open when awake.

As Fiona dragged at the shutters across the open windows she mentally sped forward a decade and imagined the puberty years. Fiona was certain they'd be in London by then. She hoped they would, although the transition from a pre-pubescent girl galloping wildly around the house like a horse and neighing, to a teenager who'd suddenly taken to practising snogging her pillow would be a strange one, wherever they lived.

Stretching her legs in her warm bed she scanned the papers once again. She was becoming obsessed with London, despite the reports of congestion charges and violence. She was aching to try the new celebrity haunts and had fully subscribed to the 'Cool Britannia' brigade.

She'd read how Primrose Hill was now patrolled by paparazzi and Hampstead Heath had become the new Brit-pack's picnic retreat. She was desperate to try the pubs in Chelsea and SW3 as she'd read that Madonna and Billie Piper all loved the roof terraces there. She'd already heard about the new gastropub in N1 where Jude Law, Johnny Lee Miller and Sean Pertwee frequented. And then there was the Primrose Hill gastropub – she wasn't entirely sure what a gastropub was, but it sounded fab – favoured by Kate Moss, the Gallagher brothers and Sadie Frost.

As she wiggled further beneath the light cotton covers even the bed moaned and she was reminded of her excess weight. She was resigned to the fact that she was one of life's hamsters, always a little paunchy in the face and simply *guaranteed* to get a double chin and disappearing eyes long, long before she'd worked up a spare tyre. She was a Renée Zellweger when she wanted to be a J-Lo, the owner of the platinum of all fats, that smooth, mocha and toned Latina fat. She knew the difference between good and bad fat. Good fat meant plenty of boob and ample hips with those demon extra inches in all the right places. She'd read that it suggested an active sex life, wealth, and never, *ever* settled on cheekbones, collar bones or hourglass proportions.

"Shit," she cursed, "I can't even have the luck to have the right kind of bloody fat!"

She tugged at the light switch and snuggled down, fidgeting in the bed space. She still hadn't got used to sleeping alone, but with her mum acting as her conscience there was no sign of any company during the night, so she figured she'd have to get used to it. The muffled music from the bar down the street snaked in through her slatted shutters. She was kept from sleep by the sounds of the Bee Gees and realised that Joao was having another of his seventies revival nights. She'd gone out with Joao too. Only once. Once was more than enough. He was a nice guy, a great landlord, but a crap date. He wore glasses. Big deal. It was as run-of-the-mill as saying he had arms and legs. Fiona had no preference one way or the other when it came to glasses. But the date had started badly. He was late. And he only lived downstairs. The threat of being stood up by someone who only lived downstairs was deeply distressing, but once he'd called up to her window she'd cheered up, even taking delight in the Romeo-and-Juliet-style beckoning. Joao had been endearingly self-effacing and interesting, regaling Fiona with his life history. No, really, she *did* want *all* the details. No, *really!* He told her how he'd once lived in Birmingham and had worked as a Samaritan and a builder, and even for the hygiene department of the local council. She hadn't been sure whether she fancied him, but after they'd staggered down the main street together, in the heady, warm early hours, the sounds of the crickets an exotic percussion to their stroll, she thought it might be worth sleeping with him. Just so that Luís wasn't her last. Just to have it on record that she *did* have a life after Luís. But it had all gone wrong once they'd got into his bedroom. She'd felt like a contestant on *Mr and Mrs* as they'd fussed and undressed either side of the bed, her grappling with the combs that held her hair up and him wrestling with his shoe-laces. And then they'd got into bed. Side by side. Very polite. And he'd kept his glasses on.

"Don't you take your glasses off in bed?" She had tried to sound casual, as if she were asking a question as simple as 'Will I go on top, or will you?' but she hadn't banked on his reply.

"I do," he'd smiled, already rubbing her shoulders and moving his hands swiftly down towards her bare breasts, which she was desperately trying to keep hidden beneath the light cotton sheets, at least until the lights were out. "I do, usually," he'd wheezed, "but I like to wear them during sex. I find it a turn-on. You know, the naughty secretary thing?"

She'd been puzzled. "Shouldn't that be *me* wearing them then?"

To which he'd looked slightly embarrassed and had shrugged, smiling, "I know, but I like them."

Fiona knew there and then that the chemistry had fizzled out. If there was any to begin with she wasn't sure, but somehow she felt instantly sober and wanted to be out of there. She'd cajoled him, buying time, "Just take them off for a second. I'd like to see you without them."

It had been the worse thing she could have done. Without the camouflage of the specs his eyes were so close together she thought he was a Cyclops. And so it had been another embarrassing situation where she'd had to bale out, making excuses that she wasn't ready for this as she quickly pulled on her trousers, putting her two legs in the one as she hurried to scuttle out of there.

And so now, in the quiet of her warm room, she listened to Joao's music and watched as the insides of her eyelids ran a clip of her teenage years. She could remember as if it were yesterday how they'd queued around the block in the wind and rain to see *Grease*. Soaked to the skin they'd endured sticky seats, the tinny sound and theatres full of cigarette smoke to watch Olivia Newton John go from ugly duckling to poodle-haired sex-bomb. And then there were the gangs of schoolgirls suffering from Pink Lady Syndrome as the boys fought with their James Bond envy versus T-Birds cool.

She didn't stop the tears as they gathered in the corners of her closed eyes while she mourned a life that she'd enjoyed and that had gone. She fell asleep with damp eyes.

Chapter Fourteen

The next morning was bright and sunny, the first signs of spring blossom, the pinks and whites, polka-dotting the sides of the streets and covering the ugly white circles of chewing gum on the pavements. Charley got up early, still aggravated at her email mishap, and dressed in her grey trousers and white T-shirt. Securing a leather bootlace necklace, from which hung a polished dark stone which rested elegantly on her collarbone she ran a brush through her long hair and then grabbed her mobile. She wanted to walk today. Winston had told her about a gospel CD that she simply had to buy from HMV on Grafton Street and her head needed the fresh air.

She was still berating herself. As she walked she rang

work and made a compromise to go in later. Her priorities had to lie with her family and she was determined to sort out her sisters, although she hadn't planned on being distracted by the window display in Zara in her bid for fitness. Humming gospel tunes, willing her voice to improve, she punched in Helly's name into her phone. It began ringing.

Helly answered, her voice low and subdued,

"Helen. We need to talk."

"Oh Charley," she whinged, "I've made a proper fecking eejit out of myself."

"Excellent!" Charley sat down on a low brick wall and crossed her legs. "Can't wait to hear all about it."

Fiona was stressing about her flagging, sagging appearance. She loved the winter months in Cascais when it was still warm, but 'the done thing' to still wear polo necks and cord jackets. So now things were hotting up and even hardened Lisboetas had started to strip off. It wasn't such a problem on the beach, more when she was walking around the shops or in town. Her sub-zero self-image had plummeted further with the impending arrival of Helly. Despite her tan, Fiona felt pale in comparison to the locals. She could have a fridge *crammed* with low-fat meals but still wouldn't lose a pound.

Yet to the many women and children standing by the kiosk that sold the coffee and cakes, Fiona, Adriana and Claudine looked the very image of serenity as they strolled in the morning sunshine. Fiona swung Adriana up onto a stone wall beneath the heavily scented orange trees as she secured her sandal strap for the hundred and third time. Her exasperated expression was hidden as she turned her back to the crowds. Claudine wandered across the street to admire the window display in Mango, appreciating how they'd incorporated the high wrought-iron balcony in the overall shop window effect. The bright sunshine reflected sharply off the glazed, green tiles that fronted the impressive shop and Claudine regretting yelling at Xavier now yearned for another job, so she could afford the new summer fashions that had been imported.

Fiona hauled Adriana off the wall, the slow pace of life irritating her. They'd spent most of the morning on the beach and she'd felt slightly guilty as the grains of soft white sand grated between her toes, especially after Charley accused her of being a beach bum and her denying it. She wondered whether she needed to look at the place with fresh eyes – perhaps she wasn't appreciating what she had here. The turquoise sea, scattered with orange buoys, lapped, whispering its way up on to the sand daily, and how she loved those sounds.

They'd wandered up to the imposing Cascais Village Shopping Centre, its tinted blue windows standing grand against the backdrop of the lush trees and tiled bungalows. Fiona tensed, as usual, at her close proximity to Luís' house that stood opposite. The pain was deepened by the fact that it had been her home too, and now she knew Bella was enjoying the high-walled enclosure and enormous swimming pool. She cringed to think that Bella was sleeping in their bed – *her* bed – and wondered what changes the bitch had made.

Claudine clasped Adriana's warm, soft hand as they hopped on the small escalator just inside the main doors of the Shopping Centre, fully prepared for the tug and mini-tantrum as they bypassed the 5-screen cinema. Adriana was always begging to go to the cinema, but Fiona simply couldn't afford it. Instead they window-shopped in H&M and Throttleman, dreaming and fanta-sising about being able to buy something, knowing full well if they could, they'd have absolutely nowhere to go to wear it. Most of their time was spent in Lara Millani as they stroked, fingered and examined the fantastic soft leather shoes and boots. Adriana soon began to whinge, fed up and keen for something to eat, and tugged Claudine to go up to the Food Court on the 3rd floor. Fiona's inventive and coercing skills, which were second nature since she'd became a mum, scurried to the fore-front as she managed to encourage her out of the shopping centre and along the white and grey cobbled winding streets, back to their favourite café on Rua da Palma, where a sardine salad cost only €4 to tourists, but a friendly €2 to Fiona, Claudine and Adriana. Navigating the scattered al fresco diners that were bunched in clus-ters along the swirly cobbled avenues Fiona quickly grabbed Adriana, dragging her backwards into a slippery shop front, where a woman knelt as she hand-scrubbed the marble tiles. A kingfisher blue motorised trike wailed as it approached them, much too fast for the pedestri-anised street and everybody froze as it came dangerously close to clipping Fiona and Adriana.

"You pig!" Claudine shouted at the swiftly disappearing trike, its buzzy rattle now an octave lower.

Joao ran out from his café and rubbed Fiona's arm. She couldn't help but notice how great he looked in his crisp white shirt and smart trousers.

"You OK?"

She was shaken *and* stirred, trying desperately to keep the tears from her eyes.

"Yes, thank you, Joao. Who was that?"

He shrugged, unable to look her in the eye. "I did not see. Only heard. You are OK though?"

She was far from OK, but was determined not to show it. She'd said before that it'd take more than one of Luís' sidekicks to frighten her. She despaired at his childish behaviour, sick of his control over Cascais, irritated that his financial status meant more than his lack of humanity.

"Yes, I am fine. Are you all right, baby?" Fiona crouched, making eye contact with Adriana who was grinning, excited by the fiasco. "Silly lady on the bike, Mummy. Mummy? I'm hungry, Mummy."

"Come on, Claudine," Fiona exhaled deeply, puzzled at why Adriana thought it had been a woman, "let's go and get some lunch."

They walked on, passing once-whitewashed buildings that now stood derelict, the brightly painted yellow, terracotta and blue buildings that had been converted into small apartments, internet cafés and then intermittent remains, crumbling walls covered in graffiti. Every avenue off the snaking street was marked with a tiled name plate, decorated in blue, yellow and red mosaic. The filigree balconies remained suspended along the length, sometimes adorned with deep green shrubs, otherwise rusting, rickety and holding on by a thread. As they passed Largo da Praia da Rainha she realised that she was carrying an empty purse. Not unusual, but this time it was completely empty.

"I need to get some money from the bank."

"Money! I did not think you had any money in the bank." Claudine was surprised that she even *thought* she had any.

"I've got €10. You two sit and order. I won't be a minute."

Adriana squealed as she saw Vitor, dressed like a 6' penguin, cockily strutting, menus in hand, as he touted for business. The café was in a line of three and so competition was rife, but fun.

"Vitor!" She ran toward him and he placed down the menus and swung her into the air.

"Adriana. You getting more pretty every day." He frowned at her, teasingly, "Are you sure you are not ten already? You are very beautiful little girl and so grown up now."

"No," she giggled, "I'm not ten. But Mummy says I'm pretty too."

"Ah, she is very, very clever lady."

Claudine dragged out a chair noisily and sat down at a table, lighting up a cigarette. The Banco Espirito Santo was beside the café and as Fiona looked over toward Vitor he caught her eye and winked at her. It warmed her how fond Vitor was of Adriana and knew that he'd often got scowled at for playing with her rather than serving his patient customers. Claudine ordered three sardine salads and as she was doing so didn't notice Fiona muttering at the ATM machine. Fully aware that she was in full view of the lunch-time diners, she was deflated to see 'nil balance' being flashed in neon before her eyes. She was surprised that the machine hadn't copped on to her at this stage and was programmed to burst into a rendition of 'You Can't Always Have What You Want' or 'Dream'. She began to panic that Claudine may have already ordered their lunch, so she quickly ordered a mini statement. It was at least something to stuff into her purse. Mentally scowling at the machine as she walked away, she was acutely embarrassed as she plastered on a face with no obvious expression.

She slumped down opposite Claudine.

"Looks like it'll be lunch at home."

"Why?"

"No money. I was mistaken."

"Shit! I've already ordered our salads."

"Well, I'll just have to go in and tell him to cancel them. It's only bloody sardines. Hardly as if they won't be needing them in the next twenty minutes!"

Fiona strode into the dark café, finding it hard to re-adjust her eyes after the brilliant sunshine. She heard Adriana giggling and blinked repeatedly until she could make out her daughter playing a game with three coins with Vitor.

"Mummy!"

Vitor turned and stood up. "Fiona, sorry. She is such lovely child."

"No, no, no bother." Fiona shook her head, dying inside at the prospect of having to cancel their food. "Look, Vitor. The order for three salads. I need to cancel them. I'm sorry."

"Oh, you have problem?" He looked extremely concerned, his kind, brown eyes wide.

"No, no problem. I have forgotten that I need to be home early. Sorry, Vitor."

"Oh come, Fiona," his tone was warm as he playfully pinched her on the arm, "you can spend ten minutes to eat. It is important you eat."

She flushed, embarrassed at the discussion about food. Awkwardly she looked down at herself and said, "Oh, I don't think it'll kill me. I could do with losing some weight."

"Not at all," he spoke deeply, "I will not accept your answer. Please, go sit down and I will bring your salads."

"But –"

"No accept! My love, you are friend. Adriana is friend. Please, you take your lunch here on me. I no accept your reply."

Fiona felt the tears rush to her eyes, desperate for some TLC from the kind Vitor. "You are a lovely friend, Vitor. Thank you."

She smiled at him, overwhelmed by his gesture, even if it was only for €6 worth of sardine salads. After the scare with the trike on the main street earlier she was starting to think she'd become paranoid about everyone in Cascais being on the side of Luís.

Amid the clatter of cutlery, the wafts of cigarette smoke and the smell of garlic cooking, they tucked into their unusually large salads.

"You know," Fiona remarked as she cut the metallic, shiny sardine, "food really does taste so much better when someone else cooks it. Why is that?"

Claudine shrugged, her mouth full, as they smiled at each other.

Fiona continued, "Who gives a damn, anyway. Let's just enjoy it."

"Yes," whispered Claudine, "especially as it is freebie."

"What's a freebee?" Adriana shouted.

"Sssh," they both gestured, trying to keep the food in their mouths while they laughed.

Three young mums walked along the seafront with their children and Fiona looked up at the sounds of buggies being pushed along, the vibration of the wheels on the cobbles. She used to love wheeling Adriana on the pinks, yellows and greys of the cobblestones, her small voice vibrating as she 'aahhhhh'd with glee. The comparison between those happy times when they'd lived in Luís' fine, huge house and her pathetic lifestyle now made her feel extremely sad. She had only recently come to terms with the fact that Luís had been probably already seeing Bella before she herself had left the imposing six-bedroomed house, and that she'd been living a lie for quite a long time.

"I can't wait to see Helly. I can't wait to talk her into letting me stay with her back in London."

"But what about Luís? He won't let you." Claudine crunched through a mouthful of olive-oiled lettuce.

Fiona ignored her. "You'll have to come and see me, Claudine. You'll love it. The London Eye, Tower Bridge lit up blue at night, the neons of the West End."

"Don't you think you are gun-jumping? Luís has said he will not let you go."

"Gun-jumping?" Fiona sniggered. "I think you mean jumping the gun."

"So? It's the same thing!"

"Helly will help me work a way around it." Fiona had finished her salad and was leafing through Claudine's CARAS magazine, delighting at the wicked close-ups of celebrity spots, cellulite and bad-hair days.

She frowned in the intense sunlight, blinded by the stark white page, and popped on her mirrored sunglasses. "Does an eyelid tuck really count as surgery?"

"Fiona. This is ridiculous. You are beautiful. Why mutilate yourself? You will only end up losing respect for all things natural."

"Claudine, it's 2005! Wake up and smell the Perlane."

"If your surgeon has a bad day at work you will be wearing it for the rest of your life."

Fiona gazed up at the sky as she daydreamed. "I don't know why, but sucking and tucking really appeals lately. I've tried dieting, anti-ageing creams and cellulite lotions. I'm not getting any younger."

"You 'ave more important things to be worrying about."

Fiona ignored her. "I'd kill for lipo on my tummy and

legs. You know, the lunch-time facelift may still be some years away but I've read that the lunch-time wrinkle-filler has arrived. Dermal fillers are the new needlework. It fills all the lines."

"I have heard all about it. In France they call it 'soft surgery'. My sister has had it."

"My God! You never said. What did she think of it?"

"She actually said there was little pain, little blood and little mess. It just plumped up her skin."

"Fantastic. Just get me back to London and I'll work all hours God sends. I don't want anything drastic, just a subtle glow where people just think I'm looking good lately."

"So when does your sister arrive?"

"Tomorrow. Coming with me to collect her from the airport?"

"Love to. I could do with a day in Lisbon."

It had been a living nightmare for Charley in Zara. She'd pulled a pair of knee-length boots onto her normally slim calves, confidently pulling the boot on and tugging the zip up. Terror had struck when, two thirds up her leg, the zip had stuck. A crowd of fellow assistants had been called in to help the impatient snooty cow that was 'looking after' Charley, although she used the term loosely. She'd been mortified, twenty minutes later, when the manager had appeared with a pair of scissors and had wrestled with the zip. There was nothing less funny than getting your calf stuck in a €500 boot that you were just trying on for fun!

Flopping down on the settee in the pub she texted Helly.

Her phone bleeped with a swift reply and, as she checked it, it read,

'How do hedgehogs know when they're at the top of a hill? Do they know it's safe to start rolling?'

Charley was no fool. She knew something had happened between Helly and Nicky but couldn't quite put her finger on it. She had little doubt that Helly had spent the entire day cooking chillies, spag bols and curries ready for freezing ready for her imminent departure to Fiona's. Despite her planning she could only imagine the nightmare that Dan was going through this evening – the night before Helly would be leaving them for a week.

I was choking up as I kissed the boys in bed tonight.

The truth is, I'm torn apart at the prospect of leaving them for a whole week.

I feel like shit.

The house is completely silent with sleep and I managed not to cry as Dan snuggled up to me in bed, whispering how much he'd miss me and how we must spend more time together. He even said he'd like to talk to me about maybe starting to try for a daughter when I get back. He's sure that a week apart will really build it up for us.

He says he's hardly able to keep his hands off me now. Christ knows what he'll be like after a week though.

I feel so sad and rotten.

It shouldn't be like this.

Should it?

Perhaps it'll do me good to get away for some time to think about what I've done.

Or what I'm going to do.

Chapter Fifteen

Charley hollered the air from her lungs at an impressive rate as she sang as loud as physically possible without straining something.

And she still couldn't hear herself over the speakers.

She had stayed in O'Riordan's pub for a couple of hours and had managed to write a fab new ear-wax-cleaner jingle, with the help of the lush in the corner and the cute barman. She'd taken great delight in ringing in work to let them know she wouldn't be in today, that she had signed off the ear-wax job. But while on the phone she had been cajoled into helping out a friend of a friend of a work colleague and had allowed herself to be set up on a last-minute blind-date for the evening.

So now, hopping and wiggling around to the music in her bedroom she felt a new lease of life, as she shoe-horned herself into her burgundy wrap-around dress. She knew she looked good. As usual she wrapped it tight as possible, making sure it clung to every curve. Her dark hair shone and swung weightily as she twisted and turned to the music. Stopping in her tracks she moved closer to the mirror, irritated at the way her fringe was starting to lift.

"Bloody cow's-lick!" she cursed to her reflection, grabbing a tub of Extra Hold Wax and scooping a large gloop into her palm.

She was excited about her blind date – especially at such late notice. She didn't usually 'go blind' but had recently blurted at work, "I've gone through half of my life without sex. I don't intend to go through the other half without it," which had unleashed a flurry of suggestions, friends and fourth cousins-once-removed who would be 'just great' for Charley. And so she was booked up for the next few weeks. And she was really looking forward to it all. She was sure she'd heard them placing bets in the toilets as they wagered her chances with each of the nominees, but where she had once been cautious with regard to blind dates, she had offered to go on this one as a favour for a colleague. All she'd been told was that his name was Barnie, he was a second-cousin of Sorcha from Accounts, and he was an actor. Of course, the squeals in the office had ricocheted off the filing cabinets as they'd teased her about him. Maria from Marketing had cackled that maybe with a name like Barnie she could expect a huge purple dinosaur, like the kids' TV character. And how they'd laughed.

But a huge, purple 'dinosaur' was exactly what she got. Barnie wasn't so much an actor, as an out-of-work actor.

Big, *big* difference.

His tall, imposing frame had been impressive from behind, but when he'd turned at the bar and revealed his jelly-belly as it wobbled beneath his ill-fitting shirt, his bulbous purple nose and acne-scarred skin she'd nearly choked. Her mind raced to figure what parts he might act, how he'd be typecast. Spontaneously she came up with two options, either the Evil Ugly Baddie In A Secret Agent Film or the Gormless Eejit That Nobody Likes In *Fair City*. And then there was the not-so-small matter of his thrown-together ensemble. Red trainers, cream combats and a short-sleeved shirt. He'd looked delighted to meet her. Hardly surprising. Charley noted his my-ship's-just-come-in smile. He stepped forward to shake her hand, and surprised her by kissing the back of it instead.

She knew instantly the whole thing was a mistake.

"You look beautiful," he'd intoned. "I've got us a table for nine."

She discreetly checked the clock behind the bar and realised she had an hour to kill with him. "Great," her smile slipped much quicker than her knickers usually did.

She hadn't realised he'd meant nine *people*.

As they'd bustled in through the bright red doors of Tex A Go-Go, Barnie pushing himself forward, leaving the door to swing back in her face, she had cringed at the crowd of anoraks who were waving frantically from a centre table. She had really, really plastered the false smile on as she'd been introduced to Izzy, Noddy, Ollie, Chrissy, Sky, Kenyo and Noah, all of whom were also out-of-work actors and spare-time kite-flyers.

As she pushed her chips around the plate she despaired at how the phrase 'out-of-work' actor meant that she was dining in the overdone Tex A Go-Go rather than the Shelbourne. This wasn't what she'd expected. Her burgundy dress was more fitting for a place where simply removing a cork triples the price.

Despite his alarming appearance, his charismatic presence was appealing. At least it seemed to be appealing to Izzy, Chrissy, Ollie, blah blah! As he gabbled on about his favourite hobby, aside from himself, she ignored the mundane references to their kite-flying fetishes. Picking up only the odd word here or there she stared over his shoulder at the metallic prints of Marilyn Monroe, Clint Eastwood and Rock Hudson as she feigned interest.

"Stunt kites . . . ultra-light weight fabrics . . . powerful quad line and dual line."

"Mmmm, right. Oh I see, yeah," Charley humoured them.

"And then . . . parafoil kites pull along . . . roller-blades or surfboards . . ."

"Look," she interrupted, resting a hand on his knee, "fancy a club?"

"A club?" He looked as if she'd asked him to sell a kidney on Ebay.

"Yeah," she shuffled, tugging on her jacket and grappling for her bag, "this really isn't my scene."

"Oh, OK then. Where did you have in mind?"

She looked him up and down, checking out his crumpled combats and Nike footwear. "Oh, I don't think trainers and bottle of water will get you in. Looking like that, you're going to get short shrift from the false eyelashes at the door."

She'd hoped that might deter him. She was having second thoughts, but he seemed keen.

"Oh, let's try anyway. We'll find somewhere. What do you reckon, everybody?"

As they discussed the idea at length, she unclipped her handbag, rooting in the depths to check her mobile.

1 MISSED CALL stared at her from the display. Hurriedly she pressed the buttons to check who she'd missed only to see *NO NUMBER*. As she fired the mobile back into her bag, it rang again. She grabbed it.

"Hello?"

She heard Steve's husky voice. And just when she'd begun to write him off for not ringing her. Barnie and Noah were counting out coins on the table as they attempted to split the bill to the last half-cent, and so she stood, taking her bag with her, and went outside to take the call.

"Jesus, I'm bored shitless, Steve ... yeah, bloody Barnie! Don't laugh .... No, I don't know what I was thinking of .... I was set up! Yeah, I wasn't counting on an evening of *whine* and dine .... Look, great, I'll meet you in half an hour ..... No, outside Madame Ya Ya's ..... Steve, you're a lifesaver ..... See you then! Bye."

Excuses were no problem to Charley, who had always been particularly inventive in getting out of something she wasn't happy with. She was sure that Barnie and his boring buddies weren't pining for her, that her vacant chair had already been pushed out at a sharp angle as they'd tucked in closer to each other around the table.

Lighting up a cigarette, she stood by the O'Connell Bridge, stepping from one high-heeled shoe to the other as she waited for Steve. She checked her watch. She'd been waiting for nearly an hour and there was still no sign of him. And she couldn't even ring him, as his number hadn't been logged on her mobile. She leaned against the wall, trying her hardest *not* to look like a prostitute. She closed her eyes and breathed deeply, drawing in on the cigarette again as she tried to calm herself. Her thoughts drifted to Helly, as she suffered from PNS. She smiled at the irony – where she usually had PMS, she was now suffering from PNS – Post-Nuptial Syndrome. They'd used to enjoy swapping boyfriend horror stories, and now it was all in the past. She hated the way her sisters lectured her, as if *she* was the one in the wrong. As if *she* was the stupid one, for going out and having fun, while they tended to their 'men' and their sad house-wifey lives. Helly and Dan had been heading towards 'nauseating-couple-of-the-year' for ages, which had started with their 'cute' joint email. Charley had roared when Helly had sent her an email from *danandhelly@dono.com*, and had laughed even more when the mail had mentioned how they'd been shopping together for a garlic-crusher. Charley very rarely got a pang of yearning for someone to accept her as she was, someone to grow old with, but she had to admit the advent of her fortieth birthday was rattling her.

Three hours later Charley was throwing shapes as she

danced alone in Bar Cuba, her red wrap-dress askew, revealing much too much boob and way too much leg. She'd finally given up waiting for piss-taker Steve and hadn't noticed her phone illuminating, flashing and ringing frantically in her bag. For the fifth time. She was now on another planet and wanted nothing to do with the waster as she rubbed up against the men and women who danced their cares away. She'd got in with a crowd whose severe lack of technique was made up for by their over-enthusiasm. She tried desperately not to dance like her mother. She knew by midnight that she'd never make it to the 6am closing time and so left the club alone and began to stagger towards home, muttering to herself as she tugged her dress back into shape. Passing the shop-fronts, the homes to the homeless, their greasy woollen blankets twitching oddly, she seemed oblivious to the dangers of walking through Dublin alone – at night. She stepped on crumpled McDonald's wrappers, kicking aside the discarded empty beer bottles, ignoring the hedges and flower-displays littered with cans and rubbish. A car pulled up alongside her. She continued walking without a sideward glance. She might be drunk, but she wasn't stupid. A voice called out into the noisy, busy night, asking for directions.

"Feck off!" she snapped. "Buy a fecking map like every-one else. What do I look like, a fecking tourist guide!"

"No, darlin'," an irritated voice shouted back, "you look like a washed-up old lush! Get a life!"

She gave a great 'two fingers'.

Chapter Sixteen

Helly felt like a million dollars and absolute crap, both at the same time. The Air Portugal flight was virtually empty and she had reclined her navy blue leather seat to its fullest, as she stretched out and looked out of the small rectangular window. She felt as if she were floating on her back, above the clouds. The book she'd bought sat untouched on her lap as she looked out at the clear blue sky and the carpet of cotton-wool cloud that lay below them as they flew out of London. Her eyes still stung from the tears she'd shed as she'd clutched onto her family and said her goodbyes, although that had been three hours earlier. She was hoping that the break would help her to reassess her life, while at the same time helping Fiona to sort out hers. She tried so hard to be a good mum and yet felt she was falling short. She knew that she still loved Dan, but tried to make sense of the over-used cliché of loving someone but not *being* in love with them. She tried to fathom her confused emotions. She knew the Nick thing was purely lust-driven but couldn't figure how Nicky + her children equalled guilt, whereas Nicky + Helen equalled feelings of liberation and lust that she hadn't tapped into for years. She couldn't quite calculate what Nicky + Dan equalled as she found herself comparing Nicky favourably against the live-to-work, busy, busy Dan. She questioned herself, once again, about the sense in having another child. It was obvious that it wouldn't bring her and Dan closer, so why sign up for extra responsibility? She already had more than most women her age, and she wanted to give as much as she could to her boys. As she thought of Toby and Jack she began to yearn for Ireland. She seemed to miss it so much more since she'd became a mother and supposed what she really missed was all that had been so familiar in her own childhood. She knew the boys loved both London and Dublin and yet she wanted more for them. She knew they had the material things in life that were so 'important' in these days of consumerism, but felt they missed out on the more natural aspects of their lives. She missed the huge fields that had surrounded her as a child, the long garden they'd had as children. She recalled the numerous summers and the fun that was to be had up the apple-tree and how they'd set up a den at the bottom of the garden where it had curved around out of sight. She remembered Dad's veggie patch, how he'd dug up a huge old tin box one year which they'd gathered around to crack open – to find it stuffed full of really old letters tied with ribbons.

As she lay back in the leather seat, a tear emerged from

the corner of her eye. It sat there, heavy and wobbling, until it finally sped down the smooth contours of her cheek, splashing as it fell on her arm. She remembered Mum's heavy hand-knits – the clothes that sat on you with the flair and cut of a blanket that had shrunk in the wash and how Fiona, Charley and she had thrown many a tantrum at the prospect of being forced to wear them. She wondered why they'd all turned out like they had. Her parents had set a fairly good example for matrimony, if not for parenthood. As far as she knew there had been no affairs or indiscretions, no violence or abuse and it puzzled her why Charley found it so hard to commit. She thought of Fiona, stuck in a country that she did nothing but complain about, and wondered why she couldn't be satisfied. She had her health, a beautiful daughter, a loving family.

And then she looked at herself. She still despised herself for the night in the taxi with Nick. In her many years of marriage she'd certainly looked and admired, but had *never* kissed or been with anyone but Dan. Until now. She wondered what had possessed her. She knew she should be happy too, what with her fantastic home, her flourishing antique clothing business, her successful husband and cherished sons. But she wasn't. She had memorised a poem years ago that she tried to raise her children by and gently ran through it in her mind as her body relaxed but her mind fretted. She tried daily to teach her children values. She recited how to teach honesty by helping children respect the truth, justice by encouraging them to make amends, empathy by teaching them to consider others and self-esteem by nurturing their confidence. She felt guilty at the line in the poem which advised to teach love by being generous with your own affections and once again Nick was there, an image on the inside of her eyelids. She'd convinced herself that nothing sexual had taken place on the basis that there was no physical evidence, apart from the severely smudged lipstick, and that there hadn't been enough time. Feeling sticky under the collar once again she snapped her eyes open as the groomed stewardess handed her the *croissant de queijo* and the *queque* that she'd ordered just after take-off. She breathed in the delightful smell of the cheese croissant and admired the chubby cake that oozed over the sides of the small plate. As she bit into the light buttery croissant she thought back to home again.

After being together for so long, I feel that Dan defines me in so many ways. We were so young when we got together so I suppose it's inevitable. And yet I completely despise myself for what happened with Nick. I've never even thought of making love, or kissing, or even flirting with another man since the day I married Dan. We were so happy together – so perfect – that I didn't feel the need to. So although he doesn't go along with my enthusiasm for a daughter, I'm certainly not bored with my marriage. Perhaps I simply need to separate myself from him entirely for a few days. I know this will mean I'll probably feel lousy and lonely, but I'll just have to suffer Lisbon and concentrate on doing my best to help Fiona.

The plane landed and Helly watched as the heat evaporated in hazy snakes up from the lush grass and scorching tarmac. The reality of her time in Portugal suddenly smacked her straight between the eyes.

I can't wait to see Fiona!

They chattered non-stop on the 6km bus ride into Lisbon. Helly thought Fiona looked brown and well, although her eyes were slightly puffy and she looked tired. It upset Helly, the sight of her sister's shabby jeans and poorly cut hair, but she'd hugged and kissed her while deliberately not looking her up and down. Fiona felt dowdy alongside her. She *had* looked Helly up and down, complimenting her on how great she looked in her beige vest and combats. She'd slung a pastel pink denim jacket around her waist and Fiona knew she wouldn't be able to fit *her* jacket sleeves around her waist as a belt. Helly had been a little disappointed at first when she saw that Fiona had bought along her friend, Claudine, but twenty minutes later she'd decided she was cool. Fiona had explained how Adriana was with her dad for the morning, much to Fiona's resentment, but Claudine had persuaded her that it would make for an easier morning if they were child-free. The bus stopped at the top of a lengthy hill which Fiona had said was Avenida da Liberdade and Helly was glad that she hadn't brought her enormous heavy suitcase. As they stepped out of the bus, Helly put down her smart holdall, pulled out a handle and began to wheel it along behind them, as it stuttered loudly over the cobbles.

"Bloody hell, Helly. Can't you lift that? I thought you said it wasn't heavy."

"It's not!" She was forced to raise her voice slightly as the wheels of her bag rumbled over the endless cobbled streets of Lisbon. "I just love the noise of it."

Fiona linked arms with her sister, stopping her in her tracks and grabbing the light bag from her. "I'll carry it for you. Such an attention-seeker!" Helly clutched Fiona's face, squeezing her cheeks together pudgily, as she puckered up and kissed her squarely on the lips.

"You're just the best, Fi. I've really missed you."

"Come on," she laughed, pulling away, "and you're still as charming as ever. Let's get the train back to Cascais."

"Oooh," moaned Helly and Claudine together, and then laughed.

Helly continued, "Can't we spend some time in Lisbon?"

Fiona frowned, "But I've left Adriana with Luís."

"And?"

"Well," she shuffled, "I hate having to ask him for help as it is, without taking advantage of the situation."

"Don't be daft. He is her father after all. He has no idea how long you'll be. Anyway, there's no harm in being pleasant to him. Especially if you want me to talk him around to letting you come back to London. Let him enjoy his daughter. It's still only early, so why don't we stay for some lunch and head back early afternoon. Please? I haven't come all this way *not* to see some of Lisbon."

Fiona conceded, "OK, come on. Especially as it's the first time you've *ever* been here. I've only lived here for eight years! Even Charley's been!"

Claudine could sense an atmosphere and stepped in. "Why don't we take you on a tram first? Fiona does not like walking up the hills here."

"Hey, speak for yourself!" Fiona was embarrassed at the truth behind Claudine's statement. She always felt chubby in Lisbon but wasn't prepared to make it public. "I'm running around after a four-year-old every day, don't forget!"

The heat soaked into their clothes and Fiona cursed that she'd worn her long-sleeved black T-shirt in comparison to Helly's spaghetti-strap vest and couldn't stop herself from glancing sideways at her as they strolled, her stiletto heels occasionally getting stuck between the cracks of the light grey cobbles. Helly soaked it all in, watching the moving shadows as the crazy city drivers rumbled over the tram lines in the road. They soon came to the bottom of the hill and Helly was surprised to see that they were standing on the edge of a large square, its tiled name plate boasting Praça Dom Pedro IV. Helly squinted at the huge bronze statue, she presumed of Dom Pedro, in the centre.

Fiona paused for breath and noticed Helly reading the name plate. "Ignore the name plate, they call this area Rossio. Fancy some lunch?"

"But it says Praça Dom Pedro."

Fiona smiled, "Listen. Lisbon is easy enough to get lost in as it is, but it took us years to get used to the fact that many streets have more than one name."

Claudine interrupted, "And some streets have *no* name at all!"

"So how do you know where you are?" Helly couldn't grasp the concept.

"You don't! Sometimes. I mean, if you went south from here, you'd start leading down towards Rua Do Ouro, which is also called Rua Aurea. It's called both!"

"I got a taxi once," Claudine said, "and asked to go do Largo Trindade Coelho. It seems simple enough – there's actually a taxi rank there. But the driver took me to Rua Nova da Trindade, also called Largo do Carmo."
"Why?"

"Because Largo Trindade Coelho is only the name on the street sign. Everyone actually calls it Largo da Misericórdia."

Helly grinned, loving the eccentricity of it all.

Fiona continued, "The craziest thing of all is the road that runs east from the Baixa district up to the *miradouros* overlooking Alfama."

"What's a *miradouros*? And what's Alfama?" Helly interrupted.

"A *miradouros* is a look-out point. A place to stand high and soak up the fantastic views over Lisbon. And the Alfama is Lisbon's oldest quarter."

"Can we go there?"

"Of course. It's a warren of narrow streets and blind alleys though."

"Sounds great! OK, carry on."

"Well, I don't think there's one person in Lisbon who knows the name of this street. The one from Baixa to Alfama. In one lengthy stretch it changes name from Largo da Madalena through about eight or more name changes. It changes so many times that it actually seems to have no name at all!"

"How exciting! I love it. I can see that a few days simply won't be enough!"

"Oh Helly," Fiona sighed deeply, "I wish I still felt that way. I've been stuck here for so long now the magic's disappeared."

"Come on. Let's forget lunch, I want you to show me some more of Lisbon."

They stepped inside a yellow building marked *ascensor da bica* on Rua de São Paulo as they waited for the funicular that would take them up the steep street to Bairro Alto.

"Is this one of the trams?" Helly asked, excited at the sight of the atrocious incline ahead of them.

"Not exactly. This is more of an elevator. Tram etiquette is something completely different!"

"How d'you mean?" she asked, paying her paltry fare as they stepped up and into the small side doorway of the graffiti'd yellow car that had just slowly crept its way down to them. They sat sideways, their knees almost touching as they slid on the highly polished wooden seats. Fiona continued, as a crowd of Japanese tourists clustered on, "The gritty urban etiquette of tram-travelling is to never jump the queue – you'll only get the brunt of a finger-wagging lecture. And hold on as if your life depended on it."

"Christ, it sounds scary."

"When I first came to Lisbon I was on a tram and a poorly attached pensioner was thrown across the car, landing with a thud."

"Feck! If that was in Ireland there'd be a compo claim in before you could say 'I slipped in the supermarket'!"

"I think they're just used to it here. She was immediately pulled to her feet, completely unhurt, by the usual 'tut-tutting' passengers."

"Poor woman!"

The fifteen or so Japanese men and women were chattering excitedly amongst themselves, their carrier bags clanking with bottles as they began click, click, clicking, photographing each other.

The tram jerked into life as the driver pulled closed the slatted door behind him, and the gaggle of tourists all '*ahhhh'd*' with excitement.

What a fantastic place! I can't understand Fiona's distaste for it all. The funicular is drawing us up one of the steepest hills I've ever set eyes on. And as we draw our way up, passing quirky side-streets, I'm amazed how much steeper they are! The plaster is literally falling off the unpainted walls of the buildings that we pass and yet the cars, parked nose to tail on the cramped cobbled sideroads are all shiny and new-looking. On this part of the hill we're virtually going up vertically. It's just sooo steep. I think I'm in love!

"There's WIP." Fiona pointed out a place, halfway up.

"And what's that?"

"It's a three-in-one kind of idea. Bar meets clothes shop meets hairdresser's. It's a great place though."

"Sounds fantastic! Do you go there regularly then?"

"No." Fiona looked away, at some unidentified focus point in the distance.

"Fi? I said do you go there?" Helly turned to face her sister only to see her looking down at her knees. She looked at Claudine. They shrugged at each other.

Helly nudged Fiona. "What's up?"

"I used to go there with Luís. It was such fun. Its marble-lined walls and shiny, happy people. I used to love watching the Bairro Alto bohos sitting around the glass-topped tables and the DJ's were fantastic."

"Oh, let's go one evening."

"Helly. My life simply isn't like that any more." Fiona's voice was louder than necessary.

"Well, it should be! Why isn't it?"

"Oh, and yours *is*, I suppose?"

"No, it's not, Fiona. And that's exactly the point. We've only become mothers! We haven't been tied to the sink or lost the use of our legs – we've only given birth! We *should* be getting out and having fun."

"Yeah, well, that's easy to say for you. You're here on holiday and it all seems different. Take it from me, I know. I was new here once too, remember!"

The funicular reached the top of the hill and Helly looked back through the end window at the terracotta roof tiles that capped the skyline below them.

"I know. And I was so happy for you. It all seemed so romantic and such fun."

"You know, Helly," Fiona replied as they stepped out into the sultry warm air once again, "I initially kidded myself this was the European San Francisco. I'd been caught up in the magic of it all. I'd been taken in by the similarities between the Pont 25 Abril bridge that stretches across the River Tagus and the Golden Gate. And then the trams and the hills. I was just waiting to bump into Karl Malden or Michael Douglas! And all I got was Luís and his handcuffs!"

Claudine grinned, hoisting her handbag up onto her shoulder and tying the belt on her jacket, "Oh Fiona, you never told me you were into that!"

Fiona frowned, but catching the smirks on Claudine and Helly's faces, realised that she had to lighten up.

"So give me the low-down! I want to know all about the nightlife, the shopping, the districts – the bloody works!" Helly was working herself up into a frenzy. She had intended to throw herself at Lisbon in a bid to forget about the potential mess she'd left behind in London. But she wasn't expecting to actually *like* the place.

I mean, Fiona's lived here for years and for ages I've heard nothing but complaints about it.

And she wants to move from here to go back to London!

The woman's demented...

"OK," Fiona sighed, exasperated by Helly's energy, as she tried to summarise, "in a nutshell – Baixa is 'the bloody works'."

"Hold on! Where's that? Is that the Baxa word I've seen on my map?"

"Probably. It's pronounced bay-ee-sha. It's known as the lower city, the commercial heart of the city with its pedestrianised streets and traditional shops and there's the Chiado district, which is the chic shopping area."

"Well, I want to go to everywhere!"

Claudine smiled as Fiona huffed. "God, this is going to

be knackering, having you around!"

"You'd better count on it! So where are we now?"

"We're making our way to the Alfama district. You wanted to see that, didn't you?"

"Well, I want to see it all, now that you've done such a great tourist-guide job on me! You really should think of starting up a tour company."

Claudine butted in, delighted, "See? Didn't I say you'd be great?"

Helly saw the flash of annoyance on Fiona's face and decided to let it go.

Sitting outside the bustling café, beneath a pastel-pink canopy they watched the lunch-time diners and office workers as they strolled past, mingling with the tourists. Fiona ordered them three coffees, impressing Helly with her Portuguese. She knew her sister could speak the language, but to actually hear it 'live' was amazing. The waiter deftly plucked up a beer mat, folding it into half, and then half again and surprising Helly as he crouched at her feet. They watched curiously as he lifted the wobbly table and placed the folded square beneath the offending leg. As he sprang to his feet again, he pushed down lightly on the table, winked at the three women, and darted back in through the smoked glass doors of the café, and reappeared in seconds with their miniscule coffees and gargantuan cakes.

Helly grimaced at the bitter coffee. "Jesus Christ! That's rotten."

Fiona burst laughing, "Here, you probably need half a dozen sugars. Most Portuguese do."

"Bloody hell. I'm surprised they've got any teeth left after that! Christ, that'd strip the enamel off all right."

"You'll get used to it."

"Don't think I ever could. I'm a tea-lady myself. Well, not literally a 'tea-lady' as such, but I prefer tea to coffee. It's the Irish in me."

"There are a lot of similarities between here and Ireland, I think," Fiona mused as she stirred so many sugars into her coffee that Helly suspected the spoon would stand up on its own.

"You're not serious. How could you begin to compare this with Ireland?"

"It is a very devout Catholic country," Claudine whispered. "Fiona says worse than Ireland."

Helly sniggered, "Go 'way. Really?"

"Put it this way, if you've ever felt the need for your very own saint, you're in the right place. They have one for absolutely everything."

"Such as?" Helly spat fluffy fragments of filo pastry from her mouth as she spoke.

"Such as safeguarding fishing trips, warding off plagues or curing sick animals."

Claudine continued, "Every village has its own saint and saint's day. Even in Cascais the launching of a small, rickety fishing boat gets a ceremonial sprinkling with holy water."

"OK, so they're mad keen on the saints, and they're Catholics. What else?"

"Nepotism."

"Feck off!" Helly blurted, shooting pastry flakes across

at Claudine and then, embarrassed, wiped her mouth with the back of her hand.

"I'm serious! Cousins in the town hall, or friends at the electricity company. It's a known fact that the majority of one of the Lisbon banks employees are all from a few streets in the same district."

"Great!" Helly threw back the last of the bitter coffee as she washed down the cake, "sounds like we should fit in just fine then. No wonder you and Luís got it together."

"Hmph," Fiona's eyebrows jumped a good five centimetres, "the only thing Luís and I have in common is Adriana."

"Well, Dan's father always said, 'Never try to impress a woman, for she will only expect you to carry it on for the rest of your lives'."

As they all cringed, Helly's phone bleeped in her bag. It was a text from Dan, reminding her how much they were missing her already. She quickly replied, sending a series of xxxxx's, and tucked the phone back into her pocket.

Fiona carried on, "I think the only time a woman ever really succeeds in changing a man is when he's a baby."

"They're always bloody babies!" Helly grabbed the bottle of mineral water, and poured herself a full glass.

Fiona squirmed, pulling at her waistband.

"What're you doing?"

"My bloody jeans feel too tight."

"Why did you wear them if they're uncomfortable?" Helly couldn't understand the sudden change of subject.

"You're not pregnant, are you?" she teased, recalling Madame Lydia's prediction earlier in the year.

"No! Don't be ridiculous. They felt OK this morning. I'm just desperate to lose some weight. That's another reason to get out of this country."

"Well, you can go on a diet just as well here as in London, you know."

"I have low-carb, high-carb confusion. Helly, I'm blinded with science by the Atkins, the F-plan, the Scarsdale, the Hampton. I mean, should I be aiming for high protein, low fat, high carbs? It's all a foreign language to me."

"D'you remember that revolting cabbage diet?" Helly began to laugh at the memory. "Do you know, Claudine, she got Charley onto it and she took flasks of cabbage soup to work every day and completely stank the place out every lunch-time."

"At least it was the cabbage, and not my feet! Unlike *some* people."

"Oh, I'm only joking. Don't be so sensitive. So come on, what's with this London fixation. What can I do to make you see sense?"

"I've read all about Botox in a lunch-hour."

"You're wanting Botox, Charley's needing detox, and all I need in life is Radox!"

"I miss all the girlie things from London."

"Such as?"

"Cellulite-busting lotion, scrummy salads rather than anything involving salted dried cod or sardines, and cheap candy-coloured underwear for the spring. And, I'd love to be measured properly for a bra. I've been wearing the wrong size for years and I've got bulges where they're not supposed to be. Oh, just give me Rigby & Peller any day!" Fiona closed her eyes and shook her head theatrically.

"Well, I'd say it's less of a case of not being able to do those things in Portugal, more than you can't afford to. I'd say London means more accessibility to a job and earnings than anything else."

"Of course, it does. It's my freedom. Let's raise our glasses to toast the idea."

"To London!"

The three women clinked their sparkling glasses of water and Helly added, "And to Charley, for whom one is too many, and a million simply isn't enough."

After their lengthy coffee break they hopped on a bus to complete their journey across to the Alfama district. Fiona had already decided to drag Helly away from the west side of town and across to the east, with the intention of making their way back to the train station for Cascais shortly after.

Irritatingly, Helly's phone rang in her pocket. She silenced it with a grab and a swift press of the button.

"Hello?" On hearing the caller her voice was reduced to a whisper, "Nick! How did you get my number?"

Fiona and Claudine pretended to look out the windows as the bus jerked its way across the city while they listened in as Helly explained that she was in Lisbon and would be back in a few days. Shortly after, as she disconnected the call, they didn't fail to notice how she also pressed the larger button to switch the phone off completely.

Christ! Nicky has only asked Dan for my number! And he gave it to him! He said that he'd lost his spare key and needed to ask me whether I'd picked it up in the taxi the other night! The nerve of him. And the lies too. What's even worse is, he's worried that I'm avoiding him. Quick off the mark, isn't he? But that's not the real worst of it. He says he told me he has a sister in Lisbon. Well, I'm sure I can't remember him saying that, although I can't remember much of that night -- except parts of the taxi ride home. Anyway, it gets much worse. His sister's husband is unwell and he's coming to Lisbon to see them.

And what's even worse still?

He's coming tomorrow. . .

She found it hard to concentrate again after the call but, as Fiona and Claudine punctuated the journey by pointing out landmarks and statues en route, she was worrying, and hoping and wishing that Nick wouldn't dare to ring her again. She wasn't so sure she could control herself. Although she was already in a state of heightened excitement as she wondered whether she'd packed her lacy underwear and looked up at the sky, thinking,

How quickly could I get a light tan? By tomorrow maybe?

By the time they reached Alfama she'd had the extensive transport system explained to her, and had heard all about the Metro and its four lines – the Seagull line, the Sunflower line, the Caravel line and the Orient line.

They finally arrived and hopped out of the jammed bus. They were immediately struck by the scents of jasmine, geranium, lemon and jacaranda hanging in the air, producing a heady fragrance. Helly looked up at the old five-storey, terraced buildings, the washing buffeting in the light breeze and canaries twittering from cages hung outside small widows. She was immediately aware of the lack of traffic sounds as she watched children running up and down the narrow streets while adults chattered outside tiny shops and cafés, many of them little more than holes in the wall.

The three women walked in silence as they soaked in the terracotta-fronted and then suddenly pastel-pink terraced houses which then blended into a whitewashed grey and then once again changed to a virtually derelict section where the plaster had all but fallen off completely. They turned down the narrow Rua de Sao Pedro and walked into the weekday fishmarket where they listened to the sing-song banter between the fishwives as they dodged the trays of slippery squid.

"Isn't it great that the cars can't get in here? It really makes the area." Helly was delighting in this district of Alfama.

"Morning rush hour in Alfama is probably the sounds of birds and footsteps of workers as they trot towards the Metro."

"So how do the tourists know where to go?"

Claudine replied, "Oh, don't worry. The coaches stop at the bottom and tip out the camera-clutching tourists. In the summer evenings the crowds pack in here, looking for outside tables and dinners of grilled sardines and red wine."

As they climbed one of the winding, narrow inclines Fiona stopped for a breather and they took the chance to look back at the view from a height. Helly noticed grape vines growing at the back of some of the houses and wondered what the Alfama district was like at night.

"Oh, don't be taken in by its sleepy daytime air," Fiona advised. "It's supposed to be buzzing with nightlife here, what with the old *fado* houses and the old dockland areas that are now a favourite haunt of the trendy clubbers."

"Perhaps we'll get the chance to see for ourselves?"

"Ooh," Fiona groaned, "she's not back onto that subject again, is she?"

Chapter Seventeen

Poke, poke.

Charley had thought she was dreaming. She was lying on a scorching sun lounger beside a glistening pool. That bloody irritating waitress had a trayful of cocktails for her.

"Jus' leave them down," she had mumbled.

Poke, poke, poke.

She'd frowned in her sleep. She hadn't been ready to wake up yet. She had been so comfy. But yet she wasn't. Wiggling, she released her feet from underneath her, stretching her legs and knocking her ankles off something cold at the same time.

Poke.

"Oh go away, please! Do I look like I'm ready?"

The waitress had spoken, her over-made-up face grinning and Charley was shocked as a 40-a-day gravelly voice barked, "I don't give two fucks whether you're ready or not, missus. You're back at the depot. Shift yourself, luv."

Charley had opened her eyes to see it was far from scorching sunlight. It was an early half-light, a sooty pink sky and the gaudy fluorescence of the bus depot glaring at her through the window. The unshaven conductor stood before her, his uniform creased and bristly. She'd shaken her head, the reality of the evening creeping back on her. She'd got on the bus for home and had fallen asleep on it.

Again.

"C'mon, luv. Weren't you the one who done this last week?" The conductor had leaned in closer to her, trying to catch a proper look.

She shied away, irritated. "Yeah. So? You bloody know when I asked to get off. Why don't you come and check!"

"Go on, get outta here. I've a home to go to, even if you haven't!"

Staggering to her feet she had grabbed her bag, which had been tucked beneath her, and wobbled her way along the top deck and down the narrow stairs of the bus, checking her phone at the same time.

"Can I go in there and wait for a cab?" She had pointed toward the depot as she punched in the taxi number.

"Reckon it's the safest bet. I wouldn't want any of my family walking around here at five in the morning. Go on in. Say Billy said ya could."

"Thanks, Billy."

Straightening her clothes she concentrated on putting one foot in front of the other, desperate to look 'together' before meeting any other conductors, drivers or even cabbies. She was totally oblivious to her mascara'd panda eyes and clumped hair where she'd been resting against the cool window.

As she stood inside the depot, beneath the cruel lights, she heard a voice behind her.

"Another one living in the shadow of the bottle eh, John?"

She turned to see two bus drivers walking past, laughing and yet shaking their sorry heads.

She felt sick at their jeering. Sick, embarrassed and bloody angry.

She'd give them shadow of the bloody bottle! Wasn't a girl entitled to go out and have some fun? It wasn't her fault the driver had been so slow that she'd fallen asleep, was it?

Steve pulled on his leather jacket, his arms shooshing through the silky, quilted lining before they emerged at the other end. He gathered together the paperwork from his desk and filed it all into a brown folder, slinging it into the top drawer until the next evening. He hated doing the night shifts, especially ones like tonight. The regulatory drunks, prostitutes and teenagers trying to nick stuff from the 24-hour supermarket were becoming mundane. As he made his way through the carpark he met his fresh-faced colleagues about to start the morning shift. As much as he wanted to, it was too early to ring Charley. He felt terrible about last night. He'd only wanted to teach her a little lesson. He was trying to tease her, make her sweat a little. He really liked her, although she worried him, her vulnerability poorly hidden as she looked for her dog in Phoenix Park. He had only meant to keep her waiting at Madame Ya Ya's for an extra twenty minutes, but then he'd got stuck in traffic. As he'd tried then to ring her repeatedly, he felt bad that she wasn't answering and hoped everything was all right with her. Madame Ya Ya's wasn't a particularly pleasant hangout. He wasn't sure whether she'd have gone home after he'd stood her up, or if she'd gone off with her friends and enjoyed another crazy night.

Getting into his car he decided he'd head home and wait until later to ring her again.

Charley squeezed her forehead as her stomach swilled with every left or right-hand turn. The cabbie had his Dublin FM radio on extremely loud and the exuberant, sing-song voices of the DJ announcing it was five forty-five grated off her irritability. She was becoming sick of these 'blackout' periods, when she struggled to remember the nights before, and she had to admit it now, they were becoming more and more frequent. She fought with her conscience, which screamed at her that the trigger for her excessive drinking had caused the split with her last 'proper' boyfriend, Donal. She had a huge problem to come to terms with, and the drink had helped her to. Anyway, she'd always come second in his life. He always came first in their relationship. They'd had numerous arguments over stupid things when she'd been on the sauce and she'd finally realised how he was slowly chipping away her resolve. She could never have told him what had happened to her in Portugal. He wouldn't have understood. He would have said it was her own fault.

She'd always loved a good night out and a few drinks, but Donal complained that she didn't know when to say no. He moaned that enough was never enough for her. It had broken her, when he had walked away from her. And now Charley wished more people understood her relationship with alcohol and was often aggravated at a general lack of understanding at why the Irish wouldn't drink with the reserve of the Spaniards or even the Italians. As she crawled out of the cab, pressing a twenty into the driver's fat palm, she didn't notice Steve drive past her flat and turn off into a side street a few houses down. She mumbled to herself about the crack of dawn, and how everyone was getting ready for work, and she was just getting ready for bed. The key in her hand shook uncontrollably, forcing her to hold her wrist still with her other hand as she negotiated the key into the lock. Kicking off her shoes onto the soft hall rug, she flicked back in her mind over the last few weeks as she tried to recall how often she'd felt hungover. She knew it was a lot. She was aware at work how often she thought about drink at inappropriate times of the day, and knew that by four o'clock she was beginning to count-down the minutes. Her days of trying to alternate her drinks with mineral water with ice and lemon were long gone.

She tugged off the wrap-dress, chucking it onto the wooden floor and watching it glide and then hit the wall in a heap. It went without saying that it'd mean another quick call in to work to promise to be in just before lunch. She simply *had* to get some sleep. A few hours curled on the itchy, back seat of a double-decker just didn't count.

She'd lost track of how many hours she'd promised to make up at work now. As she stood in her underwear before her bedroom mirror, still blind to her make-up ravaged face, she slipped her arms out of her bra straps and swung the bra around her torso, grappling between her breasts for the clips. She always insisted any one-night stand remove her underwear in a bid to disguise the fact that, at forty, she still put her bra on and took it off at the front and then turned it around. She'd resigned herself to the fact that she'd never be dextrous with the clips now, at her age.

She cringed at the thought of work, grimacing at her reflection,

"Look! And the fecking facial hair sprouting the minute my back is turned!"

Sliding beneath the cool duvet on her rumpled bed she winced as the goose pimples rose on her bare skin. Suddenly everything hit her, as if her eyes had been prised open, when all they wanted to do was sleep. Her face contorted as she lay, staring at the ceiling, and the tears welled in her panda eyes. It took a few minutes for the pressure to build up, but as she flipped and buried her face into her pillow, ignoring the stale scent of Miguel-the-waiter's aftershave, her emotions burst from her in loud, body-racking sobs as she wailed. She cried for Donal, for what could have been, what had been before she began drinking so heavily, and what existed after it. She cried for what had happened to her a year and a half ago and now she worried about Helly too. She cried for Fiona, stuck out in Portugal with the bastard Luís. She hated him more than she'd ever thought possible and yet hated herself for letting her sister stay there with him. He'd changed her life for the worst and she despised herself for letting him continue to ruin Fiona's. She cried for the mess that she was making of her life. She missed Donal so much. He'd been someone upon whom she depended and yet had needed to get away from.

As next-door's clock chimed six in muffled clangs, Charley's mobile began to vibrate in her bag.

Steve was sure that it had been her he'd seen getting out of the taxi around the corner, but wanted to check.

Even if it had meant that she'd spent the night with the horrendous blind date that she'd been trying to escape from, he at least had to know she was safe.

Charley snored deeply, her nose blocked from the crying and her head full of jumbled thoughts.

And she still hadn't rung work.

Chapter Eighteen

Beads of sweat lined up in a crease on Dan's frowning forehead. He had taken the boys and Diego to the park in an attempt to knacker them out. Helly had only been gone a day and already he was stressed. As he wrestled the muddy school uniforms into the washing machine he regretted not making the boys change into their 'home clothes' earlier. If Helly had seen them in the park wearing their grey trousers and blue V-necked jumpers she'd have gone ballistic! As he shoved the entwined clothes into the machine he remembered how, when she'd been pregnant and they had been testing out names for their babies, she had insisted on trying to find names that couldn't be lengthened or shortened. And now, she'd only been gone twenty-four hours and he was already calling them all the names under the sun and was really, *really*, missing her. He'd been toying with girl-names all afternoon, forcing himself to give in to Helly's obsession with another child, perhaps a soon-to-be-conceived daughter. His daydream was called to a screaming halt by the muffled sounds of bickering which came in spurts from the bedroom.

"*Laaads!*" he hollered, his head almost in the 'O' of the washing machine as he fumbled with an inside-out trouser leg. A thud, and then the claxon of a cry.

"Shit!" Dan sprang to his feet and strode to the foot of the stairs. "Lads! Get yourselves into bed! I'll be up in a minute."

Toby appeared at the top of the stairs, his hair ruffled and his pyjamas creased, "Dad? How soon will I be old enough to do what I want?"

"Ha. Son, I don't know. I don't think anybody has lived that long yet."

"Oh, Dad!" Toby whined.

"Look, son. Get into bed. Please, mate. I'll be up to tuck you in."

"But Mummy always reads us a story." Jack appeared, red-faced under wet cheeks, at Toby's side – suddenly they were friends again.

Dan arched his eyebrows. "Does she?" It smacked him painfully in the gut as he realised that he wasn't familiar with their bedtime routine and wished that she was there so that he could lose himself in front of the telly, or in his office, as usual.

"OK, choose a book and I'll come and read it to you."

The boys charged back to their bedroom, once again arguing and debating over which book would give them longer before lights out.

My legs ache from so much walking.

My jaws ache from too much talking.

And my neck aches from looking up all the Lisbon hills!

We were off the Lisbon streets and lying on a towel in Cascais in forty-five minutes. The train journey was only €1.30, and for the first half of it we were accompanied by two guys playing accordion and tambourine. I'd thought I was back in Dublin for a minute there. Fiona had recommended that we sit on the left for the best views of the sea. I'd been surprised at how many small fishing boats wagered their claim to the sardines, and I was surprised at the size of the Disciples statue as we passed Belém.

So Cascais?

Take no notice of what Fiona says. It's beautiful.

Fat-ankled wives wearing Sophia Loren sunglasses, hanging onto the arms of crombied men. Powdery sand beaches, fresh, clean air, immaculate cobbled streets and loads of shops.

Why haven't I been here before?

And why didn't Charley ever say how lovely it is?

Charley had gone into work very late. Begrudgingly, but at least she'd shown her face. She hadn't discussed the Barnie affair, and the girls knew better than to push it. Her body language screamed 'Leave me alone!' and they were afraid to do otherwise as she delivered her uninspired ear-wax jingle which was nothing like her usual work. As always, when she felt low, and when she was sober, her thoughts went back to the abortion that had taken her to London just over a year ago. She'd hoped that by now she would have been more sorted.

The thought alone made her snort in disgust. As she stared at the blank white pages, forcing herself to channel some kind of concentration on her work, her mind wandered back to that very day.

She had felt ridiculous, at her age, as she lay in the rickety hospital bed in the private ward at midday. The small ward had only four beds and she watched the other three girls, she'd supposed all under twenty-five, as they'd lain back in their beds watching the small telly suspended high on a bracket. The disturbing sounds of *Crossroads* and *Holidays from Hell* filled the room and she knew that their minds were elsewhere. It seemed surreal that they were watching such pap, and yet a small thread of each of them was grateful for something to take their mind off the next hour or two.

She'd felt ridiculous. At her age too. Shouldn't she have known better? As she'd forced her mind not to comprehend what she was about to do, she'd hated herself too.

It had all marked both the beginning and the end of a relationship.

In more ways than one.

Nick was looking forward to his early morning flight and promised himself an early night, but there were things he had to do first.

Perhaps if his ego hadn't been so fragile he wouldn't have felt the need for his soft-top vintage Mercedes. His self-esteem had persistently struggled to stay afloat and so, the soft-top had seemed like a necessity. Up until now, he'd felt it reinforced his image, his sense of self. Or at least the image he hid behind. It was becoming more of an effort lately, as he yearned for Helly in his arms, in his life again. He parked his car on the double yellow outside the North London tanning shop and he virtually shuddered as his conscience pricked him. He'd forgotten the concept of 'conscience' over the last few years, and it jarred him. Only slightly, enough so that he could brush it away, but he knew his reasons for flying to Lisbon weren't only of the Good Samaritan nature that he'd dressed it up as. He wasn't usually so obliging as to rush off to help his sister, but the jet-setting, fly-by-the-seat-of-my-pants of it all appealed to him. And he had to try and see Helen again – away from the conscience of her home-life. He had to have the chance to talk to her alone – away from her family commitments and responsibilities. He needed the chance to talk to Helen – not Helly, or Mrs Donovan or Mummy, but his Helen. His sister had been overwhelmed when he'd offered to go and help her out for a few days. He was always great with her children and with her husband's health problems she had more than enough on her plate.

As usual, he went to great pains to make sure that he didn't resemble a burst mattress when he took his shirt off and was fully clued up on new arenas of male competitiveness. He was no stranger to the beauty therapist where he went for "male" treatments such as back waxing, facials and manicures. He was aware that there was no longer a direct correlation between his salary and respect from his peers and realised it was now more about lifestyle and comfort. He'd done his twenty-hour days in the office and now prided himself that his job offered natural perks – like the freedom to take time out. He winked at the orange girl on the front desk and grabbed his towel as he made for the Mist-On tanning booth. He'd already prepped himself at home. He'd exfoliated the night before and had made sure he was wearing his black T-shirt and black combats. He knew the rules. Don't breathe in, close eyes, press buttons, wait for loud hiss of fake tan, and then four seconds to change position. And then no shower for twelve hours.

As he closed the booth door behind him and braced himself for the tanning experience he grabbed his manhood in his palm and rearranged it, shrugging with cockiness as he did so.

Chapter Nineteen

She'd had a tough afternoon at work and, now back home, she felt depressed. She didn't recognise the signs, but it was common after a drinking binge. Her half-eaten pasta salad sat on the floor beside her as she tried to focus on the jigsaw. She had begun to sort cardboard edge-pieces into a pile separate from the rest of the jigsaw, scratching her head as she tried to prop up the lid of the box. She knew she'd have no hope of getting it right without a clear view of the finished picture. She hated jigsaws, couldn't see the point of piecing together fragments of something that had been deliberately broken, but felt decidedly fragile and was desperate for something to focus on. The large glass of red wobbled on the rug at her side and she hummed lightly to the Nina Simone CD she was playing as she fingered and caressed the odd-shaped cardboard pieces. She'd left work a little early and had managed to spin them a jingle all of her own about how she'd started on the latest ditty to advertise the 'new fab' incontinence pads now and how she'd have a full presentation ready for them on Monday. There wasn't much to say really, to help sell incontinence pads, and she was vexing over how to use the same over-used clichés a different way. She hadn't expected it to be so difficult. It always was when she was least reckoning it to be so. As she began to snap together the small pieces to form the shape of the lady's hat she worried about Helly in Lisbon with Luís and Fiona. Whenever she thought about him her stomach churned and she cursed herself for not warning Helly what a pig he really was. She knew that Fiona was always banging on about how rotten he'd been to her, but she was sure only *she* knew the true extent of his nasty streak. She checked her phone for new text messages and, on seeing it blank, she set about keeping in touch with Helly by text. Mid-flow her phone bleeped loudly, making her jump and throw it into the air. It landed on the jigsaw, dislodging the horse's head into even uglier fragments. She read her latest message from Steve as she wobbled to her feet, the pins and needles in her ankles prickling like mad. It had taken him several texts and missed calls, but she finally agreed to let him come over in the hope that they'd sort out the mess of last night, and he was on his way. She tried to avoid her bedroom, but the large mirror called her and she soon found herself spritzing her hair with a glossing product, squirting darts of perfume around her neck, across her chest and even a quick burst down her top for luck. She plunged her hand into the cups of her bra and jostled her breasts into a higher, more pert position and then smoothed down her Abercrombie & Fitch T-shirt over her new high boobs.

She was ready for him when he knocked at the door. She recognised the I'm-hiding-a-bouquet-behind-my-back pose and waited to be presented with the lilies or roses or whatever he was about to spring on her.

"Dinner?" he grinned as he brought his hands forward, dangling a transparent bag full of silver take-away cartons. The sweet, hot smell shot up her nostrils. She'd have preferred the flowers, but wasn't going to send the Chinese back.

"Yeah, great. Come in." She forced the smile onto her face and noticed as she turned how his eyes fell and rested on her chest.

Their lips were shiny from the greasiness of the prawn crackers, the sauce of the mushroom-chicken. Their cheeks were incredibly close as she leant over the table, craning her neck to check whether the horse's legs looked OK. She'd forgotten how addictive jigsaws could be. Steve had got stuck straight into it with her, to the point that the Chinese take-away was more like a second thought as they dipped and prodded at their food, completely distracted by the scene from Ascot.

"Of course," he spoke with his mouth full of spring roll, "you realise that this lady on the left is probably going at it with that guy in the tweed jacket?"

"What? The one holding the tissue to her eyes?"

Steve nodded, a Cheshire-cat grin wide on his face.

"Don't be ridiculous! She'd never go for a fogey like him!"

"Don't be so sure. You'd be surprised at what people would go for."

"Well, I know *she* wouldn't go for *him*. He's about twenty years older than her for a start. He'd never push *her* buttons." She paused as she contemplated the scenario before she added, "Anyway, she looks like she's crying."

He held a small piece between his fingers as he lifted his face to look at her at close range. "You do know that if women cry during sex it's a sure sign of orgasm?"

"Hah! Hardly. Jesus, is that your experience? Women crying during sex?" Charley laughed out loud. The first time she'd laughed and been completely relaxed for weeks.

"I don't mean they cry all the bloody time, just at that crucial point."

"Well, Stevo, take it from me, honey, if they're actually crying at *that* point then they're faking it, babe."

"So, what about kids?"

"What about kids? They're always crying, aren't they?"

"I mean, what do you think about kids?"

"Well, you know what they say about not being able to eat a whole one."

"I'm serious!"

Charley forced her heart to slow down as it banged in her chest. It was a bit early for this kind of conversation. She'd only met him the other day. She didn't want to think about children. Despite lecturing herself not to, she still checked how old her baby would have been on a monthly basis, what kind of little personality might have been developing and whether he or she would have had the dreaded cow's-lick. She often worried about how she would have fared as a single mum.

She remained focussed on the jigsaw, laughing as she spoke, "You know I'd sooner keep putting in the practice rather than have the screaming end result!"

"OK, so what about love?"

"Love schlove. Isn't love something you make?"

"Is that what you think? You're really not the romantic type, are you, Charley?"

She was uncomfortable with the image that she was giving off, and disgruntled with his probing questions. "Oh stop the questions! Why don't you open another bottle of wine?"

"Feckit yes!" he said. "You know what? Why say 'no' when you can always say 'yes!'"

Charley smiled and raised an eyebrow.

Steve continued, "You might not realise, but there is actually one 'f' in 'Ireland'."

"Is that so?"

"Of course! Most celebrities of Irish descent 'feck'. Take Bono, Colin Farrell, John Lydon, Sinead O'Connor, Shane Mcgowan, Roy Keane – they all 'feck'."

Charley grinned at him and he winked, "But hey, not like I do …"

Charley was caught unawares by the butterflies that flipped and fluttered across her tummy. This wasn't something she was used to. She didn't like it.

"You're right," she tried to force the conversation on, "we're known for peppering our speech with charged words and phrases. What's the problem? I mean, think about it? What kind of country offers 'a hundred thousand welcomes' when for every other country 'welcome' will do?"

Steve laughed at her reasoning and was still laughing as the doorbell rang. He stared down at the jigsaw again and felt rather stupid when he looked up and saw a huge black guy, his tree-trunk neck strung with numerous gold chains, standing before him.

"Winston, this is Steve. Steve, Winston."

Steve scrambled to his feet, trying to make a hundred thousand steps look like a cool two. He held out his hand toward Winston.

Winston cracked his leathery palm down onto Steve's with a force,

"Yo bro! You the new home boy?"

"No, man," Steve threw his arms out to his side lazily and then frowned, wondering why he'd started talking that way, "I'm just a friend of Charley's."

"You any good at singing, man?" Winston directed his question to Steve, but held his hand out towards Charley. "I've got a cool new CD here for you, babe."

Steve laughed, "Only if I'm watching the rugby. I've been known to lose my voice singing 'Swing Low Sweet Chariot'."

"Go, Stevo!"

Charley gathered together the empty silver food cartons as she explained,

"Winston's in the Killiney Gospel Choir with me, Steve. Fancy a go?"

"No. Thanks. Think I'll leave the singing to those who know how to do it."

"Hah," she spat, her voice echoey from the kitchen, "you think *we* know? It's just a big excuse for a piss-up!"

Steve wondered why he wasn't surprised ….

Helly sat on the low brick wall and closed her eyes, raising her face to the sun. The intense scent from the orange trees in the square was filling her nostrils and she realised that she hadn't felt as good for ages. The small kiosk to her left was still fighting off the customers as they sold alarming amounts of coffee and cakes. Helly checked her watch. Five thirty in the afternoon and still the cafés were packed and the pastries were flying off the shelves. She held her cool bottle of beer tight in her hand, and read the label. Sagrés was similar in taste to San Miguel, that tinny flavour that all Mediterranean beers had. She'd die for a decent pint of Guinness right now. She's spent a particularly exhausting afternoon as she'd tried to educate Fiona on the rules of a good relationship. They'd spent hours discussing the merits of men being good communicators over being able to see eye-to-eye over money. Although Helly felt lucky that at least Dan took responsibility for that part of their lives, if nothing else. Fiona had realised the importance of "me" and "us" time and, Helly had to give it to her, she certainly was no stranger to being flexible. It seemed perhaps their biggest problem had been sexual incompatibility. It surprised Helly as Luís always seemed so sensitive and physically affectionate toward Fiona. And yet Fiona was almost giving an impression to Helly that Luís was rather selfish and shoddy in his sexual technique. Helly tilted the bottle, pouring the frothy remains of the beer into her mouth and grimacing slightly as she swallowed. Hopping to her feet she walked across the cobbled square, between the tables and throngs of people drinking and eating, and dropped the empty bottle into a bin. She began to make her way back toward the slight hill that led to Fiona's apartment. She looked up at the masses of terracotta roof tiles and smiled as she inspected the many flowers that grew on the roofs and sprouted from the guttering. She felt the tension of the gases in her neck and allowed herself some sound as she burped lightly.

"'Ello, my dear Helen."

Helly jumped as a deep, rich voice sang extremely close into her ear. She turned to face Luís, immediately blushing and wishing she hadn't just jumped so vigorously. She forced on a smile, hoping he hadn't heard the belch.

"Luís! I was wondering whether I'd see you. How are you?"

She scanned his face for signs that he'd noticed her alarm. Thankfully he was either excellent at forcing on a fake expression too, or he hadn't noticed it.

"I am well, Helen. You are looking as beautiful as ever. You are here to visit Fiona?" He shook his head dolefully.

"Yes, I am."

Prick! As if he thinks I can't see through his amateur dramatics.

"Fiona is not a happy girl right now, Helen. She thinks she wants to go to work, and she thinks she is not happy here. But why not be happy here?" he said, lifting his voice and raised his hands.

Helly suspected he was trying to emulate 'the man from Del Monte' whereas in reality he looked like something out of a cheap Australian telly ad.

"Beautiful place, beautiful country. Adriana can see her father and her mother. Her family is here. It would be stupid to move away from Cascais, yes?"

Helly suspected she was being manipulated and wasn't about to agree with him.

"Luís," she charmed, linking arms with him and strolling slowly alongside him, "how about I take you for a nice coffee somewhere and we can talk properly."

His face was awash with flattery as he squeezed her arm, slightly too tightly, as they walked slowly toward the nearest café.

If he noticed her flinch, it didn't worry him.

Nick wasn't the only passenger to get off the plane *with* a fake suntan already in place, but he was the only guy to. He'd jumped onto the bus and was in Lisbon within minutes. He got off at Praça da Figueira and walked across the large square, peppered with ravenous pigeons. His Magnum boots strode confidently across the chequerboard cobbles as he walked, flashing from sunlight to shade as he whizzed beneath the small canopies that hung over the shop fronts like little Hitler moustaches. His painfully skinny sister was waiting for him at the house and was barking at her children to go play out on the street with the other children. She'd always been stick-thin, but Nick was surprised at how gaunt her face had become since he'd last seen her. As he hugged her and kissed her he was aware of the hollows of her cheeks beneath her cheek-bones and her twiglet shoulders.

"Nick, thanks for coming over. You really didn't need to."

"I know I didn't, but I wanted to. How's Alfonso?"

"Oh, he just needs to rest really. I'm most worried about the paperwork side of things, Nick. We've let it go for so long and now we want to sell, I just can't get my head around sorting the books. And I can't let him know how bad it's gone."

Nick was willing to help, but also eager to achieve what he'd set out to.

"Look, I'll sort out the books for you. I've got four days here – that should be enough time. There's something I just need to do before I start. Here, take this €50 and take the kids out for something to eat and give Alf some peace for a few hours. Then when I get back I'll get stuck into the paperwork. It'll all be sorted before I go – I promise."

For the first time in weeks her face relaxed into a smile and she hugged her older brother.

"Where do you need to go?" She looked at him through slitted eyes, knowing full well a woman was involved.

"I just need to catch up with someone in Cascais. I'll

be back later." He ruffled her hair to distract her. "You go and round up the chaps and get them out for some fun."

As she busied herself with a quick tidy-up Nick pulled his mobile from the large side pocket of his combats and sent a text to Helly. He just *knew* she'd be bowled over that he was in Lisbon too. If he had anything to do with it, they'd be sharing more than texts before the three days were up.

Helly could feel the heat from Luís' leg under the small table. She was irritated at his incessant 'accidental' brushing of her arm as he toyed with his coffee cup. She forced herself to hide her annoyance as she spoke,

"And so you see, Luís, we think it's important that Fiona, *and* Adriana, spend some of their time with us too."

She instantly realised how lucky she was to have the unleering, faithful Dan.

"Of course, I understand, Helen," he charmed, "but I am not happy that Fiona may decide to stay away from Cascais."

"Well, aren't her assurances enough for you? Could you not agree for her to spend part of the year in Cascais and the other part away? I don't know whether Fiona will go to Dublin or London, but part of her will always love Cascais. And you're right – it *is* Adriana's home, but she has the right to know Fiona's side of the family too."

He suffocated her slim, white hand with his hot, hairy one and rubbed them together quickly and suggestively, "I think, Helen, that you are the most attractive of your sisters. It is only a shame that I, perhaps, picked the wrong one."

Helly was fit to burst with fury, but forced herself to keep her composure. For a few minutes more, anyway.

"Oh. come on now, Luís. You know that would never have worked. You and Fiona were great together. You still could be if it wasn't for .... Well, let's face it, you've got Bella now and Fiona's got, em, nobody."

"It is her own fault. She could not be a Portuguese wife."

Helly snorted. "Well, she never got to find out, did she? You never asked her to marry you?"

"I did not. Adriana is my daughter, and always will be, but Fiona? She could never have been my wife."

Helly was sick with his leg-brushing and hand-rubbing and constant leering. She felt uncomfortable in her spaghetti-strapped vest, feeling virtually naked as he continually stared at her chest. She stood abruptly as she drew the sickening scenario to a close.

"Well, Luís, you are a clever man. Please, consider Fiona's position. You have my promise that Fiona will bring Adriana back to visit you. I will personally make sure that Adriana keeps up her Portuguese and is reminded of her Portuguese roots. Please, just think about it?"

Luís stood, blocking her exit, and cupped her face in his hands. His hot, coffee'd breath was stinging her nostrils at close quarters but she still forced herself to smile,

"I will think about what you have said. But I am not happy about it. You know the Hague Convention –"

Helly interrupted, "I know all about the legalities of it. Luís, she's not planning on abducting Adriana! She simply wants her to know both countries. Is that so wrong? She's hardly giving her a good life here, is she? You won't let her work, and she has few friends. Please, you're a reasonable man, Luís. Please, consider it."

He kissed her on the cheek, holding his lips to her skin for just a second too long, which made her feel uncomfortable, as he whispered hotly in her ear, "I will think, Helen. And I will meet with you again before you go back to give my decision to you."

Helly took a deep breath, thankful that it was all over. "Thank you, Luís. Thank you very much."

As she slung her bag onto her shoulder and turned, a look of relief fell on her face while the insides of her head screamed as she tried to figure what her younger sister had ever seen in him.

But in her hurry to get away Helly didn't notice the slightly orange-tanned man wearing the black combats, standing in the doorway across the street.

He didn't want her to see him.

Not just yet.

Nick wondered why Helly hadn't replied to his earlier texts. He thought she'd jump at the chance to meet up away from the responsibility of husband and kids. Especially after the groping on the Tube train and then the scene in the taxi. He'd hopped on the train to Cascais and knew he'd find her somewhere. He hadn't reckoned on seeing her enjoying an intimate coffee with a robust, and obviously wealthy, local. He was both surprised and yet disappointed. He didn't have her down for the kind to play away, and yet the very suggestion that she did only made it all the more exciting for him. He hadn't stopped thinking about her since the first day they'd met and had obsessed ever since. He so wanted her and wondered whether he would get her into bed before their return to London.

He always reached his targets....

Helly stood high on the cliffs of the small private beach sucking down as much fresh air as she could ingest without bursting her lungs. Her mobile in her pocket would have flashed '5 new messages' and '3 missed calls' if only she hadn't turned it off after Nick's call.

Fiona was on a high. She had met Vitor earlier and he had hugged her and kissed her cheek. He was a good friend and knew how important it was for Fiona to have Helly around. She'd nearly fallen over when he'd said, "Fiona, I will baby-sit for you tonight. I will look after Adriana and you go out with your sister. Go and have fun. I like to see you smile again."

She had taken his hands and held them tightly as she tried not to 'whoop' with joy. "Vitor, you are very kind, but I can't ask you to do that."

"You have not asked. I have offered. I will come to you at eight o'clock. But will she be asleep by then?"

"Well, I can easily make sure she's asleep."

"No need to." His warm brown eyes smiled at her.

"There is no need. She is a lovely girl. I don't mind if she is not."

"Vitor, you are a very kind person and a very good friend. Thank you so much for this. I will make sure Adriana is asleep and I promise I won't be late home."

"This is good for you, Fiona. You have been looking so sad for so long. I am very pleased for you."

"Thank you."

And she had kissed him on the cheek again and was now desperately pouring cheap vodka, Bacardi and fruit juices into the blender – in generous, but dangerously unequal quantities. Seeing Helly again had only made her more desperate to return to London with her and she was certain that a few lighteners this evening would set the ball rolling. She only had to get Helly a little drunk and she could then convince her to talk to Luís for her. She sang at the top of her voice, competing with the screech of the blender as it dismembered the strawberries, oranges and kiwis, whisking them into the alcoholic liquid.

Chapter Twenty

It's 3am and things are going missing.

Common sense.

Sobriety.

Followed swiftly by my underwear.

My fantastic Georgina Goodman sandals, with their iconic tattoo design, are waiting patiently at the foot of the bed and I just know that if they could, they'd be tapping impatiently on Fiona's cool ceramic tiles.

And I'd hear them loud and clear.

My hesitancy, you see, is irritating us all.

My problem is, it's taken me only a few hours to get to this stage. I've been angry and righteous, have flirted and fancied him and now, typically, Doubt is screaming between my ears and Realisation is exhausted from smacking me around the face like a wet fish.

The wake-up call is slightly belated though.

He was so romantic and impetuous, following me to

Portugal. I'd been furious at first. The presumptuousness of it all! But our flirtations have Barbara Windsor'd since we started on Fiona's punch— we've become all cheeky and saucy. He's surprised me with the lack of suave tenderness that I've grown to expect and I've surprised myself at being attracted to this new, mature version of Nicky. I'm blaming it on the sultry Portuguese air.

And here I am in Portugal, supposedly rushing to the aid of one of my problem-riddled sisters and Nick has followed me and got me into this lusty situation.

And look at me – chickening out like a TV reality-show contestant, all giggles and nerves.

Sod him and his suggestion of 'getting nekkid'!

Him and his warm, compassionate humour, and his con-summate know-how of all things trendy!

But his hands are smooth and luscious against my back. Despite the blanket of heat and lust, I'm aware of my skin puckering up into taut, receptive goose pimples as they prickle all over my body. His body is better than before, his touch more mature and knowing. For old times' sake, isn't that what they say?

But now I can't concentrate.

Inconsiderate of him really. Here I am trying to reprimand myself; attempting, against much resistance, to have a little chat with myself and now he's licking and gold-fishing at my neck - 'bob, bob, bob'; no, it's more of a Southern drawl, a kind of 'bahhhb, bahhhb, bahhhb', but why split hairs, it's delicious.

Reality makes a last-ditch attempt and chucks an image of my husband and kids slap bang on the inside of my eyelids. I *snap my eyes open and am slowly reminded of my surroundings through the soft-focus of pissed vision. It's not so much 20/20, more 96% proof.*

Fiona's spare room, early hours, Portugal.

I have to pull away, much to his irritation.

"No, wait," *I can hear myself panting and playing for time,* "I want to talk."

Nick's fantastic blue eyes twinkle in the semi-darkness as he smiles at me, his eyes glazed with desire. He lifts the light sheet slightly, nodding his head downwards, under the covers.

"OK, so we'll talk," Nick grinned, nodding toward his aroused condition, "but would you mind telling him what the delay is ..."

"Nick, I need the truth. About when we were together."

"Helly," his eyes were lusty as he smiled, "the truth is very much over-rated."

Charley pulled on her thin shirt, making sure she hadn't fastened the three buttons at the top. It was times like this she wished she *did* have a dog to walk, but decided instead some early evening air would do her good. She was restless and fidgety and hot. She knew why. It was tormenting her that Helly was over there, probably talking to Luís. She stepped out into the hot evening, wishing that she could roll back the clock, wishing so much that she hadn't gone to visit Fiona in Portugal. Most importantly she knew she hadn't come to terms with things, and suspected she wouldn't be able to move forward unless she did. She'd gone to Lisbon to visit Fiona and it had been the start of the ugliness of her innermost thoughts and fears now. When Helly had announced last week that she was off to Lisbon Charley desperately didn't want her to go, and yet she hadn't wanted to go with her either. But yet, after her horrendous experience with Luís, she'd told nobody, not even Donal, and that was why he had never been able to make sense of her drinking. It had been a mystery to him why she was an embarrassment to her family and why she secretly detested herself. But she couldn't change the past. Lost in her thoughts, she stared at the paving slabs and the fast food wrappers crumpled in the gutters, as she walked.

She felt only a little better after her few drinks in Finnegan's and was desperately trying to put Lisbon out of her mind. The wine helped fill her head with other, less important things. She decided it was high time to relax and perhaps try her next man-trapping tactic.

Despite throwing open all the windows in the pub the afternoon had been freakishly hot and so she'd staggered home, showered, pulling on her jeans, her green Morgan T-shirt and her Gina stilettos, with a sprinkling of diamanté. The evening was still overpowering and warm and she had embraced the approach of summer by pulling out her extensive shoe collection. She worshipped at the heels of Gina, swore allegiance to Manolo Blahnik and had rearranged her shoes by kitten heels, boots, flats, pumps and highs. The plan was simple. She was to prove to be irresistible – a curry and a chilled six-pack on the front seat.

And spark plugs in her pocket!

All the cute guys would be fighting to help her…

An hour later she was disgusted that she'd worn her fantastic pea-green top. She'd gotten it oily and stained as she'd messed about under the bonnet, which she hadn't planned on, and she was fighting the beginnings of a headache. She had once calculated that on her 'cost-per-wear index' the T-shirt had cost her €70 three months ago and she'd worn it only once. Unlike her necklace that had cost her €170 but that she'd worn every day (bar three) for the past 11 months, making the 'cpw' 50.8cent - and a bargain. She'd hopped into her car and drove it to Ballsbridge, stopping on the way for a takeaway and some cans of beer. She'd flicked the bonnet up, swiftly removing the plugs which were then stuffed deep into her pockets.

Shortly after, Charley was bent in under the bonnet, acting helpless as a fifty-plusser with grey hair and an ill-fitting suit was tampering with her car. She was desperate to get rid of him, certain that any eligible guys would immediately assume he was her father. The trilling of her phone was a welcome distraction.

It was Fiona. "Hey, Fi, what's up?" she slurred.

"Nothing really. Just thought I'd check on you. Helly's out."

"Where is she?"

"Don't know. But I'm sure she's fine. Probably enjoying the sunshine, don't you think?"

"Yeah," Charley sneered, angry at her sisters for not listening to her, "probably. Well, let me tell ya, it's beautiful here today, too. Not so that you'd notice if you listened to everyone."

"Why, what's happening?

"C'mon. You know when summer's arrived here, because you can hear the moaning from miles away."

"It rains here too, you know."

"I don't mean because of the bloody rain. I mean the Irish aren't equipped to deal with hot weather!"

Charley leaned back on her car, flicking her hair and checking out the passing talent. In the light of the awful man who was rooting around in her car, there was nothing like a spot of posing while she was chatting. "We crave the summer for eight months of the year and when it arrives the first thing we do is drag out our sandals from the back of the cupboard and the second thing we do is moan because it's too hot."

"Well, you need to take your cue from Portugal then. Hot summers are a way of life and homes are cool, calm oases of tranquillity."

"Go on." She smiled at the passing Transit van, crammed with dusty builders.

"Shaded terraces, tiled floors, enormous squares of canvas 'sail' are strung from crossbeams to filter out the UV rays."

"Yeah, go on, wind me up. Don't tell me, the barbie replaces the cooker and you're forced to close the shutters and keep the rooms locked up till sundown in preparation for those long sultry nights."

"You got it!"

"So why do you want to go to London then?" She watched as the old fella began to get frustrated and she started to lose her cool with him *and* Fiona.

"It's one thing wanting to bring your child up in a foreign place, but another watching them turn into a foreigner. I want Adriana to know Mum and Dad and Ireland, and I also want her to appreciate England, but I still would like her to be familiar with her Portuguese family too. That means filling her life with all of these things. Honestly, Charley, it's not nice hearing your young daughter rattle off Portuguese, and not being able to understand everything she says."

"So has Helly been able to talk to you about it?"

"I think she's going to try and talk to Luís for me, but I thought *we* were going to talk about it first."

"Well, let's hope she manages to do that, rather than him taking control of her."

"What's that supposed to mean?"

"Nothing. So how's Helly liking it there?"

"Well, we just had a few too much to drink last night. Some old friend of hers, Nick, turned up here unexpectedly and we all got pissed. He's a great guy."

"What 'old friend' Nick?" Charley was unaware that she was screeching. The man helping her had noticed that her spark plugs were missing and had begun to suspect he'd been set up. Indignantly he was punching in the local police station number into his phone, irritated at this eccentric woman who had removed her spark plugs.

Fiona continued, "I don't know who. He knocked on the door here last night and said that he was looking for his old friend Helly. He was really nice, but I don't think she was too keen on seeing him?"

"So did she send him packing?"

"No, he stayed here last night."

"Holy shit!"

"No, Charley, nothing happened. Helly wouldn't do something like that. It was just drunkenness."

"Yeah right. This sounds like déjà moo to me."

"What do you mean?"

"I mean, I've heard all this bull before."

Charley looked across at the man who was barking his location into his phone and realised something had gone wrong.

"Look, Fi, have to go. Talk later."

She pushed her phone back into her jeans pocket and winced as something dug into the top of her leg. She rooted in her pocket and pulled out one of the spark plugs. Her rescuer watched her.

"And, officer! She has the spark plugs in her pocket!"

Charley blushed. "Who are you talking to?"

He disconnected the call, "I've reported you to the police for causing disruption and blocking the roads. I don't know what your game is, lady, but you need help. And quick! The police are on their way."

"Shit, shit, shit!" Charley cursed, just hoping and praying that Steve wouldn't come charging around the corner.

Chapter Twenty-One

Charley had fretted herself into a frenzy. She'd dashed back home after the incident, scurrying to replace her spark plugs and tearing home before the police had arrived. It'd be just her luck for Steve to show up again, embarrassing her. As if it wasn't embarrassing enough. How was she to know that stupid old sod was going to try and help her? Why didn't he just walk away if he didn't want to go along with it? She was so worried about Helly and had tried to take her mind off things and had only got herself into more trouble. As she fiddled in the kitchen, mixing large amounts of vodka with orange juice and Jack Daniels, she fought the urge to book a flight over to Cascais, but realised that she needed to be there *now*, not in eight or nine or ten hours. The phone had been virtually glued to her ear for ages as she'd rung, rung and rung Helly, only to get her answerphone repeatedly. She rang Winston, asking him to come back around and if he fancied going out on the tear. She knew she could rely on him; he said he'd be there in an hour. Grasping the full potent glass, she drank as she walked into the bathroom and was horrified to see a caterpillar growing on her top lip.

"Feckit! I'm growing a bloody moustache! Jesus, it's only getting worse."

Flinging open the bathroom cabinet she grabbed the crème bleach, mixing up the correct quantities of powder to crème over the sink, applying it liberally above her top lip. Wondering how she could kill the required ten minutes, she plucked a straw from the box in the kitchen and proceeded to suck down the remains of her drink. As she poured another one the foaming fluffy marshmallow began to slightly sting her skin. Only three minutes into the process she jumped at the sound of her doorbell.

"Shit!" She panicked, looking around the room, not really knowing what for, and moved to her front door, calling through the wood, "Who's that?"

"Steve. You OK?"

"Em, yeah. I am. OK. Yeah, I am."

"Charley, was that you in Ballsbridge earlier?"

She didn't reply.

He continued, "Only, I heard that a car similar to yours had broken down in Ballsbridge. Something about a drunken driver and fake spark-plug removal?"

"Hang on. I'll be a minute. Em, just a minute Steve." She paused, grinning as she moved closer to the door that stood between them, "Steve? Are you in uniform?"

"Yeah."

Her voice rose an octave or five as she squealed, excitedly, "Hang on right there. I'll only be a second!"

She dashed into the bathroom, grabbed a flannel and removed the bleach concoction from her lip with a single swipe. She knew the box said 'rinse with tepid water' but she hadn't the time or the forethought. The skin between her lip and nose was red, but she dashed for the door anyway, flicking her long hair from her collar, composing herself.

She opened the door,

"Steve! Hi!"

He walked in, looking around suspiciously. "You OK?"

"Yeah, course. Why?"

He eyed the red skin beneath her nose. "Mind if I use your loo?"

"No." She remembered the bleach-clogged flannel on the toilet seat. "Oh," she darted in front of him, feeling like John Cleese, "just hang on a minute." She dashed in, flinging the flannel into the laundry basket, then holding the door wide open for him. "OK, sorry."

She breathed deeply while he was in the loo, swigging at her full-bodied drink.

But his face looked severe as he came out of toilet.

"You been doing coke?"

"What?" She giggled. "Diet Coke, Cherry Coke, what?"

"I'm serious, Charley. What the fuck's going on with you? First I get a call to say that someone resembling you is acting the maggot in Ballsbridge, then I come around here and you won't open the door. When you do you've got traces of white around your nostrils and now I find white powder in your sink. Don't make more of an arse out of yourself! What are you doing?"

Charley exploded, "How dare you! Who the fuck do you think you are? Coming in here!" She stormed to the bathroom, plucking the flannel from the basket. She stuck it under Steve's nose angrily as she hollered, "Look, you ignorant fuck! Bleach! Look! I've got a shagging moustache to bleach, OK? So don't you come in here acting all high and bloody mighty. I wasn't hurting anyone in Ballsbridge, it was just some innocent fun. OK, so I'd had a few drinks. What of it? And all the time," she gasped for breath as she began to lose control, "I'm sitting here shiteing meself about my sisters out in Portugal!"

She flopped down into the chair and began to cry. Loud and wailing, "You don't understand. Nobody does. He's a bastard."

Chapter Twenty-Two

Regret tasted foul.

It turned the orange glow of sunlight into a stark, fluorescent glare.

Helly perched on the seawall while the insides of her head gripped tight. The wall felt dense and cold beneath her and so she swung her legs up, resting her white Birkenstocked feet on the wall. It irritated her, her Mum's voice ringing in her head, warning her about getting piles from sitting on the cool wall. At a time like this too. She'd fully intended on thinking over last night and here she was with her ma's voice squeaking through her head. She watched the brightly coloured fishing boats – the *moliceiros* – and the reds, greens and yellows reminded her of Charley's Rastafarian scarf that she said she'd taken to wearing most lately. Fiona had pointed out the *moliceiros*, explaining about their curved, high prows which were usually decorated as a gaudy figure-head featuring women or marine motifs. She rubbed her hands across her forehead and then lightly over her face as she sighed and attempted to go through the evening in sequence, recalling how she'd got back to Fiona's only to find her and Claudine singing loudly to Robbie Williams and drinking, and Adriana having fun running between them, probably excited at seeing Mummy laughing for once. Fiona had said how her child was a weapon of mass destruction as Adriana took full advantage of her distracted mother. Helly had mucked in and helped them to prepare more punch and alcoholic smoothies and she knew they'd drunk most of what they made while they were making it! Within half an hour they were all having a great time. Vitor had turned up to baby-sit Adriana and then the 'party' had sped up a level as Fiona had dragged out her Boney M and Abba tapes and the three of them had unbuttoned the top few fastenings of their tops and had karaoke'd themselves dry.

Her thoughts of last night were interrupted by a craggy old woman, her deeply wrinkled face the only skin evident from beneath her black dress and headscarf, as she hummed to herself while she lay out numerous sardines to dry on huge trays in the sun. The fishy smell wafted quickly up into her nostrils and her stomach churned at the prospect of the fish soup, *caldeirada*, or the much boasted 365 ways to cook cod. She stood up from the wall and wandered around the curve of the bay towards the private yacht club. As she strolled she looked down and across at the bright colours of the *moliceiros* reflected in the thick sea, them fragmenting and then rejoining with each light 'chop' of a wave. She thought back to last night again and tried to remember what time the knock at the door, which had heralded the arrival of Nick, came. She had turned on her phone after seeing Luís and had already received his texts from earlier in the evening, choosing to ignore them. She was appalled that he was in Lisbon already, and had decided she had no intention of seeing him. And how he'd laughed and charmed Fiona and Claudine with this explanation of how he'd been looking for Helly and her gorgeous sister in Cascais when he'd heard them singing from the open window of Fiona's apartment! Cascais was only a small village. It had been easy. Fiona had invited him up for a few large glasses of punch and before long he was working his act, persuading them to go out to the bars for a few drinks. Helly had been relieved when Fiona explained how skint she was, but then disappointed when New-Mr-Flash-Nick had offered to pay for the evening. She only had to look at Fiona's face to see the girl needed a decent night out. And so they'd gone on a bar crawl. Which had led to them getting in well after two. Which had meant that Helly felt so drunk she wasn't sure whether she needed to pass out or be sick.

Which had meant that she'd, somehow, ended up in bed.

With Nick.

Naked…..

She had by now walked across to the marina, where she sat on one of the small posts, trying to ignore the vivid splash of neon sick on the pavement and then the dog-poo beside it. The tanned, muscly torsos of the fishermen caught her eye and she watched them as they sat on their boats, hands in laps as they repaired their fishing nets. They were virtually motionless except for the muscles in their forearms as they flexed and twisted beneath leathery, hairy skin. She looked at the younger man's hairy chest and immediately thought of Dan. And then of Nick. A wave of nausea washed over her again and she swallowed hard to keep it down. She grabbed her phone from her denim jacket pocket and set about texting Dan and the boys.

Right at that moment, she would have given anything to be back at home with Dan ignoring her.

Things must be bad!

Nick was upset by Helly's swift disappearance the next morning. He had woken in a strange bedroom, with a banging headache, and it had taken a good few minutes of concentration to remember that he was in Helly's sister's apartment. He searched on the floor for the pearly-swirl evidence of safe-sex, but when he saw no sign, assumed he'd simply forgotten. That or she'd already flushed it away. He lay alone listening to the sounds of Fiona mumbling to her cute daughter. The smell of stale alcohol hung heavy in the room and his tongue was parched and stiff. He felt down to his crotch. His early morning stiffness wasn't confined to his tongue. He scrambled in his memory for evidence of Helly the night before, feeling like a love-struck teenager again. He wasn't used to this. He had to get back to his sister's house.

He needed to get a grip. She was married for Chrissakes! If he was honest with himself he was surprised that she'd sprung out of bed so early and immediately worried that she was already regretting it, and hoping that she wasn't.

She was obviously a cooler cookie than he'd given her credit for.

Helly made a decision. It went without saying that she had to talk to Nick before he went back to London. If he was daft enough to follow her to Portugal, then who knows what he'd tell Dan? She had walked up the winding hill to the train station at Cascais and hopped on for the forty-five minute scoot to Lisbon. The digital display in the chrome carriage informed that at 8.45am the outside temperature was 14°c and they were heading from Cascais to Cais do Sodré, Lisbon. She was surprised at the serenity on the train, knowing full well that any London train at this hour would be jammed with commuters, treading on each other's toes and breathing in each other's faces. She looked across at the beautiful middle-aged woman with shoulder-length blonde hair who was knitting a baby-blue creation on a round needle. As the train rumbled off its starting block she rested her forehead against the cold window, allowing her teeth and the insides of her skull to vibrate in time to the beat. She was at the Lisbon destination before she knew it and had already texted Nick, asking to meet him in Lisbon to talk. She wasn't sure whether he'd still be in bed at Fiona's or if he might even be on the same train as her, but she knew she couldn't talk to him in the small town of

Cascais. She hadn't yet figured what excuse she was going to give to Fiona, but put it to the back of her mind – for now. Nick seemed to be enjoying playing cat and mouse with her, and had texted back, suggesting that they meet at the gigantic Cristo Rei statue, across the River Tagus, at midday.

She enquired at the train station only to find that she could get the ferry across to Cacilhas, and then she needed the 101 bus to the towering religious statue. Glancing at her watch, she wondered how she'd kill two and a half hours and so she meandered to the nearest café and ordered a *bica*, which she sat outside to drink with the locals. She watched the impish packs of freeloaders as they hung off the back of the trams, which clunked and whirred their way through the incessant, fast traffic as if they were supposed to be there. It seemed the scruffy, mucky-faced kids were ignored by the driver, who was obviously used to their presence.

Nick tugged on his combats quickly, hopping on his left foot as he struggled to direct his right one through the black-tunnelled leg. He cursed as he hopped onto his mobile and it jabbed into the soft arch of his foot as he landed.

Fiona was too busy trying to persuade Adriana to go back to sleep, whilst convincing herself that she didn't have a headache, to notice Nick's departure.

But Claudine wasn't. As she sat on her balcony a few doors down from Fiona she watched as the tousle-haired Nick tucked his T-shirt into his trousers and frantically pushed the buttons on his mobile as he joined the queue outside the coffee shop for early morning pastries.

By eleven thirty Helly was buzzing on strong coffee and sitting on the noisy, hot ferry for the short sail across the river. The 101 bus was easy to find and she enjoyed the ten-minute ride up and up the winding hills, past the kids in the school playground and through the residential areas up to the point where the copy of the Brazilian Cristo stood high, its arms outstretched as if welcoming visitors to Lisbon. At the bottom she joined the few tourists and took the lift up to the top, where she immediately saw Nick, his back to her as he leant on the railings and admired the panoramic view.

"Glad you could make it."

They stood side by side, Helly feeling sicker than ever, but unable to make eye contact as they leaned in to the side walls of the open-air viewing gallery at the foot of Christ, and looked in awe at the impressive views across Lisbon.

"Course I could make it. Don't be ridiculous. So why did you really come to Portugal?"

He wasn't fazed. "To help my sister out. She and her husband are trying to sell the family business and she needs some help tidying up the books."

"Bullshit!"

"Huh, don't be like that, Helen. You started this."

Her voice was low. "Don't fucking patronise me, Nick. OK, so I made a huge mistake in the cab with you back in London, but I can't believe you've got the gall to follow me here! And didn't Dan think it strange that you asked him for my mobile number? What the hell did you think you were doing?"

"Don't sweat. Christ, you were never this uptight."

"I wasn't *married* back then!"

She turned her back on him. He stepped around her, facing her once more.

"Helen. I love you. I've loved you forever. And I was upset when I saw you yesterday in the café with the Portuguese guy. He couldn't keep his hands off you."

"That is my sister's ex!"

"You like to keep it in the family then?" he grinned.

She hated herself for it, but she had to smile.

"Feck off," she smiled. "Nicky, why did you come here?"

"I told you. I came to help my sister out. But I came to see you too. I still love you, Helen. Making love with you is what life is all about. We fit together, Helly. We're like a jigsaw. Our bodies were made for each other. I'd like to have sex with you again. Well, ideally I'd like to have sex with you and then I'd like to make love to you, but that's neither here nor there. Something really happened last night, didn't it?" He paused and watched her struggle to take in the information before he added, "Don't tell me you didn't feel the chemistry. Just the same as all those years ago, Helly. You still do it for me."

Her eyes darted anxiously as she tried to read his face. He was so groomed and together – so unlike the straggly-around-the-edges Nicky from so long ago, and yet he was right. She'd felt the chemistry. Their bodies fitted together in a way that she never experienced with Dan. But she was terrified by his presence.

He began to walk away, stopping and turning as he grinned, "Oh, and you still hum in your sleep, babe. I need you, Helly. My life isn't complete without you."

Helly felt sick.

Shit! What if he says this to all the women, though? That night I went out with them there were plenty of adoring hangers-on. But what about Dan? He's a good man. Just because he doesn't fancy me any more. And Toby and Jack? How would they feel if they knew what I'd done? What about all of my harping on about another child? What about the daughter I've kept on about? What the hell am I thinking of? Of course, I know I've been neglected in the bedroom lately but that's just him trying to discourage my baby-making ideas. But yet, could it be more than that? Could it be that he doesn't want me any more? Am I just a habit to him? Because it's easy? Comfortable? Routine? Could that be the very reason I'm tempted?

She rushed to the lift, following Nick down and catching up with him at the bus stop.

"Listen, Nick, don't try that one on me. What happened between us was a huge, huge mistake. In twelve years of marriage Dan and I have stayed faithful. I won't be railroaded by you and your flattery. I'm married and I would seriously advise you not to try and jeopardise it. You will only come off the loser."

"Helen," he smiled, touching her hand lightly, "it's not about coming off the loser. You left me twelve years ago for Dan and broke my heart; changed my outlook on life.

277

I've been around you for a few weeks, and already you've changed it back. You've reminded me what I want in life and it's not materialistic. You mean everything to me, Helly. I love you."

She waited for the next bus, refusing to get on the same one as Nick and finally got off the ferry at Cais do Sodré an hour later and still felt like she'd been wrung out. She felt confused, abused and betrayed and couldn't make sense of her feelings, wishing the new suave Nick had come with a health warning. She'd had a couple of texts from Fiona asking if she was OK and had simply replied that she'd gone into Lisbon to sort out the mess she made of last night. She'd have to explain more later. She couldn't face heading straight back to Cascais and the probable inquisition from Fiona and Claudine, and so hung around outside the station, watching the trains come and go, and the buses queue at their stops. She watched as a young couple disappeared into the solitary public toilet together, the young woman tugging and giggling at her boyfriend as she paid her money and then dragged him in behind her. She watched the drunkard as he held his pinched fingertips over the top of his bottle of beer, tipped the bottle upside down and then smeared his damp, beery fingers through his yellowing, white hair. He was moaning abuse in Portuguese and Helly seemed to be the only person taking any notice of him. The sun began to bear down on her blonde head, and she felt the tingling of sunburn begin. She spotted a boutique across the road and figured she'd get a hat, and so she got to her feet, and made her way across. As she went to cross the frantic road a large car screeched to a halt beside her. She felt embarrassed until she realised that, unlike London, nobody had given it a second glance, the sounds of cars screeching, braking and hooting in Lisbon was par for the course. The shrill sounds rose and melted into the hot air, whereas back home they would have cut through the chilly air and hung there. She turned, her face flushed, to see Luís smiling at her through the tinted windscreen. The driver's side window slid down effortlessly.

"Hey, you no look happy? You OK?"

She smiled, relieved at the friendly face. "Yeah, I suppose so."

"You no look OK? Problem?"

Helly made her way around to his open driver's window and leaned down to speak to him. "Not a problem as such, no. What're you doing in Lisbon?"

"Oh, I come twice a week. For my business. I go back to Cascais now. You like lift?"

The thoughts of a ride in his air-conditioned, cool leather-seated car calmed her crinkled mind and she agreed instantly. She slid into the front seat beside him and pulled on her seat belt as he screeched away before she'd even had the chance to plug it in. Luís obviously thought he was a seventies cop as he screeched and skidded through Lisbon. Helly tried to remain calm, but it was hard. She watched the passers-by through Luís' tinted windows and was amazed that his cop-show driving drew no attention. If she'd driven through the streets of London or Dublin in such a way, it would have been expected for them to get out of the car wielding guns and wearing rubber Tony Blair and Ronald Regan masks! She nervously struck up light conversation in an attempt to distract herself from the hair-raising ride. She noticed his neatly folded camel crombie on the back seat as she listened half-heartedly as Luís made small-talk about his coffee empires and Helly nodded and coo'd in what she supposed were the right places. She lost herself in the sights of the ladies dressed in traditional dresses which looked like doilies and the locals as they mixed with tourists darting in and out of the enticing delicatessens.

He suddenly took her by surprise when he rested his hand on her bare knee. Her heart banged in her chest as she struggled to understand what the hell he was thinking of, but she retained a cool exterior as she removed his hand, raised her bum slightly and tugged down her hemline. It was hard to stop the skirt from riding up her legs a little on the shiny leather seats, but Helly clenched her cheeks and sat tall.

She changed the subject. "What's the *padaría* and the *talho*?"

Luís replied, his voice thick and smooth, "The bakery and the butcher."

"Oh, right."

The silence hung heavy in the air and she placed her hands on her legs, worried now that Luís would slime his hand back in her direction.

As Luís accelerated along the straight road through Belém back to Cascais she rested her head back on the leather headrest and thought back over her meeting with Nick. She felt exhausted, realising that she may as well have had the conversation with her mobile phone rather than talking to him. She regretted last night so much.

"So?" Luís cut into her thoughts, "You are probably wondering what I think about Fiona?"

I wasn't actually. Not at that moment, but hey, let's change the subject. After all, that is why I'm supposed to be here.

"OK," she said over the tinkling music that warbled from his radio and forced herself not to wonder about Nick and her infidelity.

"Well, I have made no decision yet," Luís went on, "because I would like to talk to you properly about it. Would you meet me for dinner this evening?"

"Luís, if you don't mind, I won't. Not this evening. I am very tired and had a bad night last night. Perhaps we could talk tomorrow?"

She watched him hunch in annoyance. He stared at the road in front as he replied, "I am busy tomorrow."

"Look, Luís, you're a reasonable man. Why don't you just let Fiona and Adriana come back with me for a few weeks? They can stay at my place and perhaps the time away will put things back into perspective for her. You can't hold her prisoner here. It's not right."

"I don't know. I am not happy with this arrangement. She might refuse to come back, and then what will I have to do?"

"Please don't go on about that Hague Convention again. There's no need for such drama. Just give it some thought, please?"

He nodded, still stiffened as he stared at the whizzing road before them. Helly turned to the window and looked out at sea, watching the sardine fishermen, the size of salt and pepper pots out on their boats, but her mind wasn't really taking it in. It was working at 100mph as she tried to make sense of the last twenty-four hours. She didn't notice when Luís continued past Cascais rail station and headed up toward the Cascais Village Shopping Centre, as he made for his huge, high-walled house halfway up the hill.

Charley hadn't gone to work that day. She couldn't relax and was pacing. Something was wrong and she knew it. She had tried Helly's phone and couldn't get through. The vodka bottle on the table was more than half empty and she poured another glass of it, gulping it down in one go. She was on the verge of obsession with her phone. She tapped it against her leg impatiently as she rang Helly's number for the third time. Was it her phone that was playing up or Helly's? She dialled her again, not expecting her to reply this time. She did.

"Hi." Her tone was clipped. Charley knew she was in company.

"Helly! You OK?"

Helly looked sidewards at Luís who dragged on a cigarette as he drove, "Yeah. Fine, thanks. You?"

"Helly, you're going to think I'm cracked, but you're not with Luís, are you?"

"Em," she kept her voice light and sing-song, irritated at another of her sister's drunken calls, "yes, I am actually."

"Oh Christ, Helly, please get away from him. Please!"

"OK," her tone was playful and patronising, "you go and sleep it off again, love. I'll call you later."

"Helly!" Charley hollered in the noisy Dublin street as Helly clicked off her phone.

She hyperventilated, her fingers shaking with nerves as she tried to punch in Fiona's lengthy number.

Fiona answered immediately. "Charley?"

"Fi, where's Helly?"

"What?"

"Fiona! I've just rung her and she's with Luís."

"What do you mean? She went into Lisbon for the day."

"Fiona," Charley hissed, "just get your arse around to his house and see if you can find out where they are. I know you're hearing me, but you're not listening to me! Please Fi, if I ever ask you to do something again and it's shite, then I'll let you off, but just this one time. Please?"

Fiona hesitated. "OK, but she's probably just chatting to him, getting over her hangover."

"I don't fucking know. All I know is that she's with him now. You must go and find her, please!" Charley began to sob, "Please, please," as she hung up.

She cried into her glass, hoping that she could change the future.

If she wasn't already too late....

Fiona was worried about Helly and took Adriana for a walk to the beach to get her head straight. Especially after Charley's crazy call. She knew that Helly had mentioned her drinking bouts, but hadn't realised she'd got to

283

the stage of Incoherent-Phone-Calls-In-The-Afternoon.
And yet Helly had been completely out of character last
night and now she'd been missing all day. They'd texted
each other earlier and Helly had assured her that she'd be
back later to talk, but Fiona was still unsure.

Helly wasn't comfortable in Luís' huge, silent house. As
he'd pulled onto his driveway, obscured by the high stone
wall decorated with pink flowers, Helly had felt confused.
He had turned off the ignition and twisted in his seat to
pull his heavy coat from the back seat, holding her gaze
at close range for a split second too long. He'd asked her
in, his brown eyes sparkling, his smile warm as he
suggested it was time that they discussed Fiona and
Adriana's future.

Helly was puzzled. She knew Luís lived in a male-dom-
inated world and it was unusual for him to treat any
woman as an equal.

Charley's insane drunken call rattled in her head as
she got out of the car, following him into the impressive
house. As she walked through the terracotta-tiled hallway, the solid oak beams and cream walls breathed a
serene, relaxing ambience. It seemed strange thinking
that Fiona had once lived here. She had gone on through
to the lounge, as he'd instructed and looked through the
impressive stone archway cut into the back wall and
admired the colossal, inviting swimming pool. She had
wondered where Bella was.

He interrupted her silent admiration of his home and
entered the room with two large glasses of port, holding

one out to her as he smiled. She took it from him, looking at the brickwork staircase, the cool marble floor. It
was magnificent. And yet in this enormous, vacuous
house, which threw their voices back at them, hollow
and strange, Helly began to feel decidedly ill at ease. It
was the way Luís looked at her. It was his strange
familiarity. The inappropriateness of it all. She had been
aggravated at Charley's call, although it was hardly
uncharacteristic. Still, it had given her the willies at the
time.

*Honestly, I go away for few days and instead of being
pleased for me, her reaction? To get rat-arsed. I don't know
why she always has to be jealous.*

Anyway wasn't she here last year?

It's not as if she's never been to Cascais...

Luís asked her to sit down, nodding his head at the
cream leather sofa.

"I have something I need to talk about."

"OK." Helly lowered herself down onto the edge of the
sofa.

*He then told me about how pretty he thought I was and
how he thought that he'd got together with the wrong sister.*

*I told him I was leaving and then he necked the whole
tumbler of drink, slowly placing the empty glass down with a
woody thud.*

Helly felt she was moving in slow motion as she looked
down at the oily liquid clinging to the sides of the glass
and slowly sliding down towards the bottom.

*I stood and put down my full glass. I felt sick. It was more
than instinct. It was that churning panic, that surge of*

adrenalin when you look into someone's eyes and know.

You just know…

"Luís, I'm leaving now. I don't quite know what your game is, but I'll explain this only once, so please listen. I'm leaving this evening and I'm taking Fiona and Adriana back to London with me."

He grunted, a deep, loud sound as he tried to interrupt her, his arms lifting from his sides like a puppet.

She continued, speaking over him. "There's no need for you to distrust me, or to worry. It'll only be for a few weeks – perhaps that's all Fiona needs to decide what's best for her and Adriana. There's no need to quote Hague Conventions or politics to her, but just as Adriana is entitled to see her family here in Cascais, she is also within her rights to see her family in London and Dublin too."

She saw the hatred in his eyes and knew that it would be best if she got out of there immediately.

Chapter Twenty-Three

Helly wished that Adriana would keep still beside her. The little girl was so overwhelmed with excitement at being on the aeroplane that she was hopping and fidgeting and banging into the glowering black bruises on Helly's arms and ribs.

She tried not to wince, not wishing Fiona to notice her discomfort. She was relieved when the stewardess had finally crouched beside Adriana's seat and handed her a colouring book and crayons. Helly reclined her seat slightly, settling back into the plump seat and closed her eyes. The second they were shut she could see Luís' angry face. She could virtually feel him slamming her against the doorframe as he lunged and grabbed her.

She'd been terrified.

But something else had kicked in.

Apart from her left foot straight into his nuts.

For once in her life her sense of responsibility

overwhelmed her. As he shouted at her, his voice hoarse and frightening, she knew that she couldn't, she *wouldn't* allow him to ruin her life. She had Dan to think of. And Toby and Jack. And, yeah – even Charley and Fiona and Adriana.

As he'd doubled up, clutching his ugly self, Helly had run for the door, slamming it behind her and then trying to half-run, half-walk along the seafront back to Fiona's. She didn't want to attract any more undue attention, but wanted to get away from him as quickly as possible.

Thank God, she had managed to.

Her stomach did somersaults at the prospect of returning to Dan. Apart from trying to hide the bruises that Luís had marked her with, she had no idea how she'd ever manage to keep an innocent expression on her face when she faced him. She was sure that Nick would be written all over her – her skin, her touch, her scent. She was certain that Dan would take one look at her and see that she was a woman who had been sexually satisfied. For the first time in months. Not to mention a woman who had fought off a potential attack! She sat upright in the blue leather seat of the plane, cutting a completely different shape from the languorous, relaxed one who had travelled a couple of days before.

Fiona had been relieved when she'd seen Helly, asleep on her bed. She had walked the streets of Cascais looking for her, unable to actually approach Luís' front door in the name of this alarmist goose-chase. She'd been tormented by Charley's insane phone calls, and was glad to see that

Helly had made it back to her apartment.

Fiona had been overwhelmed with excitement when Helly had instructed her to pack, but she hadn't hung about.

"Don't you worry about Luís," Helly had snapped. "He's sorted. I've sorted it."

And so Fiona had rallied Claudine, persuading her to take in everything that she couldn't pack – her telly, her kitchen utensils, some of Adriana's toys. She was ecstatic. She'd hoped for Helly to talk to Luís, but hadn't intended on flying back to London with her. Helly had assured her that Dan wouldn't mind, that there was room at their house for her and Adriana. She'd hurriedly packed her essentials, their clothes, a few CD's, Adriana's toys and her violin. Claudine had been great, offering to take her key and hand it over to Joao on the condition that Fiona promised to come back soon for the rest of her stuff and keep in touch. They'd kissed and hugged and had wiped each other's tears. As excited as they both were, they'd been best buddies for a while now and would miss each other desperately. Although, Fiona had joked, she wouldn't be missing the art class, which they'd now called 'the arse class' after Fiona being forced to flash her butt at the students.

But Helly seemed strange. She was tense on the flight, almost withdrawn and moody and Fiona was feeling uncomfortable. Helly insisted on insisting that nothing was wrong every time Fiona tried to ask her why they were leaving so quickly and then she'd been shocked when Helly had snapped at the stewardess and then at

Adriana. It was so unlike her, the mood swings, the extreme irritability. Almost afraid to look sideways at her Fiona glanced out of the corner of her eye to see Helly, sitting upright with her eyes closed, and a bubble of tears settling in the corners of her eyes.

Panic attack at 38,000 feet. I'm swamped with tiredness and yet every time I close my eyes I either see the handsome, lusty face of Nicky or the angry hideous one of Luís. Fiona probably thinks I've gone bananas.

I can't wait to see Dan, to hug my children. The reality is petrifying. You never think it'll happen to you. Isn't it always 'someone else'? It's not about what happens to us, but how we deal with it, isn't it? Right now Toby and Jack, Dan, Pink Turtle and Quattro seem a million miles away but they are my future, and that's what I'll concentrate on. I came to help Fiona — little did I know I'd be bringing her and Adriana back with me.

What else could I do?

Leave them there?

Charley hadn't cried for months. Probably over a year, she couldn't remember. Steve had hugged her as she'd answered his probing questions, crossing the line from potential-boyfriend to friend-and-counsellor. She had to answer 'yes', she had kissed someone she wouldn't fancy if she was sober and 'yes', she usually had a few drinks at the end of the day. She *did* look forward to a few drinks with friends to reduce stress, to relax, to achieve orgasm and 'no', she didn't consider that it amounted to problem drinking. She nodded, her head in her hands, as she listened to him spurt statistics and advice, probably drummed into him as a rookie policeman – how alcoholism knocks fifteen years off a woman's lifespan and how women drinkers tend to be more devious than men. Charley had attempted to fight her corner by explaining how she was renowned for her love of cocktails and her opinion that everything is temporary.

"You don't understand how difficult it is to meet a decent man in this city. You've either got the ones who can't get an erection because they're on bloody Prozac, or the ones who can't get rid of it cos they're buzzing on cocaine! I am lonely, I admit it."

As much as Steve was trying to help her, he was also alienating himself from her. She was already holding him mentally at arm's length, deciding to cool their friendship. He already knew too much about her. She smiled, forcing her stilted grin,

"OK, so I've been a fool."

Steve smiled too, rubbing her shoulder. "Well. you know what I always say, never underestimate the ingenuity of fools!"

"Thanks," she smiled, desperate to be rid of him.

As her phone rang the doorbell went too. She went one way to answer the phone, indicating for Steve to answer the door for her. As Winston 'yo dude'd' with Steve they both turned to see Charley's face turn pale.

"You're not fucking serious!" her voice sounded hollow as she whispered. "Why?"

Feeling awkward, they sat on her sofa and waited.

The pause seemed long until she spat,

"Well, fuck you!"
Slamming down the phone she turned, her face drawn,
"I've been fired."

Chapter Twenty-Four

Helly lay in bed, curled in the foetal position. Her bruises weren't so painful now; the arnica she'd taken must have helped. But the muscles in her groin still ached guiltily – a strange stiffness and yet tenderness which she felt in whichever position she rested her legs. She was overwhelmed with tiredness and yet her irritating prickling mind wouldn't allow her to sleep. She nestled her hands between her tucked-in knees, warm against her soft pyjamas. Dan used to have issues with her going to bed in her thong and vest, but now she'd taken to wearing her pyjamas in bed. She didn't know what he was thinking. She didn't really care. Minimal skin contact was the name of the game now – her favourite bras buried at the bottom of her underwear drawer in disgrace. She was sick at the thought of what she had done.

Besides, she felt a fraud, ashamed that both Dan and Fiona thought her strong and persuasive enough to talk Luís into letting Fiona and Adi come back to London with her at the drop of a hat. She'd heard Fiona telling Claudine that Helly's idea to leave there and then was so ridiculous, it was either completely mad or worth a go.

Thank God she came, though. I don't know what I would have done if she'd refused. I could hardly leave her there, could I?

I had to get out of there, and if that meant them coming with me, so be it!

I know that Dan is impressed that I supposedly "got around" Luís. He's never liked him and he is proud of me. Shame I don't feel so happy about myself. Luís was awful, but my left foot's always been my prized weapon, and getting away from him had been scary, but not a problem.

But Nicky? What the hell was I doing? What an idiot! Wasn't I laughing at all his crap jokes and innuendos? I hadn't exactly got up and marched out, all indignant, had I? I hadn't said 'Oh no Nicky, please go', had I? No, I bloody well hadn't. I'm obviously giving off the signs of a desperate woman! Look how he'd assumed I'd jump into bed with him and let him take advantage of me when I was pissed! But who am I trying to kid? After all the flirting, I was just as 'up for it' as Nicky was.

I used to dread going to bed in case Dan turned his back on me again, but now it's just worse! I soooo want him to hug me and yet simply can't bear the physical contact. Guilt is prickling at my skin and I want to cry and sob and let out this secret inside me, but I'm afraid what it'll do to him. What it'll do to us. What if Fiona or even Adi let slip the fact that Nick was in there in Cascais? Imagine, if he starts questioning me and I have to admit that yes, Nick was at Fiona's, and yes, I was undressed, and no, I wasn't insisting that he leave. I have a desperate need to share it, but I know he couldn't deal with it. I have to block this out. I must concentrate on my life, my family's lives. And I must ring Kaz tomorrow. Quattro are what I need to take my mind off Nicky.

"So you've spoken to Luís?" Dan's voice was subdued under the late-night blanket of quiet in the house. Even the telly was on low and Fiona was reading by the light of the corner lamp. Since her return from Portugal Helly had taken to going to bed extraordinarily early and tonight was no exception. She wasn't even staying up to watch *House In The Sun* otherwise known as *Trade In Your Crap Life For A New One Somewhere Hot.*

"Yes, I rang him yesterday."

"And?" Dan lifted the beer can to his lips.

Fiona shrugged, swinging her feet up beneath her on the sofa. "And he seemed fine about it. I can't understand it really, with all the fuss he's made in the past. Helly must have really done a job on him."

"Yeah," Dan frowned, "I'm surprised though. I didn't think she'd be able to talk him round."

Adriana woke from her sleep, her high-pitched crying zooming down the stairs and into Fiona's ears before Dan was even aware of it.

"God," Fiona sighed, dragging herself to her feet for the fourth time that night, "she's awake again!"

"Jesus, I can't even hear her. It's a Mum-thing, isn't it? Being able to hear your children's cries before they've even started?"

Fiona smiled at Dan, resting her hand on his shoulder as she passed by him. "I may as well stay up there this time. Night, Dan. Thanks once again for everything."

"Night, Fiona, sleep well."

Dan sat in the quiet room, the buzz of the all-but-muted telly the only sound. He channel-hopped, pausing to look at the boobs-and-bums as they joggled around the screen on the late-night game show. Flicking his finger on the remote control, he switched the telly off.

Something didn't seem right about Helly and he couldn't put his finger on it. She'd returned from Portugal two days earlier than planned with Fiona and Adi and, since then, something wasn't sitting right with him. He wasn't sure whether her distant behaviour and early nights were because of the pressure of having Fiona and Adi around, or whether she was still tired after the trip.

And he wondered why Nick had wanted her number.

There was definitely a sniff of something wrong here, but right now Dan wasn't able to pinpoint it.

Adi lay cradled into the crook of Fiona's neck, the curve of her little knees resting on Fiona's tummy.

Fiona loved Helly and Dan's spare room, adored the

bold green walls and wicker furniture. It seemed so modern, so homely, after her tiled, impersonal apartment. She already knew she was going to love this new life, even embracing Adi's new name, as coined by Toby and Jack. It was nice to see Adi playing in the garden, on the grass, with her cousins rather than in the sand or on the beach. She'd waited a long time for this opportunity and she wasn't about to mess it up. She would go looking for a playschool and a job tomorrow.

She just wished Helly seemed happier about things, but then felt guilty – they'd never discussed the night that Nick had stayed over but she had noticed a change of personality in Helly since then. But perhaps she was imagining that. She felt so unsure about things – the arrival of Nick, Helly's surprise meeting with Luís and then the swift departure back to London. Not to mention Charley's crazed phone call.

Adi sighed deeply in her sleep and smiled as she nestled into her mother. Fiona felt a glow of contentment wash over her body, warming her soul in a way that the Portuguese sunshine had never been able to do.

Fiona was cooking breakfast and Helly missed the usual smoky aroma of bacon sandwiches as Fiona fiddled with fresh fruit and yogurt, showing off her new-found smoothie skills. She assumed she wasn't pouring liberal amounts of vodka and Bacardi in, as she had done in Cascais. She usually loved people in her kitchen, took pride in it being the hub of her house and yet, strangely, she resented her presence there.

Was it just that she was a constant reminder of Cascais?

More like a permanent reminder of extra-marital!

Charley had had enough. As if it wasn't bad enough that Steve had mutated from Potential-Shag-Partner to Let's-Talk-Sensibly-About-Your-Drinking-Counsellor, she'd been fired. She supposed she knew it was coming. It was only last week, when she'd rung in sick – again – that the director's secretary had snapped something along the lines of "Well, I hope the straps on your hammock snap! *We're* stuck in the office."

And yet this wasn't at the forefront of her mind. She knew there was only one place she wanted to go, and now with the excuse of work out of the way, she had every intention of going. She dropped her keys off at Winston's, entrusting him with her enormous CD collection and fully-stacked drinks cabinet and got on the bus to Dublin airport.

There was only one person to see at a time like this – the Olympic Flame, the one who never goes out and has no life apart from her family – Helly would sort it all out for her …

Chapter Twenty-Five

By late afternoon the boys were home from school and Helly could hear them squealing as Adi splashed them with water from the inflatable paddling pool while they kicked the football in the back garden. Helly didn't feel as good as she actually looked, in her brown pinstriped trousers and tight cream T-shirt, balancing on a step-ladder at the front of the house as she watered her loaded hanging baskets with the hose attachment. She stepped down to water the conifers and laurel that stood proud in aluminium buckets outside her front door. They seemed dark brown through the heavy tint of her large sunglasses. She sidestepped to pour the trickling water into the window boxes.

I often feel that green reflects my mood.

Sometimes it's a rich, lush green but then it seems to turn into a purple, broccoli tinge. In an early morning light it even seems yellow sometimes. Today I'm a dull, sad moss. A dirty grimy grey-brown.

She felt ridiculous in her sunglasses.

I need them to hide behind. I feel I'm baring my soul every time Dan looks into my eyes.

She was squeezing herself into the imaginary box of denial, forcing herself to keep a smile on her face and put it all behind her.

I'm not sure what's worse, the actual deception or the way that I'm trying to trick myself into believing it didn't happen.

And that I didn't enjoy it.

Loads.

It felt shit though, seeingToby and Jake's faces when I first got back. No matter how 'together' you think you are, you can't hide from your children. It's all about the power of the mind though, isn't it? I'm sure I've convinced Dan that I'm back into my humdrum routine. I just wish he'd stop fussing, saying how much he missed me. How sorry he is for taking me for granted. You know how, when someone's nice to you, it makes you cry? I haven't got time to cry. It's not on my agenda. I'm too busy to stop and cry about this. Anyway, I'm not sure what I'm crying for

Sorrow?

Or guilt.

She couldn't bear to be around Dan or Fiona today. He was in the back garden with the kids, mowing the lawn, losing himself in the loud drone of the mower, and she was unable to watch, wondering what he was thinking. They'd had many summer nights under the massive oak in their garden. It had become their secret, their illicit, naughty and yet deeply romantic place of love-making and now seeing Dan tending to the grass around 'their' oak tree flooded her with the most gut-wrenching emotions.

She was irritated that Dan had taken the afternoon off work to meet up with Nick and Gav. They'd been asked to play at a huge South London venue and were delighted at the prospect. Dan had roared with excitement when he'd come off the phone: "The boys need to meet!"

She'd left Fiona upstairs running a bath for Adi who was covered in choppy shards of grass, her feet decorated with a dirty polka-dot of green. As she came in through the front door, placing her watering can just inside, she heard Fiona calling Adi from the backdoor and cringed at the thought of the child's dirty grassy feet pressing into the runner on her stairs. Everything seemed to irritate her usually calm psyche. Now seemed a good time to lose herself in the housework. She had no intention of coming face to face with Nick in this state. She climbed the stairs, wearily clutching the pile of ironed clothes that needed to be put away. Entering her bedroom, she caught sight of her reflection and hated the guilt that made the tears spring to her eyes without warning.

Fiona didn't think it was as warm as Dan and the boys seemed to. She figured that she'd got more used to the heat in Portugal than she'd realised. Adi threw off her clothes in a flash, leaving crumpled piles of soft cotton folds on the bathroom floor as she cocked her leg and clambered into the bubbly bath. They'd been without a bath in their apartment and suddenly Fiona felt the urge to get in with Adi. She pulled off her clothes, leaving larger piles on the damp floor. It was by now very stuffy and steamy in the bathroom. She stood in the bath to open the sash window, desperate for a waft of cool, fresh air. She pulled at the top of the stiff window, her arms high above her head, her bare breasts squashed against the glass, jostling with her jerky movement. She noticed a red Mercedes coming down the street but then went back to cursing and pulling at the stiff wooden window. At last she managed to shift it, and watched the steam as it was sucked from the room, escaping quickly to the cooler, outside air.

She recognised the face of the guy who got out of the red Mercedes. It was Nick.

He got out of his car and did a double take, seeing a naked woman at Helly's top window. Fiona watched as his face stretched into a wide smile and he raised his hand – and waved.

Startled, momentarily oblivious to her joggling boobs and wobbly tum, she waved back.

"Morning!" Nick called, his voice clear through the now opened window as he put his hands over imaginary boobs. "Three of spades, is it?"

Fiona's face flashed beetroot, her eyes pulsating in her head so fiercely she felt sure they'd fizzle and melt. Rooted to the spot, she looked down at herself.

Mortified.

Jumping back from the window, she sat down in the bath with Adriana, certain that she heard the water hiss as she got in.

I wish I'd grabbed Fiona earlier and got out of the house
before he arrived
But it's too late now.
He's rung the bell, and that's it.
Nick is in the house.

Scowling, Helly listened to the cheery banter as Dan chatted with Nick downstairs. She was dreading Fiona meeting him again, especially after their night of indiscretion. She just knew he'd be lapping up her attention and Fiona would be delighted to see a friendly face that wasn't a blood relative! Stamping across to Toby's bedroom she grabbed the duvet, flinging it high and letting it fall, parachute style, onto his bed. She turned to the window only to see Dan standing right beneath the oak. Talking to Nick. The nausea rose and fell in her in an instant.

Seeing them both together is just too much.

I feel so bloody awful. And more so because we were so good together. Just like before.

It had all seemed so consuming, so terrible when I'd spoken to Nick in Lisbon, at the Cristo Rei statue. And now, here at home, watching him talk to Dan, it feels even worse.

Forty minutes of bed-making, toy-clearing, laundry-folding and cobweb-inspection was pushing it by anyone's standards and Helly knew she'd have to face the men sometime. She was lying on her bed, leafing through a magazine, when she heard Fiona come out of the bathroom with Adi.

"You asleep in there?"

Great! Shout it as loud as possible. Make it plainly obvious

303

that I'm hiding up here.

She's getting more like Mum every day!

She cleared her voice, preparing to sound light and breezy. "Just coming now. Could you put the kettle on, please?"

She couldn't delay it any longer and figured it better to go downstairs now, rather than when Nick and Dan were both in from the garden. She gathered up the dirty washing in her arms and skittered down the stairs. As she turned at the last step she didn't notice the wafting bedsheet hanging in a huge loop from her pile, and then her left foot was stuck in it and she was already tripping, falling, landing on the polished hall floor, rugby-tackling the washing as she slid along. She looked up to see Nick, Dan and Fiona gaping at her from the kitchen, amazed at the grand entrance.

Nick broke the silence. "Falling for me, Helen?" he quipped while Fiona began to giggle.

"Leave it out, mate," laughed Dan. "She's my wife, so she's falling for *me*." He stepped forward and helped her up. "You all right, babe?"

Helly tried to smile, but it wasn't easy. Her knee hurt, but she knew her pride had taken more of a beating.

"Yeah," she tried to laugh it off, "I'm fine. Christ, you couldn't do that if you tried, could you?"

She limped past Fiona and crouched in the kitchen as she stuffed the mixed load into the washing machine.

Dan opened the fridge door, pulling out two cans of beer, cracking them open and Helly pretended not to watch as he and Nick walked back out into the garden.

"Hey, are you all right there?" Fiona joked. Then, following Helly's gaze, added speculatively, "I've just been eyeing Nick up. Tasty, isn't he? I wouldn't kick him out of bed." She paused, then when Helly made no response, added, "Mind you, after what he saw an hour ago I wouldn't say he'd be jumping over people to get to me."

"Why, what happened an hour ago?" Helly hadn't meant her voice to be quite so sharp, and surprised herself.

"Hey, keep your cool! What's wrong with you?"

Helly stopped forcing the laundry into the washing machine with the vigour of a shopper after the last parking space and stood, turning to face Fiona. "Nothing, sorry. Open up those HobNobs over there and tell me what happened before they come back in."

I didn't mean to snap at Fiona. And no – I'm not jealous.

Me and men are done from now.

All men.

Even Dan.

Helly was relieved when Gav finally arrived. It meant that the guys took their instruments into the lounge and she was excused from being the loyal wifey. She and Fiona had earlier agreed to go for a short walk, just to get out of the house.

Well, if she could prise her sister away from the lads.

"Fi," Helly faffed and fluffed with wet towels at the lounge door, "would you come and help me with these?"

Fiona didn't hear as she continued chatting with the fellas.

Helly tutted, "Don't worry. I'll text you!" Her sarcasm

was lost on deaf ears.

She hung out the towels, then went back up the stairs and started organising her clothes, grabbing her phone a few minutes later and texting her sister.

The hollow sounds of wooden heels on wood accompanied Fiona's approach.

"They're some laugh! What a great crowd of lads!"

Helly tried to appear nonchalant. "Yeah, they're OK. Suppose you'd get fed up with them if you saw them every week."

"No, I wouldn't! They're right fun! And Nicky is sex-on-legs! Better than chocolate! Though I reckon you already know –"

"Reckon?" Helly interrupted sharply. "I reckon he's well capable of a tenuous relationship with the truth when it suits him. Like most men."

"What's that supposed to mean?" said Fiona, realising that Helly had cut right across her oblique reference to Nick's night in Cascais.

Helly flopped down onto her plump bed, and it slightly bounced beneath her. Fiona pushed an empty suitcase to one side and sat beside her.

"What's up, sis?"

"Oh, nothing. I'm just being silly. I suppose I just feel resentful sometimes that he's so taken with them all."

"But they seem really nice guys. What's the problem? Isn't it better he gets beered-up away from you, rather than in your face?"

Helly shrugged.

Fiona continued, "Look, being away next week will do

you good. It's just what you need –"

"I think it's bad enough that I left my family for a week to go to rescue you, never mind going off again now!"

"Sorry. I didn't realise it was so difficult this end for you."

"Sorry, Fi. I'm just feeling guilty about leaving them for the week. And I'm worried about Charley. And you! I'm worried about you and Adi too."

"Look, don't worry about me! But you're right about Charley. Perhaps now I'm here we can try and talk to her every day on the phone. I might be able to talk some sense into her."

"Yeah, maybe. I'm sorry. I'm just not feeling too happy at the moment."

"No worries," Fiona stood and readjusted her too-tight jeans. "Happy is temporary. You have to ride the theatre of life."

"Or in Charley's case, ride anyone that's interested."

Fiona laughed, "Oh, she can't be that bad. Can she?"

Helly stood beside her and began folding her clothes again, "Well, from now on my first priority is that I'm a mother."

"Come on then, Mum, let's get out for that walk."

"OK, I'll just go to the loo."

"I'll wait downstairs."

Fiona grinned, winking at her strangely irate sister, glad to see the suggestion of a smile on her face again.

As she waited in the hallway for Helly, Nick appeared, on his way to the front door.

"Oh, leaving already?" she asked, deliberately trying to

act normal after exposing herself to him. Although, in the light of the art-class scenario, she wasn't as mortified as she'd expected.

He smiled as he replied, "Not at all. Just need to grab something from my car."

"Not your inhaler, I hope. Especially after that episode at the window."

"Far from it," he grinned. "Nice tan."

She waited for him to come back in and as he did she stepped in front of him, "So what do you think of our Helly then?"

Completely unruffled, he shrugged. "I think she's lovely. Why?"

"No reason. I just wondered."

He walked past her, throwing in, "I think she has a huge charisma that she's completely unaware of."

"Most definitely. But, tell me, why do you think she's avoiding you?"

He turned to face Fiona square in the eye. "I wasn't aware that she was."

Fiona raised her eyebrows.

He continued, "Is she? How do you know?"

"Oh, just call it sisterly intuition. It hasn't gone unnoticed anyway."

"I can't imagine what you mean."

"Maybe give it some thought then."

"Right."

"Oh, and Nick? Dan's a great guy. They're a fantastic couple. There are plenty of impressionable single women out there to work your charm on."

"Implying what, exactly?"

"Implying nothing. Just a friendly statement. That's all."

Fiona and Helly took a walk around the tree-lined streets, viewing the four- and five-storey white Victorian houses. They'd loved walking in Ireland, but found much more sport in it in London. It was intriguing looking in through people's windows and checking out their choice of interiors. Most of the white stucco houses around Belsize Avenue had been converted into flats and they both yearned for one of the pretty multicoloured houses around Chalcot Square in Primrose Hill, one of the area's best addresses. They wandered past the attractive mews cottages tucked off Belsize Lane and then headed back.

They turned the corner approximately three minutes too late. Any earlier and they would have seen it and had less of a surprise when they got home. They would have seen Charley looking like something out of The Priory knocking on Helly's door. They would have seen Dan's mouth contort into a goldfish 'O' and then how he'd swiftly remembered to smile at yet another sister. They would have heard the whoops, laughter and banter as she'd walked into the kitchen and met Jono, Gav and Nick.

After hearing so much about him all those years ago, she finally got to meet him. And she thought he was dead cute.

The last person I need to see right now is Charley and she's here!

*Flirting and laughing and giggling with Dan and Gav . . .
and Nick . . . I can tell that she likes him and she's lapping up
the charm. And don't I feel pathetic standing in the kitchen
with my bloody sunglasses on! My face probably looks like it's
reflected in the back of a dessertspoon, it feels so puffed up.
And great – there's my knickers on full view, rotating at the
window of the washing machine for all to see as it jerks into
mega-vibrate mode. Dan offers them biscuits, grabbing at the
rattling tin. I watch their faces beam at the chocolate
HobNobs and Jammy Dodgers. And I was trying to save
what's left of them for when the boys get in from school! Did
you ever feel like your house was being taken over? And I
daren't ask where Charley's expecting to stay. It only takes
one look at her, perched up on the high stool giggling, the two
huge pink suitcases beside her, to know. They'll hardly miss
me if I go upstairs now and make up Toby's room for her.*

Just for a few days though . . .

"So what's with the sunglasses?" Charley's voice
clipped into the merriment.

Helly froze. The silence was painful as she turned,
crowbarring a smile onto her face.

"Oh, just forgot to take them off. Still got a bit of a
headache from earlier." She pointed towards her forehead
as she spoke.

"Yeah," Gav's voice was warm, "Dan said you were
quite the hero, bringing back your sister from Portugal."

Helly looked awkwardly at the faces, all waiting,
anticipating her story.

"No." Her voice was extraordinarily light. "No, I don't
think so. Just persuasive, you know."

310

She turned to leave but Charley spoke again.

"So I take it you *did* agree it all with Luís? I mean, was he OK about it? OK with *you?*" She stared at Helly intently, and then, remembering her audience, attempted a sinister expression, "I don't have to go over there and sort him out, do I?"

Dan interrupted, "See what I've got to live with now, lads? You've heard of the Mafia – well, meet the Murphia!" Everybody laughed at him, which only encouraged him to continue. "Yep, I'm now signed up for weeks of interrogation, turf wars over who wears what top and intense questioning about every single thing that anybody might say at any time. The Murphia have arrived! That large family group who tend to take over wherever they go. They're not so bad, one at a time, but bring them together? Bullies," he teased, "just bullies. It's bad enough having 'the Don' ringing from Wicklow every other day, but now, the three of them under the one roof? It's only a matter of time, lads, only a matter of time …"

Helly was grateful to Dan for unwittingly changing the conversation. She was used to him calling her family the Murphia. He'd done it for years, ever since he'd met her extraordinarily large family of extended cousins, aunts and uncles. She smiled across to Charley. "Charley? Got a couple of minutes?"

"Sure." Charley hopped down off the stool and followed Helly, knowing with every inch of her body that the guys were checking out her backside as she shimmied out. She addressed the back of her sister's legs as she followed her up the stairs. "So will we get out for a bit of dinner and a few drinks? You, me and Fiona?"

"Hardly."

"C'mon, we haven't been together for years. We have to get out and celebrate."

"My life isn't like that any more, Charley. I've got the children to think about, I've got bills to pay. I don't have so much disposable income these days. Anyway, is that the first thing you can think about, drink?"

"My treat. You can't refuse, can you? Anyway," she linked arms with Helly at the top of the stairs, "you could do with a few bevvies to lighten you up. I know I could."

Helly shook her head in resignation, disappointed that Charley's opening shot had been one regarding alcohol.

The truth was, though, that Charley had been slightly perturbed by what she'd read in the in-flight magazine from Dublin to Stansted, about women and alcoholism – how drinking was linked to breast cancer, higher risk of miscarriage and cirrhosis of the liver. She knew she regularly exceeded the recommended fourteen units per week max. But none of that stopped her raiding the small bottles of Smirnoff that the powder-faced girls had trollied up and down the aisle for the duration of the hour flight.

Charley did very little to help Helly as she set up the camp bed in Jack's room for Toby and remade Toby's bed for Charley.

The boys are going to be ecstatic. They were happy enough about Fiona and Adriana, but Auntie Charley's a completely different thing. And by the looks of those two giant suitcases this isn't a weekend visit.

"So how long are you planning on staying?" Helly tried to keep her voice light, but was sure it betrayed her true feelings of irritation.

"How long?" Charley sounded surprised. "I'm here for good, Hel. I'm outta Dublin. Sick of the shite weather. And the lack of decent men. I'm here for good, babe."

"You can't stay here for good! What about your job?" She no longer pretended to be casual about this.

"Oh, I know. Give me a few weeks to sort myself out and I'll be outta your hair. I couldn't stand working for that slave driver anyway. I just need to sort out another job, get some money together. Although I've brought my savings with me, just to keep me going."

"Jesus!" Helly sighed as she wrestled the duvet into its brightly coloured cover.

Dan's called up the stairs, his voice muffled slightly as it bounced off the walls and corners, "Babe, we're heading down to The Eagle to talk. Fiona's in the garden with the kids."

Charley hopped up, suddenly bought back to life as she checked her watch, "God, yeah look. It's beer o'clock . . ."

Helly followed her to the doorway, watching her trot down the stairs.

"Mind if I join you?"

Charley's voice was syrupy and Helly knew they wouldn't mind at all. If it had been Helly or Fiona that was asking, the answer would certainly be different. But

Charley was charming, flirty, one-of-the-lads, and she knew it. Within minutes the house was, once again, in silence.

By early evening the children were asleep. Helly was delighted – *EastEnders* hadn't even finished! She felt as though her hair was sitting limp on her head but she was much too tired to wash and freshen it.

Instead, she relaxed with Fiona in front of the telly.

As she lifted her large mug to her lips, then discreetly spat back the cold coffee – she hadn't realised it had been sitting there for so long – she heard the front door bang and Charley 'coo-eee' just too loudly as she walked up the stairs. Helly prayed that she wouldn't wake the boys. Losing herself in the predictable East London Bad Boy/Indian Family Market Stallholder argument she didn't notice when Charley came into the room, eyes adorned with Gothic black make-up, dressed in an inappropriate miniskirt with kick pleats at the front.

Fiona spoke first. "My God, are you turning back time or holding back the years?"

Charley laughed, throwing her head back theatrically, her long dark hair swaying in a glossy mass. "As I get older my fashion sense has simply become more risqué and adventurous. And what's wrong with that? I like to make the effort. So, girls, are we hitting the town tonight? You look like a right couple of sad-acts there."

"I thought you went out with the fellas?"

"I did," she smiled. "I'm back. I came back to get you two."

"Well, you can go," Helly didn't look away from the telly, "but I'm staying put."

"Come on! Don't be so old. Dan will be back in half an hour and he's already told me he'll mind the kids for you. And if he doesn't, I can guarantee it's gonna be a night worth booking a baby-sitter for. We're heading for the West End!"

They both groaned, but at least Fiona rose to her feet as she did so.

"What do you reckon, Helly?" she asked her, completing ignoring her statue-like I'm-Hypnotised-By-The-TV pose.

Charley marched across, flicking off the television and sitting on the coffee table in front of Helly.

"Look," it was obvious she'd had a skinful in the pub with the lads earlier, "when I was on my way home from the pub I was stopped by a gypsy lady selling pathetic little sprigs of lavender in tinfoil. Well, she told me that I should be with my family tonight and we'd have fun. I then told her to feck off, and that I didn't believe her and guess what? I bloody tripped over!"

Helly looked up at her, wishing not for the first time that she could raise one eyebrow. "And your point is?"

"My point is, Helen, that she could be right! Once I'd told her what I thought of her, she made me trip and so she must be right about the fun night."

"Charley, you probably tripped because you're half-pissed. Honestly, I can't believe you go for all that crap."

"You can talk. What about Madame Lydia at Mother Redcap's? That was all your idea, wasn't it?"

"Was it?" Helly suddenly remembered the prediction – travel, pregnancy in the family and sex with a handsome stranger.

My goose pimples are like hedgehog spines! Could she really have foreseen me going to Portugal? Fiona and then Charley coming to London? But sex with a handsome stranger? That couldn't be Nicky, could it? He's not a stranger . . .

And a pregnancy? Maybe I was right about Fiona's tight waistbands!

Holy Jesus!

Charley interrupted her thoughts, "Come on, don't make me put your arm up your back. I promise you'll have a great time. You see, the trouble with you is you're assuming you're not going to enjoy it. You should never *never* assume."

Helly snapped, "Oh Charley, don't give me the 'ass of u and me' speech. What next? There's no I in team?"

Fiona and Charley looked perplexed at each other as Helly stormed up the stairs, they hoped, to get ready.

She was so scared of what she'd just realised, that she was angry.

Chapter Twenty-Six

The Stag was packed. Charley was in her element, chatting and flirting with the barmen and customers as she ordered three Sex On The Beach cocktails.

"Sex On The Beach or Sand In Your Bum Crack?" she guffawed, causing everyone around to laugh at this loud, attractive Irishwoman who was so entertaining.

Helly tried to relax. She stood in the corner with Fiona, surrounded by the hot bodies, feeling herself being brushed against as people cut their way through the crowds. She had noticed the way the guys had looked at them when they arrived – Charley with her short skirt, great legs and silky dark hair, Fiona with her all-over sun-tan, bronzed arms and neck exposed in the spaghetti-strap floral dress and herself – well, she had deliberately dressed down and worn her faded-beyond-belief 501's and navy blue T-shirt with JESUS LOVES YOU, BUT I'M HIS FAVOURITE on the front of it. The only way she'd complied with the 'rules' of the evening was by wearing the strappy stiletto sandals that Charley had insisted upon. She'd initially slid her feet into her powder-blue Birkenstock mules but Charley's yelling soon put paid to that. She had used the term 'taxi shoes' as Helly came down the stairs, comfortable in her mules, declaring that they were all to wear shoes that were only comfortable enough to hobble from the house to the taxi and then the taxi to the pub. So now they all teetered in gorgeous, but uncomfortable shoes.

They heard Charley's return before they saw her, weaving her way through the crowd, holding three large drinks precariously as she yelled cheerily at people to make way.

"You know. The guys here are such a laugh. Why didn't I come earlier?"

"Can't we sit down somewhere?" Helly was uncomfortable in the crowd.

And my shoes are already pinching me!

"Sit down?" Charley screeched. "What, and miss all the fun? No chance."

Helly opened her mouth, inserting the straw, clutching it between her teeth as she sucked down the chilled sweet drink – completing the transaction in only six long slurps.

"Finished," she breathed, holding the empty glass out to Charley.

Charley and Fiona laughed. "Fecking hell!" said Charley. "Aren't you the dark horse?"

Helly simply shook her head, "If you're wanting me to

get into the spirit of the evening, then best you get me a refill. Make it an extra large one."

By the third round Helly was more than merry, and for the first time since the 'incident' was smiling and relaxed as she listened to Charley's tale of being sacked.

"I didn't bother to work any notice – I just got out of there. Wanted to see my sisters, didn't I?"

They laughed as she told them about a new 'friend' whose number she'd decided to delete off her phone. "You see, it's important to avoid Drunken-Phone-Calls-To-Unsuitable-Men Syndrome."

"What's that?" Fiona asked, embarrassed that she felt so amateurish at the contemporary rules of flirting but full of anticipation of improving her tactics now, influenced by the well-practised Charley.

"You've been off the scene too long, babe," Charley smiled as a hunky skinhead slipped past her, slightly too close for politeness. "Before mobiles, a girl needed to cover her phone in yellow Post-It's saying *'Don't ring Paul'*, or *'You'll regret it in the morning'*, but now, having the number on your mobile means drink-dialling is so much easier *and* then there's the 'last dialled numbers' reminders the next day too!"

Helly laughed, knowing she was too loud. "So what're you saying? 'I Just Called To Say I Love You' isn't appealing any more?"

"Course not. It just strokes their over-inflated egos."

They didn't notice her voice soften as she told how she'd done the very same with Donal just after their split, how she'd whipped out her Ericsson T28 and called him

319

to say she was coming over, her excuse being that she'd left something behind when she'd moved out!

"It was all OK until he'd asked what I'd left. Guess what I said?" Fiona and Helly were transfixed.

"My mobile! As if!"

Their laughter rang around the thronged pub and Helly teetered through the cigarette smoke to the bar, wobbling on her heels, for more drinks. She was beyond caring about how little disposable income she had or whether Dan was OK looking after the sleeping children. Or even that she had completely forgotten that she'd stopped taking the pill! It simply didn't bear thinking about. Not tonight, anyway. As she returned to their corner, spilling most of the cocktails on the way, she decided to challenge them both.

"So, why London? What do you think is here that isn't anywhere else?"

Fiona smiled widely as she launched into her favourite subject, "Well, I can't wait to get a job and save enough for some cosmetic surgery."

Charley screeched. "You're not serious! You're going to actually *do* it?"

"I am too. I dream of Botox, Perlane, dermabrasion and tummy tucks."

"Jesus, do you think you have that body dysmorphia disorder? It's a psychiatric condition, you know."

"Course I don't. I just don't like most of my body. What's unusual about that? Aren't most women that way?"

"No!" Charley and Helly answered together.

"You'll end up like those hideous Hollywood women," said Charley, "addicted to the surgeon's knife. What's her name? That New York socialite who they call the Bride of Frankenstein or something?"

Helly knew – she'd read the *OK, Hello!* and *VIP* magazines too. "Jocelyne Wildenstein. And it's the 'Bride of Wildenstein', that's the joke. She's spent about £100,000 so far, so they say."

"Yeah," spat Charley, "and she still looks shit."

Helly slurred slightly as she spoke, not noticing the slight dribble run down her chin. "Well, Fiona, forget about the plastic surgery. Let me tell both of you about the reality of life in London: exorbitant council tax, rain one day searing heat the next, damp-morning-induced frizzy-hair condition, cancelled Tube trains, over-stretched NHS, speed cameras, congestion charges, ATM machines that swallow your card, wheel clamps with hundreds of pounds release fees. You wait, it won't be long before you'll have Watched-Kettle Syndrome – you'll be waiting for your lives to change again."

Helly was interrupted as a middle-aged man approached them. He was sweating profusely. Charley lit up another fag, the orange flame dancing as reflection in her eyes, and Helly, leaving Fiona to practise her stand-offish body language on the Man From Atlantis, hopped on her. "Another? That must be nearly ten gone already!"

"Well, you can't smoke in pubs in Ireland any more. I'm making the most of it."

"But have you even *tried* to give up?"

Charley shook her head. "Can't."

"What do you mean 'can't'? Have you tried the patches?"

"Oh yeah," Charley smiled as she drew in deeply, "the nicotine patches are great." She exhaled the smoke slowly, catching Fiona's eye as she spoke. "Stick one over each eye and you can't find your fags!"

Charley had booked a taxi and surprised her sisters when she announced that it was waiting outside. Already Helly was fighting off 'spinny- rooms' and Fiona was slurring her words. They hoped the cab was taking them home.

But Charley had other ideas …

The queue to get into the West End club was ridiculous.
Especially in these shoes!
I haven't queued outside a club since I was a teenager. But I've no intention of telling Charley that – she'll only take it as a sign that I'm even more of a real saddo.

Helly and Fiona found the cool evening air diluted their plastered state, inducing sobriety quicker than you could say "I'll have another". Charley was already trying to queue-jump as she stood near to the entrance, laughing and chatting with a crowd of guys from Liverpool who were down for the weekend for their mate 'Tommo's' stag weekend. Charley was obviously part of the entertainment for them as she squealed and giggled when they tried to throw coins down the front of her low-cut black vest.

"Hey, hey, Tommo, look! We've got a new game 'ere, pal – 'boob slotties'! Come on and try!"

Helly cringed at the sight of her forty-year-old sister jutting out her chest like a porn queen as the wobbling men got closer and closer to aim their loose change at her tits.

They shuffled forward in the queue, thankfully quicker than Helly had expected, and soon stood near the entrance, below the blue-tinted brick walls, which absorbed the neon lights. The honking of black cabs, the pungent smell of drains and spicy takeaways stung at Helly's nose and she wished, she really wished, she could go home.

My feet are literally killing me! It's the first time I've worn shoes like this in years and I'm half afraid to take them off. I'm going to have enormous blisters in the morning and if I look down at my feet now they're probably swollen over the edges of my so-delicate sandals. Even the feel of my jeans lightly touching my feet is agony! And for what? A hangover the next day?

Aware of Fiona mumbling away at her left ear, Helly nodded and 'mmm'd' in the pauses and looked around at the buzzing nightlife of the city at a time when she was usually in bed listening to her husband tucking the duvet in around himself in a bid to avoid skin contact with her. She was transfixed by the yellow-haired tramp across the road as he yelled abuse at passing cars but her spell of voyeurism was broken by Charley as she tottered over, grabbed her by the shoulders and frogmarched her to the front of the queue to stand with the Liverpool guys, introducing her as her sister, 'the Olympic Flame!'.

At which they all guffawed!

"Charley," Helly hissed, "please! I don't want to spend the rest of the night with them!"

"Don't be so fucking miserable, Helen. They're great lads." She spoke through gritted teeth into Helly's ear, "At least we'll have a laugh with them. Better than spending the evening with a crowd of middle-aged, sad married men with post-nuptial-syndrome. Be nice!"

The 'Fandango Club' wasn't quite what Helly had expected. It was so hard to tell with these London clubs – what they looked like from the outside so often gave no indication of what to expect on the inside. They sat with the stag weekenders and in the end Helly was relieved – it gave Charley someone else to irritate rather than her and Fiona. The drinks flowed and the fuzziness of being drunk wasn't long in coming over Helly again.

"So, Tommo," Fiona ventured, "when you getting married?"

"Next weekend, love. We've just spent the last few days in Las Vegas. Lads' week, you know. We hired ourselves some tuxedos and played the machines."

His spotty pal interrupted, "Yeah, and Tommo didn't really take advantage of the deals there. What was it, Tommo? Two 'ladies of the night' for ninety-nine dollars!"

They all roared with laughter as Helly kept a straight face and remarked,

"Christ, they can't have been much good if you needed two of them!" The blond guy who sat opposite from Helly grinned at her subtlety and winked at her.

Jesus! That's all I need! I must have it written across my

forehead or something.

Tommo was rugged and extremely good-looking. And he knew it. He got up and staggered as he spun, trying to determine which way the bar was.

"So?" Charley spoke loudly above the background music. "What is it with men's legs when they're drunk?"

"Hey?"

"Well, don't you guys forget how you walked when you were sober? I mean look at yourself. You're lurching, banging your arms off your sides. And you haven't a clue what to do with your hands."

"Yeah," Fiona joined in, standing in a wobbly fashion as she lifted her empty glass, "your legs don't know you and your arms are droopy. You look dead stupid. It's a man thing, isn't it?"

Fiona's remarks hung in the air, ignored by the crowd as Charley sniped, "Well, Fiona, by the looks of you, the answer is 'no', it isn't just a man thing!" She leaned across and tugged at the back of Fiona's dress which she'd inadvertently tucked into her knickers the last time she'd been to the loo. Fiona hadn't noticed, and neither had they – until she stood up.

Helly laughed, watching Fiona zigzag her way across to the toilets again, and half-listened as she caught the tail-end of Charley's flirtations.

Charley was leaning in, onto Dave, rubbing her hand up his leg as she shouted, much too drunk to make any sense, "Look at you, babe. Your hairline's nearly history. What is it with men and their hair? It's either parted, unparted or departed!"

To which Dave leaned across and said something into her ear. Helly cringed, feeling sick once again as she watched her sister yell while she caressed Dave's upper thigh, "So, what do you mean? You think your body's a temple or what? Well, babe, mine's a bloody amusement park!"

They settled back at the round table and watched the frilly-knickered girls can-can to the music of the violin-playing cowgirl onstage. Fiona clapped the whole way through, chewing Helly's ear as she moaned how she hadn't practised enough in Cascais. The Liverpool lads whooped as the violinist finally joined in, stripping out of her suede skirt and gingham blouse, revealing suede nipple tassles and a cowhide G-string. It was all really bizarre.

Helly felt she was at a freak show. She didn't know what to expect next. A saxophone began to squeal as a troup of tuxedo'd men marched onto the small stage. Tommo hollered to his mates that's how they'd looked in Vegas last week, just as he stood and made his way to the bar. Helly's stomach lurched at the prospects of yet more drink. She felt exhausted and rather sick. The mixed audience clapped both in and out of time as the tuxedos were thrown off and then the white shirts until finally, the fever-pitch atmosphere exploded as the suntanned, six-packed hunks finally pulled off their trousers to reveal outlandish stockings and suspenders. Feeling extremely bored and tired, Helly couldn't see the humour in it. Least of all when Charley stood up and clapped, laughing hysterically. The gaudy performances were irritating

Helly and she began to worry as the waves of nausea washed inside her stomach. Charley was thrilled, rubbing her hands together as one of the suspender'd hunk stepped down off the stage and made his way toward her, his muscle-bound torso gleaming under the coloured lights.

The innuendo is making me feel ill. All this bare skin! I daren't say anything to Fiona or Charley, but I'm just not ready for all this sexual tension. I don't want to feel sexual right now. I want to be biological, physiological. But not sexual. My body is not like that at the moment.

And could you blame it? It's probably in severe guilt-mode.

The place erupted into laughter as Charley got down on her knees, the stripper's stocking'd legs solid before her as she rolled down the silky threads from him, revealing tanned and shapely thighs. He thrust his significant pouch forwards into Charley's face. She laughed along with the rest of the crowd.

Except for Helly. The tears flooded to her eyes. Nobody noticed. They were all too busy clapping and laughing at the 'great sport lady' who was still smiling as the oiled body of the stripper lay on her, grinding at her pelvis through his red silk thong. Helly felt her muscles contract right from her stomach up to her neck.

Nobody heard her chair scrape on the floor as she stood.

Nobody noticed as she clapped her hand over her mouth, her eyes bulging with panic as she ran towards the toilets.

Nobody missed Helly as she puked a good thirty quids' worth of alcohol into the toilet bowl of The Fandango Club.

Nobody heard her retching and crying as she struggled to eradicate the guilty memories of Cascais.

"Fuckit, my skirt and top are ruined!" Charley swiped and wiped at her pleated miniskirt and silky top as she noticed the darkened oily patches that the stripper had left her with.

"Well, what do you expect? Letting him lie all over you like that!" Fiona was able to say what Helly was thinking. Helly was unable to talk. As they wobbled along the uneven pavements of London in the early hours, Helly and Fiona had been forced to remove their shoes and were desperately trying to avoid the many sick splurges that had hit the pavement like paper bags filled with vegetable soup. The mere sight of them made Helly's stomach churn once again.

"Still," Charley teased, waving a small scrap of paper at them, "at least I got his phone number! Although I'd say Chaz'll be ringing me before I ring him."

"Chaz!" Fiona belted. "What kind of a bloody name is that?"

"Who gives a shit!" laughed Charley. "It's not his name I'm interested in anyway."

Helly grabbed Fiona quickly, diverting her away from a small puddle of sick, the sudden movement making Fiona jump and swerve in the wrong direction. Their drunken feet moved clumsily and Helly just managed to avoid the mess herself. But the sight of it caught her and she once again found herself clamping her hand over her mouth and praying and begging not to be sick.

Fiona and Charley laughed at her as she struggled to fight it. "Really Helly," Charley spoke much too loudly as she linked arms with her, "we're gonna have to get you more used to drinking, babe."

Chapter Twenty-Seven

The sun was splitting the stones the next morning. Helly cursed it. She could have done with a drab, grey day to go with her drab, grey perception of life. Her head felt constricted and her stomach churned. Still. By the time she had struggled with the Weetos and milk for Toby and Jack and had begged and pleaded with Dan to drop the boys into school, the headache had subsided. But the nausea hadn't.

It seems so unfair! Charley and Fiona are still in bed and it's their fault I'm in the state I am! They'll probably be there till lunchtime. Still, I suppose I shouldn't complain. It'll be nice to get down to Portobello and not be disturbed by either of them. I'm looking forward to some peace and quiet, and don't like the idea of Charley getting too friendly with the locals. She won't do my image any good. Just because she doesn't have anything to do. Mind you, I heard her persuading Fiona to try out the new Sporta Gym with her – perhaps once they've recovered after last night they'll head down there.

Anything – as long as they leave me alone.

Fiona had emerged half an hour before Helly left home. Dan had mumbled in annoyance, but had agreed to drop the boys off at school. She was grateful. She wasn't in the mood to listen to the mums bitching today. She'd left Fiona in the kitchen, propping up the worktop, sharpening her eyeliner pencils with Helly's best paring knife and praising herself for the less severe than expected headache and complimenting herself that her jeans felt less tight than usual.

As Helly's head squeezed, she looked forward to the prospect of peace and quiet at Pink Turtle today. It was becoming the only place that she could call her own. No sisters, no husband, no reminders of Nicky – heaven really. As she walked around Notting Hill in the sunshine she felt herself relax, aware that she was no longer breathing in short gasps, but pausing to take deep fulfilling breaths. As she walked along the familiar row of second-hand clothing shops and antique silverware displays, her feet cringed in competition with her head as they tried to recover from the damage done by the confines of last night's sandals. She heard her mum's voice in her mind as she was reminded how she insisted they break their shoes in at home.

It was hell at the time. As if the school shoes weren't black and ugly enough, the three of us had to clomp around the kitchen lino in them. We weren't immediately allowed in the kitchen, mind. It was a good two days on carpet first, so as if they weren't right we could still take them back without having marked the soles. It put me off the idea for life.

Appalled at the recollection, she fought it back. The warmth of the sun soothed her and, despite her swollen feet, she enjoyed the light breeze as it made her skirt dance and her T-shirt ripple in the sunshine. She by-passed the manic Abba2Zappa shop, the loud obscure Polish electro-music causing the walls to vibrate, and paused at the window of Notting Hill's coolest café, the boho chic Lisboa Patisserie.

Suddenly Nicky was there in her mind again. Her thoughts snapped straight back to Cascais and how fantastic his hands had felt on her. A cluster of olive-skinned teenagers came out of the café, ripping open the paper bags, eager to get to their breakfast. Helly looked as their dark hair glistened in the sunshine, their geometric hairdo's reminders of the 1980's. As she watched them she realised that she was probably their age when she'd first met Nicky. When she'd had the brief affair.

I honestly thought I'd never see him again! Although there have been so many times I wanted to He was so full of life, so vibrant and brimming with exciting ideas, I imagined he'd gone off travelling the world or something equally challenging. I hadn't expected him to knock on my door twelve years later!

She was soon at Pink Turtle and, as she twisted the key in the door, Penny from next door came up behind her.

"Hey, honey. How was Lisbon?"

She shrugged, non-committally, "Oh, it was OK. You know, sunshine, port and sardines."

"So how did you get on with your sister then? Did you manage to help her sort it out?"

"Fiona? She came back with me last week. They're all staying at my place."

"All? How many of them did you bring? You didn't pick up any hunky young men too, did you?"

Jesus, hit the nail on the head, why don't you!

"Fiona and her daughter Adi came back with me, and then Charley arrived from Dublin. Dan calls them the Murphia."

Penny didn't get it. "Why?"

"Well, Mafia – Murphia. They carry weapons and throw their weight around. Not really, just because he likes to wind us all up. And I suppose they do take over to a certain extent."

"And they're all staying at your place."

Helly pulled a tight mouth and rolled her eyes upwards.

"Look," said Penny, "I'll get us a couple of cappuccinos from Costas and you can tell me all about it."

Great! Just when I wanted to forget.

By the time Helly had filled her in on the briefest and most boring version of Cascais – *best to keep it boring in case I let anything exciting slip* – they'd not even finished their coffee. Helly was delighted for the distraction as the bell above the door jingled, the percussion to Kaz's entrance.

"Hi, there!" Her smile was wide and friendly and Helly

was delighted to see her.

"You're looking great!"

Kaz looked down at her light pink jeans and her cream Faith sandals. The fake tan and teeth-bleaching helped too. "Thanks. It's nice to be able to wear something summery. Makes a change. Either of you fancy a coffee? I was just going over to get a giant one."

"I've just had one." Penny hopped up from the stool as she spoke, lifting the large cardboard mug from the counter, the remains of cool coffee swilling around inside it. "I'll catch up later, Helly," she smiled, weaving her way around Kaz as she left.

"OK, Pen, thanks! Yeah, I'd love another coffee, Kaz, thanks."

"Give me a couple of minutes, then I'll be back to chat."

While she was gone Helly jumped up and quickly rearranged her display, pulling the funky and pricey antique clothes to the front of the rails, and pushing back the cheaper pieces. Kaz soon returned with two enormous coffees.

"So how was Lisbon?" she smiled as she sat on the high stool that Penny had vacated.

"Great. My sister and her daughter came back with me."

"Excellent. That was the plan, wasn't it?"

"Well, yeah. Although I'd expected it to take weeks to persuade her ex-partner to let them. He said he wouldn't allow it. He even accused her of child abduction!"

"How awful! Has she agreed to let him see the child?"

"Of course, she has. She has no problem with it, only she was so desperately lonely and unhappy there. Hopefully she can start getting on with her life now."

"Great. You're a good sister, aren't you?"

Helly blushed.

Shame I'm not as good a wife!

"So, there's a charity gig next month for Cancer Research. Before we talk about Quattro I want to talk you into donating a piece."

"No need to talk me into it. No problem. How about that three-quarter-length velvet coat in the window?"

Kaz looked around and beamed. "Fantastic! Thanks."

"No bother."

"So have you given any thought to Quattro's tour?"

Helly smiled. "Loads." She stood and picked up her keys. "I need to show you something down the road."

They walked through the market, Helly stopping a few times to talk to her stallholder friends as they made their way up to Jessie's. Helly had already spoken to Jessie about using the flirty gingham short skirts that she had in the window and Kaz was delighted when she saw them.

"They're absolutely perfect! Excellent."

"And I'm going to team them with some quirky chiffon, off-the-shoulder gypsy tops that I picked up in Paris on my last trip. The girls will look fantastic, Kaz."

"Helly, you're a legend. Thanks."

They took a slow walk in the sunshine back to Pink Turtle, distracted as they chatted to Caleb who sold the exotic fruits and Barry who made crêpes to order with an impressive range of sweet or savoury fillings. By the time they'd got back to Pink Turtle Helly felt better than she had done in months.

Challenged, excited and full of anticipation for the Quattro tour. I know we've got another eight outfits to pull together but this is what I was made to do! I was born to be a bloody stylist!

"OK then, Helly –"

Helly took a small folded square of cardboard and wedged it under the door of the shop to keep it open. The late morning sounds floated into Pink Turtle on the sunny breeze. She felt great.

"So I like those choices for the girls," Kaz continued. "Now time is starting to slip away from me and I need to sort out some more stuff for the record company. Do you think I could leave you to pull together seven more funky-chic outfits? I'll bring the girls in here next week for a fitting session, but they're all standard size ten's so it shouldn't be a problem. Only Letitia and Lesley, they've got great long legs, so I'm not sure how short the gingham skirts might be on them."

"Don't worry, Kaz. Drop them in on Wednesday morning, say about ten-ish? I'll have the tour clothes ready here for them to try and we can take it from there."

"Fantastic. Thanks, Helly. You don't know how great it is to have someone you can rely on in this business. You're a gem."

"Thanks, Kaz. But I really, really enjoy doing this. I've always loved clothes and thought Pink Turtle was what it was all about for me – but now?"

"Hey, go easy," Kaz laughed. "Keep on like that and I'll think you're after my job!"

"You never know, Kaz. Watch your back!"

They laughed as Kaz picked up her straw bag from the counter, flinging it over her shoulder in a wide sweep.

"See you Wednesday then?"

"Done. I'll have some great stuff here by then."

"I don't doubt it, Helly. I really don't."

"Thanks for the coffee."

"No problem. See you then?"

"Bye."

Kaz skittered out of the shop, her sandals thudding on the bare wooden floorboards. Helly was on a high. She waited until she was sure Kaz wasn't about to spin around on the pavement and come back with some forgotten request, and then she squealed, jumped up off her stool and began dancing to the Kelis CD that was playing as background music. Her skirt swung as she ground her hips and wiggled her bum to the beat. Her short blonde hair jumped a little as she funky-chickened her head, jutting her neck back and forth, her eyes closed as she rotated on the spot.

Like a needle being scratched across a record she jumped at the sound of a man's voice.

"Nice. Very nice. What do you do for an encore?"

Helly spun around to face the door, her facial muscles slack with shock, her mouth open in surprise.

The split second that she saw Nicky standing in her doorway she felt the blood rushing from her toes to her face, settling in unattractive clusters of blotches across her cheeks, forehead and neck.

Great, isn't it? I can't even rely on my blood to be in the right place at the right time. And what about my feet and legs? How're they supposed to run on empty? Maybe that's why they're feeling like jelly – there's no blood left in them . . .

I need to sit down.

Like a rag-doll she flopped down onto the high stool, staring at Nick.

He grinned.

Fuckit, he's good- looking.

Her voice came out in a breathy whisper, "What are you doing here?"

"Well," he teased, "I'd heard there was a brilliant antique clothes-shop where the owner provided entertainment. Mind you, I was expecting more Britney than Blazin' Squad."

"You shouldn't be here, Nicky. What are you doing?"

"I'm looking for some clothes." He turned to the rails, pushing each item along on the chrome bar as he pretended to take great interest in everything.

"Fuck off! This isn't fair. What if anyone sees you here?"

"I'm allowed to shop, aren't I? Anyway, nobody knows about us, except for us! You're paranoid."

She jumped up, fully in control once again. "I'm angry. You can't just swan back into my life after twelve years and expect to carry on where we left off! I made a mistake in Portugal. We both did. Just accept it and carry on. I'm married to Dan and that's the way I intend to stay."

He turned to face her, calm and measured, "Yeah,

you're married to Dan, but you missed a word, Helly."

She looked puzzled as she went over what she'd said in her mind.

"You missed the most crucial word. If that word had been in there I'd walk away now, but it wasn't there."

"For God's sake! What are you going on about?"

He stepped forward and put his hand on her cheek. She flinched.

"You missed the word 'happily'. You said you were married to Dan, not 'happily married'."

She sneered, stepping back from him, "That's ridiculous. Talk about analyse every single word!"

"You're not happy, Helly. If you were you wouldn't have ended up in bed with me in the first place. You wouldn't even have kissed me in the taxi after the gig."

She closed her eyes and exhaled deeply.

The trouble is he's right. I wouldn't have. On the most basic level of thought, it's obvious. If I was entirely happy with Dan I wouldn't even have looked at Nicky again. I would have told Dan that I knew him from years ago and there would have been no secrets. Well, apart from the fact that I had a brief fling with him in our early years, but that wouldn't have been so damaging.

Not as damaging as admitting I slept with him last week.

And all at a time when I'm trying it on with Dan too.

It's just unthinkable that I stopped taking the pill though. I really must check my dates. The potential could be completely unthinkable!

Makes it all even worse, doesn't it?

"Nicky, you have to go. It should never have

happened. I'm sorry."

"Helly, I love you. Do you hear me? I love you! I've always loved you. You broke my heart all those years ago and I won't let you do it again. Tell me you're happy with Dan and I'll leave you alone."

She stared at him, unable to speak.

He continued, "It's obvious you're neglected. Look at the situation. He goes out to work every day, brings home some money and that's where it begins and ends for him. You get no help with the children, and now your two sisters have landed in on top of you. Don't you get a life? Don't you get the chance for some happiness? Or are you just there to make everyone else's life great? Just there to sort out everybody else's problems?"

"No, Nicky, it's not like that. If I needed help, they'd be there for me."

"Who? Charley and Fiona? Hah!"

"Yes!" She was angry now. "Of course, they would be."

"I've not long left your place, Helly. I called in to collect some gig lists that Dan had printed out and do you know what was going on there?"

Helly shook her head, cringing in anticipation of the revelation.

"Charley was hollering that your butter had gone mouldy. She was cutting her toast and it was streaked with blue and green. Fiona panicked and threw it away. Then she remembered she'd been sharpening her make-up pencils with your knife and they began to argue. They're waiting for you to get home to bring in some more shopping. Charley is still hungover and they're both now getting ready to go to the gym."

Helly shrugged.

"So how are they helping you, Helly? Aren't they just out for themselves? How can they manage to go to the gym, but not be able to buy some more butter?"

"Oh bloody hell, Nicky! Ease up a little, will you? They've only been here for a few days and they're both trying to rebuild their lives. Give them a chance."

"A chance. Right. A chance. So how about them giving you a chance? Couldn't they be here with you, helping you with the shop? Doing stuff for you at home while you're working? No. They're going to the gym."

"Oh Nicky, calm down."

"I'm just worried about you, Helly. That's all. I love you."

He moved forward towards her, cupping her face in his hands again. Before she knew it she was pressed against the wall, his hands running over her shoulders and breasts. The adrenalin surged through her body and she wasn't sure what to do. He lifted her top and bent his face down towards her chest. She suddenly realised what he was trying to do and her arms pushed at him, forcing him backwards away from her.

"Jesus! Nicky, what the hell do you think you're doing?"

"I want you, Helly."

"Get out!"

He stared at her.

She flung her arm outwards towards him, knocking over the half-empty cold-coffee mug on the counter.

"Get out!" she hollered, as she watched the dark brown liquid fly in slow motion and land on the leg of his jeans, leaving a big dark-blue wet patch.

Chapter Twenty-Eight

Fiona didn't really have clothing suitable for the gym. She was a stranger to the routine and felt nervous and inadequate. Especially in the light of Charley and her over-confidence. Charley paid for them at the plush chrome counter and Fiona trotted in behind her, her light combat trousers and T-shirt feeling decidedly wrong compared to the slick lycra of the women who pounded the treadmills.

"OK, so gym for an hour and then a swim?" Charley was full of it. Fiona couldn't quite figure how she could be so effervescent in the shadow of the over-indulgence of the night before. She herself felt weak and still had a headache. "Whatever you think. I'll follow you."

"Great. Come on then."

Fiona knew she shouldn't be, but she was surprised to find that Charley even flirted at the gym. The dark-haired instructor stood beside the recliner bikes for the full twenty minutes and chatted to her whilst they pedalled. Fiona couldn't join in. She was having trouble catching her breath as it was. She had a lot to learn. After half an hour she had only managed to tackle the recliner bike and the treadmill and already she was exhausted. As the sweat trickled down her back and sat like clingfilm on her face she looked over towards the huge turquoise pool and yearned for it.

"Charley, I'm done. I'm going to shower and have a swim."

"OK," she called across from the mats where she was doing sit-ups, still chatting to the instructor as he lay his tanned hands on her flat tum while she grinned through gritted teeth. "I'll see you in there."

Fiona didn't like being seen in transit between the changing rooms and the camouflage of the water and so she slipped and slid on wet tiles as she attempted to walk in a hurry, only highlighting her juddering cellulite rather than disguising it. She slipped into the water, looking down at her still hanging-on-in-there tan. She began to swim in the lane at the side of the pool and became confused by the sign which instructed her to swim clockwise. As she swam alone in the lane she struggled to imagine a clock face, wondering which direction she should be going in. She was relieved to see Charley appear, looking like something from Monaco in a gold cozzie.

"Here! Charley, here!" Fiona stood in the water waving her arms at Charley and regretting it immediately as she felt her bingo-flaps shudder on her arms.

Charley smiled at her, confidence oozing sickeningly.

"Let's get into the Jacuzzi first."

"Shit," Fiona spoke to herself quietly, "now I've got to get out of the bloody water again!" She attempted to hoist herself up on the pool side, failing miserably and falling back into the water with a clumsy splash, nearly knocking herself out with her own out-of-control hand. Charley had already walked toward the Jacuzzi and was laughing and chatting with the four or five strangers in there. Fiona wondered how she did it. She resolved that once she'd lost her weight she'd replace it with heaps and heaps of confidence.

"Shit!" Nick cursed as he rubbed at the wet mark on his jeans. He was due in at the office in less than an hour and he had no intention of either turning up late for the important appointment with a potential new customer or arriving with a wet leg. He nipped down a side street and impressed himself with his powers of positive thinking as he steered himself into The Admiral pub. He noticed the barman look up and wink at him as he made his way through the small clusters of men who were laughing and drinking. He was irritated at how they failed to move out of his way as he cut through to the toilets. Once in the toilets he hit the large chrome button to activate the hand dryer. As it roared into action he lifted his leg, allowing the warm air to blow onto it. Five minutes later his leg was burning and the dark patch seemed no smaller.

"Bloody Helly. She was always stubborn!" He looked at his watch: time was running out fast. He walked along the four cubicles, pushing the doors open as he checked he was alone. In a flash he unzipped his jeans, pulling his feet out through the legs carefully. Standing in his boxers he pushed the button once again and the dryer started. No sooner had he held the coffee-stained leg up to the hot air than the toilet doors opened and two guys came in. Nick rarely blushed. But as the two men stood beside the mirrors Nick overheard their conversation.

"Well, I'm not having it any more. He either leaves him or leaves me. I'm sick of him and his two-timing."

"You're right, of course you are. He can't keep his hands to himself. Even Andy told me that last week. He was all over him at the reunion."

Nick shuffled awkwardly as it all fell into place; he realised he was standing in his boxers in the toilets of a gay bar. He'd never pulled his jeans on so quickly in his life.

Fiona ached from the gym. She was barely able to lift her arm to scratch her nose as they headed back to Helly's on the bus. Charley, on the other hand, was full of energy.

"Think I'll go up to Portobello and annoy Helly for a couple of hours," Charley quipped as they sat on the top floor of the double-decker and checked out the guys in the Lebanese cafés smoking their pipes.

"You're not still raring to go, are you?" The pain in Fiona's voice was evident. "I'm knackered. Anyway, Dan's minding Adi for me. He said he'd be there all afternoon, he had some paperwork to do. I'd better get back."

"You lightweight," Charley teased. "Well, I noticed

Hel's bike in the shed. Think I might cycle there. It's been a gorgeous day and I'm hoping it'll last."

"On these roads? You're insane."

"Maybe," Charley giggled, "but at least I'll be *fit* and insane come the great weather."

The wicker basket on the front showed the beginnings of mould which Charley had scrubbed at with a wire brush that she'd found beside Dan's tool box. It was only when she'd got to the end of the road that she realised the brakes weren't up to much either, but she was determined to carry on. As she cycled on the busy roads, dodging the buses and motorbikes, she soon became used to weaving between the traffic and hopping up onto the pavement to avoid the constant streams of traffic-lights and one-way systems. Before she knew it she was cycling down Pembridge Road, her dark hair flowing behind her and her backside pert and tight in her shorts as she hovered slightly above the hard seat. She didn't know Caleb on the exotic fruit stall or Barry who sold crêpes – yet – but they noticed her as she whizzed past. In fact most of the male population of Portobello Road noticed her as she stopped at Lenny's flower stall and bought a bunch of tulips, laughing with Lenny, throwing her head back as she did, and then cycling across to Pink Turtle and leaning the bike up against the window.

As she hopped off the bike she snatched the flowers from the wicker basket and spun around to go into Pink Turtle. She was immediately faced with a muscly wall, which smelled of Clinique Happy for Men. Stunned, she dropped the flowers as she fought to remain standing.

A deep rich voice spoke, "I'm sorry, lady. Here."

She watched as a black, shiny head lowered itself before her, picked up her flowers and gave them to her gently. This bald guy was gorgeous! At least six-foot-four he had a presence that wasn't all because of his height. Charley took it all in – the three-quarter-length tan leather jacket, the cool shades. She felt like Dorothy on finding Toto. "Well, thank you."

"No problem. I'm sorry about that."

"No. Not at all. My fault. Always in a hurry, you know."

"Can I buy you a coffee to apologise?"

"Sounds great! Hang on there, I'll just run these into my sister, just a second."

And so instead of presenting Helly with the flowers as a 'thank you' for everything, she dashed in, plonked them on the counter and muttered something about being back in half an hour, she was going for a coffee.

Helly didn't see Charley again until she got home.

And that was after five. She'd been gone for a coffee for over two hours!

She came back to the house with the bike but Helly wondered how she'd got back in one piece.

She'd been in the pub – again! First with James, the guy she'd bumped into, and then with Barry and Caleb and Lenny and half the bloody market! And now it seems they all know her and think she's great. And she's probably publicised my new nickname 'the Olympic Flame' and they all can't believe how a boring shite like me could have such a gregarious, fantastic sister! Just wait till Fiona tells her that her mobile's been ringing all afternoon.

We don't know who Steve is but he's been persistent.

He's only rung seven times this afternoon.

Charley hadn't shown excitement or horror at Steve's phone calls. Helly suspected that her emotions were numbed due to the afternoon drinking spree, but she decided to make a point of bringing up his name again in the near future. She felt a little jealous of Charley – of her freedom and her vivacious nature. And her complete lack of guilt for doing whatever she wanted – whenever.

I used to love sitting outside a pub in the summer evenings, the hanging baskets heavy above our heads, the sprinkles and clusters of pinks and yellows amongst the greenery. If I was ever in the mood for a few drinks, tonight would be the night.

"So come on, girls, we're out for a few drinks again tonight. My feet have just about recovered from last night."

Charley, Fiona and Dan looked up in amazement as the theme tune to *Emmerdale* rang out of the telly.

"What?" Dan who was sketching out some new designs for a new company logo seemed more worried than the other two.

Probably because he's going to be on baby-sitting duties again!

"Yep, you heard right the first time. We're out tonight." She looked over. "It won't be a late one like last night though, love. Just a couple of hours out, that's all. You don't mind, do you?"

His mouth said 'no', but his body language and attitude screamed 'yes'. I pretended not to notice.

So by early evening they were sitting outside Cargo, under the red-bricked viaduct where the trendy wine bar/café/music venue was situated. Wobbling their seats on the uneven pavement they watched the tourists in T-shirts with London Underground maps on the front. They were all in great form, especially considering the hangovers that had been dragging them down only that morning and, in the new sisterly tradition, they'd all managed to dig out fantastic shoes that rubbed in completely different places to the ones from last night. Fiona was wearing her Georgina Goodman sandals that Helly had bought her for Christmas two years ago, Charley had on her Diesel slip-ons and Helly felt great in her Miu Miu ankle-strap shoes that she'd got second-hand in Camden for less than fifty quid.

"So did you know The Sister Brothers are playing at the Forum tonight?" Charley asked out of the blue.

"Who?" Fiona and Helly both looked confused.

"The Sister Brothers. Don't tell me you haven't heard of them? They're great."

"So how do you know about them? And how do you know they're on tonight at the Forum?"

"James told me they were on tonight, but I've heard them on RTÉ back home."

"Well, I don't know them." Helly sipped at her white wine spritzer.

"That's no surprise really though, is it, Hel?" Fiona cut in, making Helly feel even worse than she already did.

Fiona felt a little guilty the minute she'd said it. She blamed Charley's piss-taking influence.

"Cheers, Fiona. OK, so what time are they on and how do we get there?"

"James said that we should be at Kentish Town by seven if we want to get a proper seat. Otherwise we'll be standing at the back and they'll only look about six inches tall."

Ever the sensible one, Fiona interrupted, "But what about Dan? You said we'd only be a couple of hours."

They were both surprised at Helly's insensitive retort, "Oh fuck him. He'll be OK. As if I never sat in for hours waiting for him to come back from a gig or a night out with the lads. It'll do him good."

And so they downed their drinks and made for the Tube station.

The place was mobbed and Helly loved it. It had once been a small theatre and the Anglo-German architecture was amazing.

"So what's with Nick?" Charley's voice was loud over the music. They picked their drinks up from the bar at the rear of the Forum and took fairy-steps down the small stairs that led to their seats.

"I bet these walls have soaked up some memories!" Helly shouted.

"Don't change the subject, Hel. I said, what's with Nick?"

Helly frowned at her, glancing to where Fiona sat waiting for them. "Fiona doesn't know about me and Nicky.

Shuttup, will you? Anyway, nothing's with Nick."

Charley laughed. "What do you mean Fiona doesn't know! Didn't he spend the night with you *at* Fiona's?"

"I mean she doesn't know about all that twelve years ago! And I've not spoken about what happened in Portugal. So just leave it."

Charley smirked. "OK, I'll leave it. For now. But Helly, remember. *I* know about twelve years ago. I know that you're lying when you say nothing happened in Portugal. And, I know that you're still mad about him. But OK, I'll leave it. For now. But even Fiona's noticed that you're avoiding him."

Helly hated her cocky sister sometimes, and came back with a quick retort, "Thanks. And while we're on the subject, who's Steve?"

"No-one."

They reached their seats and sat down. Charley sipped her drink and looked ahead at the spot-lit stage.

"The 'no-one' who rang you nearly ten times today!" Helly persisted. "C'mon, Charley, who's Steve?"

Fiona huddled in closer, enjoying the camaraderie. She missed Claudine and their girly banter.

"Steve is a jerk. He's a copper."

"Oohhh," teased Helly as Fiona giggled. "Is he a jerk because he's a copper? Or a copper because he's a jerk?"

"Neither. He's a great guy, a great copper but he's decided to try and be my new-counsellor-friend rather than fuck-buddy."

"Right, so that makes him a jerk?"

"Correct."

"And has he showed you his truncheon?"

It took a couple of seconds for Fiona to catch up. "So why does he think you need a new-counsellor-friend?"

"Beats me," Charley quipped, lifting her glass to her mouth and downing the double Jack Daniels in one. "OK, so who's for another?"

Helly and Fiona looked down into their full glasses in silence.

Charley shrugged, then sidestepped her way along the seats and then trotted back up the stairs to the bar.

"Fi," Helly shouted into her ear, "did you really need to ask?"

The Sister Brothers were fantastic. Kind of light rock with a bit of R&B thrown in. Obviously James has good taste. In music at least. Charley was annihilated by eleven, although me and Fiona weren't far behind her, but she was drinking two to our one so it was no surprise really. We'd got in with a few arty types who were heading on to Fabric for the rest of the night and, although I hadn't really wanted to go, it had been two against one. Charley was moaning the whole time about the Draconian drink-licensing laws and how if you found the right pub in Dublin you'd be there till the next morning. She had no intention of being back in bed by midnight – not her own bed anyway. I went on to the nightclub with them but left shortly after. The guys had got pissed and the flirting thing was just winding me up. I looked at my reflection in the toilets and didn't like what I saw. Here I was, a husband and kids at home wondering where the hell I was, an illicit night of (great) sex tormenting me and what was I doing? Sitting at home trying to make it work with my family? No, I was half-cut in a

*London nightclub chatting to guys who were only after one
thing. A sobering thought.*

I got the next taxi home.

Alone.

Fiona had been propositioned at Fabric by an Orlando
Bloom-a-like. She'd been on the verge of self-combusting
in panic, which resulted in him walking on by, mainly
due to the fact that she was unable to string a few words
together without stuttering. She was slightly put out that
Charley was so surprised that he'd approached her in the
first place – even more surprised than she was herself. But
that wasn't the point. She'd chickened out. Charley
laughed at her and told her she was mad as they stopped
and started, the cabbie cursing the late-night traffic.

"The guy was gorgeous *and* loaded. The perfect shag-
formula."

"Charley! I'm not like that. I don't care how much
money they've got in their back pocket. It's not just about
that, is it?"

"No, not *just*. But it helps. So what's your problem?
You're not still saving yourself for a reunion with Luís, are
you?"

"Course not! Just because I'm not jumping into bed
with the first guy that's asked me in ages, doesn't mean
I'm pining for Luís."

Charley just raised her eyebrows sceptically.

Fiona continued quietly, "Anyway. I can't cope with
one-night stands. I'm crap at the etiquette. All that
tension. The build-up is great, all the chemistry, but

uninhibited one-night-stand sex is shadowed by the awkwardness afterwards. And anyway, it's only made worse when you get back to their place only to find that they're a great laugh but too pissed to 'perform', so you're resigned to spending the night with a drunk, snoring stranger. That *and* trying to get rid of them afterwards."

Charley laughed, catching the cabby's eye as he waited at the traffic-lights. "Jesus, Fi, that's the easy bit. Just ask them if they've already booked their cab, or would they like you to do it?"

Fiona cringed at the thought. It simply wasn't her style. Although she didn't really know what was.

Charley continued, smirking at the cabbie with the gorgeous blue eyes,

"Anyway, you'd have to go back to *their* house, wouldn't you? I mean, you'd hardly take them back to Helly's. Christ, it's as bad as being back at Mum's."

"Charley, I'm just not like that."

"Bullshit. Every woman is. Tell him from the start you're only using him for sex. Men love the idea of female as predator."

Nick lay in his leather-framed bed staring up at his ceiling, watching the orange lights of the occasional car-lights slip over the ceiling and down his wall like fried eggs in a greasy pan. He wanted Helly more than ever, and it was keeping him awake. He was puzzled by her. There wasn't a week that had gone by since she'd told him to go all those years ago, that he hadn't thought of her. He hadn't expected to see her again – ever. But he wasn't entirely sure if it was the challenge of the chase or whether he'd really never got over her.

But in Cascais she'd talked about needing "the truth" about "when they were together" twelve years ago, and he'd steered the question away. At the time he hadn't a clue what she meant, and it was now the cause of his insomnia. He had to find out. He fidgeted, the cool cotton duvet gathering in clumps around his ankles and pissing him off. He would make it his life's work to get her alone and get her to tell him. He'd been thinking about that a lot lately and it was taking over his mind. What did she mean by "the truth"? He supposed she could only mean whether or not he had truly loved her. That was a question he could easily answer. Why had he shied away from it? He made a decision to ring her. Tomorrow. First thing. No, maybe not *first* thing. Perhaps he'd wait until the children were at school and she'd be alone. He'd ring her in the afternoon.

Chapter Twenty-Nine

Helly waited in the rain outside the school gates. She stood beneath Dan's ridiculously large orange golfing umbrella, in a tangerine glow, as she gave some shelter to the mums who had forgotten their brollies. Amongst the high-pitched sounds that came from the masses of women talking at the same time, she picked up the trilling of her mobile. Lodging the cold metal handle under her chin she cocked the brolly backwards, nearly taking Georgie Jones' mum's eye out, grappled with the phone and answered it. She'd already pressed the button to connect when she noticed the name 'Nicky' on the display.

"Hello." She was abrupt, wishing she hadn't answered it. Especially in the company of the other women.

"Where are you?"

"Outside the school waiting for the boys to come out."

"Oh, nothing's changed in the last twenty years then?" he teased.

She wasn't about to be won over that easily. "My boys."

"In the rain?"

"Yep, thank God for umbrellas, eh?"

"Helly, I won't keep you then, I know you've got your hands full but I've got a problem. Do you fancy helping?"

"That depends on what it is." She could hardly hear him over the noise of the chatting and the traffic.

"D'you know, it took me ages to get your coffee out of my jeans the other day."

She laughed lightly, "Well, it served you right, acting up like that in the shop."

"I thought I was a right chap, nipping into the pub around the corner to try and dry them under the hand-dryer."

She laughed again, suddenly not so conscious of the mums around her, "It doesn't work, does it?"

"No. I took off my jeans and stood there in my silk boxers only to realise too late that I was in a gay bar."

"Not The Admiral?" her eyes were wide with shock.

"Yep."

She laughed louder, now attracting glances. "You divvie!"

"I know. Told you nothing had changed."

"So what's this big problem then? They'll be out in a minute."

"Well, I've got another stain to sort."

"God, sounds disgusting. Are you sure you want to ask me?"

"Yeah, course I do. You see, it's a tough one. I only went and spilt some stain remover on my jacket. How the hell do you get *that* out?"

He laughed at the sounds of her laughter. Just like it used to be. Free and spontaneous.

Well, it broke the ice again anyway.

At that split second Toby and Jack came running out of the school, the noise levels manic as the children swarmed out like ants.

"They're out. I have to go."

"OK. Helly, I have to talk to you. I'm sorry about that in the shop the other day. I'm all over the place at the moment."

"Me too. I have to be in control, and you took that from me."

"Me too. But I can't relax unless everything's sorted."

"Jesus, are we anal or what? So what do you want to talk about? Isn't it just prolonging the agony? Can't we just leave it like it is?"

"No, I need to know what you meant the other week when you asked me about the truth."

Toby and Jack ran up to her and piled their schoolbags on her, scrambling and pushing to get under the umbrella as they kicked water from the light puddles at each other. Helly went quiet. She didn't know what to say.

I know exactly what he means though. But I was drunk and I wish I hadn't said it.

"Helly? I didn't know what you meant. I was just joking when I said that the truth was overrated. What *did* you mean?"

"Nothing."

"I know you. Something's bothering you. I need to know."

"OK, ring me next week, give me some time to think about it. We'll meet up and chat. No monkey business though."

"*Ooh, ah ah ah ah ah!*" he squealed down the phone, forcing out his monkey impression.

Her ears suitably accosted, she pressed the button to disconnect the call.

As if I was going to continue the conversation in front of my children, anyway!

She opened the front door and held her breath. She wasn't sure what to expect these days.

But it looked promising.

Silence.

She nagged at the kids to kick off their wet shoes in the hallway and she did the same, shaking out her umbrella and removing her coat. It seemed too good to be true – time alone at home? Miraculous. She felt strangely lifted since the call from Nick. Just to hear his stupid sense of humour once more made her feel good. She'd forgotten about her bad-hair day, and even walking in the puddles hadn't bothered her. He was still having an effect on her. She wasn't sure how she felt about that. As she went into the kitchen she wondered where Fiona and Charley were. It was only a fleeting wonder though – there was plenty she wanted to do while she had the chance.

It was simple sorting the boys out after school. While they changed out of their uniforms and into their jeans and T-shirts she whipped up a quick sandwich for them. Just to keep them going till dinner time. They were already squabbling about which TV station to watch. Helly walked in bare feet, the bottoms of her jeans wet as they clung onto her heels. As she kissed the boys on the head, she handed them each a sandwich and a sugar-free drink.

Great. Now perhaps I'll get the chance for a quick bath and some well overdue defuzzing. I simply can't get into the bathroom these days. I don't really know who's the worst, Charley with her bulging make-up bag or Fiona with her love affair with exfoliators and face creams? Anyway, I'm getting in there now and I've told the boys not to disturb me – whoever might turn up or phone. I'm not available!

As she turned to climb the stairs the phone rang. She thought twice about answering it but just had to look and see whose number was flashing on the display. It was her mum.

"Shit!" Helly closed her eyes and ran her hand through her hair. The last person she wanted to talk to. Her conversations always went on forever – and just when she was trying to grab some time too.

I'd better answer it. She's probably got a million questions about Charley and Fiona. It might be easier to talk when they're not in the house. Here goes . . . .

"Hi, Mum."

"Helen. How'ya love?"

"Great. You?"

"Oh you know, can't complain. Although my arthritis is playing up these days. So how're my daughters? It must be lovely, all of you living under the same roof again. You're a hero, Helen."

Helly snorted. "Jesus, Mum, you're the only one who thinks so. I think they've got muddled. Are you sure you never told them I was running a B&B?"

"A B&B? No. Never. Well, at least I don't think so, Helen. Why on earth would I have told them that?"

The concept of irony obviously hasn't reached my mother yet!

"So, Mum. Got any news?"

"Not much, love. Your father's annoyed with me again. I've only gone and agreed to go to Lourdes with the ICA."

"So what's his problem?"

"Oh, he's jealous. You know what he's like. I've promised to cook him loads of shepherd's pies and stews. The freezer'll be full of stuff for him while I'm away."

"How long are you going for?"

"Only a long weekend. You know – the usual."

Helly nodded, though aware that her mother couldn't see her actions.

"You'd love it there, Helen. So peaceful, so beautiful. Did you never think of going?"

"Not really, Mum. I'm not that religious. I think it's all about being a good person, a kind person. Isn't it?"

"Mmmm, well, there is that."

"Anyway, you don't see too much about Lourdes over here. I think the English can't understand the Irish's fascination with Lourdes. And no-one even *wins* anything there!"

"Wins anything? What would you be winning?"

"No, Mum, it was just something that one of the guys in Dan's band said a while back. Dan was telling him about his mother and aunt going to Lourdes and Kyle thought he'd meant Lords."

"Lords."

"Yeah, Mum, as in the cricket ground?"

"Oh, Helen, what are you talking about? We don't play cricket in Ireland!"

I'm clearly wasting my breath here…

"So how is my lovely son-in-law?"

"Dan's fine, Mum. And the boys are too. Getting bigger every day. I'd swear Toby's nearly as tall as me."

"Go 'way. Jesus, he's not even a teenager yet!"

"Far from it. No, Dan hasn't changed. He still tells everyone I use the smoke-alarm as a timer when I'm cooking and takes great delight in making me look stupid in front of the lads. But it's all in good fun, Mum. I'm used to it."

"And?" Her mother lightened her voice and began to speak in a high-pitched, broken manner. "Any chance of the pattering of more tiny feet, Helen? I've always said how great it would be if you had more children. And I can't rely on those two sisters of yours to give me any more grandchildren now, can I?"

Christ. What is it with mothers? How can they hit the nail right on the head without even meaning to?

"Oh, you wouldn't be so sure. I've been on about wanting another. But it's not entirely unconditional. I'd like a daughter. Nothing like being choosy, eh?" Helly laughed, trying to lighten up the conversation.

Her mother was having none of it. "Well, you'll never know till you try. Anyway, it'd be great for you to have a big family. Just like your father's family. And it's not like you don't have the room there, is it?"

"I don't know about *that* at the moment! Between Charley and Fiona and Adi moving in I'm fairly full here right now."

"Ohh, that's only temp'ry. They'll have their lives sorted soon. And then you can really concentrate on giving me another granddaughter. Oh, I really like the sound of that, Helen, and she'd be a great playmate for Adriana."

"Mum, leave it, will you? It's not a good time for me right now and we'd never even agreed on the two we have! We never discussed or planned it, as such. You see, all my friends have kids of similar ages. Maybe it would be ridiculous for me to be thinking of starting back at square one now. And then, think of Toby & Jack! How would they react?"

"Well, I think it sounds like a great idea. And since when did you follow your friends? P'raps you should think about it, Helen. Just think."

THREE OF A KIND

And so I wish I'd never said anything.
Especially in the light of the most recent activities . . .

Chapter Thirty

A few days later Helly was standing beside an empty rail in Pink Turtle, humming along to The Sister Brothers as she sorted some of the outfits for Quattro. She was chuffed with her choices and delighted that she'd picked up the delicate yet funky pieces from the Parisian market. They went perfectly with the urban-style combats that she'd got in Brighton and the jewellery from Camden market. Things were certainly falling together for her. Gonad sat once again in her doorway, this time inside on the distressed floorboards, as he sheltered from the latest shower-burst.

The bell tinkled and she turned, a smile of satisfaction on her face, only to see Kaz. She didn't recognise her at first, what with the kagoule hood up and the drawstrings pulled so tightly around her face.

"Kaz! You weren't supposed to be coming in till Wednesday!"

"I know. S'OK."

"No, it's not OK! I haven't got them all ready yet. I've just sorted five outfits so far."

Kaz waved her hand dismissively at Helly who only then realised that Kaz was looking ghastly.

"Hey, are you all right?"

"Yeah. Well, no. Not really. I've come to ask you a favour, Helly."

"Go on."

"My father's sick. Really sick."

Helly stood and poured a glass of sparkling water from her bottle, handing it to Kaz. As she sipped at it, Helly turned down the music.

"How sick? What's wrong?"

Before Kaz could reply, two large American tourists came in to the shop, wearing cameras around their necks. Kaz lowered her voice as Helly pushed the volume dial slightly, reintroducing the music.

"They think it's his heart. They're not sure. But I have to go and see him. I have to be there. My mum and he split up a few years ago and he's got nobody. I'm all he's got."

"Of course, of course you have to go. What can I do to help? Do you need a lift somewhere? Where is he?"

"San Francisco."

"Fuck!"

The two tourists looked around at Helly frowning. She ignored them as Kaz spoke quietly, "Yeah. I need you to help me."

"Anything, go on. Just ask."

"Quattro."

"What?"

"I need you to take over the tour for me."

Helly flopped down onto her high stool, holding onto the side of the till for support. "You're not serious! Me! I can't. I wouldn't know what to do."

"You'd be great. The tour starts the week after next so I'll go through the outfits and schedule with you later, don't worry about that. You'll love the girls, they're great – no egos, no bullshit. Just decent young girls."

"But where? For how long?"

"Well, about four weeks in total, but just the UK for now. London, Birmingham, Manchester, Cardiff, Belfast, Dublin. Then there's always the possibility of going international after that, but we're still waiting on final dates from the record company."

"I can't do that!" Now the colour drained from Helly's face.

Kaz was confident. "Of course, you can. I'll be back within the month anyway. Hopefully it'll only be a couple of weeks. Please?"

Well, isn't my mind suddenly awash with complications! Here I've been, yearning for freedom, for a life of my own, and then when the opportunity is put in front of me, a thousand hurdles get in my way. They weren't there a minute ago though, so who am I trying to kid?

Charley whizzed by the window –

– on my bike! – looking like something out of a magazine!–

and Helly realised that the rain had stopped.

It sickens me though. It could only happen for Charley.

Helly looked across at her clock and realised that Fiona would be arriving in less than five minutes.

Shit! I need to make a decision quick.

"Kaz, can I get back to you later? I need to think about this. I'll have to organise my family, my life, you know?"

"Of course, but Helly, I really need to know before the end of the day. If you can't do it I'll have to find someone else, but you're ideal. You're so tuned in to my way of thinking for the girls – and, from your point of view, it'd be a shame to waste the opportunity too."

"Hey, I was only joking when I said I was after your job!"

"Yeah, right," she teased. "That's what you *have* to say now."

Kaz kissed Helly on the left and then the right cheek before she turned and left.

Helly was in a daze as she took the hundred and thirty-seven pounds from the two American customers as they brought delicate 1960's skirts that were obviously at least four sizes too small for them.

And it would be a great opportunity to get away from everything. From my sisters and Dan. And Nick. The only people I'd miss would be Toby and Jack – and they'd miss me – but haven't they got enough people around them at the moment? I'm exhausted with everyone leaning on me and it would also mean I don't have to face Nicky with 'the big question'.I haven't had time to think – all these nights out are exhausting and I need some space. It'd be the ideal opportunity.

I'll ring her later.

Maybe have a chat with Dan first; it'd only be right to.

As the two customers left the shop Charley bounded in, all rosy-cheeked and blossoming. Helly couldn't help but notice that she was wearing her new T-shirt.

No – my new T-shirt.

"Where'd you get that from?" She jabbed the air as she pointed towards the bright red T-shirt with the slogan 'I'M JUST A SOCIAL DRINKER – BUT I DO DRUGS LIKE A PROFESSIONAL' emblazoned across the chest.

"Oh, just found it at home." Charley shrugged, knowing full well that she'd taken it from Helly's wardrobe. "Fancy a bagel?" She held the bulging bag of bagels out under Helly's nose.

Helly looked at her fake-tanned arm, which was decorated with some turquoise/silver jewellery.

"And where'd you get that?" Helly pointed to the chunky silver bracelet. "Is that new?"

"Yes." Charley spoke through a mouthful of bagel.

"You've just bought it?"

"No."

"So back to my first question! Where did you get it?"

"Calm down. Jesus, you're uptight. James bought it for me."

"James? So when did you see him again then?"

"I've actually seen him twice in the last three days. He's a dote. Do you know he lives in one of those pastel houses on the side street?"

"What, Tavistock Road?"

"Yeah."

"Fuck! They're worth a fortune."

"I know. Told you I had good taste. We're going over to his friends' house and staying there tonight. Apparently he has a great collection of contemporary foreign films – *La Haine, Amélie, El Crimen del Padre Amaro. Y tu Mamá También*."

"Since when did you –"

"Since I met James."

"Huh, you're just killing time. Using him."

"Mmmm," she mumbled as she attacked the second bagel, moving across the shop and flicking through the rails, collecting a few pieces and making for the changing rooms with them.

"Hey, make sure your hands aren't greasy."

"OK, 'Mum'. You're all right. They're not."

"And you pay for anything you want, mind."

"No worries," she replied, closing the changing room door behind her. "I'll get James to treat me again. He adores me."

"Oh, and what about Steve?"

"The eejit copper?"

"Whatever. What about *him*?"

"*La la la la la*," Charley hummed loudly, ignoring her.

She's driving me insane. And I just know that she's going to try and connive some freebies out of me before she leaves here. And just as I try to calm down, who walks in?

Fiona arrived in high spirits. And Helly had to agree, she did look good – as if she'd lost a few pounds. Perhaps the late nights and alcohol suited her.

"Guess what?" Fiona gushed.

Helly 'sssh'd' her silently, mouthing that Charley was in the changing room.

"What?" Charley's voice boomed from behind the changing room door. Helly and Fiona rolled their eyes. Nothing stayed a secret for long once Charley got hold of it.

She continued anyway, "I've just been offered a job."

"Excellent!" Helly squealed. "Where?"

"In that trendy coffee bar on Westbourne Grove." Her voice was an excited whisper.

"The one beside the tribal interiors shop and the oriental accessories stall?"

"Yeah. Great, isn't it? Perhaps my life is on the turn upwards."

"Good for you, Fi. Well done. You deserve it."

Fiona smiled. "There's only one problem, Helly."

Helly returned the smile, delighted at the news that Fiona was to start earning some money and getting on with her life.

She might even start thinking about getting her own place soon then.

But I don't mean to be rotten – it's great to see her so happy.

"Well, it'll mean I'll have problems with Adi. You wouldn't be able to drop her off and collect her from playschool, would you? Please?"

I should have known it was too good to be true!

Charley had managed to tease a bright red 1970's 'disco-era' vest from Helly on the promise that the all-singing, all-dancing James would bring in the thirty pounds tomorrow. She had tried it on again in Helly's bedroom and was delighted at how well it went with her faded 501's and Gola trainers. Picking up her glass of red wine she gulped at it. She liked having a few drinks at home before she went out. And if she was going to spend the evening with the delectable James again she needed something to take her mind off Steve. She was missing him but was determined not to acknowledge the fact. Not fully anyway. She tried to keep herself busy during the days and then busier during the nights in a bid to forget him. It had been bad enough getting over Donal but at least she'd had something to be angry about with him. With Steve, well, he'd done nothing wrong except try and help her, be her friend. She 'rewarded' herself for her strong resolve by opening the second bottle of wine in less than half an hour. She blamed Helly's huge wine glasses – she could only get two out of a bottle! Anyway, she felt she deserved it, after what she'd been through in the last year. She hid it from her sisters as much as possible and had already begun lying to them, insisting that she'd cut down, opting for the healthier lifestyle choice. She even went as far as choosing a fruit juice instead of a Bacardi Breezer sometimes. She'd spoken to Dan earlier in the day and had arranged that they'd all go to the Saturday-night gig in Antoinette's. He seemed pleased. Although she knew Helly wouldn't feel the same way. She was looking forward to bringing James along too. His presence might prevent her from copping off with the first bloke who showed a modicum of interest in her. She knew Helly would be annoyed, but she'd go along. She'd have to if all the others were. Anyway it'd be a great opportunity to see how Helly and Nicky reacted to each other. She was desperate for the chance to check out their interaction, and here it was, handed on a plate.

When Helly got in later that afternoon after collecting Toby and Jack from school she immediately smelt the booze. The house was already ricocheting with at least four different sounds and she had a headache just thinking about it all. She passed the lounge only to hear Fiona arguing on the phone.

Probably to Luís – again.

It's becoming more of a regular occurrence over the last week.

Helly stood at the foot of the stairs, looking at the pile of shoes that had been kicked off and left. She looked up the stairs. The sounds of Barry White were pounding from her bedroom upstairs.

That's obviously Charley, drinking and singing and putting on too much make-up ready for her night out. If she gets red wine on my white duvet cover again, I'll kill her. Honestly, it wasn't as bad as this when we were all teenagers. And I thought we were supposed to get better with age!

And then she caught the sounds of Dan on his drum-kit, the tinny rattling rhythms competing with the soulful bass of Barry White's crooning. Toby and Jack were laughing hysterically in their bedroom, which was a lovely sound to Helly. She just wished it was the *only* sound.

Fiona's eyes welled with tears she put the phone down on the angry Luís, Charley pouted at the mirror as she smeared on two red streaks of lipstick, and Helly stood silently amidst the chaos. At that split second she made a decision. She picked up the phone and rang Kaz immediately.

"Hi, Kaz," she spoke in a balanced calm voice. "Yeah, I'm fine thanks. You? Any more news on your dad?" She paused as she listened, before she continued with, "Yeah. No, listen. I'll do it. Yep, I'm up for it. You can rely on me."

I'm not running away, not abandoning my family. I'm probably cracking up, but I need to do this – for me! Dan will understand. He'll have to. It's not as if I'll be away every night. Kaz said that the first five nights are London gigs so I could be home every night for the first week. Then the second week is Brighton, Birmingham and Norwich, so I could come home nearly every night of week two. Third week she said, I think, it's Cardiff, Manchester and Edinburgh, so that'll mean what? Three nights in a hotel. Luxury! And week four is Cork, Dublin and Belfast, but Kaz thinks she'll be back for them. She might even be back for week three if her dad picks up. Who knows? All I know is I'm looking forward to this. I need the space and the thinking time.

Helly felt liberated and yet terrified at the same time.

Chapter Thirty-One

By Saturday night she had the seven outfits picked and was ready for the girls to come in on Wednesday, ready to meet them for the first time at the fitting session. She wasn't too pleased at the prospect of going to the gig tonight.

In the last fortnight I've been out more times that I have in the last two years! And the reality is – it's not what it's cracked up to be. I suppose that's part of the fun of going out – the occasion of it, but believe me, nearly every night for two weeks? It's knackering! Right now, an evening in front of the telly with Toby and Jack sounds like heaven. Only Toby and Jack though, no sisters or husbands or musicians.

She heard Charley on the patio screeching an exaggerated laugh into her mobile. She walked to the French doors at the back of the kitchen and watched her older sister, her legs up on the wooden garden table and her long hair hanging over the back of the chair as she reclined. She felt proud that her sister looked so good and yet slightly jealous that her manic lifestyle hadn't yet taken its toll on her – or not too much anyway. But her skin showed signs of abuse, and who could tell what the *inside* looked like? She couldn't fathom her drinking, couldn't understand what she was so angry about, or what she was running from. She squinted to see the fill-line on the vodka bottle that sat on the table alongside the 7Up and the glasses. She was sure that the bottle had been a new one, just opened, and yet it looked like it was nearly half empty! Then she was alerted as Charley laughed, in her most flirty voice, and said the name 'Steve'.

Now I'm suddenly interested!

I'll just open the door a little. No, it's not eavesdropping or earwigging! I'm just curious. She is my sister!

It had been a weak moment when Charley had answered Steve's call. It was only the third one of the day but she wasn't too fond of the idea that he could be getting bored of trying to reach her. So as she'd gulped at her drink she'd answered the call with a, "Hello? Hello? Oh hi." She paused deliberately. "Steve who?"

He'd been ready for her though. He'd been unable to get her out of his mind since she'd left for London so suddenly. He knew she was insecure but every time he thought back on her daft shenanigans he couldn't help but feel a great warmth for her. It wasn't every day you met a fantastic woman pretending to lose her dog in Phoenix Park, or reporting her car stolen when she'd simply forgotten where she'd parked it.

"Charley. I miss you! What have you been doing over there?"

"Oh," she breezed, "I've made a load of new friends around Notting Hill and Portobello Market. It's great craic."

"I've rung you loads of times. Didn't you see the missed calls?"

"Oh, no. I've been out nearly every night. And I haven't had any credits either."

"Are you pissed?" His voice cut through her light banter.

"No!" she barked back at him, slightly too quickly.

"Jesus, Charley. Why don't you come back over here and we'll sort things out?"

"Oh, you mean you'll be my counsellor and try to convince me what a crap person I really am?"

"What? No. Nothing like that. Christ, I like you, Charley. I just want to help you, that's all."

"No, you don't. You want to make yourself feel better about yourself. You want to lecture me on liver cirrhosis, hypertension, heart damage, and shagging ugly fat blokes. Well, Steve, you're too late! I already know."

"Shagging ugly fat blokes?"

"Well, you know what I mean. Everyone's lovely when you're jarred."

"Thanks."

Now she felt a little bit rotten. Not overly, just a small bit. She really liked Steve too, but didn't want to be his latest project. She turned the conversation to a lighter tone.

"Anyway, how can I give up when the science world keeps giving me excuses?"

"Go on." He resigned himself to her wafer-thin excuses.

"Don't you know that grape seeds contain polyphenols?"

"No, I don't."

"Ha. You're preaching to me and you don't even know about polyphenols! They're an anti-ageing substance fifty times more powerful than vitamin E and twenty-five times more than vitamin C. And hey, having Alzheimer's can't be fun, but there's a chemical located within the skin of red grapes that looks set to reduce symptoms."

"Feck off, Charley!" He laughed at her reasoning.

"It's true! According to some professor in Milan this chemical bolsters the activity of a human enzyme and forces the damaged nerve cells to rebuild and regenerate. Really. I'm not shiteing you, I read it in a magazine!"

His silence spurred her on. She was enjoying teasing him unashamedly.

"Scientists in Texas have been giving a mix of caffeine and booze to rats to prevent brain damage during a stroke. They say the caffeine increases the blood pressure while the alcohol dilates the blood vessels, allowing more blood to seep into the brain and reducing the possibility of brain damage by up to eighty per cent! Jesus, the doctors'll be prescribing Irish coffees next thing!"

"You're fucking cracked, Charley," he laughed down the phone, his voice warm.

"Thank you."

"OK," he calmed himself, "just do me a favour. Just one little thing?"

"Depends." She slurped at her drink while she spoke.

"Just keep an alcohol diary for one week. Just *one* week. That's not too much to ask, is it?"

"Yeah."

"Just one week, Charley. And be honest with yourself. The deal is this – if you're not shocked by the outcome then I'll leave you alone to mingle with the London Sloanies. But we'll talk in a week's time and see."

"OK, I'll do it. But only for one reason."

"Go on, what's that?"

"That you didn't laugh at me when I pretended to have lost Diego."

"There was no Diego, was there?"

"Well, there was. But he's my sister's dog and he's never even been in Phoenix Park."

"I bloody knew it all along."

"And Steve. He's not a boxer. He's a spaniel."

Helly felt sick. She wasn't sure whether it was watching Charley drink the bottle of vodka like water, or the prospect of the evening in Dan *and* Nicky's company or what. But something wasn't right.

Perhaps it's the stress of what I've taken on with the Quattro tour. Or even the tension in the house as we all try and live together under the one roof. It's a lot of responsibility on my shoulders and I'm cracking up here. Or maybe it's guilt at my feelings for Nicky – for what I've done.

She sat on the side of her bed in her underwear and

pulled her filofax from her over-sized handbag. As she flicked through the pages to check the dates for the tour she stopped, flicking back a couple.

She flicked back another four pages and began counting on her fingers, throwing down the leather-bound organiser, leaving it to backflip on the bed as she stood and scrabbled in her bedside cabinet. She pulled the strip of pills out of the box and saw the small blisterpack full. As it should have been.

No, I didn't just imagine it! I really haven't taken them for weeks!

Holy shit!

She sat back down on the bed as she started to cry in panic. Her thoughts turned to jumbled mush as she tried to make sense of the dates. She counted erratically on her fingers.

Oh my God! I should never have done that in Cascais!

Why did I blank out on the fact I'd stopped taking the pill?

How the hell could I have been so stupid?

And now I'm late.

Dear God please, please, please.

Not again.

Please . . .

She could hardly dress herself properly. The thought of what she'd put at risk for one stupid night with Nick had suddenly hit her full force.

If I'm pregnant with Nicky's baby I can't even pretend it's Dan's! He hasn't wanted me in weeks. What have I done? Jeopardised my life, my family and for what? A night of drunken nostalgia? I've not only betrayed my husband, but my children, my sisters and myself. What a stupid, stupid cow!

She swiped at her wet eyes and cheeks at the sounds of someone coming up the stairs. Quickly she spun around to face the wardrobe, dragging out her floral skirt and slipping it on over her long legs. As Fiona walked into her room she was just tugging on the yellow lacey-topped vest.

"Hey, you look nice." Fiona's smile was wide and genuine.

It struck at Helly to see her so happy once again. In that split second, more than ever, she hated Luís for treating her so badly and felt angry at his incessant phone calls. She wished he'd stop ringing and spoiling Fiona's new life, especially after what he'd tried to do to her. She desperately wanted to tell her about her bruises. She wondered whether Fiona knew what he was potentially capable of.

Shame I had to put my life at stake in order to sort Fiona's!

"That Nick's a nice guy, isn't he?"

She stood beside Helly at the mirror. Helly stiffened a little.

"Why? What do you mean 'nice'?"

"He's only brought round some new Barbie outfits for Adi's dolls. She's ecstatic, sitting down in the lounge and dressing them up."

"Nice. Yeah."

Fiona caught sight of her pink-rimmed eyes and turned to face her,

"What's wrong?"

"Nothing. Just hay fever. You know. Pollen and dust and that."

"You never had hay fever before? Since when?"

"Oh just in the last couple of years, you know. Don't know where it's come from. Probably just allergies and stuff."

Fiona looked puzzled, not believing her flippant reply but knowing when to leave something alone. "Are you coming down?"

"Yeah," she dabbed white blobs of face cream onto her cheeks, nose and forehead and smoothed them in, in upward strokes. "Who's down there?"

"Everyone!" she smiled.

She's loving this new social life, bless her.

"Jono, Gav, Nick, Dan, Charley, James."

"James?"

"Yes, Charley invited him."

"Oh, great. She's some girl, isn't she?"

"She's a nightmare!" Fiona laughed, fondly.

"So Nick's already down there?" Helly's voice had quietened.

"Yes, he is. Are you sure you're OK about him?"

Helly turned and Fiona noticed a smear of face cream on her cheekbone. She ran her finger across it to wipe it away as Helly spoke, "He's a nice guy. It's a long story, Fi. I just have to accept that he's in the band, but don't ask too many questions if I keep a wide berth, eh?"

"As long as you're OK. I didn't know what to say about the Barbie clothes. They're not brand new, but it was a nice gesture. Wasn't it?"

"Course it was. I'm fine, don't worry. I'll see you down there."

Fiona turned to leave, stopping at the doorway, "Shall I pour you a large one?"

"Yeah, lovely. Oh, em, no. No. I don't think I'll drink tonight."

Fiona frowned in amazement.

Helly turned back to the mirror as she blushed slightly. "You know, bit of a belly ache. Not feeling too hot after all the drinking in the week anyway. You wouldn't be a love and get me a tall glass of the fresh orange juice that's in the fridge, would you?"

"Leave it to me. Ice and a slice?"

Helly smiled and winked as she left the room.

So now there's the sudden worry of pregnancy! Just what I've wanted for so long. It's ironic, isn't it? Dan's avoided sex with me for so long – terrified that I'll be pregnant again and here I am!

I'll either have to sleep with Dan very, very soon, or make a massive decision.

Fiona had really wanted to talk to Helly about Luís, only she'd noticed her red eyes and knew she wasn't herself lately. Her timing was all out. It'd have to wait. She'd had four arguments with him over the phone this week and the pain of keeping it all to herself was killing her. His acquiescent mood had evaporated long since. He now bellowed down the line at her, accusing her of child abduction and yelling quotes and clauses from the Hague Convention like a big-mouthed MP desperate for pre-election votes. She had surprised herself with her

387

strength and her retaliation. It pleased her that her move to London had brought with it an increased confidence. Her new lifestyle was helping too. Adi was so happy living with Toby and Jack and they'd enjoyed many sunny afternoons out at Hyde Park, Regent's Park and on Hampstead Heath. She loved watching the Serpentine Swimming Club as they dived into the huge lake at the park every Sunday morning and she already knew that she didn't want to bring Adi up in Portugal. She didn't want her having a childhood that was so alien from her own.

And then there was Raoul. She hadn't mentioned him to Helly or Charley yet – she knew they'd scream at the name alone. But she'd met him earlier in the week in the coffee bar and they'd clicked immediately. A student at the London School of Music, he spent hours talking to her about his cello and as she confessed to hardly having touched her violin for months he offered to spend some time with her – all in the name of art. They'd talked for ages after work about bows, and how different bows make such a huge difference to the sound of their instruments. The top note was hit though when he invited her to the Academy's classical concert at the end of the month. She was elated. She'd wanted to tell Helly about him too, but decided instead to mention him later in the evening. Perhaps when Charley was out of earshot and Helly had maybe had a couple of drinks too.

As she came down the stairs she heard the banter in the kitchen. Helly felt sicker than sick. The thought of walking into her kitchen and seeing Nick and Dan standing together and laughing was almost unbearable. And all the time she wasn't sure whether she was pregnant or not. She checked her watch, wondering whether Tesco Express would still be open. She was thinking up an excuse to nip out and buy a pregnancy testing kit.

She had no hope. The second she walked through the kitchen doors the laughter hit her. Dan turned to face her, putting his arm around her shoulder territorially.

And I haven't even mentioned the Quattro tour to him yet! It's just getting worse by the minute!

Charley was pouring them all large glasses of Jack Daniels and stuck one under Helly's nose.

The silence was deafening as she spoke. "No, thanks. Fiona's got me an orange juice."

"A wha'?" Charley screeched.

Helly blushed, "An orange juice." She rubbed her tummy feebly, "Not feeling too great tonight. Think I'll stay off the drink."

Charley narrowed her eyes to slits and stared at her sister. Helly simply couldn't make eye contact.

That Charley's too damn cute for her own good.

Dan broke the silence as he pulled her closer and rubbed his hand across her flat tummy. "Hey, babe. You haven't got your wish, have you? There's not a mini-HellyDan in there, is there?" She knew he was joking. More than joking really, and it was cruel. Especially in company. Especially as he had avoided her and caused her so much pain. They hadn't slept together for weeks, but she wasn't about to whip away his male ego in front of his pals and admit that. Anyway, she was irritated at his accuracy. As she forced on a fake smile she caught Nick's eye. He held the eye contact for slightly too long and it made her feel even more sick.

What's worse is, I know he'll be pressing me to tell him what the big question is too and that's making me feel worse. If only I could get out of tonight and spend some time here alone.

I need time to think.

To panic…

She broke the silence by looking up at Dan and smiling: "I'm going on tour with Quattro."

"Who?" He smiled although he had no idea what she was talking about.

"Quattro. The new girl-band. Their stylist has to dash over to San Fran and she's asked me to accompany them on tour – just their UK tour – as their stylist."

"You're not serious!" Charley looked impressed. And that didn't happen often. "Fucking brilliant, Helly! Well done!"

"Yeah," piped in Nick, "when're you going?"

What? So you can follow me again?

"Em, week after next. Only for two or three weeks. And I think I'll be home nearly every night."

Dan's face was serious. "*Nearly* every night!"

"I might only have to stay away for three or four in the whole tour."

She could see by Dan's face that he wasn't happy, and she couldn't really blame him. First it was Fiona and Adi landed in on them, and then Charley. Helly hadn't counted on the Murphia reunion meaning so many late nights out. She could understand his anger.

"Look, love, maybe we'll talk about this later. It's no big deal. I'll just go and ring Pat and Brian. They did say they'd be here by now, so I suppose we should check."

As Helly left the kitchen Dan followed her into the hallway. Before she could dial the number Dan grabbed her and spun her around.

I haven't been as close to him as this for weeks.

"Helly. What's wrong? You've changed."

I forced myself to relax and yet my breathing was short and fast. It's so hard to lie to him – I suppose that's why I've been avoiding him. I touched his chest lightly.

"Nothing's wrong, Dan. It's just a great opportunity for me. I'd really love to do it."

"I don't mean that. I mean the way that you've been so distant since coming back from Portugal. You've looked wretched every morning for the last couple of weeks and you're just so strange lately and now this! I know you really wanted for us to try for another baby, but I have to be honest with you."

Her eyes felt huge as she stared up into his, waiting for this revelation. He continued, shuffling awkwardly from foot to foot, "Well, em. We're in a bit of a financial mess. I haven't been able to meet all the direct debits for the last few months. It's all going a bit wrong."

She hadn't been expecting this.

The one thing that is his sole responsibility and he can't even manage that! I always spend within my budget when I'm shopping, so I know he can't blame me! What the hell has been going on?

"It's even harder now, what with your sisters living here, taking over the house, and now you want to jump ship for a couple of weeks and leave me with it all? It's not on, babe."

Too right it's not.

And he said I've looked wretched in the mornings! Charming!

"It's not like that. You're dramatising it. I want to do this. I can't cope with Fiona and Charley's lives. I can't make it right for them, I can only offer to help them in a time of need. We need to talk about the money. Why are we spending more than we've got?"

"Just because the work hasn't been coming in so quickly since April. The summer months are always worse, but it's never been this bad. That's why I've been trying to get more gigs – to earn some more money."

"Why didn't you tell me before?"

"Because I didn't want to worry you. But it's started to make me feel really sick."

Come to think of it I have been feeling rather sick a lot lately. I'd put it down to the late nights.

Dan hugged her in the hallway and the guilt swamped her as he said,

"Well, I think it's time you started putting some conditions on your Good-Samaritanness. I mean they don't pay anything towards their stay. Not even a goodwill gesture to say 'thanks'. How about telling them they've got a month to get sorted or they're out?"

I can't cope with this now. And I can't say that to them.

Who knows what's ahead of me? I'm knackered every day and the worry of this possible pregnancy is virtually taking over my life!

Just like before.

Just like the last time…

Helly and Dan had waited for Pat and Brian to arrive, leaving the others to go ahead to Antoinette's, agreeing to meet them there. They sat in silence in Helly's Mini as she drove through the London streets. Her phone bleeped. She ignored it at the time, but checked her text messages once she'd parked down the side street beside the continental bar that they were gigging at.

And it was from Nick. Thank God I never looked when I was in the car with Dan! But it's worse than that. He's texted me to say how he doesn't mind being with someone with kids, how he'd even discussed it with his older brother who thought it was cool too. I'm absolutely mortified at it all.

Mortified and confused.

A pressure cooker, just about ready to blow.

Chapter Thirty-Two

Antoinette's was fantastic. From the dusty dressers that lined the walls, housing numerous bottles of wine, to the hanging baskets outside. Fiona had squealed at the giant Jenga game in the corner, dragging Kyle across with her to play. Charley had dragged three tables together and was sitting with Jono and Gav, while she waited for James to bring the drinks over. Nick and Dan disappeared to the other end of the bar where they discussed the evening's plans with the manager. There were another two bands playing and the three men sat with their pints and worked out the time slots.

Two hours later she was wishing she could get out of it. What had started off as an intimate, relaxed bar had mutated into meltdown. The place was jammed and, despite the two sets of patio doors being flung open onto the London street, it was hellishly hot. It only took a glance across to Charley to see that she was well on her way – again. And Fiona had struck up a conversation with Kyle and Gav and was throwing her hands around in animation as she explained something to them. The gig had been great and the fellas always came off stage hyper.

She looks good too. I'm proud of her and how she's changing her life around. Delighted she's away from that brute.

Dan and the lads had just finished their slot and they'd been fantastic. Helly hated to admit it, but it was true. The last time she'd gone to their gig she'd got ridiculously drunk and had –

Well, let's not go over that again, eh?

But this time she was sober. Stone – cold – sober. As she looked at Dan, his handsome face shiny with the heat, she felt her heart miss a beat. *Perhaps I am too hard on him? He's bloody good at what he does and I don't really give him enough credit. I think I'll just nip over to the loo and cool down a bit, then I'll go and make a bit of a fuss of him.*

As she opened the toilet door she was faced with a queue of women, using the waiting time to fuss and fiddle with their hair and make-up. Helly stood at the sink, running the cold water over her wrists, exhaling at the relief. She watched two black women beside her, one of whom was plastering on a fifth, or maybe sixth layer of mascara onto her bloodshot, unfocussing eyes, and lipstick onto her slurring mouth as her friend stood beside her and whinged, "Oh, do you really think that's going to make a difference, Carol? I mean, do you really think you're gonna walk out of here and everyone will stop? They'll all say, 'Oh look how good Carol looks now she's touched up her make-up!'?"

"Fuck off, Jackie," her caked friend replied with a laugh in her voice. Everyone was watching from the corner of their eyes, but nobody wanted to be caught in the act. Helly looked down at her tummy in the mirror, viewed its familiar curve and wondered whether there was a small cluster of cells inside her that were slowly forming an embryo. The nausea swept over her without warning and, without thinking, she lifted her wet hands to her face and dabbed her cheeks, then ran her damp hands through her cropped hair.

"Bloody hot in there, isn't it?"

Her thoughts were disturbed by the tall, slim lady the other side of her. She smiled, weakly. "Yeah. Fierce hot."

"I wish my hair was nice and short like yours. It must be so easy to keep nice." Helly didn't know what to say and so she simply smiled. The lady continued, rummaging in her bag and pulling out a biro. "I hate doing this but I can't bear the heat," she complained as she twisted her long hair around and up into a top knot, spearing the bulk with her biro to hold it into place.

"It looks fine," Helly reassured her before drying her hands and walking back into the club. Only a few steps out of the toilets she was confronted by Nick, who despite the rivulets running down the side of his face, still oozed charm.

"Hey, Hel. How you doing?"

"OK. You?"

"Roasting! We were just saying, do you fancy grabbing something to eat after here? We've done our stint now and I think we'd all like to go on to somewhere cooler."

It seems I'm always looking for this Somewhere Cooler place. And so far I haven't found it. Late night in London, in the summer – where would you?

Queensway Ice Rink maybe?

"Whatever. Eating was the last thing on her mind. "What were you thinking of? Chinese?"

He grinned. "Saveloy and chips?"

"Yuck."

Nick smiled at her, putting his arm around her waist and pulling her into him.

"Nick. Not here!"

"Not here?" he smiled, encouraged. "Where then?"

"No-bloody-where!"

"Yeah, you say that now. We thought we might head off to Chutney Mary's on the Kings Road. Fancy it? We could mix with the American business-types and the well-to-do-Chelsea gang, couldn't we?"

Yeah, we could if we didn't feel sick!

Helly turned to head back to their table, "I'll go along with whatever Dan's doing."

He caught her by the arm, "It's touching. So devoted. Anyway, not so fast. I thought you were going to tell me what you meant when you said in Cascais that you 'needed the truth'?"

"Oh Nick, not here!"

"Might as well be now."

Well, I suppose I might as well get it out of the way. Here goes…

The sudden grapefruit that stuck in her throat

threatened to choke her as she squeezed out the words, "All right then. Nick, I was pregnant when we split up."

"Pregnant!"

She nodded.

"What are you saying? That it was mine?"

She nodded again, speechlessly.

"But – but – how could you know? How did you know it wasn't Dan's?"

"I knew. I knew from the dates. There wasn't any doubt."

He gazed at her, horrified, his thoughts racing. He took a deep breath. "I don't understand. So how could you have told me to go? To get out of your life?" His voice was loud and she 'sshhh'd' him. "Helen?"

"That was my decision." Her voice trembled.

"But why? When you were pregnant with my child? It doesn't make sense!"

She had a sudden urge to look down and check who was squeezing his goolies, because by the shrill tone of his voice *someone* had to be. She fought it, and replied to him with a calm confidence that surprised her,

"I'll tell you why, because you'd always been going on about not wanting children."

"But I loved you, Helen! You were the best thing that ever happened to me."

"I didn't 'happen' to you!"

He shook his head, the confident man-about-town façade gone. "But why did you reject me? What had I done?"

"Nothing. But I felt you had no intention of making

any commitment to me. Admit it, your idea of commitment was to get married in Vegas and go for a curry afterwards!"

He grinned. "Oh yeah. I did say that, didn't I?"

"Yes!"

He shook his head and reconnected with her words. "But I didn't mean it, Helen. Why didn't you tell me?"

"That's what the 'big question' was. The truth that I wanted to know. I never was sure . . . whether you knew I was pregnant when I told you it was over."

"No! Why would I? How *could* I?"

"I don't know. I thought you might have noticed how sick and bad I was every time we met."

He laughed. "I just thought I had that effect on you."

"Oh Nicky. I did love you, you know. But I loved Dan too. Anyway, even Tina Turner said: 'What's love got to do with it?' It was time we moved on. You weren't serious enough about me. About us! I needed Dan." She looked down at her varnished toenails. "You were always saying how you'd prefer to be up all night having mad sex rather than up all night with the screaming mad product of sex!"

"But it didn't *have* to be that way! Oh, Helen, you just didn't trust me, did you? That was the real problem, wasn't it?"

She forced herself to meet his gaze and there were tears in his eyes.

She regretted telling him here, in front of everyone, in the anonymity of Antoinette's. She'd had years to come to terms with it, but this was new for Nick. It wasn't right. She rubbed his arm. "Please try to understand. I didn't want to make you feel obliged to commit. I couldn't have pretended the baby was Dan's. And I couldn't consider rearing it on my own. Me and Charley and Fiona used to think it was a fun game that we played with our parents every Friday when we hid behind the settee to avoid the rent man! But I couldn't put *that* on a new life! It was too precious, too special."

"So you decided to sacrifice your future for your past!"

"How was I doing that?"

"Because of some fixed notions in your head you took it upon yourself to assume that I wouldn't make the effort to support you. You assumed I wouldn't try. It was all you – *assuming!*"

"We needed security! I'd lived half my life waiting for security and the time was up! Dan was waiting for me. To this day he doesn't have a clue about you and me. And I loved him. I still do! I was wrong to even be seeing you! I wasn't fit to be a mother and I wasn't worthy of a child."

"But you were fit and worthy with Dan?"

"Yes, I was. And what you and I did was wrong."

He stood back, shaking off her tanned hand from his arm. A sudden fixation with his fingers overwhelmed him as he picked at his fingers and mumbled, "So, what did you do? Thought you'd take it upon yourself to get rid of it? You didn't think that I had anything to do with it?"

Helly couldn't find the words.

Nick looked up at her, the pain evident in his eyes.

"So what was the plan? Abort me with our baby? Get rid of your past life with the embryo? Did you really think it'd be that easy to simply forget?"

"No, Nicky. I lost the baby two weeks after finishing with you. Nobody ever knew. Dan, Charley, Fiona, nobody. So it doesn't matter any more, does it? I've so often wondered whether you really felt that way. Did you really not want children so much?"

"At the time, no, but if you'd have told me, everything would have been different. It was easy to muck about with you and my mates when it wasn't a real situation. But you were carrying our child."

"A child that was never meant to be. I just had to know if you meant it. That's all."

They were interrupted suddenly by Dan's voice, interjecting between them as he passed by, "Hey, this looks very serious. Everything OK?"

Dan put his arm around Helly, eyeing Nick suspiciously. She felt safe but stiff and uncomfortable in his hug, watching as Nick sprang back into charm mode.

"She's a great woman, Dan. She's got me in raptures here."

Dan smiled, kissing her on the forehead again. "Yep, she sure is. We're leaving in a few minutes so get over there and finish up your drink, love."

Helly smiled at him.

As Dan carried on over to the toilets Nick relaxed again, shaking his head at her, and walking away.

If only he knew history could be repeating itself.

It's taken this to make me realise how much I love Dan though.

What a stupid fool I've been!

It was gone two when they all got home. Pat and Brian looked fresh and awake in contrast to their slurred, half-pissed state. All equally drunk, except Helly – but she still felt twice as bad as they did. Charley was irritated that Helly was so against James coming back to the house and had argued with her for the whole journey home in the taxi. Charley had hissed how pathetic Helly was and how she was a grown woman and entitled to sleep with whoever she wanted, without any judgements from her prudey Olympic Flame of a sister. Fiona had been upset at Charley's tone and had been dragged into the atmosphere too. Remarkably they had all managed smiles when Pat and Brian met them in the hallway.

"Charley," Brian had gushed on seeing her again, "it's great to see you again!"

"You too, Brian. And Pat. You're certainly looking well."

"You too," said Pat. "We hear you've joined the choir."

"The gospel choir," she confirmed. "Not just the shagging choir! I was having a great time." She was speaking very loudly and Helly poked at her, indicating for her to keep her voice down. Charley pulled a face and pushed her hand away, as she attempted to whisper, "It's a great place for meeting men."

"Ah," Brian was actually flirting with her, "ulterior motives, eh?" He laughed.

"I know. But don't tell Helly. She's awful serious tonight," she whispered. "Were the kids good for yez?"

"No problem. They're lovely children."

"Helly," Charley called, once again too loudly as she

linked Brian's arm, "put some toast on. I'm still starving!"

Pat shrugged at Brian's imploring expression as Charley dragged him down the hallway and into the kitchen. Within seconds they heard the light footsteps of someone coming down the stairs, one at a time. Toby appeared at the kitchen doorway, his Action Man under his arm as he wiped at his sleepy eyes. Charley lunged at him, tickling him in the ribs, as he flung himself wildly to escape her grasp.

"Got a big kiss for Auntie Charley?" she teased, opening her arms wide for a hug.

But Toby was a little reserved. She stretched her neck for a cheek-kiss so as to avoid hair-to-hair contact, and realised that nothing was happening . . .

"Oh, too big for a kiss now, are you?"

"No," replied Toby, "but you always have a funny smell."

Helly popped out from behind the open fridge door, surprised at Toby's remark, and time stood still for a split second as Charley, Fiona, Dan, Pat, Brian and Helly glared at him.

"Toby!" Helly chastised. "Don't be so rude! What smell?"

"Oh," Toby shrugged, "I dunno. Kind of like that drink that you were all drinking the other night when Auntie Charlie was trying to sing like a black lady. When she was showing off in front of Dad's friends about the godspell choir you used to be in."

Fiona and Helly looked at each other, waiting for the volcanic eruption, but Dan clapped his hands and laughed out loud.

"Ha! He means red wine. You don't miss nothing, do you, son?" He ruffled Toby's hair and led him back to the stairs. "Go on, turn around there and we'll go back up to bed."

Toby turned to go with his dad but paused at the foot of the stairs and looked back into the kitchen.

"Sorry, Auntie Charley," Toby grinned, "but we're told to always tell the truth."

Charley forced a smile on, "No bother," she grimaced. "Good boy."

The house was quiet as everyone slept. Brian had managed to escape Charley's clutches, much to Pat's mirth, and they'd left shortly after the sobering words of Toby. Helly could see how much it had affected Charley, as she'd disappeared up to bed only seconds after him.

Perhaps that's what she needs.

They say that no-one tells it like a child.

Helly lay beside Dan, staring at the ceiling as she turned over her ridiculous predicament in her mind. She heard Fiona's mobile go off and the muffled sounds of her voice as it came from the bedroom upstairs.

"Jesus," she sighed lightly into the quiet room, Dan's beer breath choking her as he turned, "things have got to start getting better around here soon."

Chapter Thirty-Three

Usually Helly looked forward to the weekend.

Usually.

Pre Nick-Sex.

The evening that could possibly have changed the rest of her life.

She wondered whether the shop would even be open at this early hour of the morning as she nipped down the road for milk and bread, enjoying the admiring glances she got. She knew it wasn't actually *her*, more her Mini Cooper with its beetle-black paintwork and white-skunk stripe that ran across the roof and down onto the bonnet. It was one of the only things that were 'hers' these days. Her house had been invaded, between her sisters and the band, and even Pink Turtle wasn't exclusively hers any more. Charley and Fiona used it like a back-up wardrobe – somewhere to call in when they'd exhausted their own, and then Helly's personal supply of clothing. The warm breeze whipped into the car, up around Helly's arms and neck, swirling around her face and head and then darting out of the passenger window to caress the next driver. From what she noticed in the shop and on the sunny London streets, the majority of Londoners were already sporting the glow-in-the-dark red triangle on their chests to show that they'd been out in the sun. Helly pulled up outside her house and switched off the engine, silencing the rather too loud music. She got out, straightening her khaki vest and shorts. She grabbed her shopping from the back seat and, without thinking placed the flat of her hand on her tum, the reminder of doubt flashing in her head. Fiona grabbed the carrier bag from her at the door and scuttled back down the hallway, to pacify a moaning and only half-awake Adi by pouring her a tall beaker of milk.

Feeling deflated and fed up with them all relying on her to keep providing for them, she avoided eye contact, simply nodding. "So when do you start getting wages?"

I didn't mean it to come out like that – it just did. I was never especially good at hiding my feelings though.

Fiona spun around to look at her, a deep frown between her eyebrows,

"At the end of the month. Why?"

Helly immediately felt mean. After all, hadn't she agreed to let Fiona and Adi stay with them from the start? Hadn't she whisked them back to London with her, all because she couldn't bear to stay in Cascais, to get them away from the violent Luís?

Was it because she couldn't bear to be reminded of her

huge mistake with Nick? She hadn't banked on seeing him every bloody week at home!

Fiona interjected, "You're not serious! You want me to give you the money for the milk?"

Helly's stomach lurched again, "No. Of course, I don't." She shook her head as she walked across the kitchen, unlocking the patio doors to the garden. "Don't mind me. I'm not feeling too good this morning."

The sound of the key twisting in the lock seemed to waken the entire household. Within minutes Toby and Jack had raced down the stairs, delighted as usual at the prospect of another whole day off school. They were in the garden with Adi, bypassing all reminders of breakfast, drinks and instructions to remember not to throw the ball over next-door's fence. Fiona brought a coffee out to Helly, placing it down in front of her as she sat at the wooden garden table, the huge square parasol overhead giving a relaxing shade.

"Sorry I haven't been giving you much money, Hel."

Helly shook her head, tired of the worry of everything. "Don't worry, Fi. I'm just cranky today."

"Why? What's up?"

"Nothing. I don't want to talk about it." She sipped at her coffee, her stomach baulking as the warm liquid travelled down. "So, who was on the phone late last night?"

"Before I tell you that, I must tell you – Pat was telling me about afternoon tea at The Savoy. She said it was something ridiculous like £25 but it was something to be experienced. Shall we see if Charley fancies it this afternoon? My treat. It'll make up for things a little?"

Fiona was smiling over her coffee cup.

It was nice to see. Helly felt proud that she'd helped make her little sister's life better by bringing her to London. Fiona whispered, "My treat to you. Not to Charley. She's got loads of money."

"How do you know that?"

"She must have. The way she spends it on booze! Did you notice she had the shakes the other morning?"

"No?" Helly spoke loudly, and then whispered, "Well, it's hardly surprising, is it? She'd put George Best to shame!" They sniggered together and then stopped, listening to the the sudden sounds of breakfast rattling from the kitchen, sounds of the toaster springs being squeezed as two slices were dropped into the slits, the flick of the kettle, the sucky gasp of the fridge as the door was pulled open. Helly stood and looked in through the window to see Charley, her hair piled high on her head. She sat back down, mouthing the name 'Charley' to Fiona, who quickly changed the subject.

"That was Claudine on the phone last night."

"Is she OK? It was kind of late."

"Yeah, she'd been out with Xavier. They'd just got in."

"Xavier? I thought she hated him?"

Fiona shrugged. "She did. That's Claudine for you."

"So what's up?"

"It isn't her problem. It's mine. She said that Luís has started being difficult, going around to Claudine and demanding that she hand over all my stuff. Insisting that it's his."

"How ridiculous! Christ, you didn't have much as it

was. Is it his?"

"A few small bits – essentials that I'd taken when he'd kicked me out, but nothing of any value. He's just being manipulative. As usual. He was always domineering when it suited him. You know, he used to kind of scare me too."

Helly completely understood what Fiona meant by that. She couldn't get it out of her mind – that look in his eyes when he'd taken her there for the drink. "So what are you going to do?"

"Huh, it looks like I'll have to go over there and either sell stuff or bring it here."

She saw the flash of worry on Helly's face. "It's not big stuff, Hel. More sentimental bits, you know, photos and pictures and clothes and that. It wouldn't take up any room. Not really."

"So are you going?"

"Yeah. I have to really. Claudine's moving in with Xavier, so I don't really have an option."

"So when do you think?"

"Next weekend I reckon. I'll get my full week in at work and then nip over on Saturday morning. I can't go pissing them off at work already. Not when I've only just started. It's a bummer though, having to spend a whole week's wages on flights."

Charley clattered out into the garden, balancing a plate and glass of water in one hand and three mugs of coffee in the other.

And yes – she's shaking. Again.

"Morning." Her voice was flat and one look at her told

Helly and Fiona she was still half-plastered.

Helly looked down at her strange breakfast of toast, tuna and scrambled eggs, wondering how she managed to stomach it on a hangover.

"So?" Charley grinned as she bit into her golden triangle of toast, snaring it still while she gripped it with her teeth, "What's on for today then?"

"You've got the bloody shakes." Helly couldn't resist. It didn't seem fair that Fiona was working so hard toward making a new life and yet Charley did little else than drink, socialise and flirt with whoever was near at the time.

Charley avoided eye contact and wobbled the toast towards her mouth for a second bite.

Helly was irritated at her lack of response and so added, for impact,

"Again."

Charley stopped crunching on the golden toast, staring at Helly with a wide-eyed look.

It's slightly unnerving.

She usually has an answer for everything.

"What did you say?" Charley looked puzzled.

And now I feel bad once more.

"I said you've got the shakes, Charley."

She shook her head impatiently. "No, no. I didn't mean that bit. What you said last."

Now Helly looked bemused as she simply said, "Again. I said again."

Charley threw the toast down onto the plate and began to cry into her hands.

"What's wrong?" Fiona asked, equally confused by her reaction.

For the first time since Charley'd been in London, Helly and Fiona saw her cry.

"Again." Her voice was flat and weak, "Again! That's what Steve started to call me – Again."

"Why?"

"Oh it began as a joke but then it stuck. Because I was so crap at everything, I suppose. Because I'd lost something – again, because I was drunk – again. And now, because I've got the shakes – again. And I can't get Toby's words out of my head. I think I need some help, girls."

They'd sat in the garden for a while, first consoling Charley and agreeing when she'd said she needed to talk about it all later on, and then soaking up the sunshine and intermittently checking each other's arms and legs for tan-comparison. Fiona was way ahead of them both, much to Charley's irritation, despite her playing it safe in a vest and light trousers compared to Charley's two-triangle bikini top and skimpy shorts.

They'd agreed to go for afternoon tea at The Savoy for the feel-good factor, and Fiona had begged to stop at South Bank first. She'd heard so much about the National Film Theatre and the street entertainers that she wanted now to see them. Especially on such a fine day.

Fiona helped Helly to inflate the large paddling pool and fill it with water from the hose as Charley grimaced at the kids' screeching and laughing sounds. By late morning she'd retired inside the house, much to the delight of Kyle and Gav who had turned up once again to rehearse some songs with Dan.

Dan had been a bit pissed off when Charley had first mentioned that they were heading out for the afternoon, but after a couple of hours of coping with Kyle and Gav's bikini-topped distraction he was delighted. It meant that they could finally get on with their music.

By early afternoon it was scorching and Charley had showered and was dressed in her Diamond Girl killer heels and her sunflower spaghetti-strap sundress, ready for The Savoy, while Fiona went more for comfort in her flatter red Skechers. Where Charley was of the opinion that afternoon tea meant 'high and sexy', Fiona preferred 'flat and ready to run'.

As they sat on the Tube to South Bank, Fiona regretted wearing her strapless sundress, watching her reflection in the window opposite as she kept tugging the straps up. Helly looked cool and comfortable in her crocheted pink, green and white striped halter-neck, which went fantastically with her jeans and yellow court shoes. She had recently taken to wearing a few small crucifix chains together and even Dan complimented her on how well she looked. They wandered around outside the National Film Theatre, Fiona stopping to read the billboards that advertised up-and-coming events, Charley watching the suntanned guys rollerblading along the riverside. The London Eye loomed beside them, a giant white wagon wheel, turning so slightly that you hardly noticed, the glazed pods crammed with people. Fiona dragged Charley under the bridge to watch the street performers, the guys and girls who had sprayed themselves gold and stood, statue-like, hoping for a few coins. Helly stood beneath the bridge and leaned on the railings, looking into the Thames, the grey/green water chopping dark patches onto the concrete pillars as they disappeared into the water.

She knew she had to buy a pregnancy testing kit. The time had come. It was ridiculous. For the sake of a tenner she'd know, she'd be free of this torment.

Free, or handcuffed!

Afternoon tea was fun. Not quite the cucumber sandwiches that they'd been expecting, but different. Helly and Fiona couldn't fathom why anyone would spend £25 on it, but Charley got caught up in the whole idea. They sat around their linen-clothed table and chatted.

"I'm so unhappy with my body still. I've lost a stone since I've been here, but it's not enough." Fiona spoke through a mouthful of salad.

Charley slathered a teaspoonful of jam onto her half-scone. "You should come to the gym with me more then and give up on those crap excuses of yours."

"They're not excuses!"

"Oh no, course they're not." She mimicked Fiona's voice, "'It's too hot for the gym, too cold for a swim, I don't like the sit-ups – they hurt my neck' – that's all you say!"

"Well, at least I'm honest about it. You'd never been to a gym in your life until you came to London. Who're you trying to impress? James? You've become a gymaholic! You're there every day with your packed gym bag. And it's all going to end in tears! You can't go on ignoring the machine time limits, going mad if someone's on your favourite treadmill."

Charley bit back, "At least I'm working towards the body beautiful. Typical of you – you'd prefer to *buy* it! They can only do liposuction so many times, you know? You can't keep going back for more. You want to spend all day running around town, having manicures and treatments."

"No, I don't! I'm working in the café to make a life for me and Adi. I've dreamed about this and now it's happening."

"But Adi mightn't like you bringing her here. Have you asked her? Does she want to be here or Portugal? She could end up hating you."

Fiona gulped at the bone china teacup and shrugged. "Charley, as Bette Davis once said: 'If you've never been hated by your child, you've never been a parent'."

Charley scowled a little as she replied, "Well, it's easy for you two. You're natural mothers. I suppose you're tuned in to your kids. I prefer to have more fun in my life. I like my freedom. That doesn't go hand in hand with giving birth."

"Charley," Helly nearly choked on her tea, "if you think that having a child makes you a natural mother, that's as ridiculous as expecting that having a piano makes you a musician!"

"Well," she shrugged, "it's a good thing I never had one then, isn't it?" Helly noticed the pain flash across her eyes as she gruffly snatched up the scone and rammed it into her mouth. She knew when it was time to change the subject,

"Fi, have you told Charley you're heading back to Cascais at the weekend?"

Charley nearly spat out her food. "You're what?"

"Luís is being difficult and I have to go and get the rest of my stuff. He's threatening me with solicitors and stuff, accusing me of child abduction. But he agreed, didn't he, Helly? When you spoke to him, he agreed that it was OK for us to come here for a while?"

Now I feel really nauseous. You see, he didn't actually agree, as such. I mean, we spoke about it and that, but he never actually said yes.

"Well, he didn't say no, did he? You're not doing any harm, are you?"

"No, but Helly, did he actually say 'yes'?"

Helly looked down at her empty plate.

"Helly?" Charley joined in. "He didn't, did he?"

Quick, aren't they!

"No. Not actually 'yes'. No."

"Jesus! As if I'm not afraid of him enough! And now I've got to go back there and risk seeing him again?"

"Well, you must leave Adi here. You must go alone, Fiona. Make a quick job of it. Don't tell him you're coming and ask Claudine not to also. Go, collect your things and get out of there." Charley felt seriously worried once more about what Luís would do to Fiona if he knew she would be there next weekend and felt an overwhelming urge to go with her. But he frightened her too and she'd promised herself she'd never see his face again. She'd promised herself that she'd take her secret about Luís to her grave with her.

But if it meant that she'd have to use it to save her little sister – then she would.

"Don't worry about it," Fiona turned the conversation around to a lighter note. "I'll have a chat with Claudine this week and we'll arrange to get me in and out as quickly as possible. I won't even have to see him. Anyway," she began teasing the rim of her teacup with her finger, "there's somebody else for me to think about now."

She told them all about Raoul, the hunky celloist who she'd met in the coffee bar and how so unpushy he was – just her kind of guy. Charley had to hold herself back from slapping her on the back and congratulating her.

"Invite him tonight!" Charley gushed, instead, desperate to meet this guy that had ignited some love-interest in her whiter-than-white sister.

"Tonight? What's on tonight?"

"Well, I've been checking out the *Time Out* guide and *Midsummer Night's Dream* is on at the Open Air Theatre at Regent's Park. We *have* to go. It'll be a fantastic evening."

"Oh Charley, I can't keep going out. Dan's going to flip!"

"I thought you wanted some freedom in your life!"

Helly scowled at her.

Charley continued, "Anyway, I think you two should have another baby."

Now I'm bright red!

"Why? Why do you say that?"

Charley gulped down the last of her tea and gathered up her bag. "Oh, I don't know. He just seemed so happy the other day when he teased you about drinking the orange juice."

Charley and Fiona had noticed Helly's sudden change of heart when it came to getting plastered. So far, they hadn't mentioned it. But they were watching her. They knew something was up.

The ridiculous thing is, I really don't want to go. Call it the nesting instinct, but I call it the Jesus-Christ-Please-Don't-Let-Me-Be-Pregnant instinct. I'd love the idea of a night in. Alone. It'd be heaven to watch all the TV crap with a bar of chocolate and my feet up.

But hey, I know I mustn't panic yet.

At least I must do 'the test' first.

Although I always seem to fail…

Charley had been reflecting too. On young Toby's words last night. They'd stabbed at her painfully and she was shaken how it took the words of a child to put things into perspective. Somehow he'd made her realise how bad she'd got. And she knew why. She knew she'd started drinking to ridiculous excess since she'd visited Fiona last year but she'd never actually faced up to it all. The way Dan had looked at Helly when he'd teased her about being pregnant had made her yearn for a decent man in her life. For the chance to be a mum too. Up until now she had always thought she *could* be a mum – whenever she chose. But Toby's words had hit home. Reality had truly bitten. Charley realised that she'd be no good to any child with her irresponsible attitude.

And her drinking.

It was time for things to change.

The Open Air Theatre was fantastic and everyone had agreed to go. Dan had jumped at the idea and Fiona had dragged Raoul out for a Murphia family introduction, Charley had arranged to meet James there and they'd even taken the kids. It was the first time that they'd all enjoyed a relaxed, non-drinking evening out together since their arrival.

Helly loved it and felt the warmth of her family as they'd sat on the picnic rug, munching the grapes and samosas as they watched the sun go down over the trees.

I must, must buy that test tomorrow.

Chapter Thirty-Four

Sometimes really daft things bothered Helly. Sometimes she'd walk into a room and wonder how the coffee stain in the shape of Africa came to be on the cushion in the corner, or she'd torment herself with figuring how the Mexican wave started at a footie match. She knew that if she was standing in the terraces and some eejit grabbed her hand and started jumping up and down, waving it about she'd turn and tell him to go have a shite for himself. The heat wasn't helping her contrariness and she felt bad that she'd taken it out on Toby and Jack as she'd driven them to school that morning. As she followed the willowy white lady with matted blonde dreadlocks down Portobello Road she felt a droplet of sweat wiggle down her spine and she was already worrying about damp patches under her arms. She'd promised herself that she'd buy the pregnancy testing kit today, but knew she'd find a million and one other things to do instead. She'd agreed to meet Fiona at Pink Turtle after she'd dropped the boys at school – Fiona had pestered the life out of her to go to Alfie's Antiques Market with her to check out the vintage fashion, and Helly had finally given in.

More through exhaustion than anything else. My resolve is shot to pieces lately. And the more I try to put Nick out of my mind, the more I'm reminded about how I may be carrying a part of him with me. I believe him – that he hadn't known I was pregnant, that he would have stood by me. If I hadn't lost it. But what does it all matter now? The quicker I find out my condition the better, and that's what I should be doing this morning instead of passing by the chemist right at this minute rather than going in and buying the testing kit!

She thought she heard someone calling her name, but broke from her trance and looked about quickly, scanning the faces of the market shoppers.

"Helly!" The voice sounded like Fiona's but she couldn't see her amongst the mid-morning crowd. And then she saw the woman in the cotton sundress and kitten heels, her glossy dark hair piled high on her head and the highly reflective sunglasses shielding her eyes.

No – that's not Fiona. She's far too classy!

And she'd never wear that red lipstick!

"Helly! For Christ's sake, can't you wait?"

Jesus, it is her!

Helly tried not to laugh at the sight of Fiona trying to run on her narrow heels, as she jostled through the crowds across to her.

"Fuck ya!" she puffed. "Why didn't you wait for me?"

"Why? I'll tell you why." Helly rattled the key into the door of Pink Turtle and let them in, quickly punching a code into the alarm system behind the door. She turned to face Fiona in the unlit shop. "I didn't recognise you! That's why. You look fantastic, Fi! And look at you in that dress!"

Fiona looked chuffed with herself and gave a twirl. "I know. I said I'd lost weight, didn't I?"

"You were right. Jesus, Fi, fair play to you. You look great. Hope Luís doesn't see you at the weekend now. He'll want you back quicker than you can say If-I-Knew-You'd-Look-Like-That-I'd-Have-Stuck-With-You!"

Fiona sneered. "Well, he can shag off! I'm not interested and I won't be going anywhere near him on Saturday. Like I said, I'll be in and out before you know it!"

"Christ, you sound like Dan!"

They looked at each other for a split second and then burst laughing at the innuendo.

"Go on, nip over to your coffee bar and get us a couple of freebies. I want to leave here just after lunch."

"Helly! I can't get freebies! I've only been working there for five minutes. It's bad enough going in on my day off as it is!"

Helly smirked at her. "Get away with it! You're dying to get over there and show off your babe-licious outfit to Raoul. As if you didn't see enough of him last night!"

"What do you think of him, Hel?"

"Oh, let's think: tall, sexy, buffed, educated, adorable. Yeah, I think he'll do for you."

Fiona's smile was so wide that Helly couldn't help but feel her happiness as it radiated from her.

"Go on, get the coffees. I'll have a cappuccino this morning though."

Fiona turned, eager to get across and see if Raoul was in for his morning coffee.

Helly shouted through the open door as she went, "With loads of chocolate sprinkles too!"

Sitting in the silence of her shop she looked over at the Quattro clothes. She was due to meet the girls for their fitting tomorrow and the anticipation was killing her. It had been a great opportunity at the Open Air Theatre to talk it through with Dan, especially as Charley had James to distract her and Fiona had Raoul.

She was mentally set to head off on tour next week, but she had tons of planning to do at home before she could physically leave the house. At least she'd be home most nights on the first week – it'd soften the blow for Dan and the boys.

She sat on the high stool at her counter, stirring up the dust while the sun shone through the window, swiping and swirling at it. She felt slightly envious of Fiona, who was crazy about Raoul – as much as she tried to hide it – and was free to express her feelings.

Whereas I'm constantly thinking of Nick and I'm betraying everyone!

Fiona opened the door and caught her swiping at nothing.

"What you doing?" She was laden with two large cardboard mugs of coffee and a brown paper bag. Helly jerked back to reality,

"Oh, nothing. Just messing. What've you got in there?"

Fiona smiled as she rested down her goodies, and pulled two huge cinnamon rolls from the bag. "Elevenses," she grinned.

Helly's mouth watered. "Well," she smiled as she took an enormous mouthful, "you won't hang onto that new figure for long if you get a taste for these."

"Just a treat, Helly. Just a treat."

Charley was taking full advantage of the Mediterranean-style heatwave. She craved solitude and was delighted that Fiona had managed to get Adi into a play-school – it meant that she was truly alone back at the house today. Stretched out in the garden on the recliner bed she felt herself perspiring on the long puffed cushion that she lay on and so she stood, rearranging her bikini, enjoying the air on her body. Her tan wasn't quite up to Fiona's mark, but it was coming along well. She loved Helly's urban garden with its decked patio, water features and chrome planters. And then she only had to look further down the garden to see the beautiful tree and the children's swings and slide. She berated herself for about two seconds for not going to the gym, but had started to agree with Fiona's point of view when she'd said, "Oh great. A stationary bike. What's the point of that? To see how long it takes to get nowhere?"

Anyway, she'd been out on Helly's bike nearly every

day last week and enjoyed it much more than pounding away in front of a wall of mirrors. She padded barefoot into the kitchen, pouring herself another tall glass of water and sticking in a straw, pausing by the wine rack as she turned. Her instincts screamed at her to stoop and pluck out one of the numerous bottles of red: it would be the perfect complement to her sunbathing session. Or, even better, to go out to the fridge in the shed and take out one of the chilled boxes of white. But something stopped her. Tears flooded to her eyes as she felt her mouth contort into a Sylvester Stallone pre-cry shape. Toby's words had hurt like hell. But they hit home. In a way that Donal had probably been trying to, but had failed. In a way that Mum and Dad, and Helly and Dan and Fiona had tried to. In the way that Steve probably had tried to. With a deep breath she resolutely lifted her glass of water and returned to the suntrap on the patio where she crouched low and sat on the edge of the sun-lounger, resting her glass on the decking beside her. She picked up her mobile and lay back, closing her eyes while it rang. She was just about to hang up when Steve answered. By his officious tone, she suspected he was at work.

"Steve? Charley." Her voice was gentle, the abrupt confident tone cast aside.

"Charley! How's life?"

"Sunny. And shite."

"No, you have that wrong. It's Sonny and *Cher*."

"No. I mean shite! Anyway, we're not all old enough to remember them."

"Don't kid yourself there, missus!"

"OK, but listen. Steve, you were right. I need some help. I want you to help me."

There was a silence. It was obvious he hadn't banked on such an emotional plea. "What can I do to help you, Charley? Just tell me."

"I need to talk to you, Steve. You were right – I am just running away from things. I know why I started drinking like this and I need to deal with it, but I'm afraid."

"Have you spoken to your sisters about this?"

She snorted, shocking herself slightly as she snorted, grateful that he couldn't see her.

"No! Huh, no. There's no way I can tell them. Not yet anyway."

"Charley, I'm working days all week, but if you can get a flight back at the weekend we'll spend some time together. I think you're fantastic, you know that. I'll stand by you. Whatever it takes."

His kind words turned on the taps – full.

Again.

Once she'd managed to regulate her gasping breath she sniffed as she asked him, "Can I ask you something?"

"Go ahead."

"Did you ever notice that I had the shakes?"

"Frequently. You had the shakes so bad when you were looking for Diego that you kept whipping me with the lead!"

She laughed. "Feck off!"

"OK, OK, so you weren't that bad. But I did notice it."

"And didn't that put you off me?"

"Fuck no! I just wanted to put your hand down my pants!"

"Shag off!" she laughed out loud.

"I'm only joking."

"Oh, thanks!" she teased back.

"Charley, I used to be a heavy drinker. I know you can get through this."

"Jesus!" she joked. "And here was me blaming it all on the mid-life crisis. I'd been looking forward to it for years, all that contrariness and reliving your youth."

"Sorry to burst your bubble. Again."

"Steve, I'll book myself on a flight on Saturday morning. Could you meet me at Dublin airport?"

"Course I can. Just text me the time you arrive and I'll be there."

"Steve?"

"Yup?"

"Thanks."

"No bother. I'd do anything to help you. I'm just glad you're coming back to give us a second chance."

She placed the phone down beside her water, laying her head back and closing her eyes. Her eyelids burned a pinky orange as they heated up.

She was having a fab time in London. Helly was great and their 'taxi shoes' nights out were such a laugh. But she knew she was just killing time. She knew James wasn't long-term material. She decided to burst out of the twilight zone that she was in. She was tired of life in the shadow of her secret about Luís, especially if he was about to start blackmailing Fiona. Perhaps it was time for her to come to terms with it.

Perhaps a double-blackmail to Luís might buy Fiona her freedom and help to reconstruct her own vandalised mind.

Alfie's Antiques market was mobbed. Fiona was in awe of Helly. She knew exactly where to go for what as they weaved through the dealers, darting in and out of the retro and antique shops. Fiona squealed as she swore she spotted Stella McCartney and then Nicole Kidman. Helly took it all in her stride – celebs were frequent visitors to the eclectic market. Fiona was carrying the eight or nine bags of vintage bargains that Helly had already bought. Fiona supposed they were bargains – she personally would never have paid £150 for the floor-length leather coat, especially as it was probably third, or maybe even fourth-hand, but she wasn't about to question Helly's judgement.

Helly had intended to spend around £400 and was certainly getting her money's worth so far.

Especially as I won't be getting to the Paris markets for at least a month now, what with the Quattro tour!

Hark at me! The Quattro tour!!

Fiona had nagged that she was getting tired, her arms and legs were aching and her throat felt as if their sides were stuck together. It was time for a drink. No sooner had they elbowed their way across to the just-about-to-become-vacant plastic garden seats that seemed to be so popular, when a phone started to ring. They sat, ignoring the scowling faces of those-who-hadn't-been-quick-enough and then Helly went to order the lattes. Fiona watched as people around darted into their bags, pockets and briefcases to check if the irritating trilling sound belonged to them.

Then she realised that it was hers.

Helly collected the hot coffees from the counter, slurping at the hot rich drink as she watched her newly glam sister come to life.

It's Raoul.

Obviously.

"No, of course .... No, I'd *love* to come .... No, please .... Fantastic! No, of course you're not interrupting anything ... OK, I'll see you there in three-quarters of an hour. Fab! Thanks, Raoul."

It was another time that Helly wished she could raise just the one eyebrow. She'd tried a few times with Dan but he'd buckled up with laughter and said she'd looked like she was in pain, so hadn't bothered since.

"Go on?" She tried to sound pissed-off, but knew she hadn't managed to.

"Oh Helly, I have to go. I'm sorry."

"You *have* to go?"

"Raoul has asked me to go to the Royal Academy of Music with him. There's an afternoon recital on in an hour and the London Sinfonietta are playing."

"So you're abandoning me. Thanks! Who's going to carry all the bags now?" Helly smiled, slightly jealous, but also pleased for her. Fiona necked her coffee at ferocious speed, surprising Helly that she hadn't dribbled any down her front, kissed Helly on the cheek and within two minutes had disappeared.

I think she was last seen skittering down the steps to the Tube Station!

Steve was serious about making a go of things with Charley and his police buddies commented all that rainy afternoon on how his mood had suddenly lifted after her call. They all ribbed him, wanting to know who the unlucky lady was, but he wasn't giving anything away. He knew he had a lot of hard work in front of him with her, but he also thought she was worth it. He looked at his watch, willing the last hour to pass quickly so that he could get home and finish painting his kitchen and hallway, and also to start working out what he could do to help her, in the way that he, himself, had been helped before. As he looked down at his paperwork he was suddenly aware of the bright glare coming off the white pages and looked up to see that, miraculously, the grey clouds were floating off towards the east and the first rays of sunshine were gracing him.

Helly had only been joking about Fiona not helping her carry the bags. She *had* only been joking, but now it was no laughing matter. Without thinking it through she'd gone on and bought another three pieces – all lined, heavy clothes – and now she felt like her knuckles were dragging along the pavement as she tried to carry them all. Making her way down the Edgware Road, laden with the abundance of carrier bags she was sure she felt a light spot of rain. While she'd been shopping the grey clouds had taken residence and on seeing the huge traffic jams, she was doubly glad that she'd rung Charley and asked her to collect Adi from play-school and Toby and Jack from school. She hadn't sounded as bubbly as usual, but Helly hadn't thought about that for more than a minute, assuming that she was irritated by the sudden change of weather.

Sure enough, as she looked up at the mottled sky another drop fell and hit her right in the eye. She struggled as she tried to lift the many bags that she carried with her left hand, and raise her hand to rub her waterlogged eye, smearing her mascara in a musky stripe across her cheek-bone. She jumped as a driver hit his horn. She carried on walking, until they did it again, in a few short blasts. Like everyone else, Helly turned her head as she walked, to see who was tooting. A red Mercedes sat in a line on the road, stationary as it waited for the lights to change.

Holy shit! It's Nick!

Smile, Helly, for God's sake. Don't let him see your panic.

"Hey, Nick," she grinned slowing down and moving nearer to the kerb, "what you doing around here?" It was easy to talk to him with the sunroof open; it meant she didn't have to put down her bags and crouch at the passenger window.

"I've got an office in Maida Avenue. I had to call in to check they're behaving themselves. Fancy a lift?"

Shit. Just what I was dreading.

"Oh no, you're fine, thanks. I was just going to get on the Circle Line. I need to get this lot home."

"Get in! You have to change trains at least once, don't you?"

She nodded, annoyed at his quick thinking.

"So let me give you a lift?"

Helly smiled, "You think you'll get me there quicker on the roads? You're deluded."

"Maybe, but at least you don't have to look at rows of strangers as they let their knees fall apart and dribble as they nod off to sleep."

She felt another quick succession of raindrops and, all in the name of preserving her new buys from getting soaked, she agreed.

"You'll have to put all that lot in the boot though. I've got a couple of computers here on the back seat."

"OK, do I need a key?"

"No," he looked ahead at the row of traffic that he was in, their brake lights going out one by one, "but make it snappy, these traffic lights are about to change."

She hit the boot button and stashed her many bags in alongside his basketball, a pair of muddy trainers, a worn-looking laser printer and an empty petrol can. She had to admit she felt good opening the door to his swanky red car and sitting in.

"So where shall we go for a quick drink?" he smiled at her, making her melt, just as he had done all those years ago.

All those weeks *ago in bloody Cascais!*

"We're going nowhere, only Belsize Park thanks! I need to get home, Nick."

"Spoilsport. But you're mine now; I can take you anywhere."

Her stomach did flips but she was determined not to

show it. "Just home, thanks, Nick."

He took her hand off her leg and kissed her palm firmly, placing it gently down to rest on her lap once again. No sooner had he pulled away from the green light than the heavens opened.

"Jesus!" Helly flinched and blinked as the rain pelted on her through the open sun-roof.

"No problem," Nick squinted as he looked up to the roof of the car, releasing a small handle by the rear-view mirror and straining as he tried to crank it in a circular motion to close up the roof. As they joined the queue of cars and edged along in the traffic once more, Nick held his breath, his face red as he struggled with the stiff old handle, managing to force it round once, and then nearly twice when – SNAP!

It broke off in his hand.

"Shit!" he hissed, holding the rusty metal handle in his left hand as the rain lashed down onto them. Pedestrians were running for shelter in the shops. Men ran into pubs and women into cafés as they dodged the deluge of the summer storm. "Shit, shit, shit!" Nick's hair was already saturated, as was his beige linen shirt. So much so that Helly could see his chest and nipples through it already.

Fuck! Does that mean I'm the same?

She looked quickly down, speechless for what seemed like minutes, although it was only split seconds, at her yellow blouse which was also now wafer-thin. She turned to look at Nick again who was frantically trying to link up the shapes of the broken handle with what it had left behind, in a bid to reconnect it and perhaps wind the window closed. The ridiculousness of it all hit Helly square in the stomach. She began to giggle. Here she was, stuck in a car with Nicky, in his flash, show-off 1971 red Mercedes and they were both completely soaked to the skin. She began to laugh uncontrollably. His expression was not one of humour.

"Helen!" he roared, incensed by her laughing, "This is my car! My fucking car! And my fucking computers!"

Which made Helly laugh even more.

We sat there, completely helpless, as the rain poured in as if someone was tipping it from a bucket. Within minutes I could feel the water droplets pinging from the ends of my hair and eyelashes, could feel the wet as it soaked through my lap and onto the car seat beneath me. We were completely, absolutely saturated.

And I loved it with every inch of my body.

It was everything I needed at that moment – a burst of reality in the strangely unreal world that I was currently living in.

I loved getting soaked and I loved watching Nick get angrier and angrier, until finally, he too started to laugh. He threw his hands up and threw the metal handle onto the back seat, where it clonked on one of the wet computers.

"Bollocks to it then!"

And we both laughed and laughed.

Charley had been a little put out at having to do the school run. It was so *not* her scene. But she'd decided to be less selfish and she supposed it was as good a place to start as any. It had surprised her how Toby had wanted to hold her hand for the whole walk home, especially after what he'd said to her. It had felt strange at first, his smooth, line-free hand in hers, the feel of his trusting palm against hers, his biro-covered fingers gripping hers. She noticed his sprightly cow'slick and squeezed his hand a little, feeling like part of a family for the first time in years. Adi and Jack had been extraordinarily well behaved too – holding each other's hands and stopping at the kerb. All in all, they'd been a dream. She felt a strange affinity with Toby since his revelation the other night and wondered what it was about his words that had made her listen. She supposed it was the innocence of a child talking about an ugly, adult world. She'd finally come to terms with it this afternoon and was ready to admit it – she knew she was an alcoholic. And she was ready to get help for it too.

"Did you ever think of going in for a Wet T-shirt competition?" Nick teased Helly as they sat in the soaked car, feeling the chill now their clothes were saturated.

"Shuttup, Nick. That's hardly your 'new man' voice talking, is it?"

He looked sideways at her, his wet hair drying in cute tufts, "You don't believe all that, do you?"

She shrugged, "I don't know what I believe in any more. I know you're not the Nicky I used to know and yet, in some ways you are."

"Helen, it's all a bloody act. Did you never hear about Male Competitiveness Syndrome?"

"Not by name, no. But aren't men always trying to outdo each other? Is that what you were trying to do with me? Outdo Dan?"

"Don't *ever* say that, Helen. My feelings for you are real."

"But this male competitiveness, it's just a bit of fun. Men no longer limit themselves to just competing over sports and cars. Modern masculine one-upmanship ups the ante with soft furnishings and cookery skills."

Helly was finding it hard to believe he was so shallow. She felt disappointed in her perception of him.

He's falling off the pedestal!

"You know, in just the last few months I've been challenged by other men over my lack of a recycling bin. *And* mocked for thinking a flotation tank was something to do with the loo!"

She couldn't keep the bitterness from her voice as she spoke, "And that's what it's all about, is it?" She glared at him and he held his head straight, staring at the tyres of the car in front. "Nicky! I said is that what it's all about for you?"

"Em, if a man speaks and there's no woman to correct him, is he *still* wrong?"

She exhaled, putting her hand on his outstretched arm, the sudden barrier that had gone up between them as he reached out to the steering wheel.

"Nick, you've got it all wrong. Who really gives a shit whether you've got a designer kitchen or a bloody recycling bin? That doesn't give a woman the shudders, or make us prick with goose pimples."

His arm relaxed a little. He made no moves to show he was taking in her words, but she knew he was.

"Women want men to appreciate our femininity, not to *copy* it. All this New Age Man crap, all this looking for someone in touch with their feminine side. If you ask me men need to find their caveman roots again. Especially city men. These guys who mow the garden, change a tyre, and then go in and hang up their aprons and dust off their tools! All these poncey boy bands, the clean-shaven, smooth-chested pretty boys. Take it from me, women want a square-jawed hairy guy in trunks – unshaven and tattooed – and sexier for it!" She felt like Les Dawson in drag as she folded her arms in front of her, jostling her left boob as she did so.

He smiled at her, pointing to the broken sunroof, "But won't my flash car be an added incentive for the ladies?"

"I think your battered Mercedes will have more women talking to you than your skills in the kitchen."

They all flocked around Helly when Nick had finally got her home, the sight of the two of them slopping into the hallway, their clothes slapping as they hit off their skin, off the floor, making them all gasp and take notice.

Dan didn't even baulk at the sight of Nick. He really has no idea about us.

And I still haven't bought the testing kit.

Dan and Charley threw towels at them and they sloughed off the rain from their hair. Uncomfortable with the situation Helly nipped upstairs, tugging off her cold wet clothes with each step, throwing them into the bath as she passed the bathroom, and grabbing the fluffy bath sheet to dry herself. Once dry she felt a chill and pulled on a cream hoody and her matching tracksuit pants, stopping to run a blob of wax through her slightly frizzing short hair, and to smear on another couple of stripes of lipstick. She didn't know why she did that. It annoyed her how Nick's presence made her inanely more aware of her appearance, to the point where she'd started to pick up and read the home-teeth-bleaching kits and tan-flannels in the chemist. As she walked back into the kitchen Dan and Charley were making their way out.

"Hey, something I said?" Helly joked.

"I've got to book a flight. Mind if I use the internet?" Charley's voice was flat and Helly couldn't believe she was giving up the opportunity to flirt with Nick while she had his undivided attention.

Dan answered before Helly could, "No problem. The password's 'Murphia'."

Charley and Helly looked at each other and rolled their eyes.

Helly grabbed her arm and spoke quietly, "Where are you going?"

"I'm looking for a cheap flight back to Dublin. Just for the weekend." She kissed Helly on the cheek lightly and she started up the stairs slowly. "I've got some things I must sort out."

Helly felt cosy in her tracksuit pants and walked barefoot into the kitchen to see Nick wearing a pair of Dan's jeans and nothing else, as he spoke on his mobile to his Maida Vale colleagues.

And my God, how hard is it not to stare at his fantastic

chest. *His muscly, lightly tanned and slightly furry chest! In my kitchen!*

Trying to ignore his half-dressed state she pulled open the cutlery drawer, pulling out a knife, checking it first for streaks of colour thanks to Fiona and her make-up sharpening habits. Before she knew it he was behind her, grabbing at her boobs as he nuzzled into her neck.

"Kiss me, Helly," his voice was low and thick.

She felt the adrenalin race in her chest, terrified that Dan or Charley, or even the kids would burst through the kitchen door any second.

"Nick!" she hissed, "What the hell do you think you're doing? Stop it! Now!"

He kissed the back of her neck, causing her nipples to jut immediately. She closed her eyes and lost herself in the moment for a split second before she sprang back to reality.

"Nick, no. Please. Not here. Not again, no!"

"Kiss me."

She knew he was challenging her, seeing how brave she could be.

"No."

"Go on," he goaded, "just kiss me. You know you want to."

And yes, up to that point I really did think I wanted to. But then the thought of my family stopped me. My family who loved me, who trusted me and relied on me.

He wasn't worth it.

Maybe one time he had been, but not any more.

Not now.

Helly relaxed, allowing him to grope at her chest as she fiddled with the knife on the worktop.

Nick froze when she hollered, her voice composed and level, "Dan! Dan!"

He replied with a call from the lounge, "Yeah, love?"

"You haven't got a minute, have you?"

Nick sprang from her as if he'd been electrocuted, busying himself with his phone on the other side of the kitchen as Dan came in, oblivious.

"Yeah, babe. What's up?"

Helly turned, smiling, the sharp knife in her hand as she wiggled it before him. "Fancy some toast?"

"Oh, babe," he came across and slapped her arse, not noticing her erect nipples, "I'd love some."

Chapter Thirty-Five

Fiona felt the week was flittering away like the pages of a cartoon calendar, the breeze blowing them from the screen as it depicted the passing of time. Helly was so caught up with Quattro, and Charley had suddenly turned mute. Their taxi shoes lay, discarded at the foot of the stairs, inanimate objects that were no longer in favour. Fiona was dreading going back to Cascais. She never wanted to go back – ever. Since the afternoon with Raoul she'd rekindled her love affair with the violin and now, more than ever, she was in love with London. Raoul had cajoled her into thinking about giving violin lessons and had kissed her tenderly after he persuaded her to join him, making his quartet a quintet, to perform at the impending Notting Hill Carnival. Her life had become so exciting in comparison to the half-life she'd been living in Cascais for the last year and a half. She found herself suspended between what she wanted to do, and what she should do, as she moved at a slower rhythm than the world around her. It made sense for her to leave Adi in London and she began to steel herself for a quick trip which would finalise everything. She'd already made a list of items to bring back. It included photographs, sentimental items from Adi's birth and her baby days and videos they'd made when Adi was small. She wasn't so worried about the furniture and had already decided to let Claudine keep what she liked the look of and to sell whatever was left. She owed her for her help and perhaps if she could make a few euro from the sale of these items it might go some way to showing her gratitude. She sat on her bed in the spare room and pulled her mobile from her bag, texting her flight details to Claudine and asking for her to help her. She'd planned on flying in early Saturday morning, getting the bus from the airport into Lisbon and then the train on to Cascais. She told Claudine she'd be at her apartment by eleven.

And not to tell *anyone*.

Not even Xavier.

Helly spent the week on a high, her shenanigans with Quattro forcing her still-looming pregnancy concern back to the remotest corner of her mind. And when she *was* home she was making huge pans of spag bol and chilli and chicken curry, ready for freezing so that Dan and Co would have meals ready every evening. It meant that she could collapse into bed when she got home late every night whilst on tour. She'd been given an 'access all areas' pass with a glossy airbrushed photo of the girls on it, their

Quattro name in the marketing department choice of logo. She'd now met the girls a few times and thought they were great. Extremely young – but nice. Lindsey was tall and gangly with waist-length blonde hair, Laura was shorter with spiky blonde hair and a few piercings which made her look feisty and fresh rather than wasted, and Letitia and Lesley were the legs of the group, which made up for their average looks and shoulder-length high-lighted hair. Helly had laughed that they hadn't been strung with a name like The Four L's, until Laura grabbed her by the hands and told her that's exactly *what* the record company had suggested at first. It had been Lesley and Letitia that had come up with the name Quattro, and they hadn't looked back since. They'd been in to Pink Turtle a few times and they'd had great fun. Helly had locked the shop door and Penny had kept going across for coffees for them all as they'd tried on various outfits and had mucked about practising their dance routines in front of Helly's mirror. As Helly had helped them in and out of chiffon gypsy tops and pleated miniskirts, thigh-high biker boots and diamanté T-bar sandals she discovered that Lindsey and Lesley were from South London, Letitia was from North London and Laura had moved to Kent from Galway when she was thirteen. As their trust in each other grew, Helly asked the girls for tips on handling the tour, at which they'd all cackled. It was their first tour too. It was truly a case of the blondes leading the blonde. Every time they left Pink Turtle they'd give Helly a hug and a kiss on the cheek which brought out the maternal instinct in her.

Is this what it would be like to have a daughter?

Would we have fun swapping clothes and boyfriend stories?

But the thoughts of more children brought with it the nauseous wave of worry that she still hadn't taken the precious five minutes for the test that would predict her future.

And with the end of every day came the dreaded journey home. Every second that she sat on the Tube train seemed to bring with it a looming depression. Sitting on the prickly nylon seats as she careered at speed down the dark tunnel, her spirits sagged.

Home to Dan. I can't even bear to look at him lately. I feel so guilty at what I've done and yet I'm still thinking of Nick.

Home to Toby and Jack, who I'm leaving with my unstable sisters and busy husband for a week I'm resigned to only seeing them in the middle of the night, when their faces are pushed into their pillows like kissed fingertips and their minds are with their dreams.

Home to Fiona and Charley. I'm tired of looking after everyone and I cherish my time at Pink Turtle, away from the miserable reality of my life.

I'm so excited about going on tour next week and in a way I'm relieved that Charley and Fiona are clearing off for the weekend. It'll give me a chance to get ready for Monday and to think straight.

Hopefully Dan's out on a gig Saturday night, so I can get the kids to bed and flop in front of the telly in my underwear with a glass of wine!

It's been months since I've had the freedom to do that…

But maybe then I can face up to doing 'the test'?

It only seemed like Wednesday but yet the weekend had arrived. Fiona was flying out from Gatwick on a ridiculously early Saturday morning flight and Charley was flying from Stansted on a mid-morning flight to Dublin. Helly felt a little sad at seeing her sisters go, but then hissed at herself to 'cop on', that they'd be back on Sunday evening to irritate the shite out of her again. She was glad she was off on tour the day after. Raoul had arrived in the dark early hours to collect Fiona, taking her empty suitcases and swinging them lightly into his boot. Helly knew he wouldn't be as flippant with them when he collected her. She'd come back loaded down.

Helly had got out of bed to see Fiona off, hugging her in the silence of the sleeping house and holding her face, looking deep into her little sister's eyes and pleading with her to take good care and to come back straight away. She knew Fiona was nervous, but was proud of her for facing up to the possibility of seeing the arrogant Luís.

James arrived after breakfast in his Ford Focus. Just the sight of it pulling up outside the house caused Helly and Charley to cringe. They'd been playing Guess The Motor all morning, fantasising over what flash, iconic car someone as stylish as James would have. Now they sank with disappointment as the family car pulled up outside. They jumped back from the lounge window, not wanting him to see them spying on him. They both gasped as they watched him remove the two child's seats from the back, surreptitiously looking over his shoulder as he did so and locking them into the boot.

"Did you know he had kids?" Helly's voice was a high-pitched squeak.

"No." Charley shook her head, her expression flat. And slowly a large, wide grin crept onto her face as she began to giggle.

"Charley! What's funny?"

"Fucking eejit he is anyway," she snorted into her hands to try and laugh quietly. "Look at him out there, putting on his uniform. That's it," she provided the commentary to James's actions as he dressed himself on the street, "get out your pork-pie hat," James pulled it down over his bald head, "OK, and now take off your office-man driving shoes and slip on your mules," as James stood on the path, resting his foot on his car seat and untying his laces, the mules slapping on the floor as he dropped them. By the time he rang on the doorbell Charley and Helly were virtually wriggling as they tried to hold in their laughter. He stood at the doorway looking as stylish and sexy as usual.

If only we hadn't seen the transformation outside!
And the child car-seats going into the boot.

As Helly nipped up the stairs behind Charley, leaving Dan to chat to James over orange juice in the kitchen, she stopped in the bedroom doorway, blocking Charley's exit.

"Are you sure he never mentioned his kids?"

"No. Well, he lives alone so they're not with him anyway." But it doesn't matter.

"Why doesn't it matter?"

"Because, Helly, he's taking me to the airport and picking me up tomorrow night and that will be the end of that. He's OK as a friend, but I know who I want to be with. And it isn't James."

Helly's eyes opened wide. "Steve!"

Charley grinned and nodded, a serenity coming from her that Helly hadn't seen for years. She kissed Charley on the cheek and wished her good luck for the weekend. Within seconds she was in James's car heading for Stansted, her bags on the back seat where his children's car seats had sat only minutes before.

Dan finished his breakfast, leaving the greasy plates and utensils on the draining board. Helly knew he was edgy and that he would be all day.

"So where's the new venue tonight?" she tried light conversation as he grabbed his CD's from the rack in the kitchen.

"Highgate. A converted factory that's now one of the quickest rising rock and blues venues. It's a big one, Helly."

"So what time will you be going?"

He checked his watch as he fiddled with the rattling CD cases. "Jono, Gav and the lads are coming around later for a run-through and then we're heading up to the venue for the sound checks. Suppose they'll be here around two, and then we'll nip over to Highgate from four till sixish. The gig starts at nine."

"So will you all be coming back here after six?"

He shrugged, "Dunno. Never do with that lot. Could you have a big pot of chilli on, just in case?"

"No bother. How about I take the boys over to the

park for the afternoon? At least you guys can get on then?"

He put down the CD's and walked across to her, pulling her to him. She felt her flat tummy against his and the claustrophobia was overwhelming. He kissed her. Small butterfly kisses on her forehead, her eyelids, her cheeks, nose, chin and then little kisses on her lips.

"You're a great woman, Helly. Sorry I've been so uptight about your sisters and that, but I've been so stressed about the money. But it really did get out of hand there, all those nights out. All that drinking."

"I know, Dan, but it's Charley. She's a living nightmare."

"Yeah, the bloody Murphia arriving on my doorstep."

Helly giggled, praying and praying as she did so that she wasn't pregnant with Nick's baby. Praying and hoping and wishing that everything would be OK. Promising to herself that she'd never, ever be unfaithful to Dan again if she could only have this one chance.

"I know, love, I'm sorry. From what Charley said she's got the hots for that Steve policeman guy, so who knows what'll happen there."

Dan smiled. "You mean she might go back to Dublin?"

"Don't get too excited too quick. You know what Charley's like!"

He groaned as he tilted her head forward and kissed the top of her head, breathing in the floral smell of her shampoo, feeling her soft short hair.

It took ages to get Toby, Jack and Adi ready. It wasn't so

much the actual task of them getting dressed, more the distraction of Saturday morning telly. One minute Jack would have on his pyjamas, and then half an hour later he'd be wearing one sock and a T-shirt. And then she'd look and Adi would be wearing her trousers the wrong way around and she'd be trying to put on Toby's large T-shirt as she watched the telly at the same time. Overall, it took nearly two hours for them to be standing at the front door, washed, dressed and raring to go. She had initially decided to get out of the house so as to avoid Nick. But as she stood in the doorway, she realised that the thought of him no longer made her stomach flip.

Whereas the thought of being pregnant with his child most certainly did.

She needed the fresh air and promised them a bus trip, and as she watched her two sons and her niece racing ahead, she called instructions for them to stop at the third tree, or by the house with the white gate, and her mind wandered. Before she knew it they were approaching the bus stop and Toby began to hop and leap around her, causing her to stumble and stutter.

"Toby! Walk in a straight line, can't you?"

"Muumm, Mum? Can we get some sweets?"

"Can't we wait till we get there?"

Jack joined in, "Oh Mummy? Please? We'll be really good."

Just one look at their fresh skin, their bright eyes and gappy-toothed grins warmed her.

"OK," she smiled, "let's go in here and get you something to eat on the bus."

"In here then." Toby grabbed her arm, dragging her into the nearest shop. It was Boots the Chemist. They queued at the till for a couple of minutes, their drinks and sweets making their excited hands twitch, until the po-faced woman at the counter slapped a *'this checkout is closed'* sign onto the small conveyor belt.

"You're not serious!" Helly squealed. "We've been waiting here. I've only got three bags of sweets and four drinks!"

Po-face shrugged, "Sorry. You'll have to use the pharmacy counter."

"Jesus!" Helly cursed, turning on the spot and making for the other side of the large shop. As they stood in the queue at the pharmacy counter Toby and Jack chatted excitedly to Adi, exciting her with the stories of Hyde Park and how they could play 'it'. Helly scanned the shelves laden with travel-sick tablets, Calpol, diarrhoea treatment, antihistamine, pregnancy testing kits, headache tablets . . .

Pregnancy testing kits!

Her heart beat like a drum in her head, threatening to burst through her ears and start bouncing around the shop floor. She felt herself flush and then feel sick again as the smiling powder-faced lady behind the counter reached out to take the drinks from her.

It was a split second decision as Helly spoke low and fast, "And a Clearblue, please."

Powder-face smiled and turned, plucking the wrapped box from the counter.

Helly watched as in slow motion the pharmacist found

a rustling polythene bag to slide the testing kit into.

She couldn't get out of there quick enough.

So quickly, she left her bottle of Evian on the counter.

As they sat on the top floor of the double-decker bus the children bickered over their drinks and who could see the most white vans. Helly pondered how ridiculous it all seemed that one blue line had the potential of changing the rest of her life. As they stopped near Hyde Park she guided the kids down the short spiral staircase of the bus, promising to herself that she'd do the test that evening when Dan was out at the gig.

Chapter Thirty-Six

Fiona's flight had been more relaxing than her previous one, where Helly had sat tense and anxious beside her. She was pleased that she'd chosen to wear the black Gharani Strok dress that she'd picked up in Debenhams for only forty pounds. She felt slim and attractive in it, the cerise and cream swirls like a firework display against the black backdrop. Her tanned legs looked good and the cheap T-bar mules she'd borrowed from Helly emphasised her colour. She was ready for Luís, if she saw him. Her weeks in London had brought her a new, slimmer Fiona who had bags more confidence and attitude. She hoped she wouldn't need it, but was ready just the same. The second the flight landed, all her insecurities plagued her once again. It wasn't until Claudine surprised her by meeting her at Cais do Sodre, where the bus from the airport dropped her off, that she started to feel a little more at ease.

"Blimey 'ell, Fiona!" Claudine squealed. "You look *fantastique*! Look at you!"

Fiona hadn't yet mastered how to deal with compliments and so chose instead to look awkward and change the subject. "So, shall we get the next train to Cascais? I'm leaving in the morning, so we don't have long."

They chatted non-stop on the train, Claudine unable to get over Fiona's transformation, and Fiona struggling to come to terms with Claudine moving in with Xavier. Within the hour they were safely holed up in Claudine's apartment where she was surprised at how much space all her stuff was taking up. She spent the afternoon drinking Claudine's non-alcoholic smoothies and laughing over the fun times they'd had together.

Claudine came up with a great idea late in the afternoon: "Why don't I go to see Vitor and ask him to bring some food up for us? I know he would love to see you, Fiona. He has not stopped talking about you since you and Adriana left here."

Fiona wasn't so sure. She really didn't want anyone but Claudine to know she was there. "Claudine, the fewer people know I'm here the better. What if Luís hears? What if the word gets round that I'm here? I know he'll try and blackmail me into returning to Cascais with Adriana. And he'll probably go mad that I haven't brought her with me."

She didn't want to face him, couldn't handle the confrontation.

"Oh, come on!" said Claudine. "It will be no harm. I will go and see Vitor. Ask him to be discreet."

Helly had every intention of locking herself in the bathroom for five minutes to do the pregnancy test when she'd got in. She had even bought the children icecreams, which were now melting too quickly to keep them occupied. But it all went wrong. She'd no sooner turned the key in the lock and she heard Kyle and Gav cracking open beer cans in her kitchen and Dan, Jono and Nick talking through the evening's sequence in the lounge. She might have known their plans would be all over the place.

Dan looked up as she entered the lounge, immediately smiling at her,

"Hey, babe. You coming tonight? The lads were just asking me if you were."

Yeah, by that I bet he means Nick was.

Why can't he get off my case?

"Hardly." She tried to be flippant. "I've got kiddies to mind."

But Dan was persistent. "Why don't you give Pat and Brian a ring? I'm sure they'll come around again if you ask them to?"

"No, really. I won't. Not tonight. I want to prepare for Monday anyway. And I'm looking forward to a quiet weekend."

"OK, babe. Whatever."

She left the kids in the kitchen teasing Kyle and Gav and she hurried upstairs, stuffing the Clearblue testing kit into her bottom drawer, swearing that she'd finally do it this evening when the children were asleep and the guys were all out at the gig.

It had taken everything Charley had not to have a quick drink on the plane to Dublin. Just the very thought of home made her want to have a quick one, but she fought it. She knew Steve was pulling out the stops for her and she didn't want to let him down. She hated the Arrivals section at Dublin airport, where the crowds of people thronged around the sliding exit doors as they held up their name plaques and waited for long-lost family members. Charley had never had anyone meet her before and so usually marched through the crowd without making eye contact. But this time she knew Steve was waiting for her and her palms were sweaty with excitement at the thought of seeing him again. She had worn her black combats and khaki vest, Helly's collection of crucifixes hanging from her neck delicately and her hair loose. As the smoky doors slid open she felt like something from *Stars In Their Eyes* and fought the urge to say: "Tonight, Matthew, I'm going to be the New Improved Charley!" She needn't have worried. Steve was straight in her line of vision and she surprised herself by flinging her arms around his neck. He surprised her by lifting her off her feet and kissing her, on the mouth. She pulled back, looking him in the eyes, communicating, but not verbally. Slowly Charley leaned forward again and this time they kissed until the guy holding the plaque for 'MR AGAWAMA' spun around and knocked into them. They laughed at his nervous apology and then again as he shook hands formally with Mr Agawama, frowning at his laden trolley full of cases.

"So? Fancy some food?"

"I could be tempted," Charley teased, just happy and comfortable to be snuggled into his side as they walked out towards the carpark.

"Great. How about Italian?"

"Sounds yum."

She couldn't recall the drive into Dublin and the meal was probably great, but Charley wasn't sure. Like a love-struck teenager she paid little attention to what she was doing and lost herself in Steve's conversation. If anyone was worth cutting down her drinking units a week for – this guy was it.

Vitor had been overwhelmed to see Fiona looking so good and made gestures with his hands to his chest, adopting a pining look on his face as he complained that she had broken his heart. She laughed it off, kissing him on either cheek as he rested down the two full plates of Chicken Caesar Salad that he said were 'on the house'. He asked for Adriana, and Fiona promised that she'd get her to write a letter to him, sending on some photo-graphs. As she promised to stay in touch she realised that she'd never be truly free of Cascais – as long as Luís wanted to be part of Adi's life then she simply *had* to let him be. She didn't want Adi, in her teenage years, des-perate to know her father's side of the family, wanting to go back to Portugal. And however badly Luís had treated her, she had never let Adriana know what went on behind the scenes. Once Vitor had scurried back to his competitive touting for the evening tourist trade, Fiona sat on the balcony with Claudine, enjoying the crispy chicken and croûton salad. Her suitcases were bulging, packed with memories of her life in Cascais. All she wanted now was an early night, ready to head off in the morning back to London, back to Raoul, back to her exciting new life. They didn't think they were on edge, but they must have been as they jumped when Xavier rapped on the front door.

"Blimey 'ell!" Claudine complained through a mouthful of lettuce. "Why does he have to knock so hard?"

She opened the door to Xavier and he burst in, facing Fiona as he said,

"Luís. He knows you are here. He is waiting in his car at the end of the street. He thinks you have Adriana here and is saying he will not let you go back to London."

"Oh Christ!" Fiona slapped down her fork, not realising how it took a chunk out of the edge of Vitor's plate. Her eyes filled with tears of panic. "Now what am I going to do?"

"Calm down," Claudine placated her. "He can't kidnap you! He can't stop you from going to London!"

Fiona was listening, but not hearing, years of threats and taunts from Luís rushing to the forefront of her mind. "But Luís knows the legal system. Christ, he has solicitors queuing up for a slice of his money! He's always on about the Hague Convention securing the prompt return of children wrongfully removed. He knows all the loopholes!"

"Calm down, Fiona!" Claudine had heard this all before too as Fiona had been living in the shadow of the Hague Convention ever since Luís had decided that he didn't want her any more. "You haven't done anything wrong! You aren't in breach of custody rights, are you? You haven't forbidden him to see Adriana?"

Fiona was despondent now, watching her new London lifestyle disappear quicker that water down a plughole. "No, well, the question hasn't come up. But I don't think I've got a leg to stand on. Adriana was born in Portugal, one of her parents is Portuguese – I think that's enough to give him the upper hand."

"Fiona," Claudine's voice was calm, "ring and see if you can change your flight to tonight. You have to get away from here and think about what you're going to do. I'll ask Xavier to see if he can get a taxi to come and collect you from here. But first, see if you can go tonight."

She handed Fiona her phone, leaving her to try and punch in the numbers as her hands shook.

Helly was glad she hadn't agreed to go to the gig with Dan and the lads. She was feeling tired and again a little sick. Thankfully the children had finally settled to sleep just before nine o'clock, which was still an hour too late, but she was relieved nonetheless. As she went in to check on them, pulling off their duvets, feeling their clammy foreheads, she opened the top window slightly. It was a hot night and she didn't want them waking up in a sweat. She crossed the landing, entering her room and pulling the handle on her bottom drawer, taking out the rustling bag which held the Clearblue.

I want to know, and yet I don't want to.

I'll just go down and have a glass or two of wine first,

just to make sure I actually want to go to the loo before I start.

She tiptoed down the stairs, the Clearblue back in the dark of the bottom drawer, and dropped down onto the settee, flicking the TV channels as she slurped her wine.

Some time later, the phone rang, making her jump and spill her wine down herself.

"Damn!" she spat, standing and swiping at her legs as she picked up the cordless from the armchair.

"Hello?"

"Helly, babe. I've forgotten some of my stuff."

"What stuff?"

"There's a folder in the kitchen that I've been keeping to show to any record companies. It's got our demo CD's in it. Babe, I need it. Is there any chance you could nip into the car and bring it over? We're only a few miles away."

"Dan! I've had a couple of glasses of wine. I can't drive. And what about the children?"

"Oh no, don't bring them. It's too late. And it'd be much too noisy."

"Dan! I'm serious."

"Helly, I really, *really* need it. Could you ring Pat and Brian and see if they'd come over for a bit while you nip into a cab and help me out? Please, babe? Please?"

"Oh sod you, Dan! I really don't want to do this. Can't Kyle or Jono nip into a cab and come over here to get it?"

"Helly! We're on in ten minutes. Please, babe?"

"OK!" she hissed, "but I'm not staying!"

"Love you, honey. Thanks, love."

Begrudgingly she dialled Brian's number. She hated asking for favours and this was no exception. Except for that fact that she blamed it all on Dan, a sure-fire way to get Auntie Pat scurrying around here – from wherever Auntie Pat was sitting Dan could do no wrong.

Pat and Brian agreed to be there within the half hour and so Helly changed into her grungy jeans, her Jane Brown sandals and her Rogue Choppers T-shirt that she'd bought on the internet. She didn't bother with her make-up as she'd done on the taxi shoes nights out. She had no intention of trying to look good for Dan or Nick, or anyone tonight. She just wanted to get into the cab, deliver the folder and come straight home.

Chapter Thirty-Seven

The acrid smell attacked Charley's nostrils on the street outside Steve's house.

"Ugh! Paint!"

He smirked. "I forgot to mention, I was trying to freshen the place up before you arrived. I wasn't counting on the extra overtime and so I'm still halfway through it. Sorry, it does stink a bit."

"A bit!" She waited behind him as he grappled with his door key. "You know, all this time and you've only been living a couple of streets away from me. How come I hadn't seen you before?"

Steve grinned. "You probably did, but weren't looking for a man in uniform."

"Nope," she smiled, shaking her head, "I always notice half decent men. Especially if they're in uniform."

If the smell hadn't been so overpowering Charley would have liked his house. He'd gone for the strong, but muted Irish Heritage colours of Fitzwilliam Blue in the hallway, Leeson Street Red in the kitchen and Galway Green in the living room. He grabbed the bottle of lemonade from the fridge and joined her in the living-room, pouring them both a fizzing large glass. She began to giggle.

"Hey, what's so funny?"

"This. Me, sitting here with you. Drinking lemonade! I mean, Steve, all my problems aren't going to be solved by just keeping off the sauce for a couple of days. And you, all domesticated and organised. Look at you!"

"I have to be domesticated and organised. I don't have anyone else to do it for me."

"You sound like Helly!"

"Charley, I don't know why you think it's so funny. It's life."

"Well," the laughter disappeared from her voice, "it's not a life I want. Trapped in the kitchen, kids always asking 'When are we there?' and 'Can I have this?'. It's what I'm running away from, Steve. It's part of the problem."

"Why? Charley, you've got a lot of anger in you. Did you never want children? Have you always been so fiercely independent?"

"Yes, Steve. I wanted kids. I know why I started drinking and it was because of *nearly* having kids."

His tone was slightly patronising, although he hadn't meant it to be. Steve only wanted to help, but Charley was getting too emotional to listen properly.

"So talk to me about it."

"Talk to you!" she screeched, standing up and

slamming her lemonade glass onto the table. "Talk to *you*. And what are you going to do? Arrest everyone who's ever upset me? Arrest the barman for selling me a drink? What the fuck are *you* going to do? You're only a copper, not Judge-Shagging-Judy!"

At twice the speed Charley had entered Steve's home, she left, grabbing her bag on the way and swinging it, accidentally hitting Steve on the chin as she stormed out.

Pat and Brian arrived near to ten o'clock. Pat looked disgruntled, as if she'd been called out in the middle of the night. Helly was sure she'd disturbed the exciting Radio 4 play that she'd probably been tuned in to. Brian was all smiles though, glad for the excuse to come around and watch the movies on Sky.

Helly adjusted the studded belt on her jeans as she spoke, "Thanks for coming at such short notice. I won't be long. Dan just wants me to drop this in and then I'll be back."

"S'OK, love," Brian answered, already picking up the remote control and flicking the channels, "take as long as you want."

She followed Pat into the kitchen and offered her a glass of wine. She declined, asking for a coffee instead. Helly poured the remains of the bottle into her glass, almost to overflowing. It wobbled, slightly bulging from the lip of the glass, sitting like mercury. Helly saw Pat's disapproving look as she stooped, stretching her lips to the glass as she slurped the wine.

"Ooops," she joked, "eyes bigger than my belly or

what?" Her face dropped with the reminder of her belly, the reminder that if she *was* pregnant she shouldn't be drinking and the fear and dread that she might be. She knew she was being silly, but promised herself she'd face up to it all tomorrow. She'd enjoy her few drinks tonight and then, without fail or excuses, she'd do the test in the morning.

First thing!

The taxi hooted outside and she grabbed her bag, thanking Pat and Brian for their help at such short notice. Brian said he was was delighted to oblige. Helly wondered why he hadn't left Pat at home.

Charley stopped off at Doyle's pub and they all cheered when she walked in. She felt wanted here and they were so pleased to see her. The guys at the bar put their arms around her and pulled her in close to their sides as they asked where the hell she'd been for the last few weeks? And told her how well she was looking. As she sat with them, the free drinks arriving in front of her quicker than you could say I-Drink-Anything-Except-For-Gin, she felt good. She was no alcoholic! She wasn't a tramp; she wasn't down-and-out! She kept herself looking good, took pride in her appearance, kept her friends. She was just a woman who probably went slightly over the recommended weekly alcohol units for women. As she sat in the hubbub of the chattering, laughing crowds she smiled to herself.

"Yeah," she said to herself, "people *like* me. I'm not an outcast. And I'll go and make it up with Steve later and then maybe I'll put him straight on a thing or two!"

Fiona waited for the taxi in the doorway of the Panisol café. She was sweating and sickly. Thankfully, there was no sign of Luís lurking about but she still felt jittery. Claudine and Xavier waited with her, to help her bundle her cases into the taxi and make a quick getaway. She had been lucky to change her flight at such short notice and it had been a tearful goodbye as she'd hugged Claudine and promised to keep in touch.

She breathed in the early evening air, its warmth lining her mouth as she sucked it in, and her heart sank. She already knew that she'd miss Lisbon in the autumn. In the last few years she'd got used to the city filling up again as the Lisboetas returned from their holidays on the Algarve. And then it would be harvest time in the country, when she loved taking the train and showing Adriana the golden fields and the vineyards full of villagers picking grapes. Vitor had once told her that in the Douro valley they still trod the grapes and had promised to take them this year. She could almost smell the chestnuts sold then on the Lisbon streets. Her senses had been assaulted in Lisbon in a way that the London pollution hadn't managed to match up to and as the taxi drove her through the evening half-light she closed her eyes and dreamed of the charcoal-grilled sardines – *sardinhas assadas*, the cod fishcakes – *pasteis de bacalhau* and the *linguado grelhado* – grilled sole. And how she already missed the three types of table wine: the red, the *maduro* so called because of its mature taste and the light, slightly

469

sparkling *vinho verde*. But she knew she had to get away from Luís. At least until he agreed that for her to live in Cascais she had to have a *life*.

Chapter Thirty-Eight

Charley fell into a Dublin taxi, her battered Reeboks feeling heavy on her disorientated, drunken feet. As she stumbled, laughing, at the back door, the cabbie hollered at her to mind herself. She slurred Steve's address to him, not noticing how he shook his head at the pathetic sight of her. She was asleep before he could warn her not to get sick on the upholstery.

He had to poke and prod at her before he could wake her.

She rolled back to life, slurring at him and crying as she murmured, "Afterwards is worst – the build-up is great – all that 'lectricity."

"Yeah, righ', love. C'mon. You're home. Want a hand in?"

"I do not!" Her attempts at being indignant were pathetic and he took her money and sped away before

471

she'd even had the chance to get her bag on her shoulder.

But it was Charley.

She was used to it.

Fiona had climbed into a caramel Mercedes. She had once been used to travelling in style, but this was no longer Luís' top dollar transport, but a Lisbon taxi. She still hadn't got used to the oppressive August heat and as she hunched on the large back seat, she desperately tried to avoid eye contact with the swarthy Portuguese driver who stank of cigarette smoke, despite overdosing on pine air fresheners. Breathing in hot recycled air she hugged her knees and looked down at her tanned elegant feet, her toenails free from varnish as a large teardrop fell and splashed on her cheap leather sandals. She watched as the single drop trickled down and lost itself between her toes.

Helly felt nauseous as she hopped into a black London cab. She hadn't intended to enjoy the last part of the night, but had had a great time at the gig and had enjoyed a couple of glasses of wine. A niggling notion taunted her perplexed mind that she'd felt this way before. She stretched out her legs on the back seat, her Jane Brown sandals glistening in the orange glow of the streetlights as they nipped towards Belsize Park. As another wave of warm sickness churned in her stomach once again, she knew.

Just like Madame Lydia had said, 'travel, a new baby in the family and sex with a dark, handsome stranger'...

Had he been a stranger after all? A Nick she no longer knew?

She *must* do that test when she got home.

Chapter Thirty-Nine

Steve heard the mumbling from his bedroom window which was open. It wasn't particularly hot but he had to let out the paint fumes. He got up out of bed in the dark and moved across to the window, watching Charley muttering to herself, arguing quietly with her handbag as she rooted inside it. She pulled out her mobile and he watched her angrily jabbing the numbers in. A few seconds later his mobile, which sat on his bedside cabinet, lit up and trilled a polyphonic tune.

He lunged across the bed and grabbed it, answering it quietly as he moved back to watch her. "Hello?"

She fidgeted from one foot to the next, leaning up against next door's wall under the street lights.

"Steve? It's me – 'Again'. I thought I'd just ring you to let you know that I won't be coming back to your place tonight. Anyway, it'd stink too much."

He smiled in the shadows, watching her every move.

She ranted on,

"And I thought I'd let you know that I've met up with an old friend. *He's* a great guy. And I'm staying there tonight."

"Oh, right. Whatever you want." His voice was calm and steady.

"*And* he doesn't have a spare room, so I suppose I'll share his bed. His *water* bed."

"Christ, won't that make you feel sick? I've heard they're awfully uncomfortable."

She was stopped in her tracks.

He continued, "And there I was making up the sumptuous double in my spare room for you. And I had the kettle on too."

"I'm not an alcoholic, you know."

"I don't really know, Charley. That depends whether you *need* alcohol in your system or whether you simply go over the units-per-week quota. And we won't know that till we talk. But hey, you're sleeping over at your man's house, so perhaps we'll talk tomorrow. Call me when you're ready to talk. Night then."

"No, Steve, wait!"

"Charley?" He made out that he couldn't catch what she was saying. She looked comical now, marching up and down the street as she talked into her phone.

"Steve. I do want to talk to you."

"Well, it's a shame you didn't plan your evening better. You're flying back tomorrow, aren't you?"

She sobered at the thought of leaving him, of wasting her time here. She stopped at his door. "Supposed to be."

Her voice cracked and he began to feel mean,

"Charley," he talked into his phone softly as he walked down the stairs in his boxer shorts, opening the front door with a click, putting his arm around her shoulder as he spoke into her ear, "how about you come in and we'll talk in the morning."

She kissed him hard on the cheek and staggered into the house with him.

He knew the routine. Get her in the house and keep her talking while he coerced a couple of pints of water into her along with two Nurofen. He could sort the rest in the morning. The headache, the sickness, the shakes. It was nothing he couldn't handle. And for Charley, he was prepared to do it.

The next morning was a bright and sunny one. He had made himself a coffee and had picked up his Sunday paper with the numerous glossy supplements from the doormat and made his way back up to bed. He loved a lie-in on a Sunday and only paused at the door of the spare room to check on Charley. Her hair was splayed wildly on the pillow and her mouth was open as she snored, dribbling onto the pillow. It was a good sign: at least she was getting a long sleep.

Nearly two hours later he heard her moaning in the bathroom. He waited for the sounds of vomiting, but none came. Another good sign. Shortly after she paused at his bedroom door, looking dishevelled but fantastic in her khaki vest and knickers, her mascara smudged down to her cheekbones.

"What you doing?" she groaned, her voice thick and tired.

"Reading the papers. Having a lie-in. It's what I always do on a Sunday if I'm not working."

"Ugh," she disappeared out of sight and he heard her throw herself into bed again.

He gave it a few minutes and went downstairs, bringing her up some dry toast, a juicy orange and two more Nurofen. He sat on her bed making light conversation while she finished them all, and then insisted that she go back to sleep for another couple of hours. Remarkably she did as she was told.

Steve knew she needed to be looked after, and that it had probably been a long time since that had happened.

When Charley woke the next time it was almost lunchtime and she was disappointed that she was due to fly back to London late in the afternoon. She showered and put on Steve's towelling dressing-gown, curling up with a huge mug of coffee on his settee, to talk.

"Were you supposed to go to work today?"

"Not today. Anyway, aren't there more important things to deal with?"

"What?" Her voice was soft and her make-up-free face looked remarkably fresh.

"You." Steve walked across the room to her, crouching in front of her and taking the mug from her, placing it on the coffee table. As he turned back to her she felt like a little girl as he took her two hands in his, cupping them securely. "Charley, you owe it to yourself to get sorted.

People have got over worse. It's not the end of the world. You're important to me, Charley, and I want to help you."

She smiled a huge smile. It surprised her because she thought she might cry, but for some reason she grinned enormously.

"What's so funny?"

"Not funny, but nice." She released her hands from his and touched his cheek. "Nobody has ever thought I was important before. Other than my family, and even then I've been a bit of a nightmare."

"Well, I think you're important. There."

"I didn't keep the drinking diary that you asked me to."

"Why aren't I surprised?" he smiled at her.

"But I have been doing some serious thinking and I know I've got a bit of a problem. I can see how I drink when I feel under pressure, and I'm no stranger to a quick scoop for Dutch Courage."

"I was a heavy drinker only three years ago. I never bothered with an official title as 'alcoholic' or 'dependant' but I was always having a laugh with my mates in the pub – every evening. It became a habit. I didn't have the vodka bottles under the bed or anything like that, but I knew it was taking over my life."

"I used to take a little hip-flask into work sometimes." She stared at his face, waiting to see the shock. It never came. Steve nodded at her, so she continued, "I didn't see any harm in it – it was just something that I used for medicinal purposes. Shag it, that's one of the oldest ones in the book, isn't it?"

"And how did it make you feel, the drink? Happy, sad,

angry? What was the purpose of it?"

"I suppose to make me forget stuff. And it depended on the company I was in at the time. I mean there's many a time I've cried in front of a stranger when I've been on the sauce, and then other times I've made a bee-line for the cocktail list and had a great time."

Steve sat up beside her, passing back her coffee. "OK, so when you said you were drinking to forget stuff. What stuff?"

He saw the look flash across her face and realised instantly that he was on thin ice again. "Charley, you don't have to tell *me*. Perhaps you need to come to terms with this first yourself, or you could maybe see a counsellor or a doctor?"

As she looked into his eyes she realised that she had never had a friend like him. She remembered how patient and kind he'd been when she had pretended to lose 'her' dog, she recalled how he had stopped her getting into trouble when she'd removed her spark plugs, holding up the busy Dublin traffic. She knew that Steve wouldn't judge her, or stand on a moral high ground.

If she was ever going to squeeze the poison out of her body, now was probably the best opportunity she'd ever had.

Perhaps it was time.

Helly hadn't been able to get her key into the lock in time. As she'd hopped out of the cab she had fumbled with her keys, leaning up against the front door as she tried to isolate the one key that she needed to get in. Pat had been irritated that she had been so long as it was — she hated Brian watching all those tits-and-bums late-night quiz shows on Sky and had already argued with him that they wouldn't be coming at such late notice in the future. She'd muttered to herself that it was ridiculous, past one in the morning, and if that Helly thought she could come home drunk, she'd got another think coming. Helly felt the sickness rising, to the point where she simply *couldn't* get her key sorted. Just as she saw the mottled silhouette of Pat through the glass of the door she retched.

Pat opened the door with a cat's-arse mouth to match her mum's just as Helly was sick in one loud roar.

All over Pat's shoes.

Helly lay in her bed feeling terrible. She went over in her mind how she hadn't even been able to apologise to Pat properly last night, instead running past her to the kitchen sink, where she'd been ill again a couple of times. Brian had been marvellous, consoling the furious Pat and even slipping off her shoes and cleaning them up for her. He had held Helly by the shoulders as she was ill and had even been kind enough to believe her when she'd said she had only been drinking water, and was gracious enough to blame it on a bug.

She wished.

Pat and Brian had waited for Dan to come home before they'd leave Helly, although she had already gone up to bed. And she had tried to sleep but couldn't, although she'd pretended she was asleep when Dan got into bed beside her, caressing her forehead and whispering to her how much he loved her. Within minutes he'd been snoring and she lay on her side once again, cradling her tummy, knowing that she had to be pregnant. By three am she could stand it no longer and had tiptoed out of bed, opening the bottom drawer as slowly and silently as she could and wincing as the paper bag around the Clearblue rustled. As she went into the bathroom she had gone over the events at the gig, wondering when she'd suddenly felt so rough. She had been upset when she saw the lads laughing with the group of flirting middle-aged women, but it hadn't been enough to make her ill.

I'd even kept cool when I saw Nick kissing a stunner backstage. I'd expected my heart to sink, but it hadn't.

At that instant she had realised that it didn't matter whether Nick knew his Limp Bizkit from his Linkin Park and Dan didn't. She realised that the wearing of Rigby & Pellar seventy-quid underwear or lighting scented candles didn't make a relationship – that it all boiled down to the underlying issues of communication.

And she and Dan hadn't been.

Communicating.

She wished she'd listened from the start when he insisted that he wasn't hankering for a daughter. Or another son.

She wished she hadn't play-acted, going off the pill, only for Dan to avoid sex with her for fear of her becoming pregnant. Dan knew she felt rejected by his actions. She'd even joked to him last month how he always used to sleep in the nude, which wasn't a problem, except for on those long-haul flights. She knew that he was avoiding physical contact with her.

She looked down at the Clearblue box, and began to delicately unwrap it, desperate not to wake Dan or the kids. She removed the white plastic stick from the silver wrapping as she sat on the loo and read the instructions.

But she knew what to do.

Taking a deep breath and closing her eyes she held the white stick between her legs, and relaxed her muscles, as prepared as she would ever be to find out what the future held for her.

Five minutes it said.

Five minutes to find out whether she'd fucked up her life completely.

Five minutes that would seem like five days.

Luís had been lurking in his car around a corner down the street after all. Fiona had seen him as she'd passed by in the taxi. He apparently hadn't recognised her. She supposed she wasn't very recognisable in her glossy new hairdo and shades. She couldn't get his face out of her mind. She hated that he'd taken away her life for so long, but warmed herself with the thoughts of Raoul waiting for her in London. She had silently cried in the back of the taxi to the airport, the tears brimming and falling without any facial contortions or gasps. They came naturally. They had to come out.

When they'd got to Lisbon airport the driver had heaved the heavy cases out for her. She was sad to be walking away from her old life, but looking forward to her new.

She just wondered how long she could keep Luís at bay. How long would it be before she'd get a solicitor's letter, or worse still, a visit from Luís?

As she checked in her luggage to the straight-faced guy at the desk she made herself a promise to manage at least six months in London. And a year would be a bonus. She was so busy setting herself targets she didn't hear what he had mumbled as he handed her ticket and passport back to her. Catching sight of his serious expression she snapped back to life.

"Excuse me? Sorry, I didn't hear you," she smiled at him.

Remarkably, he smiled back. "Sorry, madam. We have problems with flights to London. Your flight has been delayed until two am."

"Two in the morning! You're not serious!"

He nodded. She reckoned they were trained to adopt a patronising smile from day one.

"So what do I do now?"

He indicated across to the seating area. "Madam, you cannot check in your luggage until two hours before the flight."

"That's midnight!"

"Yes. So you will have to just wait, or come back to the airport later, madam."

"Great!" she cursed, dragging her heavy cases from the scales and hauling them across to the uncomfortable-looking seating area that already had bodies strewn across it.

By seven thirty she'd read nearly every English magazine in the place and had been forced to concentrate on some serious thinking. She hated the fact that she was running from Luís, hated that he was having that effect on her, that she was choosing to be a victim to his bullying. Before she'd had the chance to think it through entirely, she dragged her case across to the public telephones and took a deep breath as she rang his number. Her heart beat in her neck and she felt slightly faint as she waited for him to reply. To her surprise he didn't answer. She did.

"*Alô?*"

Fiona froze at the sound of Bella's voice. She'd never spoken to her before and hadn't even considered that she might answer the phone. Bella spoke again, a little more loudly, "*Alô?*"

Fiona cleared her throat. "Luís?"

"*Quem fala?*" Bella's voice remained cool as she asked who was calling.

Fiona waited for her to slam it down as she said, "Fiona. It's Fiona. Luís, please?"

She heard Bella calling him, her voice echoey in the stone hallway that used to be Fiona's home. Luís came to the phone.

"Fiona! Where are you?" he all but shouted at her. "What are you doing? Where is Adriana?"

"Luís. Please. Calm down. I want to talk to you. Properly. Just us, talking. No shouting or threats."

He was silent, the concept of talking without shouting or threats clearly alien to him. She let the silence continue, determined not to be the one to break it.

He finally spoke, "OK, Fiona. We will talk. It is probably a good idea. You will meet me outside my bar in half an hour."

"No, Luís. I won't. I'm at the airport in Lisbon. I should be on a flight back to London now. I left early to avoid you. What did you think you were doing? Stalking me? I know, Luís, that you don't love me any more, though I also know that Adriana means the world to you, but you *did* love me. That must stand for something. If you want to talk, then please come to the airport. My flight doesn't leave until two. We have five hours to talk."

"All right, Fiona," his voice held a shimmer of the warmth that she had once known. "I will be there in an hour."

"Thank you."

He grunted as he cut off.

She spent the next hour pacing and fretting, worrying about what she was going to say to him, but reassuring herself that he couldn't actually stop her from getting on the plane. Not here. Not in front of everyone. She wondered whether the neutral territory was what they'd always needed to talk. There were too many emotions in Cascais.

Lots of people looked as he entered the airport. He had an air about him that commanded attention. Lots of men wore the camel-coloured crombie coats and dark sunglasses, but they didn't all get looked at like Luís did.

But for the first time ever she looked at him, striding

across the cool marble floor, and thought he looked a bit of an idiot. As he approached her she smiled, forcing herself not to make mental comparisons between him and Raoul. Especially as Raoul was coming up trumps on every count. She stood to greet him, and he actually kissed her on the cheeks, offering to buy her a coffee. But not to carry her heavy cases. He left her to grab a trolley and haul her cases up onto it, then wheel it across the concourse behind him.

Chapter Forty

By the time she'd boarded the plane she felt better than she had done in years. She was proud of herself for standing up to Luís, for making him see that Adi was *her* daughter as well as his and for not cowering and 'ssshhing' him when he raised his gruff voice.

And when she met Raoul at Gatwick airport on Sunday morning, she kissed him with a passion that took him completely by surprise.

At the same time that Raoul was running his fingers into the nape of Fiona's neck on the concourse at Gatwick airport, burying his long fingers beneath her silky hair, Helly was lying in bed beside Dan. If she were on a Channel 4 series, the cameraman would be suspended from the ceiling to get the full aerial shot of her lying there, a starfish, next to her husband. It was that kind of a moment. She lay on top of the duvet feeling her body move slightly with the rise and fall of Dan's deep breathing. The house was silent.

I waited five minutes for the results of the Clearblue.

Actually, I waited seven. I wanted to be doubly sure, so thought I'd add on a couple more minutes. You don't want to mess about with something as important as that. Although the results box didn't change in the extra two minutes, so I suppose they knew what they were doing when they instructed five.

Well, my life will never, ever be the same. From the moment that I slept with Nick – never mind that I was drunk and it was a mistake and all my other shite reasons and excuses – from that moment my life would never be the same one way or the other.

And it never will.

As she lay, motionless, on the bed her facial muscles began to twitch as her brain worked overtime. She felt the involuntary twitching first in her cheeks, and then around her eyes, until suddenly, without warning, the most enormous grin filled her face.

I am not pregnant!

Not, not, not, not, not!

And I swear to God, I'll never cheat on Dan again. I'll never be flattered by any man again in the way that I was with Nicky.

What an idiot I was!

And do you know what?

I don't feel sick any more!

And how much don't I deserve this result?

I must be the luckiest woman alive this morning.

No! I'm not messing! Really, the nausea, the stomach churning and sickness have completely disappeared.

But now I don't know whether I need to laugh or cry.

Dan snorted as she twisted on the bed, hugging him and climbing on top of him, laying herself flat on his sleeping body. He moaned, as she kissed him all over his face, his neck, his head, his ears.

"Mmmmm, am I dreaming?" he said, his eyes still closed.

"Dan. I love you. I haven't told you that too often lately, have I?"

He opened one eye suspiciously. "Has this got anything to do with you going off on tour tomorrow?"

She laughed at his way of thinking, "Nooo, I can tell my husband that I love him, can't I?"

"Any time you want, babe. It's just I haven't heard it for so long. Maybe you'd better say it again."

"I love you, I love you, I love you, Dan Donovan."

He held her shoulders lightly and flipped her onto her back, then pulled back the duvet cover and lay on the top beside her. "So? What was wrong last night? Pat and Brian said you were really sick."

She cringed. "I puked all over Pat's shoes."

"Yeah, she told me."

"I don't know, Dan, I've been feeling really sick lately."

"Well, you're not pregnant that's for sure. I haven't been near you since you stopped taking the pill."

"I know. I'm sorry, Dan. I've been rather confused the last few weeks. What with Fiona and Charley turning up and then the Quattro tour and everything. But you know,

491

I don't want another baby after all, Dan. I love our family so much and I want to build my life, our lives – not create more. I'm not ready for more children, and I don't think I ever will be."

She spoke with a conviction that he couldn't argue with.

Sure – I really know what I'm talking about, believe me!

He hugged her tight to him, so tight that she was finding it hard to breathe as he kissed her hard on the lips and said, "Helly, that's fine with me. I would never have suggested more children, but I thought it was what you wanted. I think you're right. We need to take control of our lives again. And it's going to mean changes. You're branching into something new with the Quattro tour and who knows what this might mean for you and I'm going to have to put my foot down and deal with the Murphia."

"Jesus, Dan, you know how they hold a grudge!" She smiled, feigning despair as she spoke.

He joined in the humour, "I know. It's going to mean custard-pie fights in the garden or worse, toenail clippings in the bed at night."

"OK, I can see I'm going to have to stand by you. What do you think?"

"I will have to insist that Charley finds somewhere else to live. She has plenty of money and hates spending it on anything remotely of a responsible nature. I'll give her a month, and she'll have to be sorted elsewhere. As far as Fiona is concerned, she can have a bit more time – she's got herself a job and so we'll cut her some slack. But things are going to change, Helly. I'm going to have more say in it all from now on."

"Dan, that's all I ever wanted."

"Great. Sorted then." He kissed her on the forehead, hopping up and tugging on his faded jeans, leaving the belt open and swaying as he walked. "You stay there, I'll nip out for the Sunday papers and then I'll start on breakfast."

"Christ, I am being spoiled."

And I so much don't deserve it.

"How about we take the kids out for the day? We might as well have a laugh with them before your two sisters arrive back here later on. With any luck, they'll be back before we are."

"Dan," Helly smiled, unable to remember a time when she'd been on such a high, "you're my dream guy!"

Chapter Forty-One

Charley was surprisingly chatty that afternoon. For months she'd worried that she would feel as bad as she had done on that day a year and a half ago. That day had turned her life into a mess, a pointless self-destruct as she'd thrown herself in front of man after man, her self-esteem plummeting with her sobriety. And now, for the first time, she had told somebody. Not just anybody, but her Bestest New Best-Friend. Steve hadn't patronised her, hadn't sat beside her rubbing her arms and nodding pathetically as she struggled to tell him. He had simply sat. And listened. And now she felt strangely free and liberated that she'd let her guard down. Not as in let her *garda* down, but her guard – her defence. And now she had finally dealt with it, it made her all the more determined to help Fiona. It had always aggravated her, how Luís dominated Fiona's life, how he took away her freedom, and yet all the time she had sat back, saying nothing, afraid of making herself look bad. Especially in the light of Luís' dead-certain denial. Charley had been reassured at the way that Steve coped with her news. She liked the fact that he hadn't gasped or held his hand to his mouth in horror, not knowing what to say, and so saying all the wrong things.

After all, it surely wasn't every day that he was told that his new girlfriend had once been raped by her sister's boyfriend.

"So, why didn't you report it?" Steve had sat on the coffee table, his knees wide apart and his elbows resting on them as he asked Charley the very question that she'd asked herself a zillion times.

She opened her eyes wide and spoke loudly as she sat forward on the edge of the sofa. "There wasn't a mark on me!" She sat back once again, lifting her legs up underneath her. "And it was his word against mine. And then there was Fiona to think of – she was so happy – and I was rather drunk."

"Charley, there's a thousand police rape-counsellors out there that will tell you, even if there's not a scratch on your body, rape is an extremely serious trauma and a deep injustice. No one should go through the trauma of rape alone."

"Maybe so," she shrugged, "but I felt ashamed. Everyone would have thought I led him on. I'd had a great laugh with the locals in the bar that night and Luís was right up at the front. But he was an easy target for my piss-taking – as my sister's partner, he was safe." She realised what she had said. "If you know what I mean." She took a deep breath, blowing it out in an 'O', and smoothing her hair back off her face.

Steve put his hand on her knee.

She continued, "I'd gone over to Cascais to see Fiona and we'd all been out for the night. Of course, I was staying at Fiona and Luís' and we'd gone back to the house really late. I was joking about, we'd all been drinking, and I wanted to go into the swimming pool. After some light persuasion Fiona agreed to come in too, and then Luís finally dived in. It was a beautiful warm evening and the sounds of the crickets in the grass seemed really loud. After a while Adriana woke up and Fiona had to get out of the water and go up to her. I felt uncomfortable then, in the pool with Luís. I don't really know why, just the way he *looked* at me. He put me on edge, I felt wrong there, he was creepy. So I got out and went towards the house, grabbing a towel and wrapping it around me. I was wearing my bikini, the same as Fiona. There was nothing saucy or cheeky meant by it."

Her lip trembled. Steve had reminded her that she didn't have to tell him, but she had wanted to. She composed herself.

"He dragged himself up out of the pool, following me, and before I knew it he'd pushed me up against the wall. I couldn't fight him off. He was just too strong." Her voice dipped as she wrenched her hands while she spoke, "I pretended what happened wasn't going to bother me. I convinced myself it was nothing. And that I felt nothing."

"It's common for rape victims to feel weak and wounded."

"I didn't want to frighten or upset my family. It was bad enough *me* going through it, but them too? And let's face it, they weren't exactly on my doorstep! What with Helly in London and Fiona in Portugal! And I was hardly going to tell my mum! I just felt at a loss."

"And so you started drinking?"

She nodded. "Amongst other things. I found it hard to cope with the unpredictable mood swings and drink helped. I couldn't believe I'd actually been raped. I kept questioning the word. It's such a simple word, isn't it? So uncriminal-sounding."

"It seems that in a lot of cases the rapist and victim know each other. Rape is a simple word and it doesn't always mean dark, back alleys. Rape is extremely common in a domestic situation."

"Well, I didn't want to force my family to take sides. Especially Fiona – she wouldn't have known what to do."

"So, do you think there could be other victims?"

"What?" She couldn't believe what he was suggesting.

He went on to explain, "An awful lot of rapists are serial rapists."

She found that difficult to come to terms with. Charley had been able to accept her own situation, but the thought of Luís violating other women brought her well-controlled emotions to the surface. Her face contorted as she sobbed, "That's why I was so worried about Helly going over there. Oh, my God, Fiona is over there now!"

"Calm down, Charley. You told me she wasn't planning on seeing him. Isn't that the whole idea of her quick visit? So as to avoid him?"

She cuffed her tears on Steve's cushion and nodded.

"So, Charley, would you report it now? It's still not too late."

"No," she shook her head, sniffing deeply, a determined look on her face, "but there is something I am going to do. I am going to talk to Luís, after avoiding him for over a year. There's something I need to say to him." Charley stood, the pins and needles starting in her feet as she'd been sitting on them for so long. She bent to kiss Steve, flicking and jerking her feet as she moved towards the kitchen.

He called after her, "So? What happened next?"

"Next?" She looked puzzled. She turned and looked at him. Something about the way he looked at her made her click. She knew that he knew.

She looked down at her hands.

"What do you mean, 'next'?"

His voice was level. "I mean, what happened after?"

"After? Well, I got on with my life. I came back to Dublin, back to work. And tried to put it out of my mind. Forget it all ever happened. And I found that drinking helped. It took the pain away, numbed everything." She paused and then said it: "And then I found out I was pregnant."

Steve didn't flinch. "And you knew it was his."

It was more a statement than a question and that meant a lot to her. It meant that he hadn't assumed she was an old bike who had so many men she couldn't begin to wonder who could be the father. It meant that he had a confidence, a belief in her. It meant everything.

Charley smiled as she replied, "It had to be his. I was still with Donal when I went over there and he complained how boring, quiet and different I was when I came back. I swung from good moods to bad moods, had horrific nightmares and he simply couldn't bear to be around me. And that suited me fine. I was angry and then suddenly emotional. Anyway, Donal hadn't been near me that way for nearly two months."

"So, what happened next?"

"I flew to London and had a termination. Nobody knew. Nobody. And they never will. Except you."

He stood and moved across to her, hugging her tightly. "You're a brave lady, Charley."

"No," she spoke into his neck, "I'm a coward. I've hung on to this for so long, saying nothing and letting Fiona continue to be so unhappy. I could have done something about this ages ago and I chose not to. I chose to hide behind the image of girl-about-town and I knew all along." She became angry as she spoke, "Well, he might have put me through hell, but I won't be a victim any more, and I won't let Fiona be either."

Steve had no answers.

And she didn't want him to.

She had just needed him to listen.

Fiona had spent a glorious morning with Raoul. He hadn't flinched at the call to collect her from Gatwick so early on a Sunday morning and, to top it all, he had taken her for a budget Sunday breakfast in Brick Lane, where they'd wandered through the market, nudging each other as Martine McCutcheon strode past in a baseball cap and Dr Marten's. They'd stopped at the bagel shop and each had a tuna-mayonnaise bagel and then a cream-cheese and smoked-salmon one. As they walked on the cobbled ground, browsing the stalls that sold second-hand shoes, batteries and children's colouring sets she told him all about her crazy visit to Cascais.

She told him how surprised she had been when Luís actually turned up at the airport. And then how it had all rung so true when he'd sat down to talk calmly with her, only to find half an hour later that he was losing his cool and threatening her with legal conventions and solicitors' letters. She had hoped that they could come to some adult agreement but, for Luís, that was impossible.

The kiss at Gatwick had shot Raoul's bravery levels through the roof, Fiona's public display of affection ringing his bell loud and clear. He put his arm around her shoulders as they walked and she felt slightly guilty that she was back in the country so much earlier than she'd thought and yet hadn't rushed back to see Adi.

"Hey," Raoul soothed her, "she's probably having a great time with Toby and Jack. Leave her for now. Take the time to enjoy yourself. They're not expecting you back until later anyway." He steered her toward a manky-looking café, the bricks painted a putrid yellow and the sign above the door peeling with age.

"Come on. In here – Uncle Albert's – the best cup of

tea in East London."

As they sat inside, the gross 1970's tiles offending their eyes, she had to agree; the tea was fantastic. Dark and strong and full of sugar, just like she liked it.

"You know," he smiled at her, "I'm so proud of you. You've done something scary this weekend. You've gone over there, knowing what could happen and then, at the last minute, you actually told him where you were *and* asked him to meet you."

She scratched her head. "I know. What a fool I am! It didn't work though, did it? He's still as arrogant and obnoxious as ever."

"So what now?"

"Nothing!" She was flippant and it surprised him. "I'll wait for the solicitor's letter or whatever he's going to do and I'll deal with it then. I'm not going to spend the rest of my time worrying about what *might* happen."

"So you're staying at Helly's?"

"For now. Until I can save enough money to rent somewhere. It's not ideal, but it'll do for now."

"How about if I had an idea?"

"What kind of idea?"

"A potential solution to your housing problem."

She grinned over her mug as she sipped her hot tea, "Go on."

"My flatmate is moving out next month. I mean, it's only a very small flat, but what do you think?"

"What?" she squealed.

"Well, would you and Adi like to move in?"

"Me and Adi?" She shrieked so loudly that Raoul

blushed. She felt bad, obviously making him feel awkward as he backtracked quicker than you could say Jump-In-With-Both-Feet-And-Scare-Them-Off.

"No, you're right," he gushed, "perhaps it is a bad idea. Sorry, I didn't mean to be presumptuous."

"Bad idea? It's a bloody great idea!"

"Is it?"

"Yes!" She leapt up and hugged him. "Course it is!"

Encouraged by her hug he went on, "Of course, I've already thought about this. Adi could have the boxroom. It's too small for an adult, but I'm sure it'd be fine for her. And there's no pressure on you, Fiona. We'd both have our own rooms and then, well, whatever!"

"I'll give you whatever, Raoul! You're fan-fucking-tastic, that's what you are!"

"So you're on for it then?"

"Baby," she rubbed her hands together with delight, "right now, I'm on for anything."

Charley wasn't sure how to deal with Luís. She knew what she wanted to do, but wasn't sure how to do it. And she was determined to make a decision in the next two hours – she was due to leave for the airport then. She watched the telly as Steve hummed in the kitchen, making her his speciality pasta salad that he'd promised. Her thoughts were broken as she watched the new washing-powder jingle burst onto the screen. The one she had written when she worked for the agency. Grabbing the remote she turned it up, desperate to check whether they'd used her jingle.

Her zippy jingle spin-cycled off the screen. As she sat up, trying to call Steve only to find her voice wasn't working, she pointed at the shot where the cameras zoomed onto the white sheets, flapping on the light breeze just as she'd intended.

"Jesus, I was good!" she applauded herself. As she watched the flapping white sheets her thoughts drifted back to her own childhood. She began to think about how she could still recall the smell of her mum's summer washing, and how she used to chase Helly and Fiona through the dripping sheets as they buffeted in the warm breeze. It was a foregone conclusion that Mum would scream at them, but it was worth it, and they all knew she didn't really mean it. Screaming was a mother's job – they all knew it. As Charley sat on the edge of Steve's sofa now, she could literally smell the fresh wash and the sounds of her hot childhood summers – she could all but *hear* her mum warning them about dirty hand-marks on the bedding. Without warning Charley's eyes filled with tears which sat heavy on her lower lids contemplating whether to fall or dissipate, as she wondered where it had all started to go wrong. When she had thrown herself into a crowd, only to find she was still lonely. Had it been when Helly had left for London with Dan? Was it as Mum became more and more absent-minded? Was it when Fiona went to Lisbon with Luís? Charley had often wondered how she had been left behind. She still felt bitter about it all, but didn't want to. Not any more.

Steve broke her trance as he 'ta-daaaaa'd', entering the

room with two huge bowls of pasta salad. Charley whistled as she took the bowl on her lap, eyeing the slices of hard-boiled eggs, small segments of satsuma, raisins, parmesan and shredded chicken. They sat side-by-side, completely comfortable in each other's company and munched through the exquisite salad. Once finished she snuggled up to him on the settee, dreading the thoughts of leaving him now. She knew in that instant, that he was all she had ever hoped for – and more. She felt so right with Steve.

As they both watched the telly, he spoke.

"Have you ever regretted the termination?"

She stayed put as she replied, "Never. But it's tiring trying to avoid children. I suppose that's what I've been doing, trying to be irritated with them, for fear of actually *liking* them."

"And would that be so bad?"

"Probably not. But I've been in denial, Steve. I've been fighting with myself for so long. It's hard, you know."

He sat upright, looking down at his lap. "No," he shook his head, "it's not. But if you keep stroking my arm like that it might be soon."

She punched him on the arm playfully.

He flinched a little as he asked her, "So, before all this happened, would you have liked kids?"

"Yeah. It was always me that Mum thought would pop out a few littl'uns first. But I never met the right guy. Or I was always too busy at work. There was always something in the way. What about you?"

"I don't know. I couldn't eat a whole one. And I

suppose I was tarnished by my mum's approach to toilet-training."

"How?"

"She always used to say, 'Do you want to go to the loo "properly"?'. I mean, fuckit, is there any other way?"

Charley broke into laughter at his pathetic shot at humour. "You're a real fucking eejit cop, do you know that?"

"Yup." He put his hand on her chin, tipping her face to his and kissing her tenderly.

She never noticed that as she lay beneath him on the sofa, she'd knocked the remote control and the volume had roared to number forty-two. He didn't notice that she'd also inadvertently changed the channel with her elbow and his telly now blasted out a documentary on teenage acne.

Charley had only ever had *sex* before.

And so, as Charley Murphy *made love* for the first time in her life she didn't care about anything else.

Chapter Forty-Two

Helly and Dan had had a fantastic day.

One of the best ever!

Despite the presence of three children. It was brilliant.

First we went to the Natural History Museum and then in the afternoon Dan took us to Smollensky's on the Finchley Road. The kids were in their element! Between twelve and three they were entertained with face-painters, computer games and clowns, and it gave us the chance to talk.

But the best of it was, we were actually talking.

I don't mean chatting, I mean talking. I had a good moan about living with three guys – although two of them were under ten, the principle's the same. And do you know, he'd never even considered the effect his stinky trainers might have on me.

Fiona and Charley arrived back at the house within an hour of each other. It was early evening and the children were enjoying their last half-hour of madness before

Helly chucked them all into the bath. Fiona was back first, Raoul being the perfect gentleman and carrying her grotesquely large and heavy cases into the house for her.

Helly thought she looked radiant, despite her hectic weekend. They had left the cases in the hall as she'd dragged Fiona through to the back garden, desperate for the latest news from Cascais. No sooner had Dan and Raoul joined them with their cans of beer than Charley arrived. She had asked James to drop her at the door, feeding him a story of severe tiredness after a busy weekend. She thought that James had been a little put out, but she wasn't too worried about it. After all, she knew what she wanted now.

They were all surprised to see Charley decline a drink as they sat in the garden, recounting their version of the last couple of days. Fiona went into great detail about how she'd stuck up for herself to Luís and hid her disappointment at how he had thrown it all back at her. Charley skipped the entire section about how she'd got plastered on the first night and then also how she'd experienced the ultimate with Steve on his sofa only earlier that afternoon. But between the jigs and the reels, Helly got the picture.

They both noticed a change in Helly. She seemed happier, brighter and they had quizzed her about the Quattro tour that was starting tomorrow, but she had seemed to take it all in her stride. They couldn't quite put their finger on it, but something had happened over the weekend between Helly and Dan. It made Charley and

Fiona feel a little guilty, wondering whether their presence had put unnecessary pressure on their sister's marriage.

"So!" Charley clapped her hands together. The conversation had begun to be disturbed as the children got bored and tired after their exciting day. "Who'd like Auntie Charley to put them to bed tonight?"

The three of them looked at her like she had just offered them twenty fags.

Helly and Fiona burst laughing, "Jesus, Charley, look at their faces!"

Charley wasn't fazed, and stood, catching hold of Toby and Adi's hands, "Come on. I'll read you a story."

And in a beat, they skittered into the kitchen and Helly and Fiona shrugged in amazement as they heard them singing their way up the stairs.

Charley virtually acted out the story as she read it, causing the children to shriek with laughter at her comical actions and funny voices. They were asleep by eight thirty and, quite exhausted, she tiptoed her way to the top of the stairs. As she paused, hearing the others still in the garden drinking and laughing, she looked into Helly and Dan's bedroom. Her mobile was still beside their bed, the red light flashing to show that the battery was full. She was desperate to get down to the others and convince her two sisters that it was definitely a night for taxi shoes. But before she did, she had a call to make.

Sitting on Helly's bed she scrolled through her mobile for Luís' number. It was still stored under 'FIONA AT LUÍS' and she was glad that she hadn't deleted it as she'd wanted to so many times. She breathed steadily, composing herself for this. This, that she'd waited to do for so long.

She nearly gasped when she heard his gruff voice. She wasted no time,

"Luís," her voice was low and deep as she spoke, "it's Charley. Yes, Charley, Fiona's sister. No, don't try and fucking talk to me. Just listen. You *will* listen, if you know what's good for you, so shut up and get this. You're going to make a deal with me, and you're going to do it now. Fiona is staying in London, got it? Yeah, she is. She is staying in London with Adriana and you *will not* make her life difficult. You've done that for long enough. And in return I won't report the rape. Yes, you shit-head! The bloody rape. And don't even *try* to talk. I'm talking. I'll agree not to report you as long as you leave Fiona alone. This is the way it's going to be, so listen. She is free to stay in London as long as she likes. She's making her life in London. You *know* what she's like, she'll let you see Adriana – you know she wouldn't object to you coming to London to see her. But if you ever, *ever* put pressure on her again, if you ever make her life, or anybody else in my family's life, difficult again, I guarantee you, you'll be in deeper trouble than you could deal with. I've already spoken to the police about the rape and made enquiries about procedure and I'll have no problems in pointing the finger in your direction." She took a deep breath, bracing herself for her tirade of lies. "After you raped me, Luís, I went for a medical and I've got all the evidence just waiting to prosecute you. I've got statements from two other women in Cascais to say that you have treated them the same, and the evidence against you is very, very strong. Now, I will *never* tell Fiona about this call and neither will you. You've hurt us enough, Luís. And it all stops here."

It was silent at the other end of the line.

"I know you're still there, you cowardly shit. So I'll take it from your silence that we have a deal."

She heard a murmur at the end of the phone.

And then he spoke, deep and slowly. "You are a bitch, Charley. You always were. But you win. I will agree for Fiona to stay in London, but you had better make sure I see my daughter at least twice a year, or the deal is off."

"I will make sure of that, Luís, as long as you make her life as happy as you possibly can."

"It is a deal. You are a nasty woman."

"Huh!" she laughed. "And I've only just begun, Luís. Goodbye."

She didn't give him the chance to reply, simply pressing the red phone button to disconnect the call. She replaced the phone onto the charger, standing and adjusting her clothes. Now all she had to do was get her sisters out for the night.

Helly, Fiona, Dan and Raoul were playing 'cups' on the wooden garden table. Dan had picked up the three plastic cups on his way back out from the kitchen and in their merry state they had found great delight in hiding a cork beneath one and trying to guess which.

Raoul had just said he should be getting off home, he had rehearsals tomorrow, when Charley appeared at the kitchen door.

"You guys know how to have fun, don't you?"

"Don't ever let it be said that we can't entertain ourselves," Helly laughed.

Raoul stood. "I must be going now. Thanks, Helly, thanks, Dan."

Fiona stood too. "I'll see you to the door then."

"Something I said?" joked Charley, sniffing at her armpits.

Raoul looked awkward. "No, I'd already said I had to go soon."

Charley patted him on the shoulder. "You're all right, Raoul. I'm only joking."

Fiona was gone a few minutes and returned with a smile on her face,

"So now he's gone I can tell you all."

"What?" Charley teased. "You're getting married!"

"Charley!"

She held her hands up in mock despair, "Well, I never know with you."

"Go on," Helly encouraged. "What?"

Fiona looked smug, the cat who had got the milkman, "I'm moving in with him."

"Who?"

"Raoul! Who else?"

"You're not! When?"

"I don't know," she grinned, sipping at her wine, "but

soon. His flatmate is moving out and me and Adi are moving in. Not as a coupley thing, Adi's having the boxroom and we're each having our own rooms and we'll see what happens."

Charley sniggered. "I can tell you what'll happen."

"What?" said Fiona.

"You and Raoul will be in the one room and Adi will have her own room *and* the boxroom."

"Yeah," Fiona grinned, "time will tell."

"Well, I've got some news too," Charley pulled her chair in closer to the table and they gathered around. "I'm going back to Dublin."

"Halle-fucking-lujah!" Dan hollered, his arms open as he looked up at the startings of the summer moon.

"Shove it, Dan," she joked, poking him in the ribs. "I've decided to go back and sort my life out. I'm really keen on Steve and he's a great friend as well as a, well, a . . ."

"A boyfriend?" Helly goaded her.

"Yeah, a boyfriend I suppose. Although at my age that sounds kind of stupid, doesn't it?"

"Not at all," Fiona chimed in. "Look at Liza Minnelli and Liz Taylor."

"Thanks!" Charley bellowed, hardly impressed with being compared to them.

"So when are you going?" Helly felt sad that her two sisters had already planned to move on.

Even though me and Dan had decided that was for the best, I feel upset now that I'm losing them.

It's been hard, all of us living together and coping with each other's moods and annoying habits, but I'm going to miss them so much.

"Next week, I think. No offence, Hel, but as soon as possible. I've decided I'm a bloody good copywriter and I owe it to myself to go back and give it my best shot."

"Well, fair play to you, Charley!" Fiona stood and hugged her sister.

Just as the tears welled in their eyes Charley changed the subject.

"So," her voice was getting louder again, "would you mind, Dan, if I took Helly out just one last time? I won't be able to this coming week as she's off being a big important stylist, on tour, if you don't mind."

"Go on, you mad fuckers," he smiled, lifting his can to his mouth, "go and cause havoc."

"Thanks Dan!" Charley stood, dragging Helly and Fiona from their seats as she rushed them into the house. "Don't forget now, girls, get on your taxi shoes!"

"Oh, no," Helly and Fiona groaned together.

The black cab arrived at Helly's front door thirty minutes later. They were all dressed in jeans and T-shirts but had worn the regulatory taxi shoes. Fiona in her secondhand Miu Miu's, Charley in her LK Bennett's' and Helly in her antique Pradas. Already she could feel the pinch, the arch of her foot aching with every step, but she wasn't about to break the rule. As the three of them sat, huddled in the back of the cab, Charley joked with the driver about stopping the clock and knocking a few quid off the fare. Helly's stomach danced rather than churned for the first time in ages. She felt that she'd been given a second chance and had promised Dan that she'd go back on the pill tomorrow. She knew it would mean a month before they could afford *not* to take precautions, but hey, he was worth waiting for. Fiona soaked in the London scene as they whizzed past in the taxi, cackling at the expense of the clan of Japanese tourists they saw at the traffic lights. She was excited about really kicking off her life in London, about the prospects of moving in with Raoul, about starting her violin teaching. She just hoped that she had to wait ages and ages before Luís sent her a solicitor's letter quoting her clauses and sections of jargon.

Charley felt calmer than she had done for ages. And she hadn't even had a drink. What's more, she had no intentions of having one either. She was desperate to get back to Steve, back to Dublin, back to rebuilding her life again. She didn't need drink any more.

And if she could see into the future, like Madame Lydia had six months before, she'd have known that within the next six weeks she'd be ringing Helly and Fiona, squealing with delight that *she* was the one who would be having a baby. *She* was to be the one with the pregnancy. Of course, Steve was going to be delighted and Charley was about to embrace the concept of motherhood in a way that she'd never have dreamed.

As the cabbie shoved on the brakes, Charley had cracked a funny about cabbies having leather arses due to sitting down all day.

They guffawed and laughed hysterically as the cabbie

reached back, over his shoulder, and pulled up the thin window that divided him from rowdy passengers.

At which they all laughed, even louder than before.

The End

Look Before You Leap

ALISON NORRINGTON

"I was married for 10 months, 22 days, 3 hours, 50 seconds and 1 six-week affair"

Tara McKenna was so in love with the idea of marriage that she forgot to check out one small detail . . . her future husband Simon. Stuck in post-marital doldrums, an affair had injected some life into her disappointing marriage – until Simon found out.

A year later, dumped and guilt-ridden Tara is saved by her best mates Niamh and Anna.

Declan O'Mahoney is stressed. Co-ordinating an interior-design team for his latest TV project is a real headache and ruthless, pill-popping, celebrity interior designer Ciara O'Rourke is doing her diva act. When top photographer Niamh introduces her friend Tara, Declan's TV home makeover show begins to take shape.

As Tara starts to rebuild her life her best friends stumble upon some information that hints that 'Slimey Simey' may have been much more the marrying kind than Tara ever thought.

But will Tara be able to handle the truth?

ISBN 1-84223-133-2

www.poolbeg.com

Also published by Poolbeg.com

Class Act

Alison Norrington

"I stood gawking at my hideous reflection. What a bloody sore sight for bloody sore eyes!"

Geri's life is in a bit of a rut. In its pre-marital state it was lived with passion, attitude and alcohol. Now, post-pregnancy and post-separation, it needs a good kick-start.

But, oh to be her best friend Sinéad! Refined, relaxed, high-flying Sinéad riding the corporate roller-coaster in sunny Spain… well, actually, insecure, lonely and bored Sinéad crawling from one disastrous relationship to another.

Geri and Sinéad are so busy trying to keep the lid on their own emotions, each fails to notice how the other has gone rather quiet and distant.

But Geri is about to restart her life.

NEW MAN, NEW JOB, NEW ME!

Just give her a little time to think about it!

ISBN 1-84223-086-7

www.poolbeg.com